All the
Invisible
Things

Also by Orlagh Collins

No Filter

All the Invisible Things

ORLAGH COLLINS

BLOOMSBURY

NEW YORK LONDON OXFORD NEW DELHI SYDNEY

BLOOMSBURY YA
Bloomsbury Publishing Inc., part of Bloomsbury Publishing Plc
1385 Broadway, New York, NY 10018

BLOOMSBURY and the Diana logo are trademarks of Bloomsbury Publishing Plc

First published in Great Britain in March 2019 by Bloomsbury Publishing Plc
Published in the United States of America in March 2020 by Bloomsbury YA

Bloomsbury books may be purchased for business or promotional use. For information
on bulk purchases please contact Macmillan Corporate and Premium Sales Department at
specialmarkets@macmillan.com

Library of Congress Cataloging-in-Publication Data
Names: Collins, Orlagh, author.
Title: All the invisible things / by Orlagh Collins.
Description: New York : Bloomsbury, 2020.
Summary: Moving back to London after four years, seventeen-year-old Vetty must
navigate a summer of changing friendships and coming to terms with her bisexuality.
Identifiers: LCCN 2019019159 (print) | LCCN 2019021948 (e-book)
ISBN 978-1-68119-950-4 (hardcover) • ISBN 978-1-68119-951-1 (e-book)
Subjects: | CYAC: Coming of age—Fiction. Self-acceptance—Fiction. | Friendship—Fiction. |
Love—Fiction. | Identity—Fiction. | Bisexuality—Fiction. | London (England)—Fiction. |
England—Fiction.
Classification: LCC PZ7.1.C6449 AI 2020 (print) | LCC PZ7.1.C6449 (e-book) |
DDC [Fic]—dc23
LC record available at https://lccn.loc.gov/2019019159

Typeset by RefineCatch Limited, Bungay, Suffolk
Printed and bound in the U.S.A. by Berryville Graphics Inc., Berryville, Virginia
2 4 6 8 10 9 7 5 3 1

All papers used by Bloomsbury Publishing Plc are natural, recyclable products made from
wood grown in well-managed forests. The manufacturing processes conform to the
environmental regulations of the country of origin.

To find out more about our authors and books visit www.bloomsbury.com
and sign up for our newsletters.

For Vivienne

All the
Invisible
Things

Prologue

My name is Helvetica.

Like the font.

Whenever I tell people this I wait for them to make the face: the one where their features freeze like they're hoping they misheard, then they realize *nope, she's for real* and they look sorry, like it's their fault. I bet Dad thought my name would make me sound interesting. (Graphic designers think stuff like this, I swear!) I was probably like some branding exercise and he just did it to make me stand out but in a good way. And he wasn't to know how different I'd feel already. My little sister, Arial, gets away with it because she sounds like the Disney mermaid, which I used to think was so unfair, but I'm relieved for her now. Mum must have been high on that baby gas to let Dad get away with it. But, like, twice?

Pez never made the face.

PART ONE

Back to London, back to me

Freya leans in too. "Richardson was easily the least awful of our teachers in junior year."

Liv makes a face. "She said I was trouble."

Jess shoves her shoulder. "You *were* trouble! She threw you out of her sex ed class in Year 9. Remember?"

Liv folds her arms across her chest. "I wasn't thrown out," she says. "I had to stand at the front. And all I did was ask a question."

In the boys' sex ed they get to discuss the fun stuff like actually doing it, so how's it fair that all we talk about is blood and STDs? That was Liv's question. I'll never forget because when I pointed out that boys can get STDs too, Richardson thought I was being cheeky and sent me to stand beside Liv in front of the whiteboard. "Far as I recall she got through our entire sex ed without even uttering the word 'vagina.' Not once!" Liv's voice is loud and a man behind us looks up from wiping his toddler's mouth. "She was way more comfortable with the word 'penis,'" she says, more quietly. "Preferred the feel of it inside her mouth, I reckon."

Jess takes the lid off her shake and stabs at a stubborn rock of Oreo. "What was it she called down there again?" she says, waving the now-dented plastic spoon over her lap.

Freya hooshes her stool in. "*Intimate female area?*"

"That was it!" Jess says.

Liv grabs her cup and speaks into it like a microphone. "Girls, today we're going to talk about reproductive health and sex-sue-al relations." She's got Richardson's voice exactly down and it's impossible not to laugh. "By that I mean, how to avoid touching any genitals whatsoever outside of marriage."

7

"Stop!" Jess says, bouncing on her chair. "I've got a wet patch going on here."

Richardson might have failed at sex ed, but Freya's right—she was far from an awful teacher. When I arrived in Year 8 just weeks after Mum died, she left me alone and let me thaw in my own time, which to be honest felt kind.

Liv is at full volume again. "*And* it's not like boys are the only ones with any genitals so how come they only ever talk about boys doing it?" Everyone is laughing now and I'd join in, only I seem to have missed the beginning of this particular rant and I'm not 100 percent clear what she means.

"Doing what?" I ask. Freya sticks her tongue in her cheek and makes a pretty unmistakeable hand gesture. I force a smile. "You mean ... masturbating?" The word lands awkwardly and this makes them crack up even more. I take a noisy slurp of my shake, kicking myself for opening my mouth as a reverse avalanche of freezing cold ice cream shoots down my throat. The brain freeze is so sharp I have to squeeze my eyes shut. When it finally subsides, I cautiously open them.

Liv leans closer. "Yes, Helvetica, mastur-bayy-shun," she says, in Mrs. Richardson mode again. "Feel free to share any personal experience with the class. We're all ears." I twiddle my straw, making some face back at her. She's about to take a sip, when she sits up. "Okay, real talk," she says, looking around. "Say you're at home, alone in your room, and, like ... testing your batteries or whatever, just say ... who do you fantasize about?" She glares at each of us. For a moment no one speaks and I scan the table. Jess sinks into her seat, cup raised to her mouth, but Freya looks like she's really thinking about it.

"Jamie," Freya says after a while.

"He'll be thrilled that took you so long," Liv says. "But Jamie doesn't count on account of the real-life sex you're having with him."

Freya peers up from under her lashes. "Um, we haven't actually gone *that* far."

"Whatever," Liv says. "I said *fantasize*." Then she turns to Jess, who is opening her mouth, but Liv quickly raises her hand. "I swear, Jess, if you mention that Timothée Chalamet one more time, I'm reconsidering our friendship."

Jess laughs and Liv moves on to me. "Vetty, I'm counting on you now for some real juice." Her eyes are locked on mine and I know I should just blurt out an answer but the last time I did this it nearly changed everything. Admittedly, it was in Year 8 on a sleepover at Freya's house and Liv wasn't even there, but still. I wish I could be like them and joke about this stuff but it's as though nothing I've said since sounds convincing.

I shrug. "No one in particular."

"C'mon!" Liv says. Everyone is looking at me. This could be my worst nightmare. "They don't even have to be famous. Like, how about that Pez guy? He'd count."

I groan inwardly. "Pez is just a friend."

"An attractive *friend* as I recall," she says, reaching for my phone. "There's that picture of him somewhere . . . wearing a cap." Jess and Freya peer over her shoulders, staring at the screen while she scrolls. I don't have to look. It's Pez and his dad on a red carpet somewhere. Thankfully his mum isn't in the photo or her fans would have shared it all over the internet. Me and Pez still follow each other and stuff, but neither of us really posts much now. Liv's hand flies up. "Here it is!" she says, tilting the phone in the light before shoving it toward me. Then she leans closer. "I've said it before but that boy is welcome to watch *Vampire Diaries* on my couch anytime," she says, writhing about, making some kind of sex noises.

This is just one of the reasons I don't really mention Pez anymore. None of the girls knows how close we really were, and I sit back, almost enjoying how wrong they are about all of it. Lying on the couch watching TV all weekend is exactly the type of thing Pez and I would do. Well, it's exactly what we *used* to do. Just completely not in the way Liv thinks.

Freya stops laughing and taps her hand on the table. "I've always wanted to ask," she says. "Is his nickname Pez because of those sweets? The ones with the Mickey Mouse dispenser things—"

"I had one of those!" Jess cuts in. "But Hello Kitty."

"His real name is Peregrine." It's been a while since I said Pez's full name out loud, and though it sounds unusual, I'm not sure why I ever kept it a secret.

Freya is trying hard to keep a straight face. "Like the bird of prey?"

I think about mentioning the lesser-known Marvel character Pez once told me about but I just nod. "He never liked it."

Liv looks like she's already worked this out. "Peregrine and Helvetica?" she says, barely able to contain herself.

"Dead heat for Meanest Parents Award that year. No wonder you two found each other."

I've often thought about how our names brought us together. Like, if I'd been called Liv or Jess would it have been the same? Would Pez have let me ride on the back of his BMX bike or taught me how to play Perudo when we were stuck inside on account of my broken arm? Would he have cried with me when Thomas J gets stung by the bees in *My Girl*? Would he have held my hand under the willow tree when the doctors found Mum's grapefruit? Liv pushes her cup forward and places both elbows on the table. "Things could be different now," she says, eyebrows up. "You're not kids anymore." Without meaning to, I make the kind of face Arial gives me when I say something she thinks is ridiculous. "Unless," she says, her voice softer than it's been all day and possibly ever. "You don't feel that way ... about boys."

The table shakes. "Ouch!" Liv says, spinning her shoulders around to Jess, who is glaring at her. My mouth fills with water, that way it does when you're about to be sick, and I set my cup down as casually as I can, but the shake blender behind the counter stops whirring and all eyes weigh heavy on mine in the new silence. Liv isn't exactly known for her subtlety, but *this*? "Sorry," she says, even more gently. "I'm just saying you shouldn't feel weird, if you're not into guys." Her hand creeps across the table toward mine. "We're cool about it." She stops and does something silly with her mouth. "Well, I'm cool as long as *I'm* the one you fancy, obviously."

The table trembles again. "God, Liv!" says Jess, her eyes slatted in anger.

Liv frowns. "What?"

11

"If and *when* Vetty wants to talk about . . . *this*," Jess says, lowering her voice. "That's up to her."

Liv sits back. "Well, she leaves tomorrow and I think it might help." Then she looks at me. "Get it off your chest, you know?" Her eyes are wide and earnest, like she genuinely believes this is a good idea. Jess looks like she's afraid I might cry, which I might. Freya looks confused.

"Um, hello?" she says. "Vetty went out with Arthur for, like . . . months. She was crazy about him." Arthur is Freya's cousin. He sat beside me on the bus on the way to her house at Christmastime of Year 8, a month after the awkward sleepover from hell. I was chatting away when he reached over midsentence and casually fixed my smudged eyeliner. He was dry and funny and when he laughed he had this squint and his shoulders shook violently but he made absolutely no noise. He was sweet and turned out to be a really nice kisser. We only broke up because he moved back to Birmingham that summer.

I move my hands under the table, clenching my fists tight. I may have less than twenty-four hours left in Somerset but I still can't do this. I grit my teeth, then slam a hand against my chest. "You got me, Liv! I've been dreaming about you in that panda bear onesie of yours for so long, waiting to find the right moment to tell you!" I think I'm doing a good job of sounding all theatrical but the girls stare like they're not entirely sure whether I'm joking. Okay, so, this is worse than saying "masturbation" out loud.

Jess looks at her watch, then shoves her stool out. "I better get going," she says, flashing me a quick *are you okay?*

look as she slings her jacket over her shoulder. "Vetty, you must be heading that way?"

"Just a sec," I say, freeing my bag from the leg of my stool.

I get through the goodbyes and promises to keep in touch but it's only outside in the fresh air that I properly exhale. Jess arrives by my side and we stroll silently over the bridge toward town. Outside the Co-op, I slow down and something must happen to my face because she looks guilty, making my chest even tighter. "I didn't say anything," she says. "You know? To Liv."

My spine stiffens. The queasy feeling in my stomach isn't the Aero Mint bubbles. "I was just going to . . . say thanks. That's all."

She looks relieved and places her hand on my shoulder. "Anytime, Vetty," she says, and we walk on up the hill.

Please, god, let this stuff be easier in London.

2

Still nine but a Coke can taller, Pez arrived like a gift just for me. It was the evening of my tenth birthday and I was allowed to go to the Tesco Metro on my own. Shopping alone was a treat and I was excited. Mum sat outside our flat on St. Agnes Villas holding her watch and I had a sense something big was about to happen, I just wasn't sure what. I thought about saying something important to her, like telling her I loved her, because you know . . . alien abductions, murderers, and stuff, but I must have decided that Mum already knew how I felt, because I took off without a word.

"*I'm timing you,*" she cried, and I pounded the pavement all the way there, like she knew I would. I ran even faster than the cars that heaved along on Camden Road in the heavy heat. Bursting through Tesco's sliding doors, I crashed past the security guard and managed to topple the tower of wire baskets beside him. Before I could apologize, I had to stop and catch my breath. I was bent double like this, hands on knees, when I spotted Luna Boyd at the checkout, talking to the lady behind the till and waving her hand elegantly like she was conducting the sound of her own voice. Luna was hands down Mum and Dad's favorite actress on TV, but it wasn't her I was taken with. Behind her in the line stood a boy with light-brown skin and cornrows, blowing a bubble of gum from his mouth that grew and grew until it was so humongous it covered almost all his face. I snatched a bag of Haribos from the rack, watching as he turned for the door, Mars Milk under his arm and magnificent pink gum balloon still intact. He moved spry and quick, like our neighbor's cat coming down the pipes. His eyes met mine as he passed, and he was almost at the door when his bubble finally popped! When I gasped, he spun around and I stared helplessly back until a smile cracked from underneath his cap, lighting me up like a newly struck match. His front teeth were only half-grown.

In a puff, he was gone.

I looked at the line snaking toward the tills and I knew I didn't have that kind of time. My fist opened inside my pocket and the coins slid back inside. I was out the door, back into the traffic before I could think. I wove across the forecourt toward Camden Road, panicking not about the stolen sweets under my arm, but that I'd lost him. As soon as I turned left my heart surged. Luna walked ahead, hips swaying in her denims, and the boy, on a bike now, free-wheeling down the road just meters behind her, dragging the toes of his bright-red high-tops along the ground. I galloped to catch up until the same short distance between him and Luna was all that was left between us. Seconds later she went left toward the square and in less time again the wheels of his BMX veered around the corner too.

He pedaled along the footpath in front, bouncing down the curb and narrowly dodging the huge truck that gusted out from the mews. On he rode, slinky and unbothered like one of Old Giles's cats, clattering his empty bottle against the iron railings of the playground, left hand thud, thud, thudding against the bars as he went. I was sure someone famous like Luna would turn left for one of the fancy houses overlooking the square but she walked on and the boy and his bike followed, bumping down the curb in front and soon up another. I walked faster, shadowing him so closely that I could hear his gum bursts: pop, pop, pop. All of a sudden, we'd reached the bottom of my road. My feet stopped by the bank of recycling bins because the spokes of his wheels had finally stopped. He spun around, his short, straight eyebrows sitting far up from his eyes, tilting at me like a cartoon. I counted the little lines cracking his forehead as he squinted in the evening sun: one, two, three, four.

"Gonna tell me your name?" he said, licking the slack gum from his lips and tucking it back into his mouth with his tongue.

I opened my mouth to speak, heart hammering against my ribs like his Mars Milk bottle off the railings. "Helvetica." I blurted it out and braced myself for the face people usually make. My teeth were clenched and ready, but the face didn't come. Instead another pale-pink balloon erupted and collapsed onto his nose; then he flicked the chewed gum into a nearby trash can and bobbed his head kind of slow, like he could see everything I was feeling.

"Cool," he said—that was all, but with this one word I knew we were going to be friends. Then he wheeled in closer. "Peregrine." He whispered his name slowly, lifting one hand from the handlebar and extending it toward me.

16

I repeated his name. "Pear-eh-grin."

"If you ever call me that, we're done though. Yeah?" he said, his brown eyes newly serious.

As he reached a sticky hand toward me, I nodded and, unsure what else to do, I began to shake it.

"Easy!" he said, whipping his hand back. "I was only going in for a sour cherry." Then he wiped his hand on his jeans like mine had germs before reaching for my bag of Haribos again. "D'you pay for these sweets, Helvetica?" My head moved up and down before I could think, but he sniffed the air the way Dad sniffs Vicks nasal spray: sort of quick, like he knew the truth.

"So, what am I supposed to call you?" I asked.

"It's Pez," he said, watching me even more carefully as he shoved himself backward across the street. I stared until he hit the parked cars on the other side, directly outside the blue house almost opposite our flat; the one that until yesterday had a SOLD sign stuck in its front yard. "See you round," he called out, dragging his bike up onto the curb.

"Vetty," I shouted after him. "Everyone calls me Vetty."

Without turning around, he raised the fingers of his left hand in a peace sign and clambered up the steps toward his new front door. I waved up at Mum, who stood out on the pavement, staring at the same house across the street, watching the door that Luna Boyd had walked through moments earlier.

Those sweets never tasted right but I didn't mind because from that day onward having a best friend was no longer a theoretical fantasy I'd read about in books or seen on TV. I had a real-life one right across the street and for the first time ever it felt as though I'd plugged right into life. Things started to fit and some even made sense. With Pez, I was more than the nervous *me* I was at school, I was all the fun *me*s inside my head too, because, for some reason I never stopped to try to understand, he didn't seem to care which version turned up outside his door.

Aunt Wendy arrived from Somerset wheeling my birthday present out of her van the next weekend. It was a shiny green racing bike and my eyes pricked with tears as I read the card. *Go, Vetty, go!* it said, and go I did. Term had started again but me and Pez spent every hour not at school tearing around those streets. The nasty twins in my class mattered less and less, and then, when life couldn't get any better, the weekends came around and our days felt endless. We'd get tired cycling and climb the white willow in Camden Square and drink Mars Milk and suck Haribos until our tongues burned. Before we knew it, it was summer again and we carved our names in the bark of our tree and this little den we shared felt like the center of the universe.

For four years we raced the wind along the canal to the best-ever fish-and-chips up at Tufnell Park, to the tennis courts off York Way, whizzing around the market stalls, over the cobbled bridge at Camden Lock, past the pretty houseboats, back up the canal again, and home in time for tea. On days when we felt lazy we'd lie on our backs and sing songs, or rate our favorite sweets out of ten, and if it was wet, we'd move to the couch and watch *Super 8* or *Kick-Ass*, and when we got sick of these, we'd stick on one of Mum's old DVDs: *Big*, *Stand by Me*, or *Raiders of the Lost Ark*. We'd watch them over and over again until we could play out our favorite scenes word for word. *Clueless* had some of our best lines. Pez was better than me. I'd mix up the expressions, but he'd get all the timings and even the American accents just right. At Christmas, we'd play chess and Perudo, and in the summer when it was hot, we'd hike the bikes all the way to the heath and soothe our steaming skin in the icy cold water at the public pool. It was grazed knees and full hearts until one wet April day when the doctors found the grapefruit pushing against Mum's chest.

Mum had a primary mediastinal large B-cell lymphoma. I wrote the words down carefully. Stage 4, the doctor said to Dad, so I wrote this down too. He also said it was too late for treatment, but I didn't write that. I didn't need to. His voice was like a Sharpie splotching clean paper with its black ink, the permanent kind that soaks through the pages, ruining the next and then the next. Mum started the treatment anyway, but it didn't work and quickly she became thinner and less able to talk. Pez gripped my hand under the willow tree, pulsing it gently in bursts of three, our silent code, and each of his little squeezes assured me he was there and always would be. Unlike everyone else, he never pretended everything was normal or even remotely okay. My chest got so tight that summer and I'd be so busy breathing, I never thought of words like "thank you." Three weeks before my thirteenth birthday they moved Mum into the tall hospital by Euston Road where she lay in a bed sweating and tied up in tubes. Eight days later she stopped breathing forever.

The night after she died, Dad got drunk, and when he was done shouting at the sky, he came inside and stared at the Banksy print that hung on our living room wall. He let rip at the pink Mona Lisa, roaring at her like it was her fault Mum was gone. The next morning, he sat me and Arial down and told us that in two weeks we'd be moving. Without Mum, he needed help, so we had to be near Aunt Wendy. Without Mum, I needed to be near Pez and the white willow tree and the life I knew, but nobody stopped for long enough to really think about this.

It was the first store-bought birthday cake I'd ever had. Dad, Aunt Wendy, Arial, and Pez stood around our suddenly cold kitchen, trying too hard to look happy. Dad's trembling hands lit the candles and I looked at their gathered faces, but I couldn't do it. All the tingling life had left me. I waved my arm over the hot mess, trying to kill the flames, trying to make their tiny lights go out.

"C'mon, Vetty. Make a wish!" Pez shouted it angrily like I wasn't trying. I wanted to stab him and Fudgie the Whale with my spoon. I was thirteen, not three! Besides, I *was* trying.

I didn't care much for cycling after that. Not sure I cared much for anything, and three days after this unhappy birthday the truck came and drove our life down the motorway to Somerset.

Dad finally bought me a phone; this was the extent of the good news that summer. At first, me and Pez spoke all the time. He'd share chess moves and tell bad jokes he'd learned from even worse films, but it wasn't long before those calls became messages and the days became weeks and weeks became months, until one day during the Christmas holidays we stopped communicating altogether.

Dad and everyone else wanted life to get back to some kind of normal. Pretending everything was fine felt like the easiest way, and I pretended my heart out until things almost were. I started my new school and I made friends with Liv and Freya and Jess and they helped to fill most of the empty space. It was reasonably easy to get by provided I avoided being all of myself.

I considered telling Jess about my greedy heart until I realized I wasn't ready for how different things would be if I did. I was just settling in, already the new girl with the dead mum and the funny name, who lives with her gay aunts. I didn't need another thing singling me out.

I quickly learned to keep some stuff back, but there are times when it's as though I watched those friends behind glass, observing them from the lens of my iPhone. Times I've wanted to explain that what they see isn't all of me. Times I've wondered if they'll ever know about the rest, the me who could at any point explode or take off like a rocket. Guess I never felt like explaining. I never had to explain anything to Pez. But maybe that was then, and this is now. Soon I'll be back to London anyway. Soon I'll be back to me.

3

At first Dad said we'd be gone a year but quickly he stopped talking about going back. Then, last month, his boss told him to be in the office five days a week or be fired, or words to that effect. Having supported his working from home for almost four years, it's not like the company is being completely heartless. Arial starts her school holidays tomorrow so we'll set off behind the moving van in the afternoon, driving our life up the motorway and back to St. Agnes Villas. Dad drove to London last week to help the tenants move out and he bumped into Pez on the road outside. He said everything was like it had always been; Pez had gotten bigger and his bike had gotten smaller but that was it.

"What if he's changed?" I asked. "Or he thinks I have?"

"People don't really change, Vetty," Dad said. "Not really."

I hope with all my heart that this is true.

Pez was never a boyfriend; he was a best friend and the last person I've felt properly close to. I can't stop imagining how it will be to see him again, or how life will be once I'm back. Every day I think about the stupid fun things we did and how, now, I struggle to know where to begin saying all I want to say. As kids, me and Pez wore the same jeans; we even had matching baseball shirts with our names on the back that his dad, Harland, bought for us in America. Everything felt right. I felt right. It was only when we left London that *being myself* became so complicated. In Somerset I was more girlie but I felt less right inside, and it was nothing to do with the makeup I wore or the clothes I cared about. It went deeper, an uncomfortable itch that gnawed at the pit of me, like a buried truth trying to wriggle its way out. Whether this was to do with the move or me, I'm not sure. I just know right now, I'd give anything to be that girl on her bike again, that girl who wasn't so afraid to be herself.

I'm on the couch, Dad is beside me, and Arial is sitting on the floor. It's our last night at our cottage on Aunt Wendy's farm, one of two rentals she runs with Fran, her soon-to-be wife. Without these women and this lovely place, none of us would have managed to stay vaguely sane for the past four years. Wendy is too nice to say it but I know she's relieved we're leaving. She's only human. Besides, she and Fran are getting married next month and they're knee-deep in wedding preparations. It's all that's been talked about around here for weeks. Not that anyone is complaining. We've tried different cakes and ciders and there was even a tent trial in the paddock last week. From what I've seen, planning a wedding is way more fun than getting married.

Fran's been making a playlist of their favorite hip-hop, and very late one night last week, I was crossing the yard when I saw the two of them dancing in the kitchen. I stood outside the double doors in the dark and watched as they moved around the room to "Can't Take My Eyes Off

give her a celebratory shoulder shove. "We'll wash it after we eat," I say, tying her slimy hair up in a bun. She gives me a double thumbs-up without her eyes leaving the screen.

Dad still has tiny white sticks in his ears. A lot of the time I have no idea whether he's talking to me or his phone. I follow him into the kitchen and we start our familiar mealtime dance without a word. We've become one of those families who eat the same thing on the same day each week, which, given Mum read Lebanese cookbooks and stored her homemade granola in labeled glass jars, isn't something I'm proud of. If she saw how we ate now she might die all over again.

We eat at Wendy's house as much as we can, so I can still only make six things, and Dad, for all his enthusiasm, is a lame sous chef. So Sunday is roast chicken, Monday is stir-fry, Tuesday is usually sausages, Wednesday is spaghetti Bolognese, and Thursday, today, is fish sticks. Friday is chili, but nobody likes kidney beans so it's basically spicy Bolognese with rice. Saturday comes via the Domino's app. It's written up on the fridge but sometimes we just eat cereal in front of the TV anyway. I gave Arial Rice Krispies with a side of celery sticks once. I figure as long as I include something green with each meal then she'll make it to my age with all her teeth.

She cartwheels into the room in reassuringly good health. Dad's upper body is entirely in the freezer and an icy mist gathers around his dismembered, stripy legs. "Did you see the letter about that new term induction thing you missed?" he shouts up.

"*I* showed it to *you.*"

"Of course," he says. "Forgot."

I lean over the sink, stabbing at a raisin that's been jammed in the plughole since breakfast. "And I scanned back the confirmation to the moving company."

"Good," he says, slinging a giant sack of peas onto the counter and pulling himself up to standing. "Please say they took the credit card?"

I slide the plastic ziplock along and stare in at the frosted green pearls. It's a lovely image. Comforting. Dad has tons of photography books, weighty hardback ones with beautiful covers, and I often spread them all out on the living room floor to pore over the glossy pages. Mum would buy them for his birthday and they felt like proper presents, because I knew he'd never spend that much money on books for himself. There's one photographer who only takes pictures of ordinary everyday stuff—people at the beach, plates of eggs and home fries, that type of thing—but in his photos, nothing seems ordinary; he makes you look again. He's my favorite. He might appreciate these freezer-burned peas.

"Vetty? The credit card?"

"Sorry," I say. "Yeah." He bobs his head, ticking it off the list in his mind. I grab the potatoes out of the fridge and start to peel one into the trash. Arial likes real fries, homemade like Mum used to make, but they take ages. We'll have to make a real dinner every day once we get to London. Seven days a week, three hundred and sixty-five days a year, not including extra weekend meals and Arial's packed lunches. "How was your conference call?"

I'm only being polite, but he sighs like he's thinking about the answer. "The client asked another agency to pitch.

Everyone is nervous we could lose the account, but apart from that . . ." He trails off.

I shouldn't have gone there. I only ask this stuff because I feel like I should, probably 'cause Mum isn't around to anymore. But my head is already full with other things.

He whisks Arial up onto his knee. "It'll be fine," he says, wrapping his arms around her and popping the white buds from his ears like he's up for a chat. "Because it has to be, eh? All set for tomorrow?"

I nod but my eyes veer off toward the fridge. It's a big old-fashioned one and looks like it should no longer work, but it does. It came with us from London and it's like another pillar holding us all upright. Sometimes its gentle hum will break for seconds, and the silence frightens me as much as if an actual human had stopped breathing. That fridge was Mum's scrapbook and today it's still covered with photos, bills, Arial's gym certificates, and a thousand school notices. Barely an inch of its blue door is still visible.

It's the storyboard of our family, a sort of shrine, and high up in the left-hand corner, above our invite to Wendy and Fran's wedding, is a photo of Pez and me. Luna took it on the steps outside his house. I'm wearing green polka-dot shades and my short, bobbed hair blazes in the sun. Pez's left arm is slung casually around my neck as his face squints up to the camera. Both our purple, candy-stained tongues jutting out like ten-year-old punks. It's been there for years, never questioned, never covered over. It might be my favorite photo in the world. It hits me that this precious collage should come down for the movers tomorrow, but I resolve not to move it now, or ever.

"Mum used to say you were like those kids in that film," he says, scratching his head trying to think of the title.

"*Pretty in Pink*," I say, turning around. "But I'd hardly call them *kids*. And she only said it because my hair is red like Molly Ringwald."

"She loved that film." He mumbles it to himself, pulling the chopping board toward him and slicing my newly peeled potatoes into chubby sticks. "And your hair's not red," he says, looking up.

"Auburn, whatever, and anyway Pez wasn't exactly Duckie."

Dad lays down his knife. "What!" he says. "I saw him, waiting outside on that bike like a puppy. I watched his face light up when you'd come to the door."

"That's such a dad thing to say."

"Well, it's true," he says. "Mum arrived home one afternoon bubbling over, I'll never forget." His hand covers his mouth and he looks out the window. "She'd been walking past the square from the bus stop and heard giggling coming from the swings over the hedge. She must have recognized your laugh and squeezed her head into the gap in the railing above the sign on the square." He turns to me. "You know the one?"

I've heard this story so many times but I let him go on. "Uh-huh."

"There you were, kissing Pez! *On the lips*, she said!" At this, Arial's face does the full revolted grandma and she slumps from Dad's knee. Neither he nor I protest when she edges toward the door and slinks back into the TV. His shoulders give a small shudder as the memory hits. "You'd barely turned twelve," he says, staring into thin air.

I shut my eyes. I remember that kiss, but it sounds like life on another galaxy now. It was a week before the doctors found the grapefruit and it's hard not to wonder whether Mum really had heard us laughing, or whether she stopped by the railings because she had to. She'd been getting short of breath for months. It was one of those things you only notice looking back, and I wonder whether Dad is thinking this too.

It was the only kiss. I was actually twelve and three quarters and Pez was only a few months behind. I made him pretend he was George, our new tennis teacher who was twenty-two and from Greece. I don't know what made these details so dizzying *or* how exactly Pez was supposed to *be* George, particularly given George was a girl, but this didn't bother either of us much. There were no tongues, but I made him do it over and over, quite a few times in fact, and my cheeks smolder remembering the urgent feeling between my legs and how I had to stop myself from pushing up against him in his white shorts.

"Bet he's thrilled?" Dad says, throwing an uncooked french fry at me from the other side of the table and missing.

"About what?" I ask, dipping down to rescue the fry. When I look up, he's making Arial's *duh* face, which is one thing on her, or even me, but on a man pushing fifty, is not good.

"That you're moving back."

I can't bring myself to say we haven't been in touch enough for me to tell him. "I wouldn't go that far."

He watches as I bite my lip and then he spins slowly around. "True friendship, Vetty," he says, shuffling his stack of uncooked fries, "is for the brave."

I pick up the peeler and bend back over the trash, trying to look busy, hating that my lack of courage might be so obvious. Then Dad switches on the fryer and starts humming, which he does when he's nervous. His pitch matches that of the fridge. "I watched a few episodes of the new *Darkzone* the other night," he says cheerily. "Luna does all her own stunts, apparently." *Darkzone* is in its fourth season. Dad's watched them all. Everyone has. "It'll be streaming on iPlayer, but maybe some of it is a little adult," he says, shaking *all* the fish sticks from the giant box into the pan.

I stop chopping. "Dad!"

"What?" He twists around.

"You've done it again! They don't cook properly when you put that many on at once." He turns away and stares into the frying pan, not saying anything, and my words bounce around the room. I watch his back go up and down as giant breaths fill his chest. Why isn't he teasing me about getting so wound up like he usually does?

Very slowly he returns to face me. "Sweetheart—" He stops. His face has a new expression and his soft voice only makes my words echo louder. His lips purse like he's concentrating hard as he folds up the huge, empty box. "You've taken on a lot," he says with a sigh. "You've had to." He raises a hand up to make his point, but he's holding the box the wrong way up and bright-orange bread crumbs scatter like confetti all over the tiles. It's everything I can do not to reach over to clean them up. "And the truth is you'll have to take on more once we move." He puts the egg flipper down and reaches for my hand. He looks disturbingly serious.

"I just meant we'll never eat all—"

"I'm not talking about the bloody fish sticks now, Vetty," he says. "Believe it or not"—he passes his hand slowly over the range—"after four years, I'm still working out how to do this parenting thing on my own. And I'm not sure if I'm always doing it right. I keep asking myself, 'What would *she* do?'" he says, briefly closing his eyes and moving his balled fist to his chest. "Look, I know going back to London is a big move but I think she'd agree that we're ready."

It takes me a minute to speak. "But your work, isn't that why—"

He gives the pan a brusque shake. "It's not just that. This"—he sniffs and looks around the kitchen—"was never meant to be permanent. We needed to be here. We needed Wendy and Fran. You were too young." He looks into my eyes and I feel see-through. "But we need to live *our* lives again. Does that make sense?" He tilts my chin to his face. "I'm tired of holding my breath. Aren't you?" The truth in his words knocks me but I manage to nod back. "And I'll try not to land too much on you," he says. "I promise."

I pull away and kneel down, pretending to sweep up the fish stick mess, but he bends down too, shaking the crumbs from my fingers. Then he puts his arm around my neck and we kind of slowly slump against the warm oven door, him gently rubbing my head until my eyes close. All I see in my mind are those two faces staring out from that fridge.

4

The motorway was hell. It's taken us forever to reach Camden, and now a white van is blocking the residents' parking space outside our flat. Dad pulls the car up behind it and I roll down the window while we wait for the driver to finish off-loading. Even this late in the evening the city air is thick with heat.

I steal a glance at Pez's pale-blue house across the street. It's not really a glance; I only stop staring when Arial wakes up and announces, "I smell trash," before she starts questioning the logic of us still sitting in a parked car.

Dad laughs, but she's right. I take my seat belt off and shift around, joining her as she looks out at our house, No. 6 St. Agnes Villas. Her eyes travel up and down it. "It's not *that* small," she says, sticking her head out her window for a better view.

Dad and I share a look. "Ours is the basement flat, Arial," I say. "Giles, the old guy with the cats, lives above. I told you. But we have the yard out back." I add this bit more cheerfully.

"I know," she says, her shoulders sinking. "It's just different from how I remember."

An angry dog drags a man down the street and Dad pulls Arial back inside the car. "The van is nearly an hour behind," he says. "We should grab something to eat."

I hold up the button to shut my window. "There's a Domino's on the main avenue." Food usually gets Arial's attention, but she's watching Dad, who is staring at our house like he's wondering how our stuff will ever fit back into that flat. I know this because I've been wondering the exact same thing. I'm about to say something when the van in front pulls away and I nudge Dad to get moving.

"Forget Domino's," he says, once he's finished backing up. "The Italian on Brecknock Road does the real deal."

Arial seems content, so I open the car door and step onto the street like I'm putting on old shoes, wiggling my toes and praying they still fit. Even my fingertips fizz. It's like the air itself is electrically charged. I look up and let all the blurred details come back into focus. The house was built in Victorian times, I think, and it looks every bit as lived-in as it should. A not-very-famous German guy wrote poems here two hundred years ago and there's a little blue plaque on the wall outside Giles's living room window with his name on it. It's not as tall as the other houses on the street, having only two floors above the basement, whereas some houses, like Pez's, have four floors in total. Every entrance along the street looks different, like a large front door will move to the side to make way for another window, or a top floor will slope in a half triangle with only one window instead of two, so each house manages to look unique. They all have their own shade of brick and some are painted in pastel colors, like the pale pink and the yellow ones farther up.

I love this street. I love it for more than the obvious reasons like it's where we lived with Mum. I also love that it's a hill, which is great for freewheeling *and* eating ice cream at the same time, and I love that it's two minutes from the square with its playground and climbable white willow, and I love it for the odd stew of people who live here too. Most of the houses are split into flats, like ours, but in another a dusty writer might live alone with their books. The Indian lady who Mum went to for acupuncture above the pub on Murray Street could flip among Bengali, Somali, and Albanian as well as English within the one conversation. All sorts of people live here: actors like Pez's parents, teachers, artists, politicians, and the white-haired guy who reads the news on TV, and Giles, who doesn't work anymore. When Arial was really little, a couple slept in an abandoned car right outside our flat and for months they lived upside-down days under a blanket, smoking pipes that made their eyes blaze.

Giles's window box with its bright-purple pansies is so lovely I almost don't notice how grubby the surrounding paintwork is. Apparently, the tenants who rented our flat were also big into cooking but less into cleaning and Dad had to pay contractors to freshen up the place. Under her arm, Arial clutches Eeyore, her blue donkey. He's come everywhere with us since she was two years old, but she's taken to hiding him lately, which makes me sad. He's threadbare from love and covered in stains. I suggested a pre-move spa day, but she rescued him from the wash basket and hasn't let go of him since. She's standing by the car now like she doesn't want to walk any farther and I sense the weight of her feet from here. We haven't stepped inside the flat and already this place is full of Mum. Despite the fizzing in my nerve endings, my feet feel heavy too, and it's a jittery mix. I walk around and grab our overnight bags and as we make our way down the side passage to our front door, I jangle the keys as jollily as I can.

The door opens straight into the kitchen, which in four strides leads into the living room. I drop the bags and cast my eye around the space. The light is bad, the ceiling is lower than I remember, and it smells too. The furniture we left behind looks older and the place badly needs air . . . ideally some paint and possibly a few books. How did the four of us fit in here before? I try not to think about how we will make it a home again without her.

"Where's our room?" Arial asks.

Just then Dad appears. "Arial can take the spare room," he says. "I won't need an office." Arial forces a smile, but my chest sinks with relief. "C'mon, Arial," Dad says, checking his phone. "Let's grab that pizza. Ten minutes, Vetty."

He pulls the door open with a wink and I trudge to the end of the room, thrusting the glass doors wide and stepping out into the yard that's not a whole heap bigger than our kitchen back at Wendy's. I stand there, soaking up the heat of the evening sun, trying to think of nothing, just for a few seconds. I close my eyes, and my ears revel in the hum of traffic on Agar Grove blending with a heavy drumbeat that pounds from a distant window.

It's a long minute before a cloud passes overhead and I open my eyes in the new shade. Then I see it! I blink and it's still there. An explosion of pink, feathery petals on a tiny tree, almost taller than me, bursting out from the back wall.

It's the silk tree me and Mum planted from tiny seedpods a few months before we knew about any grapefruit and I step forward and examine the flowers that fall like clusters of pink powder puffs from its large green leaves. I knelt beside her on this wall, up to my wrists in mulch, neither of us believing the photo of exotic color that the tiny plastic triangle promised.

"Look!" I say to nobody, sprinkling a smattering of showy stamens into my hand. I want to hug it for being here. I want to hug it for being alive. I take out my phone and snap, snap, snap, getting up real close. My eyes sting as mascara trickles down into them but I break off several short flowers and I wander into the kitchen to find a glass. I find one that must have come free with a Japanese beer and I fill it with water then head for my old room.

It's more Lilliputian than I remember and grubbier too. There's a narrow full-length mirror where my bed used to be, and I inspect the stubborn remains of the *Despicable Me* stickers someone stuck to the bottom. My bedroom at Wendy's was nearly double this size, with a window where I'd watch the sunrise over a field of cows. Still, there were times, in the beginning mostly, when my insides cramped with longing to be back here. Looking around, it's hard to believe I felt that way.

I place the glass beside the bed and already the room looks a bit brighter; then I wedge my head between the edge of the blind and the window frame. I pull the blind to the side and shove the sash upward to let out the stale air. I'd almost forgotten the painted white bars outside. This is the spot where I always stood. From here I can see up the whole street, but it's the blue house across the road I want to look at. His large front door is a new color but other than that the house looks the same. Faded lace still hangs from the small windows on the very top floor, where Luna and Harland sleep and where we pinched coins from on top of the dressing table like they were treasure left specially for us.

Pez would speak about his parents like they were people he watched on TV, which was at least half-right. He'd feed me snippets of their conversations like something he glimpsed through a passing window or overheard changing the channel during the ads. I never showed it of course, but sometimes listening to his stories made me nervous. Not that Mum and Dad never fought, because they did, but there was something sharp in the way Luna and Harland spoke to each other that was different.

His bedroom is the large window to the left on the floor below and his shutters are wide-open, like always. I can make out shapes of picture frames and posters against his wall and the faint glow from a TV or screen in sleep mode. It's tricky to see inside properly. It needs to be fully dark with the lights on for that, I remember suddenly. I spot the angry dog dragging the man back up the street and as I turn a tiny flash disturbs the light in Pez's bedroom. I press right up against the glass, straining to see. It's him!

I push back into my room, pacing up and down before peering back through the corner of the window frame again. He's leaning forward, watching something on the screen that casts a strange light on his face. I half expect him to come to the glass or to flash his bedside lamp like he used to; then I imagine flashing mine back and our two lights beating like hearts in the dark as we make silly faces against the glass. He reclines in the chair and as more of him unfolds into view I log all the changes I see: I can't help noticing how his body takes up more window than ever before. A loud bang makes me jump.

"Vetty!" It's Arial at the front door and I walk into the living room to see a slice of her face is framed in the letter slot. "Let us in," she shouts. "We've got pizza . . . and there's a truck full of boxes!"

Before we left the farm, Wendy insisted on a traffic-light packing system. Dad, Fran, and I laughed as she ran around the cottage labeling everything with her sticky colored dots. Boxes with green stickers have essentials like the kettle and mugs and tea bags and duvets and towels inside. These are first-tier priority, to be unpacked first, and as soon as we finished eating we started on these and kept at it until all the beds had sheets. Wendy was right. It was really useful to know which to unpack first, but to be honest I doubt we'll ever open a box with yellow dots. Reds can forget it. Come bedtime Arial wanted a story, and for some reason, I said yes.

I close *Anne of Green Gables*, which we've been reading for months, tucking down a tiny corner at the top of the page. She's watching me like she's waiting for more but I'm too tired. I stick my tongue out and reach over for her bedside light. "It's late."

"She reminds me of you," she says, burrowing into the duvet.

"Anne-with-an-*E*?" She tries to nod but her long plait is twisted behind her head. I tug it free and drape it across the pillow like a blond snake. "Mmmm . . . must be the red hair." I'm so used to people saying things like this it flies out. I'm uneasy about physical comparisons; always have been. I should probably encourage Arial to avoid making assumptions based on people's looks, but not tonight.

She props herself up on her elbows in the dark. "Do you ever imagine you had a different name?"

"Something *romantic* like *Cordelia*?"

"I'm serious," she says. "Do you like being called Helvetica?"

I roll my eyes, but the question makes me sit straight. "People confuse your typeface with mine all the time," I say. "Did you know that?" She shakes her head. "They mix them up, just like sisters."

She tries not to smile and the way she shifts about makes the stiff sheets rustle. I pinch her nose and push up off the bed. "Hey," she shouts out. "You haven't answered the question."

"Good night!" I call out from behind her door.

It's almost midnight when I finally get to my room. I should sleep but I can't. I think about rewatching *Stranger Things* but then I think about Pez and how much I'd like to watch it with him. I go to the window and drag the blind back. It's as dark as London gets outside and I can see inside his room so much better now. He's still up, sitting at his computer playing games like I left him hours ago. The strange glow is the only light and its pale beam makes his face look far away.

He looks like a ghost.

5

A clatter of smashing bottles announces the day. Hundreds of them thrash into the hungry belly of a recycling truck. I lift my arm and check my watch. 7:52 a.m. Saturday. I try to relax into the relentless *clink, clank, crash* but it's useless. When it finally stops I close my eyes but then the house gives a thunderous rumble and something seemingly endless passes very close by. Ah yes, the Overground train. Good morning, London.

I crawl out of bed, grab a hoodie from the back of the chair, and zip it up to my chin. Then I shuffle down to the window as the recycling truck trundles off, leaving the street hushed and still. Staring at his sleepy house, I imagine warm bodies in their soft beds and my early eyes blur as my mind drains to nothingness, until THRUMP! His front door slams. And I mean SLAMS, so loud that my fingers tremble on the windowpane in some imagined aftershock. I blink and move nearer the glass. I'm so close that my warm breath fogs it up.

Harland, Pez's dad, thumps down the front steps toward me, steaming tea sloshing from the mug in his hands. He dumps it on the front pillar and pats his pockets down. I slink back behind the blind until a car engine springs to life and I peer into the crack between the wall and the blind, which, not for the first time, I notice smells like some spice. That's when I see Pez standing in their doorway—stretched thin by a rolling pin and looking slept-in too, as though ripped from the bed seconds earlier. My chest tightens. If it weren't his house I'm not sure I'd recognize him. Where are the cornrows and the baseball cap? All that's left is a short back and sides, buzzed on top. I want to smile but I can't. Not when he has that look on his face. It's pure anger.

I pull back the duvet to check on Arial, my 3 a.m. visitor, and reassured by her snores, I step into my flip-flops, shoving my phone into my pocket, and then I'm out the hall door and into the brand-new day in seconds. It's cooler than I expected and as I sneak along the sidewall goose bumps dapple the length of my arm. I crouch down by the pillar at the bottom of Giles's steps, unsure as to why exactly I'm hiding. When I peek my head around, Harland squeezes his car out of the narrow space and onto the road. I press further against the wall as it passes but he doesn't look back. My eyes return to the house, where Pez is now bounding down the steps, BMX gripped under his arm, its wheels leaping about wildly.

I hadn't planned to stand up, but I do, and Pez and his bike are alone in the empty parking space. His long arms are straight and stiff on the handlebars and my heart springboards off my ribs, like it's trying to vault right out of my chest. He slings his leg over the saddle and then, like he feels my eyes on his, he looks up.

It's just us in the middle of the street, staring at each other in the early morning, and for a few seconds there's only silence as I slosh around in a torrent of words I can't get out. That's when he moves closer, looping the empty air.

"C'mon, if you're coming," he says, in a voice that's his but not his. Our first words in over three and a half years. At first my feet won't move. "Get on," he says. "Quick!"

Despite how big the rest of him is, I notice his thin wrists and how they look just as they did when he was nine. I pull my hood up and grasp his T-shirt, hauling myself up onto the pegs. I have a sudden urge to run my fingers over his new hair and feel it rough under my skin. Instead I grip his shoulders, which are thick in my hands. It's all I can do to stay upright.

"What are we doing?" I shout it into the wind.

He tilts his head toward mine. "Following him," the new voice shouts. "Hold on!"

He takes the corner wide and we dart and dive, flying into Murray Street like chairoplanes at the fairground, in time to see the brake lights on Harland's navy Jeep before it turns left into Camden Road. Pez's feet pound the pedals and we speed past the recycling trucks, toward the already steady traffic in front. He bursts onto the main road without stopping, milliseconds ahead of a duo of double-deckers heading into town. Adrenaline shoots through me and I'm suddenly more awake than I've been in my life. Once we're well on our way down Camden Road, I squeeze my eyes shut, savoring the wind on my face, allowing the roar of traffic to fill my ears. I understand now just how long it's been since I've felt this.

When I open my eyes again, the Jeep has stopped at the lights, but they go green as we approach and Pez speeds up, following it right into St. Pancras Way. After the turn, we slink up onto the pavement, weaving among the trees, hurtling along the footpath in the shade.

Roadworks and temporary lights ahead. Pez sees them

and he cuts up into Rochester Place, heading left toward the main street. Within seconds we've reached the pedestrian barrier at Kentish Town Road, where the Jeep approaches from the left and comes to another stop at the lights by Pizza Express. Pez stands firm, right foot clawing the ground, anticipating Harland's next move. When the lights change Harland goes left and Pez pounces, swooping after him like a hawk, and soon we're on his tail again. The Jeep passes the Overground station and we watch it go right. We follow and shadow the car to the top of the road, where it takes another right at the sandwich bar. At the next corner, Pez stops to peer around it. I stick my head around too.

"He's doing a loop," Pez says, and soon we've taken off again. Up ahead, the Jeep indicates left, but slows at the turning. "That's a one-way, dickhead." Pez says it under his breath and the Jeep continues ahead as we go left into Inkerman Road, bumping up onto the pavement the way Harland's car couldn't. At the junction, we stop by the pub and wait. My chest rests on his back as drips from an overhead flower basket rain into my hood, trickling icy drops down the back of my neck.

"Do either of you know where we're going?" I ask, but Pez just stares ahead. I hop off the bike, Pez too, but suddenly he reaches behind and pushes us both back up against the wall just as Harland's car reappears and turns right into Inkerman Road where it finally slows. Together we watch the car slot expertly into a tight space by the dead end, then the door opens and Harland stretches out onto the pavement. Skin color aside, Harland and Pez are like peas in a pod, their stature and mannerisms eerily close. His tall, lean frame stoops to open a small gate in front of a terraced house; then quickly he disappears inside the door in front.

Pez grinds his teeth. "Wait here," he says. "I'm going back home for something but I'll be quicker alone." He looks at his watch. "Nine minutes max. Don't take your eyes off his car." Before I've said anything, he's cycled off.

I stare at the house, trying to take it all in. I'm afraid to move, so I sit up on the table of the pub bench for a better view but there's nothing else to see and Pez has only been gone two minutes. I stare at a lonely cigarette butt floating in an ashtray beside me, wearing a trace of peach lipstick on its tip. My hands shake with excited adrenaline as well as fear as I take out my phone to check the time; then I hear a door shut nearby and I look up, but it's only a neighbor on the far side of the street. I hold my phone up, framing Harland's car ahead, and for a while I pretend to take pictures like some undercover detective. I think about how many minutes it's been as a man with a long, green hose reaches a sprinkler into the flower basket above my head. I'm moving out of his way when Pez shoots up from the top of Alma Street, between Harland's Jeep and me, his arm slinging the air again. I run toward him. He pushes the handlebars of the bike at me and fumbles in his pocket.

"Be ready, yeah?" he says.

"Ready for what?"

"To follow me!"

I'm about to ask where but he's already slid off, jeans slung low on his hips and his arms heavy, like he's still not sure how to wear his suddenly broad shoulders. He quickly reaches the house and I notice the way he bends like he's apologizing for growing so tall. Then he stops. I'm not sure what I'm expecting next but it's not for him to open Harland's car and climb inside. I'm wondering what's in there that he wants, when the engine fires and suddenly the whole giant Jeep jolts forward and crashes straight into the silver Honda in front. Alarms cry like angry bells. Two of them, ringing furiously out of sync. DING BOING DING BOING DING BOING. It's loud enough to wake the entire world.

Pez tumbles out of the car and races toward me. "Go, go, go," he shouts. I do what he says and climb onto the bike but I can't not glance back, and when I do, Harland is out on the street, his back to us, staring at his car with its door open and engine running. A woman with long, dark hair joins his side. "Move!" Pez says again, and I push off and cycle away. He grasps on tight behind me and we slip down a tiny alley into some road I don't recognize, Pez shouting out directions as we go. With a sharp left and a right, we're back out into the Kentish Town Road and I'm whizzing past the familiar sights of Poundstretcher and Superdrug, breaking the lights by Nando's, past Peanut Butter Books where we used to go with Mum and a tiny new café, painted bright orange, that's already open for business. Soon we reach the lights for Chalk Farm, where I jump the curb on the other side and we ride the empty footpath before tucking into Rochester Road. I keep going, pedaling as fast as I can, and mixed up in the fear there's a thrill too; it's like our own *Stranger Things* moment.

"In there!" Pez shouts, pointing at the residents' yard in the middle of the green. It's only once we're inside the gate and safely hidden by the bushes that he bounces down. I hop off the bike like the past four years were nothing, but as I lower it onto the grass I'm panting to catch my breath. "Shit, shit, shit!" he says, pacing around it.

"What was that? Did you deliberately *total* your dad's car? Or were you trying to steal it? I can't work out which is crazier?"

"Gimme a minute," he says. "I can't think." His voice is quiet and he rubs his hand up and down over his tight curls, just how I wanted to earlier. "I didn't mean to crash it," he says then.

I've never been in this yard and I pace the grass opposite him, watching a woman walk her dog on the other side of the hedge, praying she doesn't come any closer. When I look back Pez is staring blankly at his purple BMX. "Pez, what's going on?" He looks up, finally showing me all of his face up close. The shadow on his top lip is a surprise and there's one on his chin and jawline too. "Pez?" I say it again but he flicks his eyes back to the bike like he didn't hear me. "This is serious," I say, stepping closer and pushing him back. It's instinct or muscle memory from a hundred joke tussles and I'm expecting him to stumble but when my hand hits his chest he doesn't flinch. When did he get muscles under that T-shirt? Please say he doesn't work out. Please tell me he hasn't changed that much.

He's looking at me, looking like he's thinking, and it's suddenly clear that nobody has looked at me this way for a long time. I don't mean he's doing some staring-into-my-eyes kind of bullshit. Nothing like that. He really is just looking, but he's paying attention, like he's thinking or trying to work something out. I'm not sure what, but suddenly I'm conscious of yesterday's mascara under my eyes, even though I know that's not what's important now. I try to get back on track. "We tail Harland for miles, then you get into his Jeep and—"

I stop because his hands are on his knees like he doesn't want this interrogation. He's shaking his head from side to side, staring at his Nikes, which look fresh out of the box this morning.

I sit down cross-legged on the grass. "C'mon," I say, hoping he might sit too. He does and he glances at me, but he says nothing, and I'm left counting the lines that furrow his forehead. They've gotten deeper and more creased: like a Wi-Fi symbol etched into the space above his eyes. He pulls the car key out of his pocket and wipes it with his T-shirt, staring up at the white sky.

"Is everything okay?" I ask, softer now. It's not like I didn't see Harland's face coming down the steps before he drove off but it's been so long since I've asked this kind of question I don't know if I should. Pez finishes examining the car key and pushes it farther down into his pocket. I crawl my fingers across the dry grass toward his. "Pez?" His hand creeps back onto his lap and I watch it slowly become a fist inside his other. "I'd like to know," I press.

His jaw tightens and he inhales air sharply up one side of his nose. "*Now* you want to know?"

The face he makes twists all the strange energy around us and I realize the look in his eyes and the taut muscles around his mouth could be because of me, not Harland or anyone else, and I'm lost for what to say. I stare at the tops of the houses around us, thinking about the people behind the still-drawn curtains, yet to stir from their beds, the only thing worrying their sleepy heads being what to have for breakfast. It's like the ghost of us sits on the scorched grass between us, growing bigger in the silence, but I'm tired of ghosts and soon the words that have been circling my mind since I hopped onto that bike leap free. "This isn't how I imagined."

Pez snorts. "This?" he says, throwing his arm behind him. "Or *this*?" He points a finger toward his chest. I don't answer, I can't, and he starts to rub at the back of his neck again. "I had no idea you were moving back," he says. "Not until your dad pulled up outside the flat last week." He looks straight ahead now like he can't take my face. "He spoke to me like I knew, as though you'd already told me. You know, like a normal person would?" The word "normal" irks me but I reach a hand into the space between us again. "Don't worry," he says, shrinking away, "I went along with it. But forgive me if I'm not ready for all your movies-and-marshmallows chat just yet."

I feel sick. "I wasn't sure how to tell you."

He nods at my pocket. "Still got your phone, I see." He tugs tufts of dry grass from the hard ground, breathing out for a long time. "He's moving out," he says, scattering the short burned blades over his knees.

I let the words sink in, letting them soak up the image of the crashed cars and the lady with the long, dark hair. I haven't had an update on Harland and Luna for a long time but before I left, four years ago, Pez told me the only reason his parents stayed together was because they spent so much time apart. "That woman with Harland, back there, outside that house—"

"Forget it, yeah."

The dog walker completes another lap. "But his car, now we've run off and—"

"I was only planning to move it, to let *him* know *I* know. About her, about that place. That's all."

"I didn't even know you could drive."

He snorts. "I think it's pretty clear that I can't," he says, smiling like it's hard work. "But as soon as I heard the engine I just needed to . . . *feel* something." He whispers it, like he's talking to himself. His eyes close and I immediately want to tell him all the things I should right now, like that I'm here for him when he wants to talk. I'm working out the best way to say it when his mouth opens and he breathes out hard. "Ugh," he says. "I've had enough aggro for one morning." And he gets up, like he's decided himself this is the end of the matter.

He picks up his bike and looks toward the sky like he's checking it's still there. I feel so sad for him that his parents are separating but I feel worse for not knowing anything about it. In all this time I never thought to ask how things were and I'm kicking myself. He puts his foot down and steadies himself for me to climb up behind but I shake my head and amble along on the footpath instead. We don't talk again until we're on the other side of Camden Road.

As we round the corner into St. Agnes Villas he bounces down the curb. "It's good to see you," he says, making a face. I shove his shoulder, pushing him farther out onto the road in case he sees me smile. We're by the recycling bins when he puts his foot down again. "Can I come back to yours?"

I walk on. "We don't have any Coco Pops, just to warn you."

"But you eat them for dinner?"

"No, that was Crunchy Nut and we only did it while Mum was sick." We were never allowed those cereals until

50

the grapefruit, but then Dad couldn't give us enough sugary crap. "Things change," I say. "I'm trying not to buy them these days. Arial can put away a family box within hours."

He nods. "How old is she now?"

"Ten." *The age I was when I met you*, I think.

He shakes his face like it hits him too. "What's she up to?"

"Gymnastics. And watching TV, often at the same time. If she's not cartwheeling, she's online, watching someone else upside down."

He almost smiles at this and we make our way along the narrow path to our hall door in single file. He strolls inside, hopping onto the countertop by the sink, making everything look even smaller. I shake last night's pizza boxes and slide the heaviest one toward him. "Knock yourself out. I'll be back in a minute."

I stare at my reflection in the bathroom mirror, drying my wet cheeks with a towel, like I'm still dreaming. My head is like an upside-down triangle. Heart-shaped, I think, going from a wide, high forehead down to a pointy chin, but I find it hard to look at my whole face without getting tripped up by the individual features. If I had to choose, my eyes might be my favorite, mostly 'cause of their green color, but sometimes, especially in photos, they look too open and far apart, like an alien. Being green adds to the whole extraterrestrial thing. Best word to describe my hair is unexceptional: reddish brown, lank, not straight and not curly either, shoulder length, and blah. Brows like caterpillars. It's a fluke that people want them furry now. Mum once said I'd have been screwed in the nineties. The left one has a habit of rising up, cocking itself as though waiting for the answer to a difficult question. Like how in hell is Pez sitting out there eating cold pizza and how is having him here so normal and so strange at the same time? Like, how did I not stop to think what might have been going on for him since we left? And how is it my heart won't stop pounding and just looking at him is turning my insides out? Riddle me all that, bushy brow.

I cross the living room to the kitchen, where Pez is poured over the counter, slathering butter onto toast with no sign of a plate. I manage to keep my mouth shut. "I still don't eat mushrooms," he says, nodding to the open pizza box.

I let this go. There are too many words lined up in my mouth that need to come out, and eventually the only thing that does is "I can't stop worrying about all the trouble you're in."

"I'll deal with it," he says, taking another slice of bread from the loaf and slotting it into the toaster. Then he does an exaggerated stretch, like he's trying to look more relaxed than he is. He tosses a crust down. "I didn't think you'd ever move back," he says, looking around.

I rest the kettle in the sink and everything goes very still. It's time to say something important, like *I'm sorry*, but everything in my head is so clouded I don't know where to start. "Dad says we stayed at Wendy's three years longer than he planned." I try not to look at him, or his eyelashes, which are and have always been like a girl's. By "girl" I mean a mascara model. Nothing like mine, which are half the length and poker straight.

"You stopped posting your pictures," he says, and I freeze again. When I first got to Somerset I was obsessed with my new phone and I photographed everything. I'd post random shots of people and places like pieces of an obscure puzzle. It was nothing clever but it meant something to me and I'm so pleased to hear that he noticed. I wanted him to but he never mentioned anything. Besides, the subjects I wanted to photograph became less random and I wasn't ready for him to notice that.

"I was waiting to get a proper camera."

"So?"

"So, I never managed to save enough. Got out of the habit, I guess."

"I used to think you posted them for me," he says, thumbing crumbs off the countertop. "Not *for* me, but to *show* me. Shit, that sounds stupid."

Oh god. I did, at first. It was his encouragement I wanted the most. "But you never commented or anything?"

"Like you did on my posts?" he says, picking up the butter knife. He pops the toast up, but it's not done and he pings it back down. "We should probably drop this," he says with another huge fake yawn.

"Dad said the new *Darkzone* is amazing. Well, Luna is amazing, is what he really said." Pez is up, staring into our empty fridge, but then he shuts the door and turns around. I follow his eyes across the room, where Arial is standing in a corner, wearing pajamas and last night's ponytail.

"Look at you!" His voice is slow and quiet.

"Your hair's different," Arial says, then she finds my eyes like she's checking something. I smile and she stuffs Eeyore under a cushion, like she's only realized he's under her arm. She slowly moves forward, taking one step, then another, before wrapping her arms around Pez's waist. He kind of makes as if to crouch down but his arms hang uselessly by his sides and my body tenses. Why isn't he hugging her? I'm about to say something, when, very slowly, he places a hand on top of her hair and the two of them sway gently. I feel a sharp ache, like a stab of longing, wishing that he'd held me like that. Seconds later his hand moves away.

"Where are your braids?" Arial says, pushing her own hair back off her face.

I jump off the counter. "Um ... hang on. You said you barely remember this flat. How come you're all over his old hairstyle all of a sudden?"

She points above our heads. "From the picture."

Pez follows her hand to the fridge door, where his eyes register the photo of us and he shakes his head as though wondering how he could have missed it. His lips come apart. "When did she stick that up there?" he asks, taking Arial's hand and pulling her toward him. "For real."

"It's always been there, every day of my life." She says it so earnestly, Pez fails at not smiling and so do I. He returns to the picture, and then his fingertips lower down onto the stiff cream invitation underneath it. He spins back so quickly his sneakers squeak on the floor. "They're getting married?"

"Three weeks from today," I say, and soon there's another squeak as he pivots again, his back curved as he leans down to read where *Vetty plus one* is written in large calligraphy across the middle. All of a sudden, it's blindingly clear that Pez needs to be there with us in Somerset. It's obviously why Wendy gave me a plus-one in the first place. With him in tow, things could be so different, and maybe for the first time ever, I'd really feel like myself there. "Will you come with me?" I ask.

"Don't," he says, pulling at his bottom lip.

"Have you told him how you feel?" As soon as I've asked this it hits me that I'm not sure how Pez feels either.

"Harland's not interested in how I *feel*," he says, laughing in a way that makes me uneasy. "It's all a game to him and he only cares if I'm winning."

"How *do* you feel?"

"I don't give a shit," he says, and it's immediately clear he gives plenty.

I stare at his desk and the headphones plugged into the back of his iMac. Then I spot a series of framed sketches of a boy on a bike and I can tell by the style that he drew these himself and I really want to see them up close. I spot a stack of notebooks and his old Batman mug full of felt-tipped pens tucked away on the desk, behind the empty Coke can and a dirty plate. Lots of people, myself included, like to draw, but Pez is the only person I know who can draw a picture of someone and really make it look like them, not some basic face with vaguely similar hair. He gets the likeness in people's features exactly right. I want to ask him if he still draws Japanese comic figures and whether he's done any more work on his squad of elemental superheroes.

Eminem and the football players whose names I probably never knew have been taken down from his wall and there are new faces now: SKEPTA SHUTDOWN is printed in huge letters on a poster above a blown-up flyer for a club night on City Road. Another has Stormzy with his shirt off, bent over a microphone. I churn words over in my mouth, then point up at the poster. "He still asking for me?" I say, doing my best cheesy grin.

Pez's eyes pinch. "What are you talking about?"

"Nothing," I say, shaking my head. "Just having a laugh." He leans back and snorts. God, I feel like a dick. All I want to do is bridge this gap between us but I can't figure out where I'm supposed to fit. It's like we've skipped from kids to something else but it's not at all clear which steps we've missed and I'm making myself up as I go along and getting it all wrong. I don't know how to be around him now. High up to my left I spot the Arsenal flag in pride of place above the door. That it's still there is more of a relief than it probably should be, but the bookshelves, once stuffed full, are lined with video games and a stack of old football magazines on top.

"Where have all your books gone?"

"Mum gave them away."

"Um, why?"

He makes a face at the screen. "Because I've read them."

Pez was so proud of those shelves once. He lined up everything he'd read in order. He was particular about it too and hated when I mixed them up or put books back out of sequence, which I did a lot, mostly to annoy him. Pez was obsessed with Harry Potter and series like Percy Jackson, Artemis Fowl, and Alex Rider, anything that went on and on and on. He'd only start a book if it had a sequel, preferably eight. I was the opposite. That kind of up-front commitment made me nervous. But I guess this was a while ago. The games were taking over even before I left. Still, I ask, "Read anything good lately?"

He shakes his head like I've said something stupid. "Sorry to disappoint you."

"You're not disappointing me," I say, but this isn't entirely true. It's not so much him disappointing me as how disappointed I feel about how *different* he seems. Especially when I feel just the same as I've always been. I find another rolled-up sock in the duvet and this time I toss it in his direction but it misses and lands on an enormous denim beanbag at the end of the bed. On the shelf above it sits a large black camera. I swing my legs over the side of the bed and get up for a closer look.

"We must have better things to talk about than finals and books I'm not reading," he says.

"Seeing anyone?" I ask, standing now. It's a stupid, you-asked-for-it kind of joke and I'm about to make some crack about Jennifer Lawrence but I don't know if he fancies her anymore.

"Guess I am," he says quietly.

I lift the heavy black camera body in my hands, willing it to weight me down because suddenly I'm drifting up and up, feeling like I might float out of the open window like a sad balloon. *So, Pez has a girlfriend AND a Nikon D5300 Digital SLR now?* "Yeah?" I say, gripping the camera tightly in my hands.

"But it's not that serious," he says, tapping his foot off the bed frame.

What does this mean? He's seeing someone he's not serious about, or he's seeing someone but it's not that serious yet? Does he even take photographs? Either way it's as though I've invited one of his enormous high-tops to kick me in the stomach.

I brush my finger over the Nikon logo, then hold it to my eye and face the window. "Just wondering, that's all." I take a deep breath in through my nose while rotating the lens in my hand, acting like I'm trying to focus. "It's not like—" I'm not sure how this sentence ends, so I stop. I don't trust my mouth very much right now.

I don't know what I was expecting but it wasn't the sharp pain in the center of my chest. It's probably just indigestion from inhaling my lunch. It's not like I'd ever expect Pez to fancy me. It's not like I *want* Pez to fancy me. Breathe! Of course Pez has a girlfriend. Why wouldn't he? And I'm hardly the only person allowed to take photographs. I carefully place the camera back on the shelf, wishing I had something that cool hanging around my bedroom. A double shot of jealousy, please, bartender. I quickly swallow this down before opening my mouth. "Anyone I know?" I ask breezily, but my voice is giveaway high. I know hardly anyone around here anymore and Pez and me never went to the same school, so there's zero chance of me knowing or pulling this breezy business off.

"She's a friend of a friend," he says. "It's only been a couple of months."

A couple of months! That's practically a lifetime. That's virtually a proper girlfriend.

"It's kind of casual," he says, but the way he budges about on the bed makes me think otherwise. "How about you?"

I shake my head. There's nothing to tell. I've kissed a few boys since Arthur, but nobody significant is the truth, and Arthur was too long ago to mention. I'm not sure I've ever had a proper relationship and I'd actually really like to talk to Pez about this but I'm not ready to get into the *why* of it all right now. When we were kids, feelings came easy and quick. Like if emotions were a superpower, I would have been a freaking Avenger. But I've gotten so used to pushing that stuff down. It's not that I've been afraid of the feelings, it's more that I haven't been ready to announce that I have them.

Pez looks at his watch. "Let's go out?"

"Out?"

"C'mon," he says, already up. "I'm looking at house arrest once Harland gets here. Besides, you should meet some people."

I'm all for meeting people, but now? What if *she's* one of them? I'm suddenly tired, like I might need to lie down in this bed and overthink for a while, but then he digs my arm, quite hard, and I feel a bit better.

7

Outside in the air, it's easier to breathe.

I look down at my wheels, still caked in mud from the farm tracks near Wendy's, and I worry my tires look strangely big and wrong next to his. I never thought about having to share my half-assed hobby with Pez and I never thought I'd have to share him with anyone before, particularly another girl, and I'm not sure I know how. It sounds selfish but it's just that I could really do with all of him. I quickly hop on but when I look up from the handlebars he's already shot off down the road. He stops by the narrow exit onto Agar Grove and turns around. For a split second it looks like nothing has changed. We're both here, back on our bikes again.

"In your own time!" he says.

"Where we headed?" I ask, but as I get closer he takes off again.

"You'll see," he shouts out. "C'mon!"

He takes a right, wheeling on past the open-all-hours deli, the one with the stale cornflakes. Best-Buy-Never, Mum used to call it. Pez goes left onto St. Pancras Way, and I trace his huge arc, following under the railway bridge and freewheeling down the road all the way to the path that leads to the canal.

If Dad was right and Pez really did follow me everywhere once, it looks as though this, like everything else, has changed. Still it feels good and I push my arms up straight off the handlebars, holding my chest high into the wind. My hair blows behind me and my ears fill with the fizz of spinning spokes. It's a flash of that full-heart eleven-year-old feeling again and I hold my face to the sky, eyes closed to feel it more.

We haven't been cycling for very long but as we weave through the slipway barrier and walk our bikes down the slope toward the water, my limbs throb like we've been pedaling for hours. As we enter the canal from our usual spot the water curves and coils, twisting out on either side of us. I can hear music ahead. We wheel on past a man crashed out on the grass between two traffic cones and in a few more steps we're under the curved slope of the tunnel, where even whispers echo. I push my bike along behind Pez in the half dark but soon we're standing in sunlight on the other side. I spot the crowd of bodies gathered by a small speaker farther up on the grass and without a word from Pez I know this is his crew. Bass beats boom, warning—of what I'm not sure, but warning me all the same. If I thought my bike seemed out of place, it's nothing to how I feel now.

I keep close, pulling my shorts out of my bum as we approach, trying to do it as subtly as possible as I quickly count the faces that tilt in our direction: three boys and one girl. The couple on the far side of the speaker, with their feet dangling over the water, are deep in a kiss and have only a fleeting interest in our arrival. The boy is white with ginger hair and the Indian girl with her long, black braids and beat-up leather jacket looks like some sort of punk princess. My palms sweat on the handlebars. There's a strong smell of weed coming from somewhere else close by and I want to get rid of my gum, which suddenly feels too big in my mouth.

Pez moves toward them with a new swagger, the apology gone from him like I only imagined it earlier. He hugs and hand-slaps the two boys who are sitting on the grass, and I stand behind, flicking my ponytail off my shoulder, waiting for Pez to introduce me. Then I pull my sleeves down over my hands, which aren't quite sure what to do.

"Kyle, Lucas, this is Vetty," Pez says eventually.

The boy with the dark skin pulls his hood down and smiles at me like he might mean it. "I'm Lucas," he says, but the other, pale boy with the floppy brown hair over his eyes, who must be Kyle, seems less polite. Still, I grin back, feeling next-level self-conscious.

Pez points to the couple. "Amira?" he says. The girl looks over. "And that's Nick with her," he says to me. "Hey," he shouts, "say hi to Vetty, yeah?" His accent sounds a lot more London than it does when he's at home.

They wave and quickly return to each other. I wonder if Amira might be *the friend of the friend of a friend.*

A pretty houseboat passes us and I'm thinking how much I'd like to hop on and sail it somewhere far away from here, when another boy crosses the path to join us. Dirty-blond hair sits high off his pale face and the neck of his T-shirt is wide and low, so low that I can see the top of his chest and a string of brown glass beads tucked in behind the faded gray cotton. He looks strangely out of place but for different reasons than me. With his angular face and easy smile, he's like an actor who's stepped into the wrong scene, like he's meant to be in some American TV show but ended up here instead.

Pez sets his bike down on the grass and takes the guy's arm in a practiced hold.

"Good to see you out," the guy says, patting the back of Pez's puffer, then he reaches his hand toward me. "Vetty," he says, shaking mine. "I've heard a lot about you."

I smile back but no words come out.

"Well, now you've met Rob," Pez says, taking a step closer to the guy who must be Rob and giving him a gentle thump in his stomach. "That's pretty much it." He sits down cross-legged opposite Kyle and Lucas, so I sit down too, wishing I could think of something to say.

Pez leans over. "Here," he says, stooping to check my eyes as he offers me a Red Stripe from a pile by Rob's feet. Despite the heat, the can is cold, like it hasn't been there long. Normally I don't drink beer, but I take a slow sip, hoping it might soothe the hard edges beneath me. Besides, it's not bad when it's this cold and I'm grateful to have something to do with my hands. I take another drink and look around, enjoying the bubbling between my ears and the sharp taste at the back of my mouth.

I knew every inch of this canal once. We used to cycle to the zoo and Little Venice on one side and then for miles past Islington in the other direction, but nothing is as it was then: not Regent's Canal, not Pez, not me. The boys around me talk quick and everything feels so fast. Their voices soup together like a strange new language I have to strain to work out. I look back the way we came, where an old man fishes from a plastic crate on the other side of the bridge. My eyes follow his rod into the dirty water, then latch on to an elegant duck gliding along.

A voice crackles close to my ear. "Trailer for that new *Darkzone* looks banging." I turn around and it's Kyle talking, but I still can't see his eyes. Pez does a soft snort and looks off toward the water. He's not being unfriendly, but I can tell he doesn't really want to talk about Luna. He leans back with his elbows on the grass, closing his eyes to the low sun.

Rob moves in closer to the group. "The best bits are already on YouTube," he says, holding out his phone to the two boys. Kyle takes it, his hands cupping the small screen to shade out the light, and Lucas looks guiltily to Pez before huddling closer to the phone. Kyle slumps forward and nods like he likes whatever it is he's seeing.

"Who's the bloke with the beard?" he says to nobody in particular.

"The guilty one," Lucas explains, then he looks up, like he's not sure whether to get stuck in this conversation but he does anyway. "He's the one she's supposed to be banging up, not getting busy with."

Whatever they're watching, Kyle is gripped. "Real talk though, Pez. Your mum—I mean, I would. We all would," he says, eyeing the other boys, looking for their agreement. He doesn't have to look too hard. It's obvious Pez's friends are just messing around but I don't know how he can stand them talking about Luna like this. His face twitches in a half

68

smile but then the muscles in his neck go tight. He looks up and breathes in through his nose, like he's struggling underneath those eyes, but he holds it together. I'm tempted to say something to change the subject, when Lucas reaches for the phone. "Enough of the sexy stuff, yeah?" he says to Kyle.

"It's as close as he gets to seeing any action," Rob says, kneeing Kyle hard in the back.

Kyle glares at Rob. "'Cause there's only one Romeo round here, right?"

"You know it, man," Rob says. God, he's fond of himself.

Kyle shoves the phone into Rob's hand. "Your battery's dead."

Rob puts the phone in his pocket. "That contraceptive personality of yours really holds you back—"

"Jesus, you two, leave it!" Pez says, getting up. He kicks at the grass by his feet like he's had enough but I can see he's relieved his friends have at least moved on from his mum. He's got his back to the water now and he looks left, farther up toward the next bridge. I'm watching him, wondering what we're really doing here, when something extraordinary happens to his face, smoothing all the deep lines above his eyes. I track his stare as a girl with brown skin emerges from the blackness under the far bridge, looking like I don't know what. Bicycles and pedestrians pass as she glides toward us, like the elegant duck letting all the stinky junk float by on either side of her. There isn't the slightest hesitation in how she moves and I pull my sleeves down further and tighten the base of my ponytail because I know exactly who she is. As she gets close I see her better but nothing I see is good news. Still, I can't look away and I'm not the only one. Everything around us stops; cans are held halfway to mouths and hair freezes mid-flick as we drink her in. Jet-black corkscrew curls shoot wildly about her face and her knee-length dress is molded onto her curves so she looks like some kind of sculpture. The Adidas zip-up draped over her shoulders might as well be ermine trailing behind her. Her whole aura is next level. If Amira on my right is a princess, this girl here is the queen.

She's looking at Amira but I saw her check Pez out first and my heart is doing crazy things. It was a fleeting flash, but I caught it and I can only imagine his eyes. It's not hard to see why Pez told me about her. She sits down beside Amira and Nick, crossing her legs, shifting position, and then sitting up straight the way a dancer might. Big, wide eyes and a full mouth half-open in an irritating pout. It seems wrong that all these features were used up on the one face. "Alright," she says.

Amira elbows her. "Eight o'clock, you said."

The girl shakes her head, making her curls bounce. "Sorry, babe. Had to help with a delivery."

"It's almost nine?" Amira is trying to sound cross, but she seems as taken with her as everyone else around me.

"I'm here now," the girl says in a voice that manages to be both smooth and husky at the same time. "I only finished five minutes ago, and I ran most of the way."

Either she's lying or she doesn't run the way I do.

Amira looks at her phone. "But I've gotta leave," she says, standing up. "Dad will freak if I'm not back soon."

The girl gives a tight smile, piercing a sharp dimple into

her left cheek. "I'll come with you," she says, pushing her hands into the grass to get up.

Amira draws air in through her teeth. "Got family over. All my aunties," she says. Then she leans in and whispers something in her ear, which could be considered rude given we're all sitting around watching. "You stay," she says, louder now. Then she straightens and looks around the boys before her eyes settle on Pez. "Be nice to March while I'm gone, yeah?"

I can't see what Pez's face is doing, but March's eyes land on mine. Despite everything going on in my head, I smile back, mostly because I'm not sure what other face to make. No teeth, mind you. Soon side-eyes fly around me. Rob to Kyle, then Kyle to Lucas, and then Rob to Pez. It's like some intense telepathy. Kyle is the next to stand but Lucas pulls at his tracksuit bottoms, which are already dangerously low.

"Where you going?" Lucas asks.

"Mickey D's," says Kyle, brushing the dirt off one of his sneakers. "And you're coming too."

"Now?" says Lucas. Kyle stares at him like he's stupid and Lucas shakes his head. "How about Chicken King? Or . . ." He scratches his hair through his hoodie, like he's thinking. Even I can tell he's being slow on the uptake.

Rob rolls his eyes but Kyle's face is more urgent. "Chicken King is the wrong direction."

"But their wings are sick," Lucas says, pushing himself up and shuffling about.

"Whatever," Kyle says. "Let's get moving. I'm starving."

With a quick wave, Nick and Amira are gone. Then the

music stops and Lucas is zipping the speaker back into a bag, fighting with Kyle over the quickest route to their food. For some reason I don't want them to go, but soon they, too, disappear off down the towpath, leaving March, Rob, Pez, and me sitting on the grass, like the four of us being here is some kind of accident. It's not like I had a plan, but if I did, this wasn't it. When I turn back I've got a perfect view of Pez's face as he steals a look at March and I wonder whether anyone will ever look at me like that. The only sound is my gurgling stomach. It might be the looks Pez is giving March, or the way Rob is looking at me, or maybe it's just March turning up in July, but something is seriously churning up my insides.

Pez clears his throat. "Work busy?" he says, obviously to her. There's a slight tremble in his voice that nobody but me would notice.

She blinks slowly. It's only the tiniest flash of eye contact but I feel the current charging between them. "It's always busy," she says. "But it makes the time pass quickly."

Pez motions to Rob. "Maybe you could find a job for this waster? He's always complaining he's got no money."

Rob lowers his head. "Not everyone's parents are rolling in it."

"It was a joke, all right." The way Pez says it, I sense there's more between these two. It seems like they're close, but there's a weird undercurrent in there too.

March smiles at Rob, like she understands what's unspoken. "How are your dishwashing skills?" Her voice melts the tension and the sides of Rob's mouth widen.

"Rubbish," he says, before thumping Pez on the arm.

"See," he says. "It's not that I won't work. It's that I don't have the skills." Pez eye-rolls. "C'mon," Rob says. "Let's go back to yours, yeah?"

"If you're looking for my mum," Pez says, "she's not in."

Rob hits Pez's shoulder again. "Kyle was winding you up earlier," he says. "Anyway, Vetty's back, so you need to snap out of this slump of yours, quick." Then he twists his shoulders around to me. "So, what d'you like to watch on TV?"

"She watches everything," Pez says.

"Your favorites, then?" Rob says.

March turns too and everyone's looking at me. "Of all time?" I ask nervously.

Rob laughs, big and warm; then he nods. "Yeah, of all time."

I want to say *Stranger Things* because it's the truth, but I want to save this until I've shared it with Pez and he's part of it too. "Probably *Friday Night Lights* or . . . maybe *Doctor Who*." When I look up, March is looking at me with a new face. "But Pez is right, I'll watch pretty much anything."

"How 'bout *Narcos*?" Rob says. "You've seen it, right?" I haven't, so I shrug, and he picks up Pez's phone. "I'll show you," he says, punching in a code, but Pez reaches across his chest, grabbing it back. Rob shifts right and Pez tumbles on top of him and doesn't let go until Rob throws the phone down. "Man, I was only looking for the trailer," he says, sitting up and pulling one side of his shirt back on. "I wouldn't touch your porn. Relax." Then he laughs to himself and stands up. "Okay, everyone, that was a joke!" he says, brushing the dust from his knees and looking around.

"Let's get out of here. Reckon we could all do with some fun."

Next thing Pez is up, and soon me and March are too, like it's all been decided. He hands me my bike then walks ahead, leaving me and March to follow. I wheel along by the water beside her while he and Rob exchange an equal number of whispers and digs up in front. Whatever this conspiracy is, it's pissing me off.

March stares ahead, chin high, like she's above it all. Either that or she can't hear a word. I don't know what to say so I keep my eyes out front but as much as I wish I'd never set eyes on the girl, I feel bad we're not talking. I can't help but notice the sureness in her step, whereas I'm conscious of everything, like how I walk, how my back isn't straight, and generally how unalike we are. I should at least try to be nice, but I can't think of a single thing to say, except possibly to ask where she got all her clothes.

Without a word, Rob slinks away from Pez and back to us. It's obvious this is where March is supposed to walk ahead with Pez, but he doesn't slow down and the two of them walk along in single file under the bridge. For some reason, Pez takes the steps by Royal College Street, which aren't easy to climb with my heavy bike. Pez quickens his pace and soon he's up on the footpath alone, leaving March trailing behind. I start to heave my bike by the handlebars but then Rob grabs the saddle and the bike sails up the steps and onto the path. I go to say thanks but he's scrambled off after Pez. As we turn in to Randolph, Rob reaches for Pez's arm. "Wait up," he says.

As Pez spins around, March steps down off the pavement.

"Listen, I'll see you guys later," she says, just like that, but she's got one foot on the curb and the other on the road like she's waiting to be persuaded. I've already convinced myself she's the type who needs to be asked twice, and it's irritating me that this is exactly what she's doing, but then her other foot follows. Pez's eyes are letting him down. Clearly a plan had been built around her and she's just crushed it. Boy, this is awkward. Secretly, of course, I can't help feeling a little pleased.

Rob steps down onto the road beside her. "If you're not feeling *Narcos* we could always watch—"

Wow, this boy is not the sharpest. "Oh my god, leave it," says Pez.

Rob stands there like a lemon while March eyes Pez, who's pretending to be super interested in something by his feet. "Another time, yeah?" she says.

Pez nods without looking up but Rob isn't as quick to let her go. "I'm having a party at mine soon," he says. "I'll let you know details, yeah?"

"Alright," she says, tucking her hair behind her ear.

"Sweet," Rob says. "See you later." Then he spins around to Pez, who rolls his eyes. I raise my hand to wave goodbye but she's already slinked away up the road.

8

Pez's kitchen overlooks the yard on the raised ground floor. The ceiling is twice the height of ours, and huge industrial hanging lights drop from the ceiling like something from a design show on TV. Obviously, Harland's not here and Luna is out, so it's just us. Rob is on the island in the center of the room, sitting on the marble countertop rather than on any one of the many stools dotted around. "I can't work that girl out," he says, scratching his chin. "I thought you were right in there." On the far side of the room, Pez listens to a message on his phone while giving Rob the finger against his Arsenal phone case. But Rob's right. It was weird how March left like that. "Got anything to drink?" Rob says then, up opening cupboards.

"Try the fridge," Pez shouts, pressing the handset hard against his ear.

The way Rob moves around this kitchen, I'm thinking either he also lives somewhere like this or he'd like to think he does. As he crosses the room he glances at me again; not the intense flash of I-want-you-now that Pez was throwing at March earlier, but he's definitely looking.

Then he pulls the enormous stainless-steel door wide and grabs a carton of juice from inside.

"Cheers!" Rob says, taking a long slug and wiping his mouth with the back of his wrist. "God, that's good." He twists his wrist to read the label. "Where d'you live, Vetty?" he asks, quieter now, before looking up and raking his hand through his hair like he's slowing down time. His eyes are fixed on me. It's kind of weirdly intense and it's also impossible not to notice how not-painful he is to look at.

"Oh," I say, scraping one of the tall stools out from under the counter and perching my bum against it. "Across the road."

"We passed it on the way," Pez says, walking back into the room and whipping a baguette from the bread bin. "She moved back into her old place. I told you," he says, tearing the end off. Crusty flakes fly and he holds out a fistful of bread to me, but he's staring at Rob the whole time.

I raise my hand. *No thanks.*

"I was just being friendly," Rob says, into the fridge.

"Mmmm . . ." says Pez, walking back out the door. When Rob looks to me, we share a smile that makes my cheeks burn. I quickly follow Pez into the TV room at the front of the house, and I soon hear Rob's feet following behind. The walls have been painted dark blue and the corner sofa is definitely new. It's so big I don't know where to sit and I'm waiting for one of them to take up position but they're both up in front of the TV, trying various controls and working out what's what. I decide the middle of the L shape is a safe bet. I've only just sat when Rob plunks down too. He's so close his arm brushes off mine.

"Sorry," he says, quickly shunting down to give me more space. When I glance up Pez is dishing out a definite side-eye. I'm wondering whether this look is for me but then I spot the bottle of Fanta on the coffee table and I decide the shade is for Rob for helping himself again.

Pez throws a controller onto the couch between us. "I've got to call Mum back," he says, walking out and leaving the two of us alone.

Rob messes about with the remote and I sink back into the soft cushions, trying to process everything that's happened today. Music erupts from speakers in the ceiling, startling me at first, but soon we're both doing tiny head movements along to the beat. It's kind of embarrassing but also funny, like we're in on the awkwardness together.

"You into this?" Rob asks, pointing upward with one hand and untwisting the cap with the other. I'm almost positive it's Kendrick Lamar but it would be too embarrassing to be wrong, so I make a face I hope says *yeah*. He pours a glass and reaches it out for me to take, but I shake my head. "All the girls like Kendrick," he says, taking a long drink.

It sounds like such a line. "*All* the girls, Romeo?" I say. He smiles again and we share another look, even longer this time. It's not a look I've been giving or receiving much lately. *Holy crap, am I flirting?*

"Yeah," he says. "*All* of them!" Then he presses his lips together. "It's because Kendrick's a feminist, innit?" he says. If Pez had said this I might push for more of his take on Kendrick's feminism but Rob looks so pleased with himself, I'm afraid I might laugh, so I move my eyes around the room, feeling slightly out-of-body while trying to digest what's happening and why it feels good. "So, what's it like, being back?"

"Um . . ." I'm hardly going to answer him honestly; besides the only word that comes to me is "surprising." "Different," I say eventually.

"Different how?"

Um . . . all of it? Pez, March . . . sitting here like this, with you. "Dunno," I say, and his top lip curls and his eyebrows rise up. "What?"

He's about to say something, when Pez reappears in the doorway, making little cough sounds. "Being friendly again, Rob?"

Rob turns around. "That a problem?" he says, but jokey.

Pez steps farther into the room. "No," he says, picking up the bottle of Fanta that Rob offered me earlier. "But I told you already, Vetty's not like other girls. She's immune to your charms." He twists the cap and glares at me. "Isn't that right?" he says, smiling broadly now.

"Oh yeah, absolutely." It flies out quickly; then I swallow and look around. *Was that the right answer?* I feel Rob looking at me. Pez as well. I think I'm still grinning but I'm gripping my thighs too. Finally, Pez sits, but the two of them exchange stupid faces before Pez picks up the remote and some game fills the screen. The music is still playing, and everything feels loud and confusing. In my head I replay what Pez said. What does *not like other girls* even mean? My pulse quickens so much it's hard to think straight. I run my hands down my thighs but my head feels like a spinning bicycle wheel with a sudden puncture. "I better get back," I say, standing up.

Rob shoves his hands into the seat. "Already?"

I swat my forehead with my palm. "I have to make Arial's tea. I forgot," I say, making for the door.

When I look back Rob smiles a goodbye and Pez just raises his hand in a peace sign behind his head.

PART TWO

Not like other girls

9

The heat! My god, the heat! I lie on my bed, arms and legs stretched out wide. The blind is down but sunlight burns through the cracks like razors. I tossed and turned all night, planning how best to broach things with Pez. Find out what he meant. I ran through it all in my head, but this morning nothing feels right. Before, I'd have said something. Four years ago, I'd have come straight out with it, but it doesn't feel so easy now. I'm afraid of the questions he might ask—questions I might not be able to answer.

I decide to start one of the deep-breathing exercises that Wendy taught me to do when I felt panicky or when everything felt like too much at school. I'm picturing the clear skies above the clouds just like she said, but the fact that the sky outside my window is already swimming-pool blue makes it feel kind of pointless.

Pez saying I'm *not like other girls* is playing on a loop inside my head. Was he trying to tell Rob I won't fall for his lines, or was he trying to tell Rob that I'm ... different? And if so, how? Why do other people seem to think they know this stuff about me when I'm still working it all out? Do I give off some kind of signal? Was it a joke? Was it somehow about George and that kiss four years ago? Does he remember it as clearly as I do, or do I read too much into EVERYTHING?

My insides feel cramped, like my internal organs are squashed underneath my rib bones and these are stacked too close together. I think about how everything outside is so tightly packed too. I picture the houses along the street outside and the cars with not an inch between them, then the people on the jam-packed buses heading into town, all pressed up against one another, all of it, all of us, melting to mush. I'm processing all this feverish heat when I look down at the woolen leggings and the hoodie I slept in. Okay, so I might be inappropriately dressed for July.

Arial strolls into my room, singing. It's Jason Derulo or one of those and she belts out the words at the top of her voice. At first I'm grumpy but it's also hard not to mumble along. I start out quiet but soon I'm up off the bed, singing into her electric toothbrush alongside her. Her voice is amazing and she knows all the words but mostly I'm miming or making them up. Not that it matters; it's fun. I'm staring at us in the mirror, when, all of a sudden, she squats down and does this move, exactly like the girls in the videos. I double-take and she does it again, very slowly this time, for my benefit, and I copy her, putting my legs together, then bending my knees, while trying to keep myself in a straight line like her. She repeats it and I try again. My ten-year-old sister is teaching me dance moves and I'm actually trying really hard to pay attention. I'm crouched on the floor, sticking my bum out, having another go at curling myself back up like she's just done, but I topple over. She stands above me laughing.

"When did you learn how to do that?" I ask her.

"Ages ago," she says, pulling a piece of gum from her mouth and examining it under her nose. "Last week, maybe."

I can't not laugh. "Where?"

"YouTube?" she says, like she can't believe I had to ask, then she pings the gum back and does one more drop in the mirror before collapsing onto my bed. "I'm starving," she says. "Can we make pancakes?"

I get up and shove her out the door. "Let me get dressed!"

I drag two huge plastic boxes out from underneath the bed. Both have yellow stickers and *Vetty's Stuff* scrawled across the top in Wendy's handwriting. I crank open the first lid and rummage under old hats and hairbands to find my beloved baseball shirt with VETTY printed on the back. I press the worn fabric against my cheek; then I spot my old silk bomber jacket with the green dragon embroidery and my purple tie-dye dungarees and I lay each item carefully on the bed. These are my favorite clothes ever but it's been so long since any of them fit. I open the next box to find my current clothes, which include a far-less-loved flowery jumpsuit I bought at H&M last year because Liv said it was cute, a skirt I never felt comfortable in, and some basic jean shorts. I give these a sniff. Woof, musty, but they'll do. I toss them to the side and fish out some salvageable T-shirts and vest tops along with a striped dress and some capris. I place what represents my "summer wear" collection beside the clothes I wore when I was twelve and my heart sinks. How have I gone from *that* to *this*? What's happened? It's not just the limited amount of clothes I own but how little I *feel* for any of them that's most disheartening.

I yank my hoodie off over my head and as I'm pulling down my leggings I notice a small hole between the legs. I stand in my pants in front of the mirror with its sticky Minion remains and step into the shorts, turning to examine myself from various angles. They don't look right. Maybe they looked right before, but not here, not when I can see how far from myself I've drifted. Next, I hold up the jumpsuit, pressing it against my waist, but it's the same uncomfortable feeling and I toss it onto the bed. Then I grab the skirt, then the dress, and I can tell even by touching them that they're not . . . me. It's not that I don't like any of these clothes; it's as though they belong to someone else and I've been trying on versions of other people like jumpsuits or pairs of jeans. Technically they might fit, but none sit properly, none hang or hug me like I want them to. Besides, after what Pez said last night, it's clear that disguising myself doesn't even work. I *still* look different!

I take everything off and lie back on the bed and for a good five minutes, I allow my face to become wet, properly sodden and wet. I feel stupid, expecting clothes to answer fundamental questions or magically change my life but what's at stake feels so real. I hear Arial, through the make-shift wall, still singing along to her karaoke app. Her voice is clear and it gets louder as she moves around the room. I sit up and stare at my reflection. All I really want is to feel . . . right. I force myself up, kicking the boxes back under the bed.

The door bursts open and Arial prances into my room again. "Um, breakfast?" she says, reaching for my green silk bomber and holding it up to herself in the mirror.

d then, "Hope you don't mind?" His words sound
he's really good at saying them.
urse not."
not great on the phone, but Pez said you were into
so I thought—" He stops. "Um, anyway . . . I was
ing whether you'd like to do something."
at, like hang out?" Soon as I've said it my eyes
shut. I've watched way too many of Arial's cheesy
ws.
Saturday you said you'll watch anything and Pez
you like films, so I thought maybe we could go to
ies?"
he's locked up. Haven't you heard?"
thinking . . . just the two of us," he says softly.
back against the bed and let this sink in. So,
Pez said the other night hasn't put Rob off. Maybe
cted?
" I say slowly. It's not that I'm not up for it. I'm
that's all. Nicely surprised.
lly," he says. "Can I be honest?"

't ask Pez for your number. I took it from his

see . . ."
't sure how fair it'd be, him knowing we're out
while he's incarcerated. I was thinking maybe we
to tell him for now and when he's released, we
. He'll laugh about it then."
m not sure about conspiring with Rob like this,
end this interest in me doesn't feel good. I can't

I grab it, needlessly rough. "Give it."

She hands it back, watching me carefully. I'm being unkind. Looking at her open face, the hurt is plain to see, and I realize that Arial is one of a very small handful of people in the world for whom what I say actually matters. I sit down and she scooches up beside me. "What's wrong?"

I clear my throat, ashamed. "Nothing."

"You've been crying," she says.

"No, I haven't."

"Yeah, you have," she says, leaning over and staring up my nostrils. I turn my face away and push up off the bed. "I can tell, you know?" she says. "I can always tell."

I fold clothes, doing my best to ignore her, when my phone throbs on my bedside table. Arial reaches for it, so I grab it. "It's from Pez," she says, peering to read it as I sit back down.

Two weeks' house arrest!

I read the words quickly; then my eyes jump back to the previous date stamp—the one above his latest text. Dec 28 5:25 p.m.—over three years ago.

All those Christmases ago, he wrote, **You there?** That's all his text says and my heart jolts. I start to reply to what he's just said about his house arrest. Anything to avoid thinking about my inexplicable three-and-a-half-year silence.

Will you be allowed visitors?

I stare at the screen, waiting as his words emerge.

Security is tight but you might get past Mum.

Arial tugs my arm. "Do you think they'll be nice?" she says.

I look up and her head is hung low. I drop the phone and wrestle an old T-shirt over my head. "Who?"

"The other kids," she says.

I'd almost forgotten that Arial starts camp in Camden Square tomorrow. It was Dad's idea and he signed her up for the rest of the summer. It was the deal so that I can have some kind of a social life. "Course they will," I say, but she sighs loudly. "What?"

"It's hard making new friends, that's all."

I lift her chin. "No, it's not."

"Yes, it is," she says. "You used to talk to Wendy about it all the time."

I did, particularly at first, before Liv, Jess, and Freya accepted me into their gang. What can I say? "Just be yourself. That's all you can do."

She glares at me from under her bangs. "Is that what *you* do?"

I stare back at her, but she doesn't flinch and I finally crack. "It's what I plan to do," I say. "From now on."

"Right," she says. "Then I'll do it too."

I place my hands on her shoulders. "It'll be fun, I promise."

"Mmm . . . ," she says, squinting at me like a cowboy.

I take her hand. "C'mon, let's go make those pancakes."

10

I get back from dropping Arial
day of camp and dig out some
I spread them out all across th
over the glossy images I kn
new pictures to look at and I'
need to rejoin the library whe
Given that Pez is the only pe
actual phone call outside of
At least, he *was* the only per
still spoke . . . before. I glanc
number.

"Hello?"

"Vetty?"

Ohmygod. "Rob?" I sit u

"I got your number fron

I shake my head in the r
see me. "No," I say. "I don
there really is an emergen
bit before opening my mc

"Yeah," he says. "I've be
call you, that's all." I bite n

pretend this doesn't feel like a delicious middle finger to Pez's line about me not being *like other girls*. "I guess. When?"

"Tomorrow?"

I stop myself from saying *I'll check my calendar.* "Great."

"Anything you'd like to see?"

I haven't been to the movies for ages. "Nah ... Like I said, I'll watch anything," I say.

I picture him smile. "Cool," he says.

"K."

"K. Bye."

So, I'm going on a date, with Rob. It seems so simple. Straightforward almost, but then I look at myself in the mirror, sporting a T-shirt Fran got at a molecular biology conference in Lisbon years ago and my leggings with their hole between the legs. Gah! The urgency for a whole new wardrobe has gone from yellow to flashing red with accompanying warning sounds. I need decent clothes more than ever, clothes that say something about me, but for that I need money. So, I guess this means I need a job. And quick. And since I've never written a résumé before, I pull out my laptop and start typing. One hour and forty-six minutes later I march into the kitchen, where Dad is bent over his enormous shiny MacBook Pro, still in his pajamas. "Shouldn't you be in an office somewhere?"

"Yeah, yeah, boss," he says. "I'm about to jump in the shower."

"I'm going to look for a job." I announce it loudly.

"That so?" he says, not listening.

I step in front of him, crashing my crappy laptop down. "It's just ... I need money."

He looks up and starts kneading his gray face. "You and me both," he says.

"I'm serious."

"So am I," he says, pushing his coffee mug forward. It leaves dark rings on the countertop and I rub at them to see if they've stained. "What do you need it for?" he asks, more gently, but still staring at his screen.

"Trips to the movies and, you know . . . clothes." I don't offer further specifics. I can't bring myself to.

He looks up, then continues to type. "You've got loads of clothes," he says, like this solves everything.

"None that fit anymore." My lip trembles and I look out the window at the silk tree, hoping this might help, but thinking about Mum makes it worse. I dab at my eye with the hem of my T-shirt and mumble something about an eyelash. When I turn back Dad is nodding, like he might get it, like he sees what's really going on.

"Okay," he says slowly. "But if you get a job who'll look after Arial while I'm at work?"

So, this is how it is? Without Wendy or Fran for backup, I'll have to check my sister's childcare arrangements before I make any plans whatsoever. Dad shrugs like he's reading my mind and I walk around, leaning over his shoulder. "That from Wendy?" I ask, reading the email open on his screen.

He huffs. "It's the list she promised, about the wedding. Surprise, surprise, we've all got jobs. Arial and I are on balloon-blowing duty." He's only pretending to be pissed off. "And you," he says, tapping at his trackpad, "need to pick a reading."

I squint and lean in. *Vetty: choose a reading—something fun to read between the speeches. Thanks! xxx*

"Something fun?" I say it out loud. I love Wendy; she's the best, but for someone who's so über-forthcoming and direct she can be hard to read. Fran's the one who I'd call genuinely silly and "fun" so it's hard to know how to interpret this. I'd get it if Wendy said "cultured" or "profound;" then I'd have a sense she really wants something cultured and profound but somehow dressed up as "fun."

Dad sighs. "She's a bloody nightmare. For years she wrote poems in my birthday cards and was always disappointed not to get lengthy sonnets back. She has no idea how hard that stuff is for normal people." I give him a shove. "Anyway, she better order one of those gas-cylinder things," he says, closing his laptop. "I don't have the puff I once had."

He's looking at me like he's forgotten why I'm standing here. "There must be a job that will fit around Arial's camp," I say, reminding him. His shoulders drop and he gives one of those low groans he's so fond of lately. "You think it's not a good idea, don't you?"

"It's not that," he says. "The camp's only a few hours each day, and you have no qualifications so it won't be easy, that's all." I don't mean to look sulky. It just happens. "Don't be like that," he says, but I can't go out with Rob looking like this. Thankfully he pushes his laptop aside like he can read my mind. "Go on then, give us a look."

I drag my laptop toward him, studying his face as his eyes dart up and down the page. His silence is torturous. "What do you think?"

He rubs at his chin. "What kind of job are you thinking?"

I shrug. "You know . . . babysitting, dog walking, all the exciting shit."

93

"Vetty!"

"Sorry," I say, and he returns to the screen for a few more excruciating minutes. "I'll even do ironing."

He smiles. I can't iron. We're a strictly folding household.

"Can I be honest?" he asks, but he barrels on before I can answer. "It could do with fleshing out. A little more detail about the job with Wend, maybe. Mention punctuality too. And," he says, brushing frizzy hair out of my eye, "I'd really love to see you use your full name."

I pull away. "Maybe."

"Plus a cool girl with a rad name like Helvetica can't submit her résumé in Times New Roman. That's gotta go."

"*Rad*, Dad? You're so far from being down with the kids."

"Painful, isn't it," he says.

I fold my arms, smiling. "Not to mention superficial."

"These things matter."

"Only to insane people like you, who call their firstborn after a font."

"You were conceived in Switzerland," he says, eyes ahead.

I rest against a neighboring stool. "I was?"

He looks up. "Yeah. We were in Zurich for a design fair. Mum worked out the dates. She loved the Swiss style and she thought the name felt right."

"But—" I stare at him. I've lived for sixteen years thinking he was to blame for our crazy names. I thought he'd tricked her, gotten her at a vulnerable moment. "It was *Mum's* idea?"

"Typefaces were her thing and Helvetica was her favorite sans serif. She thought it was iconic. She suggested it as soon as we found out you were a girl."

"Seriously?"

"Oh yeah." He nods. "She'd wax lyrical about Helvetica's strength and clarity. She said it was modern yet timeless. 'Helvetica can do it all,' she said. 'Helvetica can be anything.' Then I took one look at tiny you and decided she was right." He looks out to the yard and smiles, like he's hearing her voice. My lip trembles again and I look away, letting this all sink in, but I refuse to cry today. "She was always right," he says then, snapping from his reverie and returning to his laptop. "Look, you sound like a nice kid. I'd give you a job, if I had one."

I want to walk off, but I stand there, sniffling. "Um . . . this might sound like a stupid question," I say after a minute. "But what am I supposed to *do* with the résumé once it's time to upload it?"

"In my day, we walked around and handed them to people. You know, the people we wanted a job from."

"Actual hard copies?"

He rubs his chin, sucking in his cheeks like I'm unintentionally hilarious. "Crazy, huh?"

I think about this for the rest of the day while watching back-to-back TV shows. It might not be the worst plan.

11

I skip across the road with toast in hand, excited to be close to some sort of summer-slash-life plan: get a job, earn money, buy interesting new clothes, and go on potentially fun date with chisel-faced cute boy. I don't want to speak too soon but today might be the start of a less complicated life.

My tummy is full of butterflies as I press the bell, thinking about the optimum time to disclose details of my upcoming movie theater trip with Rob. It doesn't feel right to keep anything from Pez, but I'm still a bit pissed off with him for saying what he said. Even if Rob isn't bothered, I can't help wondering whether Pez was trying to warn him off me. Most of all I'm pissed with myself because I don't have the guts to confront him with any of these theories.

Luna answers. "Hey, Vetty!" she says, enveloping me in a sumptuous caramel-colored cardigan before standing back into the doorway. She's barefoot and wearing jeans, with her hair pulled high, shining with a polish that only famous people have. Her dark-brown skin is clear without a touch of makeup. I don't know if this applies to everyone you see on TV but in real life Luna is way smaller. She's not much bigger than I am.

"Hi, Luna." I mumble because my mouth is still full of half-chewed food. Also, eye contact is tricky given what Pez told me about Harland and the talk they were all having earlier. Should I say something or simply pretend everything's normal? It's also weirdly unclear whether I'm invited in.

"So nice to see you," she says.

"You too."

"It's been way too long?" I'd forgotten how many of Luna's sentences turn up at the end regardless of whether or not they involve a question. "Gosh, you've hardly changed," she says, softly shaking her head, and I don't know whether or not to be pleased by this. "Settling back?"

I say stuff about how great everything is, smiling and gesticulating, trying to nonverbally convey that I'm appropriately sympathetic about the Harland business without making too big a deal of it, unlike Pez, who crashed his car, which—by the way—had NOTHING to do with me. The way she's looking at me makes me think I might be overdoing it. Finally she steps back to let me pass. "Go on up," she says, gently placing her hand on my back and directing me up the stairs.

When I reach the top step, I hear loud music playing on the other side of Pez's door. I take a breath and barge in.

"How's the prisoner?" I have to shout it out.

There's a thud from over by the window. "Jesus," he says. "Do you *ever* knock?"

I always used to waltz into this room but I quickly remind myself that things have changed. I see him in the mirror first.

He's wearing a sleeveless T-shirt and holding a kettlebell. *Seriously?* I had hoped those things were ornaments, for show, but, no, judging by how much he's sweating, this is a thing.

"Sorry. I didn't realize you'd be—" *How do I finish this sentence?* He looks more embarrassed than me and it's hard to look right at him. Then I remember who all this iron pumping is for and I can't help myself. "Guess I'd probably start working out if I was going out with someone *that* good-looking." He looks confused, but I decide this is put-on. "Duh, March!"

"Oh, right," he says, quietly.

He dips to change kettlebell arms and I sit down at his desk, straightening my legs out long. "D'you reckon she knows it?"

"Nah," he says. "She's cool, she's . . ." He trails off, searching for a word that never comes.

"Of course she knows it." He makes a face at this but it doesn't stop me. "I mean, she must have looked in a mirror at some point in her life." *LEAVE IT, VETTY.* He returns to his reps, lifting his left arm high, pushing the kettlebell up in the air and then extending it. His face is a knot of concentration, but his long arms look impressively muscly as they flex in and out. It's hard not to stare. "Out of ten?"

He looks up. "What?"

"Like, what would you give her out of ten?"

He rolls his eyes out loud. "She's not a new Mentos flavor, Vetty."

"I know, but we haven't played this for years."

"I haven't *seen* you for years."

"Okay, fair point."

"And, that was a game . . . for food or films," he says. "Not . . . girls."

"Well, I want to play."

"Why?"

"Because I'd like to know."

He looks at me warily. "What I'd give March out of ten?"

"Okay, if not March, then me. What marks would you give me?" *STOP, STOP, STOP!* I'm changing the rules, I'm being a total ass, but his "not like other girls" comment is like a scab I can't stop picking.

He's whispering to himself again, pretending to count but I know he's not, and he puts down the kettlebell. "C'mon, Vetty," he says, scrunching up his forehead so tight a tiny blister of sweat swells and drips down his skin.

I tip his kettlebell over with my foot and it topples onto the wooden floor. His eyes look unsure and he turns to the window. "I'm prepared to work on a few physical things, but let's keep it realistic."

He gets up and grabs a towel from the bed, smothering his face in it. "I forgot how exhausting you can be sometimes." His voice is muffled but I hear every word.

This hurts, but still not enough to stop me. "Not a ten, then, I take it?" *TOO FAR!* It's too late. It's out.

He pulls the towel down, and although there's a trace of a smile, I know by his eyes that he's tired of this, tired of me. "C'mon," he says, peeling a blue fingerless glove off his hand. "Let's not do this, yeah?" The glove is practically glued on and he has to dig at it with his free hand. I let the uncomfortable silence happen, but my words play back to me and my face gets progressively redder.

"How did the talk go earlier?" I ask, suddenly remembering myself. "How was it having Harland and Luna in the same room?"

He sucks his teeth. "Seems Mum knew about . . . the affair. He'd told her it was over but . . . well, you saw."

"D'you think they'll work it out?"

He shakes his head. "He's getting his own place when he gets back from New York. He's staying with my uncle until then."

I rack my brain for something kind to say but all that comes out is "That sucks." By the time I look up he's halfway out of the room.

"Want a Coke?" he says.

I don't want a drink, nor do I want him to walk away, but at least if he leaves I can rearrange my beet-red face while thinking of something to cheer him up. "Sure," I say, trying to sound upbeat.

As soon as the door closes I sit on the bed, but I can't keep still, and I get up to check my Dutch braids in the mirror. I put them in this morning to make myself look neat and tidy on my job hunt. Over my shoulder, in my reflection, I spy his huge iMac and I think of the funny video of the diva owl that Arial shoved under my nose earlier and I reckon that's sure to make him smile, at least.

I've only tapped the trackpad when the computer springs to life. YouTube is already open, and I scan the page he's on; it's nothing interesting, just football stuff, far as I can see, but my eyes trace along the other open tabs at the top of the screen. There's at least twenty! I have a momentary pang of how intrusive it is to look, but I quickly convince myself it's not *that* bad. It's not like I'm snooping through his search history; besides, I could do with some intel on where his head's at right now. I soon spot some blogging site, and I've been meaning to start a proper photo diary for ages so I hover the cursor along. As soon as I click, the screen fills with images and I lean in. These aren't just any images though and my eyes fly all over his dashboard, which is filled with small squares and inside these squares bodies pump and thrust and flail about; naked bodies, boobs, and bare bums everywhere!

I drop the mouse and leap from the chair. *Ohmygod!* I almost laugh. I stand back as the screen keeps flashing and blinking on repeat and my heart thuds in sync with one particularly graphic action playing out in front of me. Porn on a loop: and LOADS of it!

I perch on the edge of the chair, reaching for the mouse again, but when I hit on the next tab down, hoping to make it stop, more windows of bare flesh fill the screen. I hover along and hit the next tab and it's the same, only this window is much bigger, almost filling the center of the screen. Every brain cell I possess screams at me not to, but for some insane reason I place the cursor on the arrow and click Play. Tiny voices and grunt sounds play through the headphones on the desk as naked bodies quickly unblur. I watch, openmouthed. All I can do is stare. Now, I get that the people I'm seeing might be professional or whatever, but how is it none of them has any hair? Like, none! After games at school or swim squad, I'm usually anxious to get on with the whole showering and dressing business. I make a point of not looking around, but I'm not one of those who changes their underwear inside the towel either. Still, I hadn't realized how far out of the loop I was. If a boy looked at me from *that* angle, I'd look like a different species!

A floorboard groans somewhere on the stairs and my fingers fumble all over the keys, desperate to get back to YouTube. Pez's footsteps get closer but the screen is still lit up like a pizza shop on Friday night. Panicking, I push the chair in under the desk and jump to the window, trying to look like I've been standing there the whole time. I'm wondering how I'll ever explain this when he pushes into the room, carrying a liter bottle under one arm and some chips in the other. I whip back to his iMac and it's miraculously dark, asleep again, but Pez stares at the black screen too.

I shift on my feet, slowly rotating to stare at our flat across the street, at my room, from where I could see myself perfectly if I were at home looking up. It's as though I'm seeing myself from above, entirely out of my own body. I hear the sound of glasses clinking down onto a table behind me and when I turn back a packet of Monster Munch sails through the air in my direction. There's a strange delay and I manage to catch it. Pickled onion, my favorite, but I place the packet on the desk, careful not to disturb anything around me; then I grab my folder and cross the room. "I left croissants in the oven," I say, pushing past him. "They'll be cremated!"

I race down his stairs without turning back and I'm out that front door faster than these legs have ever carried me. I don't stop until I hit Murray Street, where I crouch by the parking meter. I'd go home only Dad mightn't have left for work yet and I can't face explaining why I'm already back, looking like this; like I've seen a ghost, lots of ghosts, naked ghosts . . . all with very little body hair. *Why did I leave? What's wrong with me? It's just porn. Lots of people watch it. Loads, probably.* It's not like I don't know this. It's not like I haven't seen stuff before. It's not as though I haven't replayed scenes from films or accidentally-on-purpose clicked on dodgy videos. But Pez? And so many screens. I think about watching him from my window this week, light shining on his face for so many hours. Is that what he's doing at his computer every night and not playing *Assassin's Creed* or *Mortal Kombat* or whatever he's into these days. The thought makes me feel weird. It's no wonder he didn't want me barging into his room. *And croissants?*

A man climbs out of a nearby car and strolls toward me, change jangling in his pocket. I stare at the folder on my knee, stuffed full of my unimpressive life summary, and I force myself up. Before I know it, I've crossed the street and I'm hovering in the doorway of Murray News, trying to think about how handy it would be to work there, trying to get my head back into job-hunt mode.

Given the only other people in the tiny shop all appear to be employees, the odds of them needing staff seem ridiculously slim and I hug the folder to my chest and scan the magazines instead. To look legit, I run my fingers over *Elle, Vogue, Glamour,* and some others, tracking along the beautiful faces as though I'm making up my mind which one to buy. I look up from the house magazines to the cars and computer ones; there's even one about fishing. Who fishes in Camden? Pez said the old guy at the canal had a magnet at the end of his rod.

I crane my neck up to the naked bodies on the top shelf, praying that the men behind aren't looking, though I suspect it's obvious. These magazines have always been here, but I've never noticed the girls' faces before. They share the same look and I stare, trying to work out what seems so unsettling about them now, until the silence finally becomes too much. I spin around, pay for some chewing gum, and leave.

Out on the street, it's like I'm sleepwalking. I'm physically here but some plastic-wrappy-membrane separates me and reality. Like a less scary version of the Upside Down in *Stranger Things* but a parallel world all the same. I pass the Irish Centre on the corner of the square where they do weddings as I recall, and lots of parties too. They might need bar staff or someone to pick up the glasses? These reasonable thoughts come as sweet relief and I'd act on them, only my head is still so full of lingering weirdness. I need to pound a little more pavement before I'm ready to talk to anyone.

I pass the community bulletin board on the square and peer in half-heartedly. Lots of stuff about adult education and the residents' association, but no jobs. Children's voices leak from the other side of the railings and Arial's summer camp group is in there somewhere so I move on in case she sees me and decides she wants to come home. Without meaning to, I retrace the route I took on the bike with Pez and soon I hit Kentish Town. Shops and restaurants stretch all the way up toward the Tube station and I hover in the middle of the street, watching a man and a young boy leaving the bookshop hand in hand. I glide zombielike toward the door they just left, running through what could, in the right light, be considered qualifications: I can read. I like books. I know some good kids' ones. Also, bookshops are safe, warm places where nice people like Mum used to go. As I tumble into the quiet, reassuring shade, I hear a bell jingle. Then again, I might be delirious.

Hello, it's me, Vetty Lake, the answer to all your seasonal employment needs is what I don't say to the man with the dainty beard and glasses who only half fills the large chair behind the desk. Instead I shuffle in his direction and ask meekly whether there might be an opening for part-time work. He stares at me like he's wondering where he left his car keys: technically he's looking but it's like he doesn't see me at all. The silence goes on so long I decide maybe he, too, watches sex videos on his computer and buys magazines from the top shelf at Murray News. I'm still thinking this when he stands up and rummages behind the till.

"Last Wednesday of every month," he says, handing me a flyer. "There's a lean toward fantasy but we cover all sorts of young adult titles. It's a fun crowd," he adds, smiling. Then he adjusts his specs, pushing them farther up his nose.

A book club? Like that's going to pay for new Adidas or the full-body wax I might now need. Except what I actually say is "Thanks;" then I trudge out the door, clutching the flyer in my fist.

Gah! Why didn't I do something useful like ask if I could leave a résumé?

I pass the window of the orange café next door, the one

I went by on the bike with Pez, and as I look inside, I decide I could do with a break and a nice, cold drink. I stroll in and stand in front of the fridge, eyeing up the fancy-looking lemonades. A pink one with an old-fashioned label looks promising but when I go to slide back the glass door there's no handle. I run my hands down the left edge on the other side but there's nothing either. I try to pull at the rim of it with my nails, but it still won't budge. I give it another go from the right. Nothing!

"You have to slide it. To the left." I look for the soft, sing-song voice, and a small woman with hair the same color as the walls smiles at me from behind the counter. "Happens all the time," she says in an accent that I think's Irish but there might be a bit of Australian in there throwing me off. I slide the door left as she suggests, and it glides wondrously open. "Ta-da!" she says, flashing her hands out like a magician. "Lord knows why they make it so difficult."

"Thanks," I say, plunking the lemonade bottle down on the counter, along with my file, as I count out my money and reflect on the simple fact that one kind person can really light up a day.

"Two ninety," she says then. I blink. Did she just say two pounds ninety, for one teensy lemonade? I don't care how pink or cloudy it is, I'm about to return it to the ridiculous fridge when I notice she's spinning my file around and pressing down hard on the luminous green plastic, trying to read what's inside. "Are you looking for work?" she says, tapping my file. "Hell-vet-ick-a." She reads my name out slowly and then looks up. "Did I get that right?"

"It's Vetty," I say. "But yes, and yes! I'm absolutely looking

106

for work." I flip the catch on my folder and slide out a résumé. "I did cleaning and admin for Tall Trees Bed-and-Breakfast full-time last month. They'll give me a reference," I say, stabbing at the part of the paper where I mention my recent housekeeping experience with Wendy and Fran. "I mean, one of the owners is my aunt, so of course she's going to say good stuff, but—"

She smiles with her mouth closed. "I've already got the weekends covered so it's Monday to Friday only. Lunchtime is when I could really do with an extra pair of hands," she says. "I pay six pounds per hour and we share tips. It'll be a bit of everything, so I hope you're not fussy?"

I laugh. I am not fussy. What I am is completely unable to believe my luck. "When can I start?"

Her laugh is quick and peppery. "Come by tomorrow, around eleven." She puts her hand out.

"Thanks," I say, shaking it hard like you're supposed to.

She smiles. "See you tomorrow, Vetty."

I back out the door, bubbling over, and I'm on the street before I realize I forgot to ask her name. Then I look up at the café's sign high on the wall above my head, and there in large loopy gray lettering it says CLEMENTINE'S.

Rob messaged and we've arranged to meet outside the Odeon in Camden at seven. Maybe I am weirdly into talking because I was kind of hoping for another call. Guess I just appreciate when someone actually dials when a message would more than do. I'm sure I'm early but when I pass the Tube station I see him leaning against the railings by the bank. He spots me crossing the street and stands straight. As

I get closer, he pushes a little boy out from behind a nearby trash can. "This is Tom," he says with zero enthusiasm.

"Where's Pez?" the boy says, staring up at me through bright blue glasses.

Rob tugs at Tom's hood. "He's not coming—I already told you," Rob says, but it's obvious from Tom's face he was holding out hope. Rob looks up at me and mouths the word "sorry."

I shake my head and look down at Tom. "Hey," I say, sizing him up. He's a lot younger than Arial for sure. "Let me guess, you're . . . seven?"

He scrapes at some gum on the ground with his shoe, trying not to smile. "Six."

Rob steps forward. "Shall we?" he says, extending his arm out, and we walk the remaining short steps to the theater together, stopping in front of the sign outside, which has the list of films showing. "That Seth Rogen comedy is supposed to be good," Rob says, "but definitely unsuitable." Then he pulls up Tom's hood and leans in. "I really am sorry about this," he says, mock rolling his eyes. "Mum had to work at the last minute, but I didn't want to bail."

"Don't worry, it's fine," I say. "Honestly."

Beside Rob, Tom is pointing to a sign for the latest LEGO movie on the other side of the theater door. "Rob. Please!"

Rob's about to protest but I jump in. "I loved the others," I say with a quick look at Tom, who draws back his clenched fist and smiles up at me.

"You sure?" Rob says, stepping closer.

"Completely." I'm not even lying.

★ ★ ★

We enter the dark auditorium, juggling ticket slips, popcorn, and drinks, and Tom makes a deliberate move to sit between us. During the movie he needs two pees and Rob escorts him to the bathroom each time. When Rob tries to switch places on the way back, Tom can't see the screen, so Rob has to swap into his original seat. Now, as we walk outside, Rob slots his giant headphones over Tom's ears and slides his phone into Tom's jeans pocket. "Don't press anything," Rob says, smiling as he ruffles Tom's hair. Tom's eyes light up as the music starts to play and soon he's mouthing along with the words. We stroll through the crowds by the Tube station on the way back up Camden Road. "So," Rob says, "I guess that was a bit of a disaster."

I shrug. "I liked the film."

"It was funny," he says. "But we met two hours ago and I haven't even asked how you are."

"I'm good," I say. "And I got a job earlier."

"Where?" he says as we pass a *Big Issue* seller outside Starbucks.

"In a café," I say, turning to him. "Just lunchtimes but it's only a short walk from my house and the hours are exactly what I needed."

"Nice," he says. "I'd like a job, but Mum works shifts. Her hours are unpredictable, and I watch Tom when he's not with my dad, so—" He looks up and drops his hand. "Maybe I should try harder. I hate being broke."

"Same. I'm already fantasizing about what I'll buy when I get paid."

"I do that all the time," he says. "And I don't even have a job." He laughs but then slows his pace. "You know, sometimes I sit in Pez's room and imagine that his brand-new kicks and his games and his gadgets are all mine. Must be nice to have two parents and a film-star salary. I don't mean that in a bad way," he says quickly. I slow down. "But d'you ever feel a bit frustrated with Pez?" he says. "For not getting what it's like. And for kinda taking stuff for granted sometimes."

I wasn't expecting this and Rob's face says maybe he wasn't expecting it either, but then I picture Pez's shiny black Nikon camera on the shelf. I don't mention it, of course. It doesn't seem right. "Dunno," I say. "I haven't seen him in so long and when we were kids I never noticed any difference in how we thought about things . . . possessions and stuff."

"I expect you'll notice now," he says, starting to walk on. "Some people can't see how good they've got it. He's even like that about her."

I quicken my pace, expecting him to say more, but nothing comes. If I didn't know better, I'd say he sounds jealous. "You mean March?" I say, trying to make it sound like she's no big deal, but then he makes this face, like he shouldn't be talking like this. Bit late for that, I reckon. "It's okay," I say. "He's told me all about—"

"Those photos?" he says. My feet stop moving. I was planning to say "their casual thing" but this stops me in my tracks. "Apparently she sent him a video too. Don't tell him I said anything though."

I want him to repeat what he's said in case I misheard, but he quickly looks to Tom then back to me, doing something with his eyes like he's checking I've understood. I swallow hard. "Sure," I say, blinking a few times. He doesn't need to explain what kind of pictures these are. His face says it all.

"I haven't seen them but they're on his phone. Did you see how he pounced on me when I was looking for the *Narcos* trailer?" I did, but I don't answer. "He freaks out whenever anyone goes near it." Having seen what was on Pez's computer this morning, I see a new image of him coming into focus. "But I can't work March out either," Rob says then. "She'll drop nudes just like that but then she acts all coy about coming over to watch TV. I reckon it was because we were there. Sometimes I think that's all it is between them. They're each as flaky as the other."

I clear my throat. "What's all what between them?"

"Sex," he says, like it's obvious.

He says it so casually, I have to hang back to let my face adjust. "Right." It's all I can say because all of a sudden, I'm winded. Thankfully we've almost reached the pedestrian crossing where I turn off for the square.

"March only appeared when Nick started seeing Amira but at least they're like a proper couple." Rob's voice continues beside me but I'm picturing Pez's face in his room earlier and all I can see is his iMac screen. Rob tilts his head, trying to catch my eye, but my mind is kind of miles away.

I stop at the lights. "Okay, well, this is me."

Rob rakes his perfect hair with his hand, that way he does. Then he bites the corner of his bottom lip. "Sorry, I go on a bit sometimes," he says.

"That's cool."

"Yeah?" he says, stepping forward. I'm smiling back when he wraps his arms around me, but then just as quickly he lets go. A micro-hug or express hug, but it was still nice. Then he nods to Tom. "I'll try to leave him at home next time."

"My sister is ten," I say. "I get it. She's my other summer job."

"Shame it's unpaid, huh?" I nod, then we sort of stand there, looking at each other, and for some reason I start grinning. Probably nerves, or the ridiculous symmetry of his face. Either way, I'm wishing I was better at this type of thing when I notice him leaning in again, just slightly, so I do too. Our faces move closer and closer until our lips are millimeters from touching, when all of a sudden Rob's body jerks backward and he whips his face around to Tom. "What?" he says.

Tom pulls the headphones off and stares up. "I didn't press anything," he says, tennis-heading between the two of us.

Rob shakes his head at him, trying to smile. "We've got to work on your timing, bro."

I step back. Whatever moment we had is no longer. "Well, thanks, I guess."

Rob sighs. "I'll message you later."

I raise my hand in a wave, then head off across the road.

I feel like I'm sleepwalking again.

12

Just sex.

I can't get it out of my head. I picture Pez's face as I left his room yesterday, only I'm not sure what I see looks like him anymore. The eyes are too hard and the face more severe. I don't know why I feel so unsettled by it. It's honestly not about March or how pretty she is and how nice her clothes are. It's not the photos she sent him either. Yeah, it was surprising to hear about those, but really, *so what?* I guess I'd assumed Pez and me would always be on the same level. Like, experience-wise. Naively, it seems, because it turns out he's bolted off down the track before I knew the race had begun.

It's not so much that he's watching porn or that he's having sex with March. It's the fact that none of it seems like a big deal. That much bodily contact without a real . . . connection. I don't get how it can all mean so little to him when it feels so momentous to me.

I need to get out the door to work, but my third attempt at a messy bun still isn't right. Arial is watching, so I yank a few strands loose then do a twirl in the mirror, smoothing my T-shirt down over my leggings. "Okay," I say. "How do I look?"

She's rifling through a toiletry bag. "Sexy," she says, twisting up an old lipstick and examining the color.

"Sexy isn't quite what I was going for. Or what you should think I'm going for," I say.

"Whatever," she says, cocking her head like a dog and giving me that evaluating look she's taken to dishing out. I'm already falling short of her expectations, I can tell. "You'll need some of this," she says, handing me the lipstick, which I can see is a fetching frosted pink. "It's waitressy."

She says it with such certainty. "Is that right?"

"Hundred percent," she says. I pretend to put it on, but she keeps watching, awaiting my transformation. "Go on," she says.

I begin painting my lips for her amusement, half hating myself and half enjoying it too. I look ridiculous, but what's the harm? I'll wipe it off on the way. "C'mon, grab your backpack," I say, but she's still eyeing me up, trying to decide whether I'll do. "Arial, we need to go!"

I reach Clementine's two minutes early and bask in a shaft of sunlight, taking in all its loveliness from outside. The orange paint bursts forth, so bright and juicy and sure of itself. Earlier rain has left drops on the sign and these glitter in the light like tiny jewels. The sandwich board outside is covered in swirly writing that's tricky to read but someone has drawn flowers all down the side and it looks cheery. Through the window I see enough bodies to know it's busy, so I quickly check my hair then step into the soft, welcoming noise. I make my way to the counter, taking in the shiny square tables with matching silver chairs and tiny white vases with daisylike flowers in the center. The coffee machine steams and chugs alongside the hum of customers' chatter and the old-school R & B that plays in the background—the kind Wendy and Fran are into. I don't know how I didn't notice these details yesterday, but I've got a powerful sense that this is a place I could be happy.

Clementine pops up from under the glass almost on cue. "You're here!" she says. "Nip around the back and grab yourself an apron. Then come help me label these baguettes."

I'm tempted to salute like a soldier, but of course I don't. She'd think I'm nuts and that could ruin everything, so I dash toward the back of the café, quick as I can. I push through the door and step into a brightly lit room, delighted at the prospect of a staff room and overjoyed with the fact I've landed such a proper job. There, on a chair, directly under the bright striplight, sits March.

March! The same March who texted Pez her bits is casually punching words into her phone like there's not one remotely unusual thing about her being there. I think about trying my entrance again. Maybe this is some surreal game of life roulette and if I put all my money on red and try walking in once more, someone else—Beyoncé, Jesus, anyone else, please—might be sitting in the chair next time around.

She looks up. "Alright," she says, low and slow.

Um, hello! I want to say. *What are you doing here at my new job?* She stands and slips her phone into her pocket. She's wearing high-waisted jeans and a plain black T-shirt that's tied in a knot to the side. A stripe of her brown skin is visible between the two and her curves fill every inch of her clothes, but instead of just taking all this in and moving on like a normal person, my brain keeps shouting *Pez has seen her boobs. Pez has seen her boobs!!!!* I feel like a ten-year-old.

"Mum mentioned she'd hired someone called Vetty. I wondered whether it was you. Can't imagine there are many of you out there."

Her mum! I take my backpack off, trying hard not to look bothered, but truly, the thought of having to deal with that face and all the madness it brings for the rest of the summer is making my head hurt. Clementine being March's mum just makes this reality sharper and makes March more . . . permanent. Only five minutes ago life looked so joyful and bright but a huge curly-haired cloud has eclipsed my sun.

I catch a glimpse of myself in a tiny mirror above the coat hook behind her head. It takes a few seconds for me to connect the pink lipstick I'm seeing with my own mouth; then I swipe at my lips until all traces of sparkle are gone. She's watching me, smiling. I do my best to cover. "Where do I find one of those?" I ask, pointing to the apron slung loose around her neck.

She opens a drawer and hands me a folded black square that's been neatly ironed. "Here," she says, staring at my lips, which I'm sure are red-raw. I shake the apron out, watching how she takes the strings of her own and loops them around her waist, and I copy how she pulls them to the front and ties them in a bow. Then she bends over and scoops all her hair up into an elastic band, leaving a pineapple-shaped stack of curls high upon her head. She doesn't fiddle with it or even check it in the tiny mirror before she leaves the room.

I follow her out and cross the floor to the glass counter next to the till, where we perch together behind an array of sandwich fillings and giant bowls of salad. I'm telling my brain to behave and wondering whether I should be doing something useful, when March takes a small writing pad and a pen from her apron. "You'll need these," she says, holding out her hand. I take them and flick through the pages. Scratches of blue ink say things like *2 x cappuccinos—1 x STRONG*—underlined a lot—and *1 x smoked salmon bagel (no cream cheese!!!)—hot chocolate—kid!!!* It's the handwriting from the sandwich board outside. I look up. "Don't worry," she says. "It's not private."

Private hadn't crossed my mind but Clementine has arrived and is standing on the other side of March. While not exactly tall, March looks it beside her mum. Her skin is a shade darker than Pez's, whereas Clementine is paler than me and her fair skin is covered in freckles.

"We do a lot of takeout over lunch," Clementine says. "Best let March do the sandwich prep today. Watch as you wrap. You'll learn a lot that way."

"Sure," I say, nodding away, like a bobblehead doll.

"Tomorrow we'll show you how to take orders, and we'll move on to the till after that. For now, just keep the tables clear and wiped down," she says, dropping some plates in the sink. "Oh, and be nice to the customers." She gives March a loaded wink. March returns the look in a way that makes it clear she's been told to do this a lot, and as her mouth returns to how it was, I notice they share the same dimple on the left side of their cheeks.

★ ★ ★

I've only been here two hours and I've already wrapped what must be a thousand baguettes. And I've learned how to froth milk properly. Who knew there are at least eight variations of what is essentially coffee with hot milk. I'm quick at turning the tables around, clearing away dirty cups and glasses, and getting them loaded back into the dishwasher. I enjoy spraying the surfaces and wiping them until they gleam, then rearranging the plastic menus behind the tiny flower vase in the center. A toddler tipped a whole bowl of pasta on the floor earlier. I got the mop out for that and even had to put up a yellow flap sign that said *Caution!*, which I thought was a little over-the-top, but who am I to argue?

A group of suit-wearing men spills through the door at one o'clock. I can tell they're regulars by how easily they arrange themselves into the chairs inside the windows. There's no break in their loud chatter as they settle in, the four of them taking up the space of three small tables. I wipe at a spot of dried pasta sauce on the table leg beside theirs, listening to their talk about buyers and vendors and sale prices.

"What've you got for us today, darling?" One of the men is out of his chair, leaning across the table to me.

I look up at the till, but Clementine is with a customer. "The specials?" I say, turning around, trying hard to remember what they are.

"I'm fond of a special," he says.

My palms sweat, and I look up to the till again, but I still can't catch Clementine's eye, and March, who is stuffing lettuce into a pile of baguettes, just watches me. I hide the dirty cloth and disinfectant in my apron pocket and force my face to look more pleasant while I try to remember what the specials are. "For this afternoon?" I say, trying to buy time while I rack my brain.

"A matinee!" the guy exclaims, and the others laugh heartily. I can't bring myself to laugh along but I worry I'm being rude, and I kick myself for having messed up already. A hand lands on my arm. "Let's hear what you've got," he says.

I pull away, pretending to scratch the back of my head while squinting at the board behind the till. "Um, spinach, warm goat cheese, and tomato," I say, clearing my throat. "That's the sandwich. It's on sourdough. And, um . . . the main is a grilled halloumi and chorizo salad." When I look up, their faces are stone. "Or there's a pasta?" I can't make out what type of pasta it is from here, or what sauce. "It's something to do with a chicken breast," I say, going redder by the second. "That is what you meant?" I want the floor to rise up and swallow me.

"He's only teasing you," says another man at the table.

I fake-laugh like an idiot. "Course. I'll get someone to take your order," I say, backing away from the table at top speed. When I round the glass cabinet and drop the dirty glasses into the sink, March's eyes follow me. Arial would have handled that situation better than I did.

"You don't have to smile at them like that, you know?" she says, stirring pesto into a giant bowl of penne.

That's what she's got to say to me right now. "Sorry?"

She goes to speak and then stops. "Just . . . don't think you have to be nice to *all* of them." She says this out of the side of her mouth.

"But—"

She places the bowl down between the coleslaw and the broccoli salad. "You'll learn," she says, walking off. I grip the sink, quietly fuming as she glides toward the broker men, moving like self-doubt has never troubled her. As she writes their orders in her pad, her body stays still, and her face is calm and professional. She doesn't smile, not once. She doesn't fake-laugh at their lame, lewd jokes. She doesn't look awkward, squirm, or go remotely red in the face either. I wish I wasn't so impressed with every bit of this.

Before I know it, it's ten minutes to four and time for me to finish. Clementine has agreed I can leave a few minutes early each day for Arial's pickup. Thankfully there was no chance for any more small talk with March, and as I leave I stuff a laminated menu in my backpack. By tomorrow I'll be able to recite the whole list along with the prices. Clementine was right; she really did need an extra pair of hands. The lunch rush didn't let up at all until after three and there was no break, not that I'm complaining. I discovered that March is well able to smile when she wants to. In fact, she smiles a lot, even at me. On one hand, having to endure her every day is pure cruelty, but on the other, I'm already fond of Clementine's sunny little café.

I saunter down Kentish Town Road, rattling the coins I earned in tips inside my pocket, but this makes me think of the man by the parking meter yesterday and then this makes me think of Pez's bedroom. I'm trying to pretend that the whole porn-watching, casual-sex business means nothing, but it's not nothing to me. I just feel so behind on all the important stuff and I wish I could talk to someone about how little I know about any of it. But at least if the tips continue this way I won't stay super broke. As I walk, I busy my head making a list of all the glorious stuff I might soon be able to afford and so far this list mostly contains clothes, decent underwear, and a lengthy list of personal grooming products.

I collect Arial from the square and we walk home side by side. I find her hand far up inside her sleeve. "So, how was today?"

"Fine," she says, trailing a small stick along the iron railings. The vibrating noise of the bars does something to my heart.

I look down and check her eyes. "Just fine?" She sticks out her bottom lip and I realize it's a long way from *fun* like I told her it would be yesterday, and I feel bad. "So, what did you guys do all day?"

Her shoulders droop. "Crafts."

"Meet anyone fun yet? Anyone—"

"No one talks to me," she says, head low. "I'm the youngest in our group."

"Oh."

As we pass by the shops on the opposite side she lifts her face bit by bit. "One of the girls can do a perfect walkover," she says, like it's bad news.

"Front or back?" I ask, because this kind of detail is important.

"Both," she says flatly.

"Was she nice?"

"I told you, no one talks to me!" This comes out angry and I let her cool off as we turn the corner into our street but then she stops walking and looks up. "So, were you a good waitress?"

"Not bad. But I didn't get to take any orders. Apparently, I have to learn lots of other stuff first."

She nods like this makes sense. "When will I start . . . growing up?" she says.

"Growing up?" I repeat. She nods again but more urgently. I walk on, smiling a bit too wide, and she tugs at the cardigan around my waist, pulling me back.

"You know, puberty, or whatever it's called."

I shake her hand away. "It won't happen for a while. Don't worry."

Her chest falls. "Oh," she says. "Like, how long a while?"

"I dunno." I'm trying not to sound annoyed but she's looking right at me, fixed eyes wide and waiting for me to say more. God knows I'm struggling enough without having to deal with Arial's anxieties on top of my own. "It's hard to say. If you're like me, at least two years. Maybe three. Ages!" This seems to satisfy her for now and we walk on for the last few steps. When we reach the pavement in front of our flat I look up at Pez's window and there he is, sitting in front of the screen.

"Can we go see him?" Arial's followed my gaze.

I push her down the side passage toward the flat. "No," I say. "Inside!"

13

Yesterday was a good day at work even though I didn't take any orders. The bank across the road had a lunch meeting and they asked for two giant sandwich platters at midday. Clementine was slammed, so she told me to make a selection. I made a mix of brown and white ones involving everything I could find: shrimp and salmon with avocado as well as the usual cheese, ham, and chicken, and veggie options too. I included some without mayo, in case anyone at the bank is as fussy as Arial. When I was finished, I sprinkled salad leaves around the edges, and when I carried them out, March made a vaguely impressed face as I passed.

Even without the sandwich-platter challenge, time's gone just as quick today. I took a whole load of orders and got them all right, and I recited the specials like they were a poem I knew by heart. It's past three thirty and I'm wrapping the filling tubs in plastic wrap when Clementine tells me to grab a drink. "Sit out on the floor," she says. "That way you can see if it gets busier and I need a dig-out."

I place a tiny teapot under the water boiler and pull down the lever, watching hot water spit inside; then I flip the lid and drop the right change for an oat bar into the till.

I make my way to a single table nestled against the wall at the back.

I've just taken a bite of my bar when March drags a chair around and sits down opposite me. When she cracks the tab on her can of lemon San Pellegrino, I can't help but notice how ridiculously color-coordinated her yellow fingernails are with her drink, like an ad someone's spent time thinking about. She holds the can up high and pours the fizzy liquid into a tall glass of ice. It bubbles into a cold, cloudy haze, making a lovely hiss as it fills the glass, stopping exactly at the rim like it was made to measure. As the very last drop drips out, she looks up at me and it feels like she's done this trick before. "Alright?" she says, which I've worked out is her signature opening.

"That went quick," I say, looking at my watch even though I know the time.

Her eyebrows rise and she nods. "Mum's pleased to have the help, just in case she doesn't say it. She wasn't sure the owner would allow her to take anyone else on. Took some convincing apparently. She said you walked in as she put the phone down. Seems like your timing was perfect."

It's the most I've heard March say in one go and as I replay her words in my head I smile for a load of reasons. "But I thought Clementine owned the place," I say, sitting forward on my chair.

She sets her glass back down. "Clementine's not a real person," she says, putting a hand to her mouth and screwing up her face. "Mum's name is Viv."

I blink and I look up at the person I now know is Viv and then back to March, who is laughing so hard. "Oh god, don't say anything, will you?" I reach across the table. "Seriously, please don't. I must have called her Clementine at least nineteen times since Tuesday!"

We're both shrieking. We're so loud that people are turning to look. We're howling so much it takes a few seconds for me to realize I'm holding March's hand in mine, suddenly feeling its heat. She looks up and I drag my hand away, tucking it safely under the table. "Who's Clementine, then?" I ask, trying to act like nothing strange has just happened.

She shrugs. "You could ask the guy who owns this place, but he's a creep."

"Yeah, why?"

"Where do I start? The way he's rude to my mum and pays her so badly, that kind of why."

This makes sense. "So, how long have you worked here?"

"I started a few months after her. So, a year, almost. I stopped around my exams, to study. S'alright," she says. "It doesn't leave much time for having a life." I go to say something about exams but she's still talking. "But I'm saving so I don't mind."

I almost ask what she's saving for, but I stop. It feels too personal a question to ask so soon.

She looks up to Viv, who's stretched over the counter, wiping it down. "No matter how hard she works or how many shifts she covers, she's always broke." She says it quietly. "I just want money in my pocket. I want to be sure it's there, you know?"

"Yeah," I say. I do.

She smiles and sits back. "So, what about you? What d'you need money for?"

Where do I start? "Um ... everything?" I say. "I've got fourteen quid in my account and nothing to wear." She laughs, but not in a mean way, more like she relates. She's quiet again, waiting for me to say more, but I'm wondering why she's being so nice and how this feels so easy. I realize it's been a while since I've said anything. I should say *something*. "Do you live near here?"

"Archway," she says. "Not far. I walk in most days. Only takes fifteen minutes and I listen to music all the way. You?"

"Opposite Pez."

"Yeah, of course, I knew that." She nods. "It's nice around there."

"Our flat is nothing like his place," I say, lifting my cup to my lips. It's not that I feel a need to point this out, it's more that I think March might be relieved to know.

She leans her elbows on the table. It might be the two high buns she's tied her hair in today, but her eyes seem bigger than usual. "What's it like, Pez's house?"

"You haven't been there?"

She shakes her head and pushes air out through her nose. "Well, his mum is Luna Boyd, so I expect his place isn't much like mine."

"But I thought you two—"

She shakes the ice in her glass. "He never asks."

I'd already pictured her in his room, on his new T-shirt-soft bedsheets, trying on his baseball caps and being all cute in his mirror. That's where my head went as soon as Rob told me about the photos on his phone and that's where I imagined they did all the stuff they've done. "You've been seeing each other for a while, I just assumed. Sorry."

"Yeah, we've hung out and stuff, but mostly at my place," she says, sounding more coy, a bit like Rob said. "He never suggests going back to his. Except for last Saturday when you and Rob were there." She looks up. "But it felt as though Rob was doing the asking that night. Don't you think?"

Maybe it did? I thought that March was the one who was acting weird that evening, but maybe Pez was being the standoffish one.

"He can be a bit . . . private sometimes," I say.

"Guess you know him better than anyone." She holds my gaze like there's other stuff she's not saying, and I feel as though I might understand this too.

I sigh. "Yeah, but it's been a while."

She gazes out onto the café floor, then looks back. "He's different than I expected," she says, before she blows into the tip of her straw. "He surprises me sometimes."

"Yeah?"

"Like, a couple of months ago, I was in Ireland with Mum," she says. "I was at my cousin's, supposedly studying, when I got a message from him. I was thrilled, because the last time we were together he'd been acting strangely, so it was a relief to hear from him to be honest. Anyway, we were chatting away when he said something about feeling down. Then he asked if I'd send him a picture, to cheer him up, he said." She looks in my eyes again and a lump of the oat bar lodges in my throat. "A photo of me, you know?" she adds, like I might need this qualification. If I could speak, I'd tell her I already get the picture but I'm concentrating on swallowing. "I knew he was like that. I'd seen that side of him before," she says, looking at me in a way that makes the chair under me feel too hard. She sits back and I try to swallow what's in my mouth. "It was unexpected, that's all, and I felt shy about it, which is stupid, I know." She bites down on her lip and stares at me.

I look away, stuffing more granola bar into my mouth, but the oats are building like a boulder in my cheeks and I can't swallow. There is nowhere for it to go and I sit there like an overstuffed hamster. "Babe," she says, reaching for the remains of the bar in the wrapper and dragging it toward her, "the ones in the packets aren't good."

I try swallowing again but the clump of oats won't go down. March tips my cup, and seeing it empty, she pushes her glass toward me.

"Drink!" she says. I start out with a sip but soon I'm guzzling away until the contents of my mouth dissolve and slide down my throat in a strange sea of super-sweet buttery lemon. "Y'okay?" she says, reaching her hand across. "Seriously?"

She's looking right at me, checking my eyes, like she's noticing every detail. "Uh-huh," I say, realizing that any efforts to keep hating this girl might be futile. She's so . . . I dunno the word. It's just nice to be around her.

"Hey, if you're interested in earning more money, I'm going to a casting next Wednesday," she says, rescuing a menu that's slipped between the wall and the edge of the table. "Why don't you come along?" I pull back, double-checking her voice for an edge I might have missed. Is all this niceness because I know Pez "better than anyone"? But her eyes are soft and her face is open, the exact opposite of mean. "Sorry," she says. "Amira thinks I've become obsessed with earning money and she might be right."

"I'd love to earn extra money!" This is true. It's also true that of all the people I've met since moving back, March might be the easiest company.

"Great," she says. "It's near Oxford Circus. And it doesn't start until six p.m. so you could drop your sister home first."

My shoulders slump. "But—"

"What?"

I feel like I fool, but I have to say it. "It doesn't make sense—"

"I guess most people who audition have other jobs so—"

"Not the timing," I say. "Look, I'm not putting myself down, but—" Her eyes scan mine and I come right out with it. "You look like a model. I don't."

Her mouth opens. "It's not a model casting!" she says. "It's an agency scouting for films, TV, and stuff. They want real people; people you'd see on any street. I saw the ad online. I'll show you their website," she says, taking out her phone. I freeze, waiting for a wave of humiliation that doesn't come. "And model?" she says, smiling. "C'mon, you must have clocked the size of my ass." Thankfully, I know better than to make any comment on this. "Mum thinks it's a scam, but the girl on the phone told me you can earn a hundred and fifty quid a day on something like *EastEnders.*"

"A hundred and fifty, in one day?"

"I know!" she says. "And you can get a whole week's work if you're picked for"—she scratches at one of her buns with her pen—"continuity, yeah, that's what she said.

And all you have to do is look normal. That's all." God, she's got no idea how far from normal she looks and I feel terrible for saying what I said in Pez's bedroom about her *knowing it*. "So?" she says. "How about it?"

"Sounds a bit too good to be true."

She sits back and folds her arms. "Not you too!" she says. "It's legit. I'm telling you." Then she takes the pen from behind her ear and starts to write a web address on a napkin. "Trust me, we'll never get rich working here," she says. "Besides, what else have you got on next Wednesday evening that's so important?"

I picture myself on my bed, lounging around in clothes I don't like, staring at my crappy laptop, or worse, out the window. Something about this picture is crystal clear. Plus Dad will be home by six and I need the money. Why am I even hesitating? "Nothing."

"So?" she says, leaning across the table.

"So, let's do it!"

14

I'm lying on my bed staring at the ceiling when Arial strides in holding her toothbrush in one hand and her Tangle Teezer in the other. In some feat of super coordination, she manages to do both tasks seamlessly. It's a few minutes before she turns off her toothbrush and spits into an empty glass. "Grace gets periods," she says.

I lift my head. "Grace?"

"The one who's good at gymnastics."

"How old is she?"

"Twelve."

"Is there no one your own age you can hang out with?"

"We're friends now," she says. "And she's not *that* much older." She puts the hairbrush down. "Can you tell me about periods? It's just, Grace says she's on it now and she says stuff like I'm supposed to understand, and I don't. Not really."

I prop myself up on my elbows and stare at her face. *How is this happening already? How are all these questions coming out of her and there's no one but me here to help?* I'd check with Dad, only neither of us needs that embarrassment and I'm not sure I want to draw attention to what Arial's missing out on by not having Mum. If he knew Arial was asking this stuff already it might do him in altogether. I had these chats with Mum pre-grapefruit, but I don't remember much of what was said. I remember her being there—here!—sitting beside me on my bed in this room. I was older than Arial but my period hadn't started either. Mum was her typical no-nonsense self, but wise and warm and all the things that I'm not. My eyes sting and I don't want to think about it. I'm not ready, not when I have so much of my own crap to work out. "Your face looks funny," Arial says. I rub my eyes, then blink a lot. "What's wrong?"

"Seems early for these questions, that's all." It comes out as impatient and she sighs heavily. "Okay, what d'you want to know?"

"Forget it," she says, getting up and reaching for the door handle.

I immediately want to drag her back and wrap her in a huge hug. "You sure?"

"Yeah," she says quietly from the other side. "I'm going to watch TV."

I roll over and bury my face in my pillow until my phone rings. It could be one of two people and for a second, I'm torn as to which of the two I want it to be.

"Whatcha up to?" says Pez, sounding super bored. I scoot down the bed and peek out from the blind. There he is, across the street, at his computer. "Because I'm over here . . . reading a book," he says.

That he's messing with me is a relief. If he'd realized what I saw on his computer, then he wouldn't act like this. "I can see you," I say, sighing for dramatic effect.

He pushes away from his desk and comes to the window. "This is weird," he says, giving me the finger with his free hand. "Just come over."

I really don't want to sit in that room. "Does your house arrest extend to the wall outside?"

"Two minutes," he says and then hangs up.

I get there first, watching as he skulks down his steep steps wearing what look like pajama bottoms that are too big. "How's captivity treating you?" My voice sounds different and I'm afraid he can tell.

"How do you think?"

"Does Luna jangle keys outside your bedroom door?"

"She's at a meeting."

"So technically there's no guard?"

He shakes his head. "This prison is psychological," he says, only it doesn't really sound like he's joking.

"Fancy a jailbreak to Tesco?"

"Amazon Fresh delivered this morning," he says, pushing himself up off the wall. "C'mon in."

"Nah, s'all right," I say. "Just fancied a walk. Any word from Harland?"

He sits back down and faces the sky. "He flew out yesterday. Least we won't have to deal with him for a while."

Pez is no way near as good at acting as his parents, and despite whatever else is swirling, I feel sorry for him. "Hey, you'll never guess who my new waitressing job is with."

His eyes follow some fast-moving clouds. "March."

I dig his ribs. "How d'you know?"

"She messaged me, on your first day," he says, rubbing the back of his head.

I jump down from the wall. "She did?"

His legs stop swinging. "Why do you say it like that?"

"Like what?"

"Like that," he says. "You said *she did?* like you were surprised."

"No, I didn't."

"Yeah, you did," he says, looking properly pissed off, and suddenly the distance between us feels greater than ever.

"D'you have a problem with us being friends?" I ask, shielding my eyes from sun that's not there.

He shrinks back. "Oh, you're friends now?"

I don't like the way he says "friends" and I also worry I'm being presumptuous in using the word. "Well, yeah," I say, because I think we are at least.

"And why would that be a problem?"

"It's not, for me," I say. "I was asking if it was for you."

"No," he says weakly, then he turns away and we both watch not much happening on opposite ends of the street. After what feels like ages he shifts back. "So, how are we getting to this wedding?" God, the wedding! It feels like an age since I asked him and I'm honestly not sure whether an entire weekend in Somerset with Pez is something to look forward to anymore. I can't look straight at him in case he's able to read this in my eyes. "Um . . . hello?" he says, angling his face in front of mine.

"Oh," I say. "Dad's driving, but I think Wendy wants me to come early."

"So, we'll get the train?"

"Yeah, I guess. I mean, yeah. That'll work. For sure."

Sun breaks through a patch of clouds above and I lean

back in the new heat but then my pocket buzzes. I'm grateful for the interruption and pull the phone out of my jeans.
Rob!

You missed a call from me at 10:56.

I switch it off mute and it *ping*s loudly with a message.

Party at mine Saturday.

Pez looks over my shoulder. "You gave him your
number?" I don't answer and he sniffs.

"What?"

"That's not an answer," he says.

I drop the phone back into my pocket. "It's about a
party."

"I know!" he says. "I got the same message, but . . . earlier."

For a moment I can't work out whether he's being mean
but then he smiles like he realizes how petty he just sounded.
It's such a relief to see his teeth that I smile too. "I'll go if
you will," I say.

He holds up his wrists like he's handcuffed.

"Err, *next* Saturday, shitface! Your two-week sentence
will be served."

He humphs and his shoulders round. I keep watching his
face until he cracks, a tiny bit. "I'll think about it," he says.

I push him back. I'm already wondering what I'll do if
Rob tries to kiss me again. Or worse, what I'll do if he
doesn't.

15

Me and March are the only two people on the 88 from Camden Town, or at least that's what it feels like. In reality the bus is packed but somehow March is the only thing I see with any focus.

"It's in Highgate," she's saying. "And all girls, which Mum, for all her right-on progressiveness, just loves. Amira's been in my class since Year Seven. We've always been friends but we never used to hang out much after school. I'm sure that's why she wants things to work out with me and Pez so badly. She's convinced if our boyfriends are friends it'll somehow bring us closer."

"Makes sense, I guess."

She lifts her knees to let someone pass but keeps her feet on the seat. "Most people say they hate school, but I like it. D'you?" she says, turning to me. I've seen this look on her face before. It happens when she asks certain questions: like her eyes get big but her mouth stays soft, like she's ready to listen and wants to know the answer. Not many people have this look and it's hard not to take note of it. Pez was always great at noticing stuff but with March I feel heard too. When I think about her question, I picture myself practicing

Wendy's deep-breathing exercises in a bathroom stall at Frome. I hid in there for weeks after I first joined, and I pray that this September, if I'm lucky enough to meet girls as nice as Jess and Liv and Freya, I might have more courage.

"Not really," I say. "But maybe next year will be different."

"Yeah, fresh start. New vibe and new subjects will help."

"Hope so."

"I went for drama, politics, and English lit," she says. "What about you?"

"Um?" I stop. I genuinely have to think. "French, sociology, and . . . history."

"I thought about sociology too," she says. "But decided politics was a better fit in the end. If by some miracle Mum and I can afford the tuition, I'd like to take it in college. Is sociology something you'd like to do after?" she says. My face twists. It's not. Definitely not. I've had few if any thoughts about sociology or college or tuition, if I'm honest. My brain can barely stretch to September, let alone years into the future. I shake my head and her face tilts. "So, why did you pick it?"

"I dunno . . ." *Why did I pick those subjects?* Wendy suggested sociology. Fran thought history was interesting and a good all-rounder, and I generally do well at French. "With the move, and changing schools and stuff, I guess I just thought it was . . . safe?"

"D'you wish now that you'd—"

"Given it more thought?" I say, cutting her off. "Or . . . made a considered choice?" She nods. "Yeah," I say. "I do. There was no reason for me not to, other than I've gotten used to waiting for other people to decide what's best for me." I don't know how March manages to do this—makes me blurt things I'd never usually say so easily . . .

"What are you interested in?"

I shrug. "At school?"

"Wherever," she says, flinging one arm wide. "What do you like? What do you enjoy doing?"

Such simple questions; I'm flummoxed. "Um . . . eating and watching TV."

She laughs. "Yeah, yeah, my two favorite things," she says. "But c'mon."

"Taking photographs, maybe? I think I'm better with pictures than with words. But I don't take many these days."

Her eyebrows rise. "And what do you like to photograph?"

"People." I say it quickly. Even though it's not strictly true. Although it's people I'm interested in, most pictures I've taken lately are of things, maybe because things are safe. An image can reveal as much about the photographer as the subject of the photo, and I think I'm afraid of other people seeing what I see.

"So why not take photography, then?" she asks.

"I don't have a camera."

She raises both hands. "*That's* your excuse?"

"It's the truth."

"Lucky we're about to get rich, then, isn't it!"

I sigh. "You make it sound so . . . simple."

"It's as simple as you make it," she says, looking at me like she might actually have the measure of me.

"They start from two hundred," the guy says, looking down at his clipboard, where he's written March's name. He's wearing jeans and a jacket that are two different denims and his long, dark hair looks like it's slicked back with syrup. He smells of cigarettes.

Four hundred quid! I say inside my head, but March says it out loud, like she's angry. "It says 'small admin fee' on your website." She waves her phone at the guy. "We've already paid a ten to the girl downstairs to fill out one of those." She points to the applications on the desk, where we've completed everything from our eye color to our waist measurements and stapled our passport photos to the top right-hand corner.

Double Denim waves his hand over the pile. "Those forms are for our background artistes," he says. "The portfolio option is offered only to the very small percentage who we feel could fit our modeling books," he says, looking only at March.

She places her hand on her hip. "And what's the difference?"

"What you're paid," he says. This gets her attention, which he takes as a good sign. "Look, you're a beautiful girl."

"Thanks," March says flatly. I'm nervous, but to her this is business.

"You could earn big from that face," he says, pulling a large black portfolio the size of one of Dad's photography books out from under the desk and placing it on top. "A lot more than the hundred-quid day rate you'd get with our Extras division." He lifts the cover of the book. "These shots are taken by our professionals in a proper studio," he says, flicking through the pages. "And they're sent to the best agencies in London, all of whom are on the lookout for actors and models, for all sorts of work," he says. "They're not just extras."

He moves closer to March so there isn't enough space between them. March steps back but her eyes eat up the open page as intently as his eyes do her. I can only see the pictures upside down but even from here I can tell they're the worst. Not wanting to sound arrogant, but I reckon I could do better.

"How old is she?" March says, pointing at one girl.

"Lauren," he says. "She's seventeen. Gets lots of catalog work. Earned thousands of pounds this year and she's in line for a big campaign with a major fashion brand."

March continues turning the pages, pressing her painted fingernail down like she's studying each of them. I step forward to see better and the headshots are as cheesy close up as from afar but it's not this that makes me want to drag her away from this creep. My pulse is racing.

She looks up at him. "How many thousands of pounds?"

The shape of his mouth changes. "Depends," he says. "The right look at the right time can make serious money." March stares at the book again, hungrily, like she wants it all too much for my liking. I watch his eyes move all over her. "We're getting more requests for plus-size. Of course, the curvy look might just be a trend but even if it doesn't last you could lose weight easily. It's something a lot of our girls choose to do once they sign up."

He lets out a long, lingering breath, but I suck mine in. *Did he really say that?* "To feel good about themselves," he adds then. "Not because they're under any pressure. It's entirely their decision. They just find they get more work, that's all."

March lifts her face from the book and fixes her eyes on

140

him. I blink and blink again. My breathing becomes quick and noisy. How wrong would it be for me to yank her away? I could make up some excuse, any excuse. Double Denim would be mad, maybe March would be too, but I want to get us the hell out of here. I reach my hand across the desk, wishing my fingers weren't shaking. Then, before my hand touches her arm, March slams the book shut, dips down to the floor, and swings her bag over the shoulder.

"Let's go, Vetty," she says, taking off across the room. "Let's go get something to eat!"

I follow her to the door. It's all I can do not to punch the air.

We ride the elevator in silence to the ground floor and we've reached the street before she opens her mouth. "Wanna get noodles?" she says.

I nod, sucking in large gulps of warm London air at the same time. I'm so relieved to be out of that room, I'll go anywhere. Besides, I'm starving.

"Let's walk into Soho," she says, taking my hand. "There's the best place."

We cross the road entwined and we stay like this as she weaves us down alleyways and busy streets. She doesn't stop, not once. She knows exactly where she's going. My heart races and my legs move with some borrowed energy. *Am I imagining the heads that turn as we pass?* An enormous photo of two long-legged girls in sportswear hangs in the window of H&M on Oxford Street. They look like they're about to step out onto the street in front of us. I slow my pace to see it better and I catch our reflection for a split second: just us, two girls walking together. Soon the image is gone but not before I photographed it in my mind.

When we reach Chinatown I follow her through a tiny door into a dark room. It's not a place I would have picked and when I look up at the enormous menu behind the counter I wonder how anyone knows what to choose in these places.

"Meat, veggie, sweet, sour, spicy, mild . . . what'll it be?" March says.

I turn my neck around and stare at the board. "I usually have spareribs and an egg roll."

She laughs. "For starters, this place is Korean. I'd recommend something, only I like to pick a surprise."

"At random?"

"Why not? It's all good," she says, leaning into the counter and catching the eye of the elderly lady serving. "Okay, so one number thirty-nine, jamppong, to go, please," she says.

"Seafood noodle soup?" the woman says. "Spicy."

"Perfect!" says March. "With lots of your special sauce please."

The woman smiles and then looks at me. "And one . . . japchae?" I've obviously mispronounced it, so I start pointing. "Number sixteen!"

"With extra sauce?" the woman says.

"Extra sauce!" I exclaim, beaming at her and then at March, who is giggling in the doorway. For some reason, I clap my hands.

These are easily the chewiest, most delicious noodles I've ever tasted. March finishes her soup quickly, making an impressive amount of noise as she slurps up the last of it. "Up for one more stop?" she says, flinging her empty box into a trash can.

I nod. "How about some ice cream?"

She takes her phone from her jacket pocket and leans her head against mine to take a picture of the two of us. I can see in the phone screen that she's screwing up her face and I try some sort of smile as she takes a quick snap; then she starts googling again like it was nothing. "There's a great place near here. We went there after the march a few months ago. Let me check," she says, licking her fingers then swiping her screen.

I stab at the last swirl of noodles inside my box, wondering what the photo looked like. "The march?"

She looks up. "Mum loves a good rally. We discovered the ice cream place after the Women's March. Chin Chin, that was it!"

"I've only seen marches on TV. You make signs and stuff?"

"Course," she says. "Since I was a kid. I wasn't great with crowds at first. I used to get claustrophobic." Her hands dance around her face like she's remembering. "But I'm better now and there's always the most insane energy."

"Is that why she called you March?"

She stands. "Nah," she says, stamping on a rogue Whopper box that missed the trash. "My birthday is on the fourth. Guess it made sense at the time."

Going home we sit on the top deck of the bus, right up in front. It's been ages since I've seen London from this height and even the sky looks new. March is still talking, listing everything she thinks is wrong with the world. It's a long list but I'm enjoying the sound of her as much as the view. Everything she's worked up about sounds worthwhile so it's reassuring that someone is getting mad about it. The bus is busy again. I start to explain to March what happened with Arial the morning before my first shift. A boy opposite us stares as if he's listening, and I'm surprised by how little I mind being overheard.

"That *that's* what she wanted me to look like was a shock, you know? Like, I'm okay with admitting that *I'd* like to look sexy sometimes, but that it's her first idea of . . . pretty— and for work—just felt, I dunno . . . kind of sad maybe?"

"We get told early," March says. "We get the signals from everywhere. That beauty or whatever is something we should be for other people. Like, it's more about what we're *supposed* to look like, as opposed to figuring out how we want to look, or even how we feel about ourselves?"

As we approach Mornington Crescent the boy on the opposite side of the aisle drops his phone getting off. March picks it up from under our seat and as she hands it back to him they bounce some flirty lines back and forth. When the bus finally stops he heads off down the stairs, looking like the cat that ate the canary. She turns back to me after, like it was nothing.

"Do you ever *not* know what to say?"

She cocks her head. "Huh?"

"It's great, by the way. I'd love to be so confident, but do you ever feel . . .?"

She presses her lips together. "Insecure?"

I wouldn't have had the guts to put it like that, but . . . "Yeah."

"Course," she says.

"Really?"

She blows air between her lips for a long time and then turns her face to the aisle. "I had this boyfriend last year," she says. "His name was Sully and he was always talking about his sister's friends and how hot or not hot they were." She stops and inspects her fingernails, which are green today like grass. "But it wasn't just these girls, it was all girls, and he could be mean sometimes. He blew hot and cold with me too and I'd question everything I said, what I wore, all that. I'd compare myself to everyone he passed comment on. It really messed with my head. I was so miserable at the end of last summer, it was unreal."

"What did you do?"

"Finished it."

"Just like that?" I ask.

She nods. "But then he started messaging me the whole time, waiting outside my house and stuff. It's so nuts to admit this, but I was kinda thrilled and I got back with him because I thought it meant that he loved me." She shakes her head. "Course, soon as I slept with him he lost interest," she says, looking down at her lap.

I straighten in my seat. "That must have hurt."

She sighs. "I regret it. I should've known it would never work out," she says, sliding her eyes to mine. "Well, he was no listener, I'll put it that way."

"What way?"

"He wasn't a great . . . communicator," she says, and the sides of her mouth tug upward. I squint back, unsure as to where this is going. "After a year of us going out he still had no idea how to please a girl." She does something with her brows. "I'm serious," she says. "He was so quick to tell me what *he* wanted but when I tried explaining to him what *I* liked he zoned out. Didn't care. Honestly, I kept telling him it wasn't my thing, but the boy was obsessed with fingering." I start to giggle and soon I can't stop. "Obsessed!" She says it again, really laughing. "I'm telling you!" When she sits back in her seat, I do too, leaning my face against the cool glass of the window, watching the traffic crawl up Camden High Street below. "Look, there's a new Shake Stop!" she says, leaning over me and pointing out the window.

I stare down, but we've already passed it. "They do amazing milkshakes, apparently. We should go there sometime."

"I'd like that," I say as we pass the Tube, sneaking another look at her face, heat rising steadily from my neck. By the time we hit my stop on Camden Road, I feel bright red. I stand to ring the bell. "See you tomorrow," I say quickly, bounding down the stairs before she notices the color of my face. I'm waiting at the lights when my phone beeps.

LOOK UP! the message says. When I do, March is pressing her face against the glass like a blowfish and as the bus pulls away she waves wildly, sticking her tongue out too, and I'm left alone, smiling at thin air.

When I get home, Arial follows me around the flat and into my room. She sits up on my bed, watching me as I change out of my clothes. It's that appraising look again, like she's sizing me up or waiting for wisdom, and I can't deal with it now. I hate making her feel unwelcome but it's late and

I want to be alone. I grab my laptop and sit on the floor, doing my best to ignore her as she plaits her hair in the mirror. If there was a tiny downside to my night out with March it's that I spent a chunk of the money I'd managed to save. But it's a small price to pay.

Finally, Arial gets the hint and walks out. I hop into bed, and to distract myself from the guilt of constantly handling her so badly, I email myself a list of the products I'm going to buy for my pre-party *operation transformation*. So far, I've got: major hair-removal product (more research required!); fake tan, to take the harm out of my milk-white legs; and concealer, sufficiently heavy-duty to handle recent chin eruption!

For at least six minutes I stop stewing over what a bad sister I am but soon my mind drifts back to what March said about her old boyfriend and how he had no idea how to please a girl. These last five words dance around in my head. It's not like I've thought about having sex *that* much, but when I do it's mostly to worry about whether I'll get it right or how little I'll look like the girls on Pez's iMac while I'm doing it. Actually, asking for what I want, or even enjoying it, hadn't really crossed my mind. Thinking about my own pleasure as opposed to what I'll look like seems almost radical. What March said about how we're taught to act in a way that we're told is attractive makes me wonder whether I've been expecting sex to be a kind of performance. Maybe it doesn't have to be. Maybe it's about listening too, and this, being a skill unrelated to personal grooming or the size of my boobs, feels like an achievable goal.

I pick up my phone and distractedly check my emails, then Instagram, then Topshop, but my mind's in overdrive again.

How will I explain what I want to someone when I have no idea what I like? Soon, I'm typing all sorts of things into Google.

I find a website that fits the bill and next thing I'm signing myself up. *How old are you?* it asks. Why, twenty-five, I say, and after a few rounds of assuring them I'm not a robot, I'm in! "What are you into?" Mmm . . . I click Fashion, on the basis that I plan to be in the future. Movies? Click. There's a photo of a chubby panda on a square called Cute—I click this too—then Photography and because Maisie Williams's face is on the TV window, I click this because *why not?*

I'm good to go, apparently, so I enter the names of some photographers I like: Nan Goldin, Cindy Sherman, then I scan through Gregory Crewdson and Corinne Day because we have their books at home and I'm not ready to search what I really want to search just yet. I keep going, scrolling, hovering, edging closer, circling around and around until finally I type in the word . . .

"PORN."

I stare at it for a minute and hit Return.

That's it for porn.

Nothing?

It must be the parental controls Dad put in place. He's been all over internet safety since Arial searched Google Images for pictures of "lovely grannies" a couple of months ago. She'd been making a family collage for her homework and got way more than she bargained for. She and Dad were traumatized. As I consider what else to try, my fingers tap through the categories trailing across the top of the screen like bread crumbs.

Okaaaaay. Wow! It's all there.

I guess they're called keywords for a reason. At first, I want to turn it off, but I don't. I keep going and alongside the multitude of dick pics are lots of people working really hard to look sexy. A lot of the girls don't do much except moan occasionally and as I watch I get the distinct impression that quite a few of them are acting how they think they're supposed to act rather than how they want to, like March said. Still I keep going, clicking and clicking, waiting to be grossed out but even though I kind of am, a little bit, I don't stop.

Suddenly Liv saying "MASTUR-BAYY-SHUN" back in Shakeaway the other week pops into my head. Is there a more awkward word in the English language? "Wanking" would have been way less embarrassing. Less clinical. God, why did I say anything that day? It's not like I'm some expert. I'm pretty positive I've never even had an orgasm, at least not like the ones I've seen on TV where it's groaning and hair flicks within minutes.

I watch one video play out, unsure I like what I'm watching—it's pretty fake—but I'm inching my hand below the waistband of my pajama bottoms anyway. It's weirdly gripping and I quickly start to feel panicky and excited, like I'm shocked and turned on at the same time.

There's a knock on my door.

Aghh!

Dad is the only one who knocks.

Holy shit.

"Just a minute!" I slam the laptop shut and shove it off my knees, frantically wriggling my bottoms back up, but they're tangled up around my legs. "Um, c'mon in."

"How'd it go?" he says, pushing into my room far too quickly.

I sit up, face like a furnace. "Um . . . the casting thing?" My voice is too high.

He sits down. "Isn't that where you were?" He's looking at me strangely.

"Oh, it was rubbish," I say, and his face falls. "But I had a good time." I drag the duvet up higher. Really, I had a *great* time, but I'm not getting into that now.

"Thought it sounded dodgy," he says, trying to look sympathetic. "But you've got to work these things out on your own sometimes." Then he leans over and fishes a dirty T-shirt up from the floor, mumbling to himself. "What else have you got?" he says. "I'm about to put in a dark wash."

"Huh?"

He looks around the room. "I can't stand putting in a half load," he says. "Pop up and see what else there is?"

Ohmygod, the "not wearing pants" part of this equation is going to get in the way of that. "Like, now?"

He checks his watch. "I need to unload the dryer before bed, otherwise those creases are for life."

"In a minute," I say, but he stands there, face scrunched, for far longer than is comfortable. "Check Arial's room too," he says eventually.

"Sure."

Then he gives me a thumbs-up and walks out the door.

A thumbs-up!

I cradle my face in my hands. You could fry an egg on these cheeks.

16

I walk into the living room and plunk myself down beside Dad. I've been up early with Arial every day and I've done five shifts at the café this week too so it feels acceptable to be in my pajamas at three o'clock on a Saturday afternoon.

Dad's reading the newspaper on his iPad and doesn't take his eyes off the article, so I just pull my feet up onto the couch and stare at his hair, which is still wet from when he took Arial swimming earlier. Then I peer at the date on Dad's screen. I've got less than a week to find a *fun* speech about love that, knowing Wendy, should ideally be deep and meaningful too. I should probably start trawling the internet but my eyes land on the kitchen clock; only five hours until Rob's party and I still haven't addressed the pressing question of what I'm going to wear.

I'm all jitters. I'd almost rather be at work and not have this much time to overthink. In Somerset, I was happy to copy what everyone else was wearing, as long as what I wore was reasonably comfortable and didn't attract too much attention. Attracting attention for clothes I genuinely like and take pride in would be one thing, but when I was trying to wallpaper myself into the background it felt wrong. I'd like to dress for myself now. I'd like to feel like I'm making a choice. What I'd really like is to look more like me. Trouble is, I'm not exactly sure what *me* looks like these days.

Unopened moving boxes are still scattered all over the flat but one corner of the living room in particular looks like an abandoned game of giant Jenga. I stare at the cardboard tower. On our last night in Somerset I saw Dad in his room smoothing Wendy's stickers onto these boxes. He didn't see me. They had red stickers, but I could tell by how he handled them that they were special, as though it was Mum herself inside. They're the boxes we may never need but will always want; boxes full of her stuff, stuff that's too difficult to sort out. Dad's keeping them for us to go through together one day. Today's definitely not that day, but there's one box in particular I'd like to see.

"Could you help me get some of those down?"

He thumbs his screen to the next page of an article. "Whatcha looking for?"

I stab the air in the direction of the boxes. "I'd like to take a look."

His neck cranes left. "Could you narrow it down, perhaps?"

"Mum's clothes," I say, before biting my lip.

He stares at me for a moment, then slinks his iPad shut, laying it gently on the arm of the couch. "C'mon then," he says.

I run the scissors along the length of the box, splicing neatly into the brown packing tape and peeling back the cardboard flaps. Mum wore men's cologne and the smell of it hits my stomach like a fist. I breathe to settle myself. Thank god I told Dad I'd do this alone.

It takes a minute before I can peer inside at the pile of old clothes. A checked shirt sits on the top, and when I press the soft flannel to my face my eyelids shut, and I picture her at the writing desk that's no longer here, wearing her wooly tracksuit bottoms and staring out into the yard. I can even smell the half-drunk coffee in her cup and a faint hint of the cigarettes she lied about smoking.

I place the shirt back and rest on my bed. Maybe I'm not ready for this and I know it's not something I should rush. I sit up to close the box but as I'm folding over one of the cardboard corners a flash of her favorite gold skirt catches my eye. I reach in and drag the silk out from under the weight of jeans and a heavy jacket. I tug and tug, like a magician on a never-ending handkerchief, until all the exotic silk unveils itself; then I go to the mirror, pressing the fabric, that's covered in clockfaces and strange-looking fruit, against me. I trace my fingers along the navy ribbon trim then hold it against my pale skin and my not-quite-reddish hair, admiring the burnt-autumn colors as I turn from side to side. Mum was even taller than Dad and the skirt spills in a pool at my feet. On me it could be a dress.

I quickly step out of my clothes and hoist the waistband up over my chest, then I grab the brown leather belt from my jeans and loop it around me, hoicking swathes of silk over my loosely cinched middle. I examine myself from several angles, holding my makeup mirror up to see the back, where my bare shoulders appear white and surprised. When I look at my face, I'm smiling. For the first time in a long time I've found something that feels special and I sit down on the bed, letting a wave of something warm wash over me. It feels like she's here.

★ ★ ★

Rob only lives in Gospel Oak but walking there is taking forever. When he's not on his bike, Pez is like a fish on land. I'm literally dragging him up Kentish Town Road; then he insists on stopping at Nando's and I have to sit there and watch him eat. I'm not sure what to say. I'm not even sure I want him to come tonight and I begin to wonder whether March really feels as casual about the whole sex thing as he does. It seems at odds with the girl I'm getting to know, the one who seems to genuinely care about people and openness. I'm even asking myself whether Pez is any better than that Sully guy she was talking about. These thoughts nag at me. I never thought I'd have feelings like this about him, but I can't shake them.

He picks at his chicken like he's not hungry, which is more than annoying. I watch his teeth bite into a corn on the cob next, causing tiny yellow explosions under his nose, and I snap a few photos of it, partly for something to do, partly because I want him to notice me taking photos again.

"Quit dicking around," he says, waving my phone away.

"I'm not," I say, still looking through the lens, waiting for a smile, but he moodily slurps up his Coke. "Just because I don't have a fancy camera doesn't mean—" I stop because I'm not sure what it means. He tilts his eyebrows up, waiting for me to continue. "Doesn't mean I can't still enjoy . . ." I trail off again.

"Enjoy what?"

"You know . . . photographing stuff."

He wipes his mouth with the back of his hand. "Whatever," he says, turning his face away.

I snap a few more photos, mostly to annoy him; then I pretend to edit them or something while staring at the last photo I took: corncob looming large in the foreground with Pez's features blurred behind. It's okay but the focus is the wrong way around. Pez's face is what's interesting, but it's harder to go there. I reach over and steal a fry. "Should we stop on the way and get something to drink?"

"What kind of something?" he says.

"Dunno. Beer? Isn't that what you like?"

He takes another long slurp. "I don't really drink."

I sit back and take another photo, of his chicken bones this time, which are piled up high. "Right. Well . . . good for you."

He sighs quietly, crumpling his napkin into a tiny ball then tossing it right at me. I look up, placing the phone down. "But I know a place that will serve us," he says. "If you want?"

"Whatever," I say, doing my best to mimic him a moment ago. He gives me a look, not quite a smile, more like the promise of one, which is enough to make me feel like I've succeeded, and I stand up, grabbing a celebratory handful of his fries on my way out.

Rob's street is lined with redbrick houses and tall, thin trees down both sides. The restless leaves above our heads dapple us in welcome shade as we walk. We're by the heath, almost at the back of the pool. If I could pick anywhere else to live in all of London this would be it. Maybe there's something soothing in the nearby water because we both seem less tense.

We stop outside a house with two slim hall doors, one for each flat. Pez steps forward and presses the buzzer on the bright-yellow one. When no one answers he pushes it open and I follow him inside.

Loud music tells me we're not the first here and we continue straight through, stepping over a colorful rug and past a bunch of framed family photographs. Nick, the boy with the red hair from the canal—Amira's boyfriend—is sitting at the bottom of the stairs on his phone, eating chips from a huge bag, but there's no sign of Amira. Three boys appear from the kitchen, laughing. Pez seems to know them and there's some back slapping before we pull into the living room doorway to let them pass up the steps behind Nick's head. Farther along the hallway, I see a photo of Rob and Tom by the sea, then another of a woman who must be their mum, in front of a Christmas tree. It feels nice that his house is so homey.

"In here!" someone shouts from the kitchen. I recognize the quick smile. "Hey, Lucas," I say. There's more back slapping before Pez slings his bag around and unloads a couple of Mars Milks into the fridge. Then he takes out a cold bottle of Corona and hands it to Lucas, who slickly pops the top without an opener.

"Welcome," Lucas says, handing me the beer.

"It's his party trick," Pez says, grabbing his Mars Milk, and together we lean up against the wall just inside the door.

I look around. It's a good spot; without moving my head I can see the whole room, into the hallway and halfway up the stairs. I notice the chairs that no one is sitting on tucked in under the dining table. I notice Pez's shoulders are slightly farther down from his ears. I notice Twenty One Pilots playing, and I notice nobody is looking at me or at Mum's crazy skirt like it's remotely weird, all of which makes me surprisingly happy and relaxed. I'm hot from the walk and I take my sweater off and tie it around my waist.

Pez turns his head. "You look good," he says. It's an olive branch and I take it. I even smile. I'm watching him pick corn remains from his teeth, when the three guys we met in the hall spill back through the door, pushing one another around like they're already drunk.

Rob follows behind. "Vetty!" he says, leaping toward us, but then he stops and stands there. I can't work out whether we should hug or something but he's studying me up and down. "Nice dress," he says after a while. "Got a drink?"

I lift my bottle. "Courtesy of kind Lucas here."

Then he leans into Pez. "Nick's been onto Amira," he says, slapping his palm off Pez's chest. "The girls are on their way." I expect he thinks he's whispering. Pez grunts but I see how hard he works to stop his lips from giving way to a grin. "Back in a minute," Rob says, heading off toward the fridge.

Just then Kyle pushes into the kitchen backward, holding forth about something or other. I know it's Kyle because of the way he constantly whips his hair off his face. He is at full volume even though Nick is literally inches in front of him, walking the right way around. ". . . but if Rob thinks he's getting anywhere he's dreaming. I mean, there's a challenge and then there's a CHALLENGE," he says, stopping in the doorway. "Not even Rob could turn that." He laughs loudly, but I notice Nick isn't laughing. He's staring over Kyle's shoulder with a funny look on his face. As I replay the words in my head, for a stupid paranoid second I get the feeling Kyle's talking about me. I look around and catch Lucas's eye.

He holds up his beer and clinks it against mine. "What's up, girl?" he says, all cheery.

I'm trying to smile back when Pez tugs on the sweater around my waist. "C'mon," he says. "Let's sort out these tunes."

"I like this song," I say, dragging my sweater from his grip, but when I look into his eyes I feel unsteady because for a split second I imagine him taking my hand and squeezing my fingers into tiny pulses the way he used to under our white willow tree. Then his hand drops and he walks off.

Lucas jumps down off the counter. "Pez's right," he says. "Those guitars are hurting my ears. C'mon!"

The three of us are by the speaker, arguing about whether Twenty One Pilots even have a guitarist, when March and Amira burst through the doorway. March is out front in a bright-white crop top and a huge puffer jacket draped over her bare shoulders. Amira follows in a minidress and silver Air Max. It's hard not to stare. It's as though the H&M poster on Oxford Street has been brought to life.

March is the first to reach me. "Alright," she says, that way she does, then she looks behind as Kyle storms out of the room. "What's up with him?"

Before I can answer, Rob walks over. "You made it!" he says to the girls, staring at them appreciatively; then he turns to Pez to get his attention but Pez does a fine job of acting uninterested and then strolls off. "Let me get you drinks," Rob says, and heads for the fridge.

Amira leans across me to get to March. "Has he even said hi to you?" She's whispering while glaring at Pez, who is opening a window above the sink. "Seriously, what's his problem? That boy needs to step up his game. I'm telling you, babe." March stays silent, but Amira shakes her head at both of us. "I mean, where are his manners?" It's pretty uncomfortable until Nick arrives and hugs Amira from behind, making his hands appear magically from the crooks of her arms. She kisses him backward before lifting the phone from the speaker dock and selecting another track. "Let's get a drink," she says, taking Nick's hand and leading him away.

"Those colors suit you," March says, nodding at my dress. It's so nice to hear this I bite my cheeks and slide my hands down the silk like it has magical properties.

Rob walks back toward us with a tea towel slung over his shoulder and holding two beers. He's about to hand them over to us, when he stops and sniffs the air; then he slams both bottles down on the nearby counter. I pivot to watch him pushing his way across the kitchen in the direction of the boys I don't know who are gathered in the far corner. Kyle has reappeared and stands with them, smoking a large spliff. Rob lunges for Kyle and lifts him up against the back door; then with his other hand he opens the lock and shoves Kyle down the steps onto a patio filled with trash cans.

"You can't be doing that shit in here," he shouts at Kyle. "This is my mum's house!" Then he slams the door shut and everyone around us laughs.

"He's fiery, that one," March says, smiling. "And sweet on you too by the look of things." She nods at the two beers. "Don't think he'd have sliced a lime just for me." I look down at the tiny green wedges stuck in the necks of the bottles; then she pokes the lime down into hers and takes a sip. We turn to watch Lucas, who has started a dance move. Actually, it's not really dancing; people are bouncing around with their arms in the air but they're having a good time and it's fun to watch. Drake is blaring out now and everyone is feeling it. Amira is dancing too, smiling like this was her plan, and next thing she's doing the same move that Arial showed me in the mirror, only she's so good, she's gathered a crowd. "Look at the boys," March says, digging me like I'm not already watching. "Amira's slutdrop brings them all to the yard." Nick stands behind Amira, gyrating up against her, and true enough the boys stand around, heckling. Then Amira does it again, lower and more dramatic, and March starts cheering too. When she's finally upright she waves March over.

"Back in a bit," March says, walking away, only she doesn't get as far as Amira because Pez, who is stationed by the oven, puts his arm out. Her hand lands where his T-shirt sleeve stops and it stays there. His lips part and then for the very first time tonight he smiles like he means it.

I'm processing Pez's spontaneous facial expressions when Rob reappears at my side, fixing his shirt. "Like he'd spark that up in his own house," he says. I should say something about what's just played out between him and Kyle, I know I should, but March has stopped mid-flow and I can't shift my focus quick enough. When she laughs, Pez leans in and her body moves closer too, mirroring his, and I can't take my eyes off them. Maybe it's best I can't see their faces. Maybe I should be glad that I can't. Pez is still playing it cool, but he's different around her; it's obvious and it unsettles me in a way I never expected. Is he different *good*? Or is he just acting all smiley and smooth?

"Vetty?" It's Rob again.

I turn around. "Huh?"

He slides a gold bottle top off the counter and flicks it

upward with his thumb. "Penny for your thoughts," he says, snatching the cap in midair and pressing it into my hand.

I turn the cap over in my fingers, listening as Rob talks on and on, even though I'm the one who's supposed to be answering questions. I'd like to be able to talk to Rob about stuff, but he definitely doesn't need to hear the thoughts that are going through my head right now. *Why am I this stressed about how to act around Pez and March when they're together? Why is it so much harder and more head-melting than I imagined?*

Rob waves a hand in front of my eyes. "Earth to Vetty?"

I shake my face. "I'm miles away, that's all."

"No, really?" he says, smirking. I try to smile back but my eyes slip away again, gravitating back to the oven. Only March and Pez aren't there. They've gone. My eyes flit around the rest of the kitchen but there's no sign of them anywhere. Rob watches me and I can't work out what words to use or what face to make or anything. "I think they've gone upstairs." His voice is so gentle, I can't respond, so I have to stand there silently digesting what this might mean. *Upstairs to bed?*

"Where's the bathroom?" I blurt it out.

"In the hall," he says. Maybe he adds something else, but I'm already walking off.

Nick and Amira are huddled by the coats on the bottom stair like some kind of sentry guards. Amira looks up at me; her face is saying lot of things, but mostly that she's pleased her Pez-and-March plan is coming together. She obviously expects me to feel the same but she couldn't know how strangely conflicted I feel.

I dash into the bathroom, close the seat, and sit down. *Breathe in, out, in, out.* When my eyes close I see Pez smile and my ears fill with March's laughter. *Could they really be having sex upstairs, like . . . now, just like that? How can they be that . . . throwaway? Ugh, get a grip, Vetty. Why do you care this much about what they're doing when neither of them seems to? It's none of your business anyway.*

I force my eyes open and look around the tiny room. Framed inspirational quotes sit alongside pictures of boats on the flowery-papered walls. There's a basket of books and magazines beside the toilet and I drag the pile onto my lap. I flick through an ancient interior decorating magazine before moving to the book underneath, which is full of pictures of dogs with their heads stuck out car windows. That's literally all it is, pictures of windswept dogs, but I go through every single page and don't stop until I reach the final image of Willow the Yorkie-poo at the wheel of a Ford Mustang. I keep my eyes on the tiny dog in a bow tie, feeling my heart slowly slow down. My head drops to my knees. How rude of me to walk away from Rob like that. He must think I'm weirdly jealous or possessive about Pez. I shudder at these thoughts and then stand. I need to apologize or at least play it cool. I need to do *something*! I return the book to the basket and wash my hands because it feels like I should.

The kitchen is almost full when I walk back in. People are shuffling about like it's a dance floor, doing similarly robotic arm movements, but I don't recognize anyone so I ramble back through the hall and peer into the living room. Rob and Lucas are sitting on the floor by a coffee table. Rob looks up and places his hand on the carpet beside him like he's been keeping a space for me. I make my way toward them, feeling grateful, but as soon as I sit down, Lucas stands.

He smiles at Rob. "I'm going to get a drink," he says, reaching for his beer bottle, which I can't help but notice is full. Rob lies back against the couch, watching Lucas disappear out the door, and I lean against the edge of the seat cushion wondering how to address my abrupt exit without making too big a thing of it. A picture on the wall catches my eye.

"Your mum looks nice," I say.

Rob slides his beer along to me then looks up to the photo. "Pez told me you moved away after your mum died," he says softly. I take a long, shaky breath. I often feel like I should be better at coping with Mum being dead by now. "Must have been rough."

It's still rough. There are times lately when it feels worse than ever, but I don't tell Rob that. Words have a habit of becoming real when I say them out loud.

"Look, I'm sorry," I say. "I don't know what came over me in the kitchen back there." He shifts around to face me. "I think I'm still adjusting to how things are . . . with Pez." He waits for me to say more but I reach for his beer, thinking about how annoying it is that Dad was right about things with Pez and me being different, even if it's not quite in the way he expected. "We're not the same as we were. He's changed, I guess. He's more—" I stop to think of a word that will fit. *Distant, maybe, but I don't want to admit this.*

Rob looks around. "Yeah," he says. "He's gotten worse. But he's been like this for a while is the truth."

"Like what?" The question pops out, but then I freeze like I'm not sure I want the answer. I wasn't expecting this to be a two-way conversation.

Rob shrugs. "Just . . . cold. Or, messed-up, I guess," he

says. "You know, you coming back is the only thing he's been excited about in months. And he wasn't *that* excited about you. No offense," he says, holding up his hands.

This conversation feels uncomfortable and I want out of it. "He's got all that stuff going on with his parents—"

"It's not just that though," Rob says, fixing his eyes on me. "Is it? C'mon, you must see it?"

I don't like the way he says this, because I do see it, but that I do and that he's right makes it harder to answer. He draws his knees in closer to his chest, lifting his chin like he's studying my face. Then he looks over his shoulder. "Look, I haven't told anyone this," he says softly, "but Luna called me, a few months ago."

My mouth falls open. "Luna?" I say. "Luna called you?"

He nods. "I know," he says. "I'd hardly said more than hi to her in four years and only if I passed her in his kitchen or whatever. I thought it was a joke at first." He shakes his head.

"But . . . why?"

He leans in. "Said she was . . . concerned about him. She asked if I'd 'noticed anything.'" He does air quotes. "In his behavior."

My heart starts to thump. It's so loud I'm sure Rob can hear it. "And what did you say?"

He shoots me a look. "Said he's been a bit distant . . . you know, harder to read. I had to," he says then, like he senses me stiffen. "I didn't say that he's been a bit of a prick or that he's become a loner at school, but like, of course I've noticed he's changed. I had to say something."

"I thought he had lots of mates."

"He does, but he feels above us all. I have to persuade him to come out, like he'd rather be alone in his room most of the time. Funny thing is, it was like she knew."

I turn back. "Knew what?"

He looks at me for a minute, biting on his fingernail; then he takes his hand away like he's decided not to say any more. "Just stuff . . ." He trails off. "Anyway, said I'd talk to him."

"And did you?"

He snorts. "You've seen how he is lately. So down on everything. The rare times we're alone or when he does return my calls, he just acts like he's being treated wrong or like he doesn't care. He doesn't make it easy. In fact, it can be hard to take. And the way he is with March—barely talking to her one minute then expecting her to get him off the next. Even Amira says it. Sorry," he says quickly, like he's said too much. Then his head drops back onto the seat and he stares at the ceiling.

"S'okay."

He sighs and loosens the neck of his T-shirt. "I didn't think he'd come tonight," he says, rolling his head along the seat in my direction. "I'm sure he only came to keep an eye on me, but I guess he's decided there are other benefits too."

"Why would he need to keep an eye on you?"

"No reason," he says, then his mouth gives him away. It's the smile from Pez's kitchen when he drank the mango smoothie straight from the carton. It's the smile that sort of liquidized my insides. "Let's just say I don't think he'd be pleased if anything was to happen . . . between us." I lean my head back too, biting my lip. I feel his stare, but I can't look at him again yet. My heart is galloping. "Trust me," he says, "he

165

would not be happy." I slowly turn my face and the way he's looking at me is such a surprise. Then he looks to the door before twisting back to me. "You've got nice eyes," he says. I push farther back into the velvety couch, letting the words seep in as the furry pile brushes against the hairs on my neck. "I mean it," he says, "I've been meaning to tell you for a while."

I roll my head back to his. "Is this where I offer up a compliment for you too?"

He raises one eyebrow. "Be my guest."

"Okay," I say. "Well, you're not painful to look at either." That is so bad I start to laugh, but he moves closer.

"So, does this mean you're not *really* immune to my charms?" His top lip does something funny, curling up a tiny bit on one side. It's what Pez said that first night, after he told Rob that I'm *not like other girls*.

I blink and then keep blinking to stop the words soaking into my brain, and soon Rob's breath is warm on my face. He tucks a stray strand of hair behind my ear. "You're miles away again," he says.

I shake my head. "Sorry."

"S'okay," he says, inching his face to mine. I lick my bottom lip, watching as his gets closer. My eyes fall shut and I feel his mouth against mine. His lips move to my cheek and words fly out of my head and I start to imagine where he'll kiss me next but then his lips are on my lips again and I start to kiss him back, slowly at first, softly and gently but really kissing, and he tastes better than I expected. There's a rush in my stomach, as though I'm standing in the sea waiting for a wave, watching the swell get closer and closer.

I reach my hand up to the back of his head, lacing my

fingers through his hair, when a thunderous noise makes us break apart.

Rob pushes himself up. "What the—?"

My dress has writhed up and I yank it back into place as I follow Rob into the hallway. When I get there Pez is standing at the front door, leaning his head against the wood. His shaking hand fumbles on the latch and I reach for his shoulder. "You're leaving?" I say, but he brushes me off without turning around.

Rob steps toward him. "What's up?"

"Open the door," Pez says in a voice so low I barely hear it.

"Pez?" We say his name at the same time.

Pez's foot kicks against the bottom of the door, making the whole frame shudder. "Just fucking open it!"

Rob leans over and flicks a small brass switch by Pez's hand, then he holds down the latch and pushes the door wide. Pez bolts out and tears off up the drive. I swing around to Rob but he's now staring at March, who is crouched at the top of the stairs, hiding her face in a sweater she wasn't wearing earlier. It sounds like she's crying. *What the hell?* I'm trying to piece it all together in my head.

I step forward, wanting to check that March is okay, but I can't get Pez's trembling hand out of my mind and next thing I'm shoving past Rob and I too am out the door.

Rob reaches for my arm, pulling me back. "I told you," he says. "Messed-up."

I don't answer. There isn't time.

PART THREE

Love is . . . something that grows

17

I race up the drive, weaving between parked cars until I'm out on the street. I catch sight of Pez turning left at the bottom by the main road.

"Pez!" He doesn't look back and I pick up the pace. "Wait!"

I shout it out, but instead of slowing, he walks even faster. I'm afraid I'll lose him if I don't speed up, so I start to jog, but he jogs too, which means I have to sprint. It's been years since I've run this fast and as I pound the pavement to the junction with Highgate Road my lungs begin to burn. I keep going, gasping for breath, but he's already at the sourdough pizza place with the tables outside. I have to stop. I can hardly breathe. "Hey, hold up!" I shout it out and I know he hears but he doesn't turn around and I can only watch as he continues on down the street, narrowly dodging an approaching couple. I can't believe he's ignoring me.

He keeps at this ridiculous pace all the way down Kentish Town Road. He's outside Superdrug by the time he looks behind.

"Pez!"

I'm practically screaming as I pass the kebab shop, much

to the amusement of two young boys on their bikes, but I'm furious and I don't care.

"Seriously, will you please stop!"

On he goes, alternating between speed-walking and running for the rest of the journey. Whatever concern I had for him leaving Rob's house is gone. *Why am I racing down the road after him when I could be back there checking that March is okay?* I'm less than four paces behind him when I realize we're retracing our steps from the first time we met, the evening of my tenth birthday, when I followed him home from Tesco. He knew I was shadowing him then, just as he knows now, but even as I shout out his name, he still won't turn around. When I finally reach St. Agnes Villas he's already at the steps to his house. I want to punch something.

"I can't believe how much you've changed!" It leaves my mouth as screams and he stops. He freezes halfway up his steps. I move closer, growing more furious with each stride, almost enjoying the fact that he's trapped because I'm so angry I could burst. "The Pez I used to know would never act like this. I left Rob's house out of loyalty. I followed you because I was worried, but it looks like I've been worried about the wrong person." His face turns but he doesn't look up. "March was crying when I left. Did you know that? Do you even care? I honestly don't know who you are anymore."

He finally lifts his face to mine. He still doesn't speak but his haunted eyes shoot chills down my sweaty back. Before I can begin to think of what to do next, he slumps up the last few steps and disappears behind the door.

★ ★ ★

When I walk in Dad glances at his watch. It's not yet eleven. He closes his laptop. "Everything okay?" he says.

I mumble something about period pain and head straight into my room but I don't go to the window this time. I've got no interest in seeing Pez stare at some computer, watching god knows what. I lie on my bed in the dark, gazing into the blackness, turning everything over and over in my head.

I could still be at the party. I could still be there, kissing Rob, but I'm not and I'm not even sure why. Then I picture March, holding her head in her hands, and I feel winded. What was I thinking leaving her? I slot a cushion under my head and scroll for her number.

Sorry for running out

I accidentally hit Send too early. Shit.

Like that.

Send.

You OK?

As soon as I've hit Send again I realize I should have called instead; then I see dots under my message and I stare, gripped, willing her words to emerge, but after a long minute they disappear and there's nothing. My heart sinks to my stomach. It would be weird to call now so I sit up again and lean against the window, peering out into the night. It's completely dark and nothing stirs apart from Old Giles's slick gray cat, prowling along Pez's front wall. I almost let myself look up; then my phone buzzes. It's March.

What did he say?

I stare at the words, thinking of how to reply; then I see she's typing again.

Just tell me, please

I quickly punch in letters.

Nothing! Honestly, I followed him home. Chased him, but he went into his house without a word. No idea what's got into him.

Bubbles . . . she's typing again.

I'll tell you when I see you. It's one for face 2 face.

I read the screen, feeling confused and hopeless.

K. But are you all right?

My chest sinks, and I lie back, a thousand thoughts sloshing between my ears.

I don't think I've ever understood so little.

18

There's a noise.

A loud noise.

I open my eyes and I still hear it.

"VETTY?" It's Arial banging on the wall from the other side.

"What?"

"Have you seen my toothbrush?" she shouts.

"What's wrong with using the door?"

Next thing she's in my room. She's wearing a leotard over her pajamas. She plunks herself down beside me and looks around. "I left it in here," she says, patting the duvet down. Next, she's kneeling on the floor and then she disappears under the bed.

I reach over her for my phone: two texts from Rob asking if I'm okay, but no more from March and not surprisingly a bit fat ZILCH from Pez.

"Knew it!" she says, reemerging with her toothbrush in hand. I throw off the duvet and go to the window and look out. His shutters are closed.

Arial joins me at the window and we both stare out onto the street. She looks up at my face. "What is it?" she asks.

Nobody but me could understand the significance of the closed shutters. "Nothing."

"Why d'you look out there so much?"

I drape my arm around her shoulder. "Just keeping an eye on things."

She pulls away. "Squirrel!" she squeals, pointing at the tree out on the path. "Look!"

Together we tilt our heads to follow two gray squirrels scuttling up to the top of the tree. The one behind's chasing the other right to the edge of a very tall branch, a bit like me and Pez last night.

"Feeling better?"

It's Dad. I turn around and he's standing in the corner of the room. He's brought his cereal with him and neither the bowl nor the spoon is more than an inch from his lips as he munches.

I turn back to the window. "Yeah." I'm not being rude. It's a gravitational pull.

"She's keeping an eye on things," Arial explains.

"Well, it's time for you to jump in the shower, Arial," he says, shoveling more cornflakes into his mouth.

"Um, excuse me!" says Arial. "*You're* not dressed. And your mouth is full."

I flop down onto the bed. "Plus, it's only eleven, Dad. On a Sunday. Does it really matter?"

"You two have shopping to do," he says, wiping milk from his chin with the back of his hand.

I check his face. "What kind of shopping?"

He pulls the wedding invite out from under his arm. "'Country glamour,' it says. I've already dug out my snazzy jacket and I don't want you girls letting me down." I don't ask him outright in front of Arial, but this must mean he's giving us money. "We'll discuss budget when you're dressed," he says, pulling the door shut behind him.

Arial looks at me, mouth open. "Yes!" she cries, jumping onto the bed. "Yes, yes, yes!" She punches her fists in the air before leaping back to the floor and doing a handstand against the wall.

I'm tempted to punch the air too but then I remember last night and I grab her legs and lower her. "C'mon. Let's get ready." She strikes a pose, then squats down in front of the mirror before curling herself expertly back up. It's hard not to stare. She gives Amira a run for her money. "D'you know what that move is called?"

She rolls her eyes. "Yeah."

"What?"

"Um . . . slutdrop," she says. "God, keep up!"

I watch the door close as she leaves. Mild panic's stirring in my empty stomach. I'm not sure how much longer I can avoid her questions. Seems like a straight-up chat is already overdue.

We catch a C2 bus to Oxford Circus and it's impossible not to be swept up by Arial's excitement as she chats away, leaning her head on my shoulder the whole time. For a couple of hours, we trail in and out of shops and I almost forget about my one-sided screaming match with Pez, my kiss with Rob, March's tears, and what she meant by "It's one for face 2 face." We hit the kids' floor at Zara, where Arial picks out a blue jumpsuit covered in tiny gold stars, and after we choose some matching gold sneakers, there's just enough of Dad's money left for the green, tea-length vintage-style dress I find downstairs at Topshop, and I pick up a few other bits of clothes with my own money too. Arial says the color of the dress complements my hair, which is nice and everything, but I can't help thinking that there might be something more interesting in one of Mum's boxes that I could have had for free.

Afterward we go to the huge Boots pharmacy on Regent Street, where I spend far too long studying hair-removal products. If I'm ever going to do more than kiss Rob, this area of my body clearly needs major attention. I eventually opt for some bikini hair removal cream for sensitive skin that promises "confidence and smoothness for twenty-eight days," which, if it delivers, is good going for seven quid. I sample some perfumes afterward, but I've already thought of a better use for what's left of my wages. It's been on my mind since Arial walked out of my bedroom a few hours ago. It's obviously time that her puberty curiosity was handled by more capable hands than mine so I'm calling in some old-school backup. We hop on a bus going home but we don't get off at our usual stop. We've walked halfway up Kentish Town Road and are stopped outside Peanut Butter Books before she notices.

"What kind of book?" she asks.

I hold the door open and she passes under my arm. "You'll see."

She rolls her eyes. "I don't even like reading," she says.

I think about pointing out how much she likes stories and being read to, but my stomach drops when I see the guy with the glasses I asked for a job. Apart from a woman

178

browsing the bestsellers near the window we're his only customers. He's sitting at the computer with a book, and his gaze flicks between the two. It's a while before he spots us hovering. "Can I help?"

I think about mumbling "I'm fine," but I could be ages trying to find what I want, and having Arial in tow, I'm determined to up my game. She wriggles away and starts rifling through gift items on a display table. "Can I have these?" she shouts out, holding up a glittery box.

I ignore her and return to the guy, who I sense might recognize me. "Yes, please," I say, trying to sound at least vaguely grown-up. "I'd like a recommendation."

He pushes his chair away from the desk. "What is it you're looking for?"

"A book about—" I search for the most appropriate word. I consider saying "sex," but I'd rather not, not out loud. "Um . . . puberty, babies," I say, careful to maintain eye contact, like I'm a mature human. A strange expression crosses his face and I realize I should probably qualify that the book is not for me. "Suitable for a ten-year-old to read alone," I add with a little cough.

He smiles without opening his mouth. "Follow me," he says, heading toward the far wall, where his hand tracks along book spines with impressive speed, pulling out titles as he goes. "These are usually popular," he says, handing me a small pile. "Shout if you have any questions."

I'm tempted to take the top one and run, but I look over at Arial sitting on the ground, spinning a globe under her finger, then at the six books in my hands. Only one isn't pink, and that one is covered in flowers. Another has a sign under the title that says BOYS OUT. *For real?* This was not what I had in mind when I thought of calling in backup. I'm not filled with confidence that any of these books will really speak to a girl who's got moves like Cardi B. I peer farther along the shelf at what seems to be the boys' equivalent and it's a sea of blue. It's like the baby card section at the drugstore.

Mum would have had lots of thoughts about this particular book choice. This is something she would have taken time over; she would have read reviews and everything, but honestly, I'd take *Puberty for Dummies* if it meant I could get out of here quicker.

Arial stands. I'm watching her get closer when my phone vibrates. Rob! Shit, I haven't replied to his messages.

Tell me he didn't give you a hard time?

I bite my lip and type.

More like me giving him an earful

Bubbles . . .

He was asking for it. Btw I liked talking to you 😊

I hold the phone to my stomach and look around.

Nice talking to you too 😊

Arial leans over the screen in my hand. "Who's Rob?"

When I look up the shop guy is on his way back. I can't deal with a conversation, so I grab the least offensive book and hand him the rest. "We'll take this one," I say, grinning hard all the way to the till.

He scans the book and I read the title upside down. It's called *Wow, I'm Amazing!* which I decide is a positive start, but Arial lifts a corner of the cover like it's a dirty tissue she wants to drop. Then she traces her finger down the chapter headings and stares up at me with a pained look on her face.

"Would you like a bag?" the guy asks.

"Um, yeah!" Arial says, eyeing me furiously.

"And we'll take those glittery notecards too," I say. She bounds off to grab her consolation prize and when we step outside she scrunches the top of the paper bag up tight and shoves it under her arm. "Why are you doing that?" I ask.

"I don't want anyone seeing it."

"You shouldn't be embarrassed, Arial."

She huffs. "Your face looked like a squashed-up strawberry in there," she says, walking on, clutching the bag to her chest. I follow behind, feeling more than a little crushed, and I'm even considering whether it's time to call Wendy to ask for some advice, but then Arial stops in the middle of the path and turns around. "But you know . . . thanks," she says quietly.

19

I'd planned to get to the café early today, so I could talk with March "face 2 face" before work, but Arial hadn't done her hair and then she couldn't find her lunch box, so by the time I arrive I'm almost late and March is already out on the floor taking orders. We spend the next four hours shuffling around like chess pieces. We smile as she hands me the lattes and cream of celeriac soup but it's hard to look each other in the eye. I'm jumpy, and she's without her usual spark, but it's so busy I don't have much time to think about how uncomfortable it is.

It's twenty to four when I finally sit down with a slice of quiche. I'm taking gulps of milk and forking pastry into my mouth when March crosses the floor.

"Have you heard from him?" she says before she's sat down. Her voice sounds different. "If you have, you can tell me." I shake my head and she bites her lower lip so hard a patch of the color fades.

"We still haven't spoken," I say, picking at a piece of burned bacon on my plate. "But whatever is going on, you can tell me that too," I say, hoping she hasn't changed her mind about what she said in her text. She pushes her coffee cup forward, studying my face. I swallow the last mouthful of pastry and crumple my napkin. "Did you have a fight?"

"Worse," she says, looking over her shoulder. "Look, you two have been mates for years, and you're super close and stuff. It's just . . . I hope we're friends too."

"We are."

"Close enough for me to—" She stops. "You're the only person I feel I can talk to about this." Her breath is jagged and I have a very uneasy feeling about what's coming next. "Can you keep a secret?" she says.

I nod. "Of course," I say, but what if what she's about to say is worse than Sully not listening. What if Pez asked her to do something porny. I almost don't want to know.

She leans in. "I think there's something wrong, with me."

I sit up. "I don't understand."

She sucks her teeth and looks away. "I don't do anything for him, that way," she says. This seems unbelievable and I shake my head but she's talking quickly. "I can't tell you how shitty it feels. And it's happened twice now."

"What has?"

She sighs. "One minute we're together, you know . . . doing stuff, in bed. We'll get to a point when things get . . . heavier, and I want to keep going but I'm also trying hard to relax and get into whatever we're doing, but I'm so nervous because of what happened before and then something just flicks, and he goes cold. Then he'll freak out and leave. The last time he didn't talk to me for weeks and it's like the exact same thing has happened again. I've got no idea what's wrong with me or what I'm doing wrong." Her chin goes like she might cry. "I've left him three messages and . . . nothing!"

I can't believe what I'm hearing and I reach my hand out for hers. "Honestly, March, this doesn't sound right." He shouldn't push her into doing things she's not comfortable with and she shouldn't feel she needs to do that stuff just to please him.

"I'm telling you," she says sadly. "It is."

"No, March. It's not." I'm surprised by the force of my words. When she looks at me I start to doubt whether I'm qualified to say what I'm saying, but I don't stop. "This is messed-up. You should talk to someone."

"Um . . . hello, I'm trying!" she says.

"How about your mum?" I suggest quickly.

She shakes her head. "I'm trying to talk to *you*."

I sigh. "Guess I could speak to him, but—"

Her hand hits the table. "No, I told you. It'll seem like I'm betraying him."

She's embarrassed and it's obvious how much it's taken for her to tell me this. "Okay."

"Promise?"

I'm nodding as the pocket of my apron vibrates. I take my phone out. It's Pez!

You think I'm the worst. And I am. But am I still invited to the wedding? Mum's asking. Something about a suit.

Oh god! I suck in a long breath, then look up at March and then back to the phone. *Honest answer? Um, I dunno! Not now.* I reread his words and I know March reads them too because she sits back and looks around the room, feeding the huge gold hoop through the tiny piercing in

184

her ear several times. "Of course, your aunt is getting married. Isn't she?"

I bob my head guiltily. I was so looking forward to the wedding once but now I wish I was going with a real friend. I wish I was taking March, or even Rob, who could be a real date, instead. I rack my brain for ways to uninvite Pez, but there's no way to do it without confronting him. Suddenly I spot the time on her watch and I reach out, squeezing her hand. "I'm so sorry but Arial finishes camp in four minutes. I've got to go."

"S'okay," she says, trying to smile. "Run!"

I pick up my plate and push out from the table. I'm so glad I've got something in my hands as I pass, because when I look at her face I've got an overwhelming urge to give her a hug.

Later, Arial is sitting beside me on the couch reading *Wow, I'm Amazing!* or whatever it's called. Her hand is over her mouth, where it's been for a while, but I can still see her lips move as she reads. I'm half-heartedly watching *The Good Place* while googling wedding speeches.

A fun speech about love? Did Wendy even discuss this plan with Fran? I search "speeches about love" and everything I click on is so clichéd. For all its endless reach, the internet spits back pretty much the same ten results no matter what I type in. I'm only sixteen and I'm already beginning to feel disillusioned with love. Suddenly Arial giggles and I look over.

"What's so funny?"

"Nothing," she says, but I scan the page she's reading. It's a double spread about the crushes and funny feelings girls have about boys. Doodled hearts filled with fuzzy advice on how to make smart "boy choices." I'm reading what's written inside the heart-shaped drawings and to be fair it seems like pretty sensible stuff underneath the fluff. Arial taps the page with her finger. "Look, they say about gay people," she says.

My eyes follow hers to the bottom of the page and sure enough there's another bubble that says—*girls who go on to have relationships with women are called lesbians and boys who have similar feelings for boys and who go on to have relationships with men are called gay.* She looks pleased about this and I smile back but something irks. I lean over and read it again but it's that same scratchy feeling and I sit back with a sigh. "What?" she says.

I frown. "Huh?"

"You're making that face."

"What face?"

"The one you make when you're mad."

"I'm not mad," I say, sounding irritated because I do feel mad. I sit forward and scan the passage one more time. Nope, there's nothing. Definitely no mention that how I feel is even possible.

"Vetty?" Her voice is soft.

"It's just—" I stop and slowly tilt my face to hers. "I'm not sure this book covers everything, that's all."

She shrugs. "I like it."

"Well, that's good," I say. "I'm glad."

"But you should tell them," she says, squinting up at me. "What they've left out."

186

I mess up her hair. "Not sure it works like that."

Her face scrunches up. "They'll never know if you don't tell them?"

It's impossible to argue with Arial's logic sometimes, and what she's just said makes me think about Pez; about how he's changed and about whether I have any right to question it or whether it's my business to give this much of a shit. I think about how simple things once were and how complicated they feel now and then I think about my tenth birthday and how we saw something in each other as we stood by those automatic doors in Tesco—something special, something unspoken and understood.

I write *LOVE* in capital letters at the top of my page and under this I scribble *One minute max!* Dad warned me that any longer and people generally lose interest. Then, because I have no idea what to do next, I sketch caricatures of Wendy's and Fran's faces in the margin of my page. I'm no artist, so I draw Wendy in side profile with her long, brown hair in a low side pony. I do big eyes, which are easy because hers are like mine. I color in all three tiny gold hoops she has on each ear with my blue pen, including the minuscule golden moon she's got in the piercing higher up too. Fran has great hair and I take care doing big, bold, wavy lines for her. It's very blond with very dark roots and even though it's only to her shoulders it's so thick and full that it's almost as wide as it is long. Fran's Welsh, but she smiles like an American, so I draw a large open mouth with big full lips. I try to capture her soft eyes but they don't turn out that well.

Wendy loves Fran and Fran loves Wendy. It's easy to see. They're there for each other like strategically placed cushions when the rest of the world feels too sharp. Like when Fran's dad had the car accident or when the farm had money problems before the Bed-and-Breakfast took off and there was all that stress with the bank. The worst was when Wendy did the test that said she wasn't pregnant and they both cried for a very long time. They didn't pretend the problems weren't there. They didn't say everything was okay when it wasn't; they'd simply lift each other up so they could see the good stuff was still there too. But wow, the fights! There was an enormous one over lunch one Sunday; it started about politics but it was soon obvious that Fran was super mad about something else that Wendy had done and the rest of us quietly left the table one by one, without clearing our plates. I hated seeing them fight but Dad said the strongest relationships can weather a storm.

I'll never love Pez in the way that Wendy loves Fran because we're friends and not a couple, but he's a friend I want forever, and maybe forever doesn't come without some thunder. Just because I don't like what he's said or what he's done doesn't mean I should walk away. A forever friend doesn't quit, at least not before calling them out or causing a shitstorm first.

Suddenly I'm taking out my phone.

No suit required. But you better set your alarm on Friday. We're getting an early train

I hit Send before I've got time to change my mind.

20

Texts flew back and forth this morning; mostly March and Rob telling me to have fun and both complaining that Pez still hasn't been in touch. Wendy suggested Pez and I come down early, which I assume means to help set up, but I'm hoping I'll get some time alone with her too.

Dad's just dropped me and Pez at Paddington Station on his way to the office and we wander into Pret A Manger to pick up snacks for the journey. I'm surveying a stack of baguettes but I can't make up my mind which to choose. I'd like to suggest that we get one each and maybe a muffin too and then we can share everything like we used to, but Pez is already at the till with a juice. I walk over and stand beside him silently and when the server gets to me I point at a cookie behind the glass that I'm not sure I want.

"Any hot drinks?" she asks.

I turn around and Pez is standing by the door. "Um . . . a hot chocolate, please."

The strange silence follows us to the huge bank of screens, where we wait for one to announce the platform for the Castle Cary train.

We've hardly shared more than two words since he

walked out of his house almost an hour ago. Dad hopped into the car at the same time as he did, so I haven't gotten close to bringing up anything that happened last weekend. Luna hugged me when she answered the door, holding me so tight I'm convinced she must have heard our argument. I'm not sure whether one person shouting even constitutes an argument but it seems like it was only the warm-up for the storm brewing in my empty stomach.

I stare up at the black screen, willing it to change. Eventually the number 10 flashes up for our train and we join the flock of passengers crossing the concourse toward the platform like starlings. A murmuration, I think it's called. People break into a run and we do too, making my back-pack bounce and my paper Pret bag jostle about, splashing hot chocolate over everything inside. I catch a glimpse of Pez's face as we run and he looks so lost among the crowd but thankfully we're soon out in front and it's not long before we're sitting at a table in the carriage by the dining car.

I settle into my seat, grumpily mopping my spilled drink with a flimsy napkin while Pez stares out the window. As the train pulls away, I take out the photography books I grabbed from Dad's room before we left. One is technical with way too many words, so I put that back. The other is called *Portraits of Conflict*, which feels darkly appropriate, but I only picked it because I haven't looked at it for a while and it was one of the few that would fit in my backpack. Inside it's full of black-and-white faces from Vietnam, Iraq, Cambodia, and I flick through the pages, staring at the images, but they're so intense it's hard to look, so I shut it and lean my head on the glass for a while.

The sky outside is still but the fields whip by like ticker

tape. Pez continues glaring into space, in some sort of trance. It's hard to believe I was in Somerset for four years without him visiting, even once. Outside, fields give way to out-of-town business parks and soon these become streets with houses and then the window frame fills up with shops and offices until we pull up at Reading Station.

I tolerate Pez's silence for as long as I can but as we're pulling away, I lean across the table. "It would help if you would say something, because it's not huge fun being ignored like this." Then an older man in a stylish suit sits down next to Pez and I sit back, defeated.

"Did you write your speech?" Pez says eventually.

I look up. "It's a reading, not a speech."

He takes a sip of his drink then digs in his paper bag and pulls out a bacon roll I never knew he had. If things weren't so tense, I'd ask for a bite. Instead I have to watch as he squashes it between his fingers like he has no intention of eating it. "And?" he says.

"And what?"

"What's it like?" he says.

"Oh . . . it's from a book." He looks at me, mock exasperated, which is kind of comforting. "It's probably a bit clichéd, but you know . . ."

He looks at the guy beside him. "I never did get a suit," he whispers. "Mum was freaking out, so I hope you weren't joking."

"It's not that kind of wedding, trust me."

At least we're talking.

★ ★ ★

191

Wendy meets us off the train. She's wearing rain boots and waving wildly even though we're less than ten feet away. I see her Volkswagen van from the platform. It's not one of those cute hippie ones; she's way too practical for that.

"Look how you've grown!" she says, wrapping her arms around Pez like he's a blood relative. He flinches for a second or two but he looks like he might appreciate it. "How's Camden Town?" she asks, like there's an actual answer to this; then she grabs a bag and sets off down the station steps with us scrabbling behind. As soon as we hit the parking lot she claps her hands together. "So, the gazebo is up! You guys can start to set out the tables and chairs." She laughs but I know Wendy well enough to realize this probably isn't a joke. The trunk is open before she's taken a breath. "Jesus," she says, looking at her watch. "The generator is arriving in ten minutes. Let's get going."

She keeps up the chat all the way to the farm and Pez watches her like he's watching TV, but she has his full attention. It's strange to see them both in the same place again. Like that game where you fold up a piece of paper and one person draws the face and different people complete the other sections of the body before finally opening it out. For sure, the picture is wonky, but it's not quite as weird as I would have thought.

When we reach the top of the long, bumpy drive, Fran is standing at the end of the courtyard in her cutoff shorts. She finishes signing a delivery note then jabs her pen into her bleached-blond bun and gives us both a hug.

"C'mon, I'll show you Wend's present," she says, heading off down the yard with Wendy running after her. I turn around to make sure Pez is following and see he's walking backward down the hill, staring up at their converted barn as he goes. Together we follow the field along by the river until we reach the spot where Fran and Wendy would take me and Arial to have picnics when we were younger. We used to launch tiny cork boats and race them all the way to the bridge. Wendy stops at a beautiful wooden bench under the oak tree.

"Fran made it," she says, running her fingers along the back of the bench.

I sweep my hand along the seat. "It's so smooth."

"It's Welsh larch," Fran says. "It's *our* bench really. I made it for both of us."

I'm surprised when Pez sits down on it. He looks like he might say something but he leans his head back and stares into the branches above his head. Wendy looks at Fran. "C'mon, we need to meet the caterer," she says, and they both head off. Wendy sounds so busy I wonder if I'll ever get time alone with her this weekend. I leave silent Pez on the bench and stroll back to the yard, where two men are tying string lights between the two huge peaks in the gazebo. Behind it, in the paddock, several tent tips twinkle in the sun and around the other side an old horsebox bar is parked up.

I step inside the vast, empty gazebo. At the far end there's a black-and-white dance floor. I walk down and tap my feet on the tiles, enjoying the sound my boots make when I dance. A gigantic mirror ball hangs above my head and I spin slowly around under it, closing my eyes, imagining it glittering in the light.

After lunch, Fran opens boxes at the table, showing us the fun stuff she's bought for the photo booth, and I'm messing around, trying on a top hat and a feather boa, but Pez checks his phone throughout. When she walks out to answer the door, I turn to him. "It's rude to be on that *all* the time."

"Huh?"

"What's the point in being here if you're not going to—" I'm about to say more, when Wendy strolls into the kitchen. "Hey, Wend," I say, smiling a bit too quick. She picks at the leftover cheese in the middle of the table as she considers the seating chart in her hands, which is covered in scribbles. "Thought maybe we could talk wedding outfits at some point?" I say. She pops a grape into her mouth and looks up. "Like, maybe now?"

"Course," she says. "You'll be all right if I steal her for a bit, Pez?"

"Sure," he mumbles, looking a bit too relieved for my liking.

I follow Wendy up the stairs, and when we reach their room she takes a large suit bag from the wardrobe and unzips it, revealing a pale-blue tuxedo hanging inside. Then she holds up the suit, waiting for me to say something.

"It looks better on," she says.

"Yeah, no, it's great. The suit is so . . . *you!*"

Her nose crinkles like she's happy and then she starts undressing. She steps into the trousers, which come up short, just above her ankles, then she takes off her T-shirt, putting on a frilly dress shirt, slim cut, with a black velvet ribbon that she ties in a long bow under a Peter Pan–type

194

collar. When she puts the jacket on it fits snugly at her waist and somehow she manages to look edgy, sexy even.

"Wait!" she says, holding her hand up before taking a pair of ankle boots out of a box. She puts them on too and walks over to the window. "So, what d'you think?" she says, twirling in the light. "Picture . . . Bianca Jagger, early seventies, with a cowboy twist." She swaggers across the room, pinging at some imaginary suspenders with her thumbs. "Squint if you have to."

I can't help but laugh. "I love it!" I say. I mean it. I do. She looks amazing. I just don't know why tears are pricking my eyes.

"Thank god," she says. "You're the only one around here with any taste." Then she slides the jacket off and sits back down, looking at me for what feels like a long time, but Wendy has always been able to see right through me. "What is it?" she asks gently.

"Sorry," I say, wiping at a tear.

She takes my hand. "Hey, I'm all ears. Always."

I look away, blinking a few times. "I don't know what's come over me. It's just watching you sometimes and . . . how unafraid you are to be *you*, and I'd so like to be more like that, but—" I stop; then Wendy presses her lips together, nodding at me to keep going. ". . . but it's been hard in London. I thought it would be easier but it's more complicated. Everything has changed. Everyone has . . ." These thoughts make my head fizz and I feel like a bottle of Sprite that's been shaken too hard and I get up and stand by the window.

"Pez is a sweet boy," she says after a while. When I turn

195

back she's scratching a sticker from the sole of one of her new boots.

"He's just a friend."

"Course," she says. "But I get that it could be tough, picking up again, after so long?"

I sigh. *Of course she needs to point this out, like everyone else.* "It's not just Pez. Not really." I take a breath. If I'm ever going to talk to Wendy about this honestly, I need to go for it. I need to put her name out there. "See, there's this girl, March, and . . . I never expected to have a connection with someone like I do with Pez, but with her, I think I could, but it's complicated because . . ." I can't even.

Wendy's head tilts. "Because?"

"Ugh . . . because everything!"

She breathes out through her nose behind me. "Is March . . . someone special?" she asks after a while.

Oh god, I want so much to be honest. I want to release this pressure in my brain and I'm trying to work out how to explain that, yes, she is, and in some ways it's the same connection as with Pez, but then . . . more. I want to explain this without Wendy jumping to conclusions. I need to, and I'm trying to think about how I can make her understand all of it, but I don't know the way in and it pops out as "Did you ever go out with boys?"

She places the other boot carefully inside the box and then gets up and joins me at the window. "A few," she says. "Early on."

I place my hand on the glass. "Was it like it is with girls?"

She looks like she's thinking. "No," she says slowly. "I wanted it to be, but, no, it wasn't."

196

I stare out the window wondering how to describe the way my pulse races when I'm around March or how my mouth goes dry when I'm talking to Rob and how good it felt when he kissed me. Should I try to explain that there's no distinction, that my mind and my body can't distinguish, or if they can, that they don't, at least not really. I feel her eyes on the side of my face and I stare ahead, heart thumping, but somehow my mouth opens. "There have been girls I've liked, but it was a while ago, mostly . . . and I thought, or I hoped, it was a phase, but—"

Wendy's hand lands on mine and the weight of it presses both of ours into the cold glass and the cap on my Sprite bottle twists, a tiny bit.

"March . . . she is special," I say.

Wendy's eyes are kind and open. "I'm so glad you told me," she says. "Coming out isn't easy."

"But Wend," I say, pulling my hand loose. "It's not that simple."

"Okay . . .?" she says.

"I'm sort of seeing this guy, Rob, and I like him a lot and I can't like March because of Pez and it's so confusing because I think that actually, really I'm—"

"Vetty!" She finds my hand again. "Lots of lesbians have heterosexual relationships before it all clicks fully into place." My free hand clenches into a fist. "Some people feel that they're defined by those past relationships, but honestly . . ." I inch back from her face. "None of that matters. It's normal to be confused. It's a huge step," she says.

I turn from her and start to walk backward, away from the window. I'm not confused. I feel like I haven't explained it properly and it's like she's seeing herself in me, and that's not it. Tears prick the corners of my eyes again but I don't want her to see me cry. Not now. I don't want any more questions. I wish I hadn't said anything. This was a bad idea.

"Guess it is," I say, moving off across the room.

"Vetty?" she calls out after me.

"I should find Pez," I say, closing the door.

I don't look for Pez. I walk out the front door, toward the gate, where I start to run and I keep going to the bottom of the lane and from there I race up the hill by the dairy, where I climb the gate and sprint all the way to the bottom of the big field. My mind is as fast as my legs. Of all the people in the world I thought Wendy might get it. I thought she'd understand that what I feel is real. My feet slam the hard, muddy ground but I don't stop running until I get to the top of the hill. It's not that steep but it's high enough for a view of the tents in the paddock and the church steeple over the top of the hill and high enough for things to slowly, slowly look different.

21

Dad and Arial arrive after supper. The cottage that was our home is rented out so they'll share one of the guest rooms in the main house, and because Wendy and Fran have decided to be traditional and sleep apart tonight, Pez and I have been dispatched to one of the tents in the paddock to make room for Fran's parents. I take Arial to bed around ten but she's excited and wants to chat so by the time I come back down the stairs Fran's family has arrived from Wales and Dad is welcoming them in the hallway with glasses of tomorrow's wine. Wendy is clearing the table when I walk back in. She takes me in her arms, swaying to some country music I've never heard before. "Y'okay, love?"

I lift her hand from my face. "Fine," I say, doing my best to avoid her eyes. Whatever the opposite of fine is, I'm that, but I'm not getting into it now; not the night before she's getting married. "Where's Pez?"

"He set off for the tent soon as you went upstairs," she says, sweeping my hair up to see my eyes. "I meant what I said, about always being here—"

"I know," I say, walking off before she can say any more,

but I've only reached the fridge when I'm punched by a fist of guilt. "Get some beauty sleep!"

I hear her laugh. "I need it," she shouts out. "Oh, and the wheelbarrow is outside on the right!"

I'm by the back door, examining the pile of sleeping bags, rugs, and pillows, all of which feel damp having sat outside for so long in the dark. I lift the handles of the wheelbarrow and trundle down the path toward the paddock, tripping over myself and cursing Pez for not being here or having the sense to get started on the beds while it was bright. I ramble on like an exhausted zombie, stumbling over the uneven ground, lulled by the increasingly distant sound of singing in a Welsh accent. Finally, I reach the wooden gate and trip into the first tent on the other side with any light. When I fling back the canvas door all I see is Pez's phone beaming out from the blackness.

He jumps up like I've walked in on something but there's no one else here. "Y'okay?" he says, reading my face.

"Apart from the new bruises from pushing this thing down in the dark—"

"Oh yeah," he says, but his eyes look far away.

I hook the lantern at head height and kick off my shoes. "Um, can you help?" I say, nodding at the wheelbarrow.

He gets up like he'd rather not, but we work quickly, laying out our ground mats. I'm hoping we can finally have a chat to clear the air, but as I throw a sleeping bag onto Pez's new bed he just unzips it and rolls over, away from me. I unhook the lantern and climb into my own bed fully dressed.

We face opposite directions, Pez toward the door and me

into the galaxy of blackness at the back. There isn't enough pillow, so I double mine over then stuff it back under my head. I shut my eyes tight, and when we both stop shuffling, all I hear is him breathing and I lie there for what seems like ages listening to a faint wheezing in his chest, convinced he's only pretending to be asleep. My legs are restless and I roll onto my back but I hear him moving and when I look left, he too is staring into the nothingness above our heads.

"Are you going to tell me what this is about or am I supposed to guess why you're being like this?"

"Like what?" he says.

I'm determined to have it out now. "Like *this*! Is the silent treatment for saying what I said outside your house last Saturday night?" He turns his face. "Or does whatever happened with you and March have anything to do with it?"

He shakes his head. "No, Vetty," he says slowly.

His body stiffens and I think I see his eyes narrow but he says nothing more. I clear my throat, then exhale hopelessly. I spoke fluent Pez once. "I don't know how to read you anymore. I used to, but I have no idea now. I don't even know what you care about." He looks away. "God, would you at least say *something*!"

"It's too quiet here," he says after a while.

I lie back and take in a deep breath. I thought that when I got here after Mum died. I couldn't believe how black the night was, or how the silence here could be both quiet and loud, and something about him noticing this too makes me soften. "Pez?" I say, but he doesn't answer and we curl in silence again for what feels like forever. I'm willing sleep to come when he rubs his nose noisily with his sleeve.

"You must miss your mum," he says.

I roll my head around to his, then back. "Every day."

"Is it harder or easier, being back in the flat?"

I think about the three of us trying to fill the empty space where she should be. "I thought being in London would help, but it's worse. In Somerset, I didn't have to look but all I see now are the shadows she's left behind. I see them everywhere." Pez squints like he's thinking. "And with Arial, there's all this new stuff, stuff I didn't have to think about before. Like how much she needs her mum, I guess."

"And you have to be like *her* mother," he says. It's not a question and he just nods like he understands. It's a glimpse of the Pez who notices stuff that other people don't want to see. I'm so relieved by all the truth we're sharing that the muscles in my face soften.

"I was mad at you," he says, looking away.

My jaw locks. "Yeah, well, you made that pretty clear."

"Not last weekend," he says. "For moving away, for—"

"Like I had any choice in that."

"I know, but . . . you had a choice whether or not to answer calls or to reply to my messages. It was like you wanted to forget, about me—" His voice shakes.

"Hey," I say, pulling at his arm.

He looks up. "The night before you left Camden, we were crying in the square. 'Thanks,' you said, all sweet, like you were grateful I was feeling for you, but I was crying for me. Mum and Harland fought every day that summer. You were the only one I talked to about any of it. But when your mum got sick you stopped asking. Losing her was the worst. It was awful for you and I get that. Of course I do. But when you

202

moved away it was like I didn't matter anymore. I've never said this to anyone, but I can't not say it to you now, because—" He stops and breathes in deeply through his nose, filling his lungs with all the air around us. "Because it . . . hurt." He pulls up the neck of his hood, closing his eyes and hiding his face.

I gulp down his words. "It's okay."

His lids open. "Nothing is okay," he says, revealing the huge whites of his eyes. "I'm not okay." He says this last sentence so slowly it scares me. "You came down here to fields and farms"—he throws his arms out in the dark—"to this Disneyland of hugs, but—" He stops and holds his head in his hands for a long time. "I'm sorry," he says finally. "I sound like a prick."

He does sound like a bit of a prick, but I reach for his hand, squeezing his fingers in mine, in our special code of short bursts, and I shake my head, because in my heart that's the last thing he is.

He pulls his hand away and looks up at me from under those lashes. "You've got no idea how badly I wanted you to move back to London, or how much I just wanted . . . you. And when you came back, without telling me, it just, like, proved everything that I didn't want to believe . . . about how little I meant to you."

I'm still shaking my head. It's all I can do. Light flashes in the darkest parts of my mind and I see it was me who kept a distance. It was me who stopped answering calls. "I'm here now."

"We'll see," he says quietly.

That he doubts me makes me so sad. "It's not an excuse," I say, leaning over, "but I felt the same. I just thought you would be fine without me, that I was the one who needed you. I never stopped to think that you might have needed me too. Not really." I lie back and warm tears drip into my ears. "I feel bad saying this, but I'm being honest." When I sit up he's looking straight ahead. "Pez?"

He sits up too, rubbing his hand under his nose again, sniffling. "I'm not in a good place."

"I get it."

"You think you do, but you don't."

"Tell me, then, so I can try."

"After you left I had no one."

"You've got tons of friends."

"I'm not myself with them."

"But they care about you, they do. When we moved here I didn't know anybody. I had to start over. But I didn't blame you for any of it."

"I'm not blaming you," he says. "Honestly. I'm trying to explain. What they see isn't me . . . nobody knew me like you and I'm just trying to understand why I feel so lonely—" He stops and looks at me as the word sits there between us, so simple and honest.

I'm so moved by how he's letting himself be seen like this, I lean over and put my hand on his cheek, leaving it there, hoping that something of me and all that I feel is passing through our skin.

"I'm so sorry, Pez." He lifts his eyes. "I couldn't go on missing you and Mum as much as I did. I had to go forward, not back. I had to let go. And I was trying so hard to hide or to be somebody else and I was afraid you'd see right through it. Besides, you were Pez . . . all bright and brilliant in your big blue house. You could do anything, draw anything, you made everything fun. I guess I convinced myself you'd be fine." He covers his face with his hands. "What?" I ask.

"Sounds like you're talking about someone else," he says.

I reach over, trying to peel his fingers away. Then I pull him closer, but he's stuck to the ground and I have to drag him.

"Pez?" He looks up, but his arms don't budge. "Come here, asshole," I say, shuffling closer. "Hug me, will you?"

"I need to sleep," he says, shuffling away.

"Pez, I'm serious. Don't make me ask again."

His breath is heavy as he slowly lowers himself back down onto the bed. *That's it?* I flop down too and he rolls onto his side. After all that I can't put my arms around him. He clears his throat, like he can hear my thoughts. "But thanks for saying what you said."

"S'okay," I say, but as we lie there in the dark, more thoughts come to my mind and I'm so inspired by how brave he's been that new words load themselves onto my tongue, eager to be let out. "Can I ask . . . just one more thing?" He says nothing, but there's a grunt, which I take as a yes. "When I walked in here earlier, what were you doing?"

His breathing gets louder. "You looked at my computer the other day," he says. "I know you did."

I wasn't expecting him to catch on that quick. I hardly knew I was going to bring this up, so how on earth did he? "It was an accident."

"So, what? You think I was watching porn when you walked in here too?"

It takes a few seconds for me to speak. "Um . . . no, I dunno. And I wasn't judging you. I—"

"What right would you have to judge me?"

"None. I wasn't. That's what I'm saying. I—"

"So, you've never watched—"

"No! Stop!" I say. "Let me finish. That's why I brought it up. I just wanted to—" Oh god. "Forget it," I say, curling up on my mat.

But I started this and I want to be honest.

I scrunch thick fists of duvet under my chin and we lie there like bizarre bookends not looking at each other and I imagine I'm standing over the edge of a great cliff. I hold myself completely stiff. Nothing moves inside or outside the tent. It's as though the wind has stopped and even the leaves on the trees and the blades of grass outside have stilled, like they too are holding their breath. I picture thoughts forming in his mind, like those ellipses when someone is typing a message. Neither of us talks but my thoughts are loud.

"I have watched porn," I say. "Quite a bit recently." When I twist around all I can see is his back, like I'm talking to his T-shirt, not him. "Pez, are you listening?"

I'm about to shove his shoulder, when he rolls over. "And?" he says, bending his elbow, propping his head up on the palm of his hand.

"And . . . I've been trying to work out how I feel about it," I say, back on my cliff, leaning into the wind and finally diving over the edge. "And, I've got questions, I guess. See, the truth is—"

I stop and he lies there watching me free-fall. "Go on," he whispers eventually.

"It's been on my mind, since I saw what I saw in your room. See, it's like my body feels one way about it and my head thinks the opposite. Maybe I've been looking in the wrong places but a lot of the stuff I've seen is kind of disturbing, you know? As though a lot of the girls are just acting like they enjoy the way sex is . . . done to them, and it's hard to get on board with that. Look, I haven't seen *that* much, but what I've seen has sort of stayed with me after I've stopped watching." He says nothing. "And then I also kind of . . . get it." He stares into the space in front of him, like he's looking through me, and I tilt my face to match the angle of his. "This might sound like a stupid question, but is it all so . . . one-sided?" I ask, and he looks up. "I can't help wondering if there's stuff out there that's a bit more . . . cheerful maybe?" I attempt a laugh, but he jolts. "Sorry, I thought you might know."

"Why would I know?" he says quickly.

"Well, you watch it more than me, so—"

"How did you work that out?"

His words sound so hard. Does he really not know that I see him staring at the screen in the dark night after night? But then, what if he's just playing *Fortnite* or watching Netflix? What if, like me, he was googling around one day and opened a ton of porn to look at and I've built this into something far bigger than it is? What if all the madness is in my head?

"Have you shared this theory with anyone else?" It's an accusation, not a question.

"No."

"Have you told anyone else?"

"No!" This isn't entirely true and my voice jerks. I've spoken to Rob and March about him. "It's been on my mind, that's all." I hear him sit up and take a drink. Liquid quickly glug–glug–glugs down his throat and this is followed by the sound of plastic being crushed in his hands.

"What d'you mean you *get* it?" he says.

"I get that it . . . *works*?"

"Works?"

Holy hell. This is embarrassing. "That it helps . . . to get you off?" I turn and study what I can see of his face but it's hard to tell whether or not he's smiling. "Please don't make me feel even weirder about this."

His face goes still. "So, how often d'you *get off*?"

I prop myself up. "Dunno," I whisper, wishing I could skulk back under the covers, but I brought it up. "I'm still . . . working myself out?" *Shudder*. I don't know how to explain it honestly. "But I guess I try about as much as guys." I'm waiting for something, a laugh would help, but he looks so serious. "Why?" I say. "How often do you?"

He leans back again. "Can we talk about something else?" he says.

I lie down. "Sure," I say, quietly fuming about the fact that I've totally overshared and now neither of us knows what to say and the silence feels endless.

I pull my sleeping bag around my face and as the heat leaves my cheeks it slowly dawns on me that I wasn't the only one to leap off a cliff tonight. It was huge of Pez to tell me he's been lonely, and as I snuggle up in the quiet, I think about how much I treasure this trust and how thankful I am.

"Good night," he says, after a while.

"Night," I say back.

208

22

Arial kneels inside the tent, stuffing a croissant into her mouth. "Is it time to put my jumpsuit on?"

It seems like only minutes ago I shut my eyes. I prop myself up on my elbows and rub my face awake. "What time is it?"

"Dunno, but Dad says you need to get up," she says, shoving in the last mouthful and using both her hands to tie the door flap open. Pez stirs and quietly announces he's going to the bathroom. I watch him crawl out of the tent and with the door open I have a full view as he slowly moves up the yard toward the house, becoming more and more vertical with each step.

Arial insists I budge over so she can cuddle in beside me. "Was it like *uh-mazing* to sleep in here last night?" she says. I don't answer. I can't. "Bet it was," she says. "But you should have brought a midnight feast." She places her face in front of mine. "Ohmygod, did you have a midnight feast?"

I pat the ground, searching for my phone. "How are the brides?"

"Haven't seen Fran yet," she says. "But Wendy's still in her tracksuit bottoms. She's stressed because her phone says it might rain." I sit up and look out at the dark clouds above our heads. "Dad can't get the helium thing to work."

I spin around. "Was that the real reason he sent you down?"

She drops her chin. "He just wants you to help."

"Tell him I'll be up in a bit," I say, remembering my own job and frantically scrolling through my phone for the paragraph I found on the internet from a book called *Captain Corelli's Mandolin*. It has a nice passage about love that lots of people seem to read at weddings and once Arial is gone I reread it slowly, timing myself. It feels clever and meaningful, but not as personal as I'd hoped. But on the plus side, the section I've picked is only forty-six seconds long.

I collapse back onto the pile of sleeping bags, closing my eyes. I want to take a bit of time to process last night, but then I remember the awkwardness with Wendy and I know I can't stay mad at her today. I force myself up and hike the path to the house. I'll make everything better after I've showered.

When I reach the courtyard, Pez has got the helium canister going outside the back door and the balloon operation is well underway. I watch him help Arial tie string to the bottom of a balloon. Then she opens the utility room door and volleys it inside before the rest of them can spill out. Pez places another limp balloon on the gas nozzle and it quickly gets bigger and bigger, but his face looks blank like it doesn't register it inflating before his eyes. I open the camera on my phone and click several times. Then Arial reappears and he hands her the giant peach balloon but instead of tying it this time, she puts it to her mouth and sucks in the gas. I lurch forward but she's already raised her head and with one hand on her hip she starts talking to Pez like a chipmunk. He laughs and so does she. She's bent double. Neither of them can stop.

When Pez looks up, I tuck my phone into my shorts and stroll over like I've just arrived. They're still giggling as I pass by and I'm tempted to turn around, to try to join in, but it was their moment.

I stroll on into the kitchen, where Dad is at the table reading his iPad and drinking coffee while people literally spin plates around him. I sit down and grab a croissant.

"Howdy, camper," he says, rubbing my head. "I'm going for a walk down by the river. Do you think Pez would like to come?"

"Ask him," I say, getting up. "I'm going to see whether there's anything useful I can do." If I can't get mad with either Pez or Wendy today, maybe Dad is the next best thing.

There are no official bridesmaids, but I find myself doing what I understand is pretty much that job, that is, telling Wendy she looks great and generally fussing around making her slightly more stressed. There's a chance I'm overcompensating for yesterday and laying on the niceness a bit thick. I've washed and blow-dried my hair and I've got my green tea dress on. Somehow, I've ended up with eyeliner and red lipstick and although my face looks completely different, I'm quite pleased. When Wendy sees me, she puts her arm around me and looks at me so kindly, I manage to push yesterday's conversation to the back of my mind.

Dad must have persuaded Pez to go on that walk, because when I go downstairs to show him my new face, there's no sign of him. I make some tea and sit on the stairs, unable to stop thinking about last night and everything he said, but after a while Fran's brother appears and tells me it's time to get Wendy moving. When her hair and makeup are done and we finally get downstairs, Dad is waiting by the door to the yard, where a path of tiny jam jars filled with flowers has been laid all the way to the door of the tent.

"It's brightened up out there," Dad says, turning around. I can tell by the way he bounces on his knees that he's nervous. Wendy takes one look at him and starts to cry. Fran's brother is convinced Wendy's crying because the sun's out, but when I look at her watching Dad, I don't think it's that.

The gazebo is full and Pez sits beside me, studying the thick card in his hand like he has an exam on the program for offbeat lesbian weddings right after. He's wearing a denim shirt buttoned up to the top and he looks neat and different, like he's made an effort, and I'm surprised by how much I appreciate it. Dad sits on the other side, with an empty chair for Arial on his right.

Then Fran's brother starts to play "Here Comes the Sun" on the guitar and suddenly Fran and Wendy emerge from the light at the side of the tent and walk up the aisle together. Fran's wedding outfit is a silky cream dress that looks like an elegant nightie. She looks beautiful, but I prefer Wendy's blue suit by a mile. Arial follows behind the brides, scattering fistfuls of gold foil stars as they walk. No one seems to mind that she's throwing the confetti already and I'm just happy to see her behaving like a kid again.

Afterward, I'm outside the gazebo scoping for Pez when

Fran strolls up and hands a glass of champagne to a friend who's standing nearby. "Aldi," she says, taking a sip from her own glass. "Eleven quid a pop!"

It seems as though the friend would like more intel on the bargain champagne but Wendy appears by Fran's side and she quickly changes the subject.

Finally I spot Arial and Pez bouncing around on our old trampoline, playing rock-paper-scissors. With some reluctance, Arial lets me join in their game, but I'm soon indecently sweaty and have to make my excuses. Dad is vacuuming up canapés when I find him and he tells me it'll be at least twenty minutes before we eat so I grab one of his chicken skewers and sit on a wall to practice my reading.

I run through it a few more times; then I look up and glimpse Pez over the top of the hedge. He's standing in the middle of the trampoline with his back to Arial, arms folded across his chest, preparing to fall into her tiny arms. We used to play this game as kids and Pez caught me every time, like I did him. The sight of them gets me thinking about last night, about how vulnerable Pez allowed himself to be, about how he trusted me to catch him . . . like I hope we're always going to catch each other. I look down and recite the lovely words from *Captain Corelli's Mandolin* to myself one last time but part of me suddenly wonders whether they're enough.

Guests have gravitated from the yard back inside the tent and soon everyone is seated apart from the brides. I spy them whispering to each other by the sign for the bathrooms. Fran points out into the room and Wendy squeezes her and smiles. Dad waves me over and I quickly scurry through the crowd, taking my seat at the top table, beside him and opposite Pez. I peer down the long row of faces to Fran's brother. He stands, microphone in hand.

"Ladies and gentlemen," he says, "please put your hands together for Fran and Wendy!" At this, the room rises to its feet and rapturous applause continues until the beaming brides are seated beside us. Once we're all back on our bums Fran's brother takes a piece of paper from his jacket pocket.

I nudge Dad. "Already?"

"Wendy wants to get them done early so everyone can relax," he says. *Relax!* I take a gulp of wine from my glass and start scrolling through my phone, mouthing the reading to myself until Dad gives me the eye that says I should really be listening to the speech that's already happening; then he takes my shaking hand and holds it in his under the table. Wendy makes her excited scrunched-up face at me before turning to hear more about the color of Fran's hair in high school.

Opposite me, Pez is buttering a roll, slowly spreading it right out to the sides like I know he likes it, and for some reason, watching him helps my insides settle. Dad squeezes my hand. "Your turn," he says.

Fran's brother is wrapping up, which means I'm next. People are still cheering his speech as the microphone is passed along the table toward me. He must have been really funny.

Finally, the mic reaches me and very slowly I stand up, but when I look out at the sea of faces my heart starts doing crazy things. I look down at my phone and the words swim around the screen but when I go to speak I can't catch a single one. Panicked, I look at Pez and this steadies me. Then I picture him on the trampoline, eyes closed, arms crossed, his huge body ready to fall back into fragile arms that could never hold him. When my mouth opens this time, I don't recite the words on my phone. New words sit upon my tongue.

"Wendy and Fran met in Camden Town." I'm stunned by how loud my voice is. "Wendy used to say she fell in and out of love with London, as though the city itself were human. Until I moved back there a few weeks ago, I never really understood what she meant. But I see now that if London is a person, then people are a bit like London too . . . We all have busy streets where buses drive down and spaces where anyone can walk around. We all have colorful, famous parts, like Camden Market or the zoo, or the pub where Amy Winehouse got up on the bar to sing." I pause here to scan the table and both brides smile back like I'm doing okay so I take a breath and keep going. "We'll happily show people around these touristy spots. But what about the secret places? Like the tunnels under the canal where it's scary after dark or the shadows of the willow tree where we hide when we're sad? These places aren't always on the map and sometimes we all get lost and we all feel lonely."

I stop. The words "sad," "lost," and "lonely" rattle between my ears and I've got a horrible feeling I've gotten badly off track. The microphone slides out of my hand, making an awful feedback sound as it crashes onto my unsuspecting plate. I run my palms down the front of my dress before rescuing it and when I look up it feels like every face in the room is staring at me. But no one is laughing; no one is doing anything. I'm wondering how bad it would be for me to just sit down. My brain races and I turn to Dad, who nods at me in a way I don't understand.

215

Wendy's face is easier to read; hers is saying *have you totally lost it, Vetty?*

But I look across at Pez, who has stopped turning his fork over and over on the tablecloth, and his eyes flash up at me, like he's listening, waiting to hear what I've got to say and what I feel for him in this moment really is . . .

"Love," I say, lifting my face to the room, "isn't something that we give or we get. Love is something that grows when we have the courage to let others into the shadows. Love is our reward for handing over the whole map, tunnels and all. Wendy and Fran, I've watched you, always there for each other, and I know love will follow wherever your road leads." I lift my glass to the room and people raise theirs too.

"To Fran and Wendy," I say, and everyone cheers.

Dad loosens the microphone from my hand. "Well done, kiddo," he whispers as he stands up, but people are still clapping and Dad has to wait until they finish.

I hardly hear all the lovely things he says about Wendy because I'm staring into space, wondering what just happened. So much stuff is still less than perfect between me and Pez, but I've found something that's been lost, something simple and honest; understanding, maybe? It's like putting on comfy leggings after wearing skinny jeans for too long or slipping back into my fake Uggs after my sneakers have given me blisters.

I eat my meal in a haze of these thoughts and only truly come down to earth in time for dessert. Soon after, people are up, gathering around the black-and-white tiles, where a six-piece band has set up on the stage, waiting for the first dance to start.

Dad stands. "They're Fran's friends from university," he says. "So, we better fill the floor." We walk over and watch the singer step up to the mic. I'm about to blab to Pez about the Lauryn Hill song when a piano and a saxophone start up, neither of them sounding remotely like the intro for "Can't Take My Eyes Off You." Then the singer belts out "Me-e-e-e aaaaand Mrs. Jones . . ." and the gathered crowd goes wild.

I watch Wendy lead Fran Jones across the floor. There's nothing showy about how they move. Fran has her hands resting on Wendy's shoulders and they turn, slowly, slowly around. That's kind of it, but the glitter ball above their heads spins and spins and the light bounces around the tent, catching the leftover stars that have settled in Wendy's hair and down the back of Fran's dress. It takes a few seconds for me to realize what's happening as people dissolve around us, becoming pairs, moving slowly about the dance floor. Pez shoves his fists in his pockets and stares at his shoes while I shuffle about, not quite sure what to do.

Dad is out there, in the middle of it all, bent low, holding hands with Arial, swinging their arms together like they're expecting someone to skip over them. Arial does a limbo move toward him and he throws his head back. Apart from two old men leaning against the tent pole like it's the bar, it's only me and Pez left not dancing.

I'm trying to work out how everyone seems to know how to slow dance and it's only when I look closer that I notice they're all doing it differently. One couple moves in urgent, highly coordinated steps, as though a very different song is playing inside their heads. Another shimmies in and out, without ever touching. But most couples just lean against each other and slowly spin around, as though the music and their full stomachs have made them suddenly sleepy. Perhaps getting it right might not matter that much. I guess it's this that makes me open my mouth. "Wanna dance?"

For a horrible moment Pez says nothing and I have to watch as he racks his brain for an excuse to say no. Then Arial and Dad beckon us from the middle of the floor.

"One song," he says with a small smile.

We move out into the crowd, taking up position next to Dad and Arial. The band starts to play something new and I put my arms out, letting them rest around Pez's neck. It's another few seconds before his hands land lightly on my hips and very slowly we start to sway. Fran's brother and his wife have all the moves and I nudge Pez to check them out, but he doesn't seem to find them as amusing as I do, so I just listen to the song, which sounds sad.

"Thanks," I say. He sniffs and adjusts his hands and we continue spinning slowly around, him studying the floor like he's still concentrating on his steps. When I lean in his skin smells clean and his cheek accidentally touches mine. I feel his breath warm against my ear. There's nothing romantic about what we're doing; I'm just relieved to be close to him again. The lyrics are soppy and predictable, but somehow they don't feel wrong.

"I'm so glad you were able to be honest with me last night," I say. "I want you to know that." He doesn't answer but I move in closer, leaning my head on his shoulder anyway. Then his breathing changes, suddenly loud and catching, and when I push back to see his eyes, his face is ashen. "You look like you've seen a ghost. Pez?"

He unlocks my hands from around his neck. "I can't do this," he says, closing his eyes like he can't look at me; then without another word he turns and pushes his way through the surrounding couples, dissolving into the crowd.

23

I'm alone on the dance floor, the only person under the glitter ball not moving, and people are starting to stare. At first, I'm too confused to know what I feel, but as I dodge arms and sweaty backs, following his path to the edge of the floor like a hunter after my prey, anger rises steadily up inside me. Pez slips through a slice of canvas at the far side of the tent but he's not getting away from me this time. I won't let him.

I crash through tables and chairs behind him. When I finally reach the opening, there's only the dim twinkle of fairy lights around the horse-box bar and tiny orange cigarette embers smouldering in the dark.

I cross the field toward the river. Fran's bench is the only place I think he might go. Music fades into the wind and its distant lyrics carry me toward the water. I can barely see my feet as I cross the wet grass, but my toes quickly feel damp inside my shoes.

I've almost reached the tree as the song finishes. In a brief pocket of quiet, I catch the rustle of his breath and I squint into the shadows. There, up ahead on the Welsh larch, he sits, panting like he's run a race. I edge closer, watching his back move up and down. It doesn't seem right not to let him know

I'm here but then I stop. It's nerves, I think. Then I remember all he said last night and I'm suddenly walking over.

I sit down beside him. "It's all right," I say. "It wasn't *that* embarrassing for me."

His elbows are on his knees and he stares at the ground.

We sit like this in the dark, listening to the water galloping past, like it too is thinking too fast. I pick up a twig from under me, scratching at its gnarly edges with my nail before tossing it into the river and watching as the stream carries it away. I place my hand lightly on Pez's back but when he stiffens I take it away.

"I wasn't honest with you last night," he says, slowly turning his face to mine. "I didn't tell you all of the truth."

"Okay . . ."

"You asked if I was watching porn and, well, I wasn't. I was on a website about how to stop watching it."

Something flutters against my spine. I check his face, which looks flat, like it's missing its usual contours and shadows. *So just as I've started to watch porn he's stopping? It's like I'm destined to live behind the curve.* I'm not sure what to say. "Would it be stupid to ask . . . why?"

"Because I'm . . . I watch it all the time," he says, rocking back and forth. "It's pretty bad."

"Like every day?"

"Before school, after school." His jaw sets and he looks away downstream. "*During* school."

"Oh." I look up at the huge branches lit by the moon above our heads.

"Whenever I'm alone, I turn it on before I can think," he says.

221

I want to say *I knew it* but this would be seriously unhelpful. "Right."

"It wasn't always like this," he says then. "Not at first."

"So, what happened?"

He shrugs. "Dunno. Something took over . . . because I can't . . . it's so hard to stop."

I take a sharp breath and look around, wishing I could say something that made sense. "But don't . . . lots of people watch a lot of porn? I mean, is it really *that* big a deal?" As soon as I've said this, I realize it was quite a big deal to me, for different reasons perhaps, but to say I haven't been worried would be a lie.

He covers his eyes with his hands. "I haven't wanked without it since I was thirteen." His words sound unnaturally slow. "But I've stopped," he says more quickly.

My eyes go wide in the dark. "You've stopped wanking?"

He shakes his head. "Watching porn."

"Shit, yeah, of course—"

He sighs. "You wouldn't get it," he says.

I don't know what to do except sit there, continuing to swing my legs under me like I'm Arial.

"I keep watching and watching until all the empty space inside my head is full. Until I'm numb," he says, squeezing his left hand into a fist. "Now I am numb, all the time. It used to be as soon as I opened my laptop, almost as soon as I clicked on Safari I'd get . . . you know?" He doesn't wait for an answer. "Now, even with the loveliest girl in London beside me . . . nothing." His nostrils flare as he breathes in and out. "It's as though if it's not on-screen I can't feel it."

Pez has had a computer in his room for as long as I remember, and I can't help wondering when all this started. Was it before I left? Then I picture him, slumped against Rob's front door, hand trembling on the lock. "How long ago did you stop . . . you know, watching?"

He turns to me. "It's day seven."

"You've counted?"

He kicks at the ground under his foot. "It's not funny," he says, but I'm not laughing. It's exactly a week ago. He stopped after the party. Is that why he left and why he couldn't face me or March? I picture him on the steps of his house, hunched over in the dark like a wounded animal, and I instantly regret every one of my cruel words. Then I picture March's eyes opposite me in the café and everything starts to make sense. Pez studies me like he sees the jigsaw pieces slotting into place. "Did she tell you?" His voice is barely recognizable.

I shake my head. "No, no."

"Bet she told Amira though. Bet everyone thinks I'm some kind of—"

"March isn't like that," I say, jumping in. "She cares about you."

Tears pool in his eyes and his head drops. He knows March hasn't betrayed him.

"I've been googling what's wrong with me," he says. "And as I'm searching I keep praying that whatever I type in won't take me to some other porn site. It's like it stalks me, everywhere I look. It's like my computer knows what I'm thinking. You've got no idea how humiliating it feels."

I shake my head. "Locking yourself away isn't the answer."

"When we lost touch, it was like you sensed I wasn't good enough anymore, like you were ashamed to know me. I haven't told anyone. This isn't something you just . . . talk about. Not seriously, not unless it's some joke."

I reach my hand out to touch him but he dodges it and I can only listen as the hurt drips down his face. This is so strange. I'm the one who cries.

Far away the music changes and Missy Elliott's "Work It" booms out over the valley. Much as I love this song, I wish it would stop. I shift my focus back to Pez. I've never seen him like this. Even last night was different.

"This doesn't change who you are, Pez. Or how I feel about you." I lift his chin. "Never. Got that?"

He nods. "D'you promise?"

"Promise," I say, leaning my head gently on his shoulder. "How's the not-watching going?" I ask. "Serious question."

He looks up. "Well, the first four nights I stayed up playing *Warhammer*. Like, I didn't stop. Then I moved my iMac out of my room and played *Threes!* on my phone until all I saw was sliding blocks, even when my eyes were closed, and then I finally slept and I was still connecting number patterns. But . . . okay."

"It's like that?"

He nods. "You said something last night, about how what you've watched has stayed with you."

"Not in a weird way. I just meant that I'd keep thinking about—"

"I get flashbacks," he says. "I was brushing my teeth the other day and I couldn't look at myself in the mirror, knowing what my brain was seeing. I sat on the edge of the bath and waited for it to go away." He stops and his head dips down.

I reach for his shaking hand. "That bad?"

"Not at first," he says. "But it's crept up on me, like I can't get enough, and then I look more and more. I'd watch anything I could, always switching it up because the stuff I'd seen over and over wouldn't work anymore. I'd search for other stuff, stuff I'm not into ... even gay stuff, whatever ... as long as it ... worked." I lift my head and examine his face. "I'm not gay, Vetty. That's what I'm saying."

"Lots of straight people watch queer porn. I read that somewhere."

"But I watched other things I *really* wasn't into and some of it was fucked-up." He looks up at the sky. "Extreme and just ... degrading. I know it's not real, but I'd freeze up inside because I don't want to treat March like that. That's not how I want to be with her ... or with anyone, but I panic that maybe I don't know any other way and I hate myself for this and I'm afraid, of myself, afraid that this darkness will always live inside my head." He's whispering, putting his two hands up against his ears. "And now that I've stopped, the empty space is back," he says. "And all these feelings are flooding in. Look at me." He holds out his shaking hands. "I'm a mess. The smallest thing sets me off. I can't bear anyone touching me; I couldn't even take your arms around me in the tent, but here I am, pouring my heart out ..." He trails off and I let the silence happen. "I haven't allowed myself to feel anything for so long. My head was so full of images I could crowd out everything I didn't want to feel, but all I can see now is how lost I've felt at home and how sad I am all the time and the worse things got with Mum and Harland the more I cut myself off. Everything is so intense. *I'm* so intense."

He closes his eyes like he's out of words. It's the most he's ever spoken about anything.

I want to hug him. It's all I know to do, but I'm not sure whether he can take it so I slowly move my hand across to his knee, praying he doesn't flinch. "You must have felt so alone," I say. "And I get that."

"How could you get it?" He says it so quietly I have to lean in. "My body doesn't work anymore, Vetty." He looks up at me and his eyes are bright like the moon. "It's like I've broken my brain."

"Some of the best relationships aren't physical."

He sighs. "I know. But I want this one to be. How would you feel if someone you liked, like really liked, kissed you and touched you, but you couldn't react? Even though your heart and your brain want to." He takes in a lungful of night air.

He's right. I have no idea how this would feel and I look back at the lights of the gazebo in the distance, glittering in the dark like a parallel world. "I'm so sorry you're going through this, Pez, but . . ." He looks up. ". . . I'll always be your friend, okay? I'm here," I say. He nods. "And you don't need to feel ashamed."

His head drops again. I don't know how long we sit like this, silently, in the dark, but it feels like forever. I'm starting to get really cold when his hand reaches around and gently squeezes my shoulder.

PART FOUR

Friends don't lie

24

We race onto the train and when I plunk down beside him, he shoots me a look. "What?" I say. "I prefer to face forward."

His eyebrows tilt, that way they do. "That so?"

"Count yourself lucky I'm not ousting you from the window seat." He rolls his eyes and returns to the window, but I catch the side of his smile. He's staring out at the passing fields again, but I settle happily into my seat, already enjoying how light and different things feel.

I flip through my phone, studying the photos I took over the weekend: Arial in the wheelbarrow, laughing. Pez blowing balloons by the back door. Fran eating toast in the kitchen on the morning of the wedding, wearing only rollers and her bathrobe. There's a new warmth in my stomach as I take them in. I continue scrolling, aware of how much I've missed capturing these unguarded looks. It feels good. There's Wendy brushing her teeth, toothpaste dribbling onto her chin. I stop and stare. I'm so happy for her and Fran that they had the wedding they wanted, a celebration that was so *them*. I just wish my conversation with Wendy the day before wasn't such a disaster. It would have meant so much if I'd been able to tell her, but now I'm not sure why I assumed she'd understand.

Our car is almost empty and we've got a table to ourselves. Pez leans back in his chair, doodling on yesterday's program, sipping on a Sprite, and saying basically fuck all. Still, it's nice to see him drawing. I keep thinking of supportive things I should have said last night but the most supportive thing I can do now is to act normal, whatever that is. I lean in to see what he's drawing but he twists around so I can't see.

"I've uploaded some pics from the weekend," I say, and his pen stops scribbling. "D'you remember me talking about Liv and Jess?"

He nods. "You mentioned them . . . a while ago."

"Well, they were dying to see a photo of you . . . something recent." He makes a face. "D'you mind?"

His eyes flick to mine. "Not really. Guess it's good . . . that you're keeping in touch with them."

"It's more like they've been in touch with me, a bit, but I haven't been giving much in return. Until now. Talking to you made me realize I didn't want to make the same mistake twice." He looks away. "Anyway," I say, passing him my phone with the picture of him alone, blowing up balloons. "Have a look. I think it's nice."

He takes my phone and stares at the screen a moment; then he shifts his entire body around to face me, looking right into my eyes. "I had no idea you were there," he says. "I like it."

"Yeah?"

"Well, I felt miserable, and I look miserable, so . . . I guess you . . . captured me," he says. "Isn't that what people say?"

He smiles ever so slightly and this closeness feels precious. If I didn't know all that I do and the risks he took to get us here, I'd probably reach over and squeeze him. What he said about Jess and Liv and Freya makes me think about how much of myself I kept back from them because I was afraid, because I didn't have his guts.

Pez hands the phone back. "So," he says. "Were you with Rob last weekend?"

I swallow. "We kissed." He snorts and looks out the window again. "What? I like him. Okay?"

"Do you?" he says.

It's such an earnest question I feel derailed. "Um . . . yes, I do." I do. "Why's that so hard for you to believe?"

He shrugs. "Just, you don't talk about him. And he's a bit . . . surface, if you know what I mean. He can be pretty shallow sometimes. I thought you'd—" He stops.

"What?"

"Nothing," he says. Then he looks up and into my eyes. "Promise you won't say anything to anyone about what I told you on Saturday night?"

I sit back. "You don't need to ask me that."

"But promise, yeah?"

"Course," I say. He nods to himself, satisfied, and then returns to his drawing. I look out the window on my left, listening to Florence and the Machine, trying to figure out the stuff swimming in my brain, like what exactly I'm so afraid of and why I never did talk to Pez or March about Rob.

A few miles beyond Didcot the train slows. There's a large bird in the sky, hovering high, focused on something way down on the ground below. Pez squints into the glass. "Look, it's my namesake. I've only ever seen one in a book."

I watch the bird soar over the field, darting expertly with impossible speed. "A peregrine? Is it really?"

"You can tell by the wing tips and the two straight lines across their edge. See," he says, leaning his nose on the glass and pointing. "They're in parallel."

As we come to a gentle stop, Pez leans farther forward and together we watch, waiting for the peregrine to swoop down. I'm marveling at how such a bruiser of a bird can hold itself so still when the train lurches forward and we get a glimpse of its magnificent wide wingspan. Then, just as quick, the bird flies off, its mind changed by something invisible to human eyes.

Hand on my heart, the only living thing I've seen move with the same grace and power is Pez on his BMX.

The rest of the journey passes in easy silence and we're waiting for the doors to open at Paddington when my phone beeps. I'm expecting it to be Rob and I feel all tight inside because I said I'd be in touch and I wasn't, but it's a text from March.

Hope the wedding was fun.
Got a call about a film job. Pls say U did too?
P.S. Work is boring without you

Pez spots her name over my shoulder and he looks up, waiting for me to say something. I hold up a finger and dial my voice mail. I'm not expecting there to be a message. March getting a call doesn't mean I did too. Pez's eyes widen but I stare back silently as a voice plays in my ear: a guy called Matt from something-or-other films says he's looking for Vetty; then he says something about background artists for crowd scenes shooting in Acton on Wednesday, Thursday, and Friday this week; then he leaves his number, asking me to call to confirm availability. I hang up and gawk at the phone as I step off the train.

"What?" Pez says.

"I've been offered a job, on a film, as an extra," I say.

"With March?" he asks as I'm already messaging March to tell her. I nod at him, still typing as we reach the ticket barriers, and I stick my hip out for Pez to take my ticket from my pocket. He slots it into the machine for me to pass through and then follows. "Have you ever been an extra?" he calls to me.

"Um, no," I say, looking back. "Obviously. Why?"

He overtakes me and turns around. "Well, it's kind of boring," he says, walking on toward the Tube.

I quicken my step. "Well, I have zero problems with someone paying me to hang around a film set for a few days. I'll even admit to being a teensy bit excited."

"Yeah, have fun," he says, jumping onto the escalator.

"Hey, are you—" I was about to say "jealous" of me spending time with March, but I stop myself just in time.

There's something wrong with the Circle Line and it takes us three trains to reach Camden Town. As soon as we're out of the station I call Dad to tell him about my new job but I get his voice mail and leave a rambling plea that goes on way past Starbucks. The closer we get to the square, the slower Pez's steps become. I'm not sure how wild he is about being alone. "Want me to come in with you?" I say. "We could watch something?"

He slings his backpack higher before looking back. "Sweet," he says, bounding on. I walk quickly behind. I already know what I want us to watch and I'm about to say it as I follow him in, but when we reach the kitchen Luna is sitting at the island with a friend.

"Hey, you two," she says, springing up to greet us. "Did you have fun?"

"Hi, Luna," I say, blabbering too much stuff about trains and Tubes and quirky country weddings, but she kisses me like she appreciates it. Then she turns and wraps Pez in swathes of that long cardigan she wears, grasping him dangerously tight. His arms don't move but his eyes close, like he's started to blink and then forgot to open them, and I end up staring at her friend and their empty bottle of wine for a little too long. "Vetty," I say, sticking my hand out to her.

The friend smiles. "I've heard lots about you," she says, not unkindly.

When I look around Luna has her hand on Pez's forehead, like she's taking his temperature, moving it slowly down his face and finally holding his cheek.

Pez lifts her hand away. "We're going upstairs," he says, and I back out of the room after him.

Pez stands over his desk, shaking everything out of his backpack and onto the floor—dirty rolled-up socks, Kit Kat wrappers, and all. Then he takes the program and puts it in his drawer before leaving the room.

He returns moments later holding his huge iMac and places it down on the desk. "*Top Boy*?" he says, on his knees, plugging it in at the wall.

I make a face. "I was thinking more *Ferris Bueller* or *Boyz n the Hood*?" This isn't really what I've been thinking, but I'm building up to what I really want to suggest.

He stands up. "Seriously?" he says. "How many times is too much for you?"

"But we haven't watched them for years," I say, pleased that it sounds as unconvincing out of my mouth as it did in my head.

He turns the computer on and opens Netflix. "How about we try something from this century?"

"*Stranger Things*!" It finally leaps from my mouth just as my phone starts to ring. I reach into my pocket and read the screen. It's from Dad.

Early meetings rest of the week. Afraid it's a nonstarter.

My heart sinks, but soon my thumbs are twitching.

Can't you do them from home?

I can't believe I've asked him this, but I'm already typing again without thinking.

Or could Arial stay with Wendy until the weekend?

The screen flashes again. Who knew Dad could type this fast?

They're off to Venice! It's called a honeymoon.

I curse inwardly.

I've already told March I'll do it

235

I stare at the screen, waiting . . .

Untell her. Home tomorrow. Talk then. Love Dad

Gah! There's nowhere to go from here. I type okay and fling the phone down onto Pez's bed. He brushes it aside and sits too, staring at me quizzically. "I can't take the job." I don't try to hide the huff I'm in. It's so unfair. "Dad worked from home for four years, but seems he can't even do a few hours out of the office now."

Pez makes a noise like he's trying to be sympathetic. "What do you need?"

I let out a long breath. "A mum."

"When?"

I check his face. He's serious. "Well . . . Wednesday, Thursday, and Friday. Dad leaves for work just before nine and Arial's camp doesn't start until eleven, and he doesn't get home until after six, so . . ." I rub at my forehead, realizing how impossible this all sounds. "What was I thinking? It was stupid to—"

"I'll do it," he says, leaning his back against the wall.

My hand drops to my lap. "You would?"

He shrugs. "Why not? Anything to get out of this room." I reach for him, spreading my arms out wide. He ducks but I manage to grab him and for a few seconds he lets me hug him. Before I let go, I hold even tighter. "Why don't you stay tonight?" he says.

I sit up. "In here?"

"Wherever. It would be nice, that's all."

My heart swells like a balloon. "I'd like that."

236

Pez falls asleep during the third episode of *Stranger Things*, which under normal circumstances I'd find unforgiveable, but I see he's shattered, in every way. The extra mattress under his bed is long gone so I make my way to the spare room, the one I slept in as a kid sometimes.

This bedroom is almost the size of our living room, and it feels even bigger because the ceiling is so high. I jump under the sheets, taking in the familiar smell of whatever they were washed in and listening to the shower in the en suite bathroom drip a beat in time with the clack of a distant pipe. I've drunk so much Coke my brain whips and whirls. Then Luna's feet are on the stairs, padding a predictable pattern past my door. It's been years since I heard this house at night but that I still know its rhythm helps me settle. It's not long before all sounds fade and I'm thinking only about how much I've missed being here and how good it feels to slip slowly into sleep as Pez snores peacefully next door.

I wake to daylight and something heavy weighing the duvet down.

A black box sits at the end of the bed, with a blue Post-it curled in a tiny wave on top. I sit up and reach for it, pressing the Post-it down to read.

Gone to Tesco to get Coco Pops. Wanted to give you this years ago, but here it is . . . later than planned but charged and ready to go!

I peel the blue sticker away and stare at the word NIKON printed in white letters beneath.

25

March and I are in the café and she's so excited about the film work, it's impossible not to be swept along. I'm so glad I went with her to the casting that day. I'm glad for a load of reasons, that we're getting to hang out together for a few days being only one of them. I finish giving her a long coffee order before I pass on the info that Matt the film guy, or second AD as he called himself, gave me about what to wear.

"Nothing 'obviously contemporary' was what he said first, but then he said not to worry, because 'the girls in wardrobe will give us a once-over.'"

"Nice one," March says. "I was so busy finding out what we're being paid, I forgot to ask," she adds, sliding a decaf flat white across the counter. "Just a hundred and twenty quid per day!" She raises the hot-milk jug high in the air and we both cheer until she lowers her arm and leans in. "What else did he say?"

"That it's crowd scenes for a film set in Northern Ireland during the nineties, or maybe eighties. I can't remember."

"But what's the film actually about?"

"'How dance culture brought young people from both

sides of the divide together' was what he said. I wrote it down but I'm not sure—"

"Protestants and Catholics raving. I like that," she says, nodding to herself until Viv summons her to help at the till.

When lunch is over we sit down for a drink at our usual table. She stares at me like she's waiting. "C'mon," she says, "I want to hear all about your long weekend."

"God, yeah," I say, making some dumb face. "It was fun." But her eyebrows stay high. "Well, the wedding itself was great. My aunt and her wife had the best time, but other parts of the weekend were . . ." I stop to think about how best to answer this. "Full-on?" I say, sitting back slowly and cracking my can of lemon San Pellegrino. I'm pouring it from up high the way I watched her do, only I must have the wrong glass, because I have to slurp some out to make it all fit.

She leans in. "How was Pez?" she asks gently.

"He had a good time, I think. It's hard to tell with him sometimes."

She sits up. "Did he say anything?" My face twists. I want to reassure her, but I can't do this without being disloyal to Pez. I promised him I wouldn't say anything, so I can't. It's that simple.

She slumps back into her chair, and if it's possible, I feel worse. She shifts around to face the floor. "He still hasn't called." She puts her hand up to her mouth and tilts her head ever so slightly. "It's stupid, but I was hoping he might say something about it when you were in Somerset." She glances in my direction. "I thought he might have given you some clue as to what's wrong."

I can't bear how sad her eyes look. "He really cares about you, March. You should know that."

She sits up again and moves my glass to the side. "So, he did talk to you about it?"

"He said some stuff, but I can't say more than that. I'm sorry—" I stop. Her eyes bore into mine, but I just shake my head.

"Please, Vetty. I'd like to know where I stand."

"I get that, but I can't." I say it again.

She pushes her coffee cup forward and folds her arms, obviously upset, but it's as though a part of her senses how torn my loyalties are. What she can't know is what a tangled mess my heart's in too. She must never learn that what's involved in making her happy has the potential to crush me.

"He's given me his camera," I say after a while, desperate to move into safer territory. "I've been thinking about getting back into taking pictures for a while and then, after we spoke about it on the bus, I've been feeling . . . more motivated."

"To take photos again?" she asks, and I nod. "That's cool."

"I've only been messing about, taking snaps with my phone, but I got some nice shots of Pez and Luna over breakfast and I was thinking—" She leans forward. "If you need some portfolio shots, maybe I could . . . I dunno, give it a go? And mates' rates too . . . and by that, I mean *free*."

She smiles. "I'd like that."

"You would?"

"Course. I'd love you to take my picture. I'd also love not to deal with creeps like the guy at that model place again." She sighs.

240

"He was the worst."

She looks up. "Is it me, or does that feel like ages ago?"

It really does, and I want to agree but her face looks suddenly sad.

"Hey, it'll be fun tomorrow," I say, taking a big gulp of my drink.

"Yeah," she says after a while. "It will. And we'll get to be together for a few days, so it's not all bad." I put my glass down, replaying what she said, enjoying how easily she said it. "Why don't you come over to mine tonight? You could bring some of your clothes and we'll try stuff on together," she says, looking at me. "And plan what we're going to wear?"

I'm about to say yes when my phone clatters around on the metal table between us. I lean in and March does too. It's Pez! I snatch it and read the screen from my lap.

Up for more stranger things later?

I stare at the words, not thinking about Pez. I'm picturing March and me in her room, trying on clothes, talking and laughing and maybe me taking some pictures, and next thing I've let the phone slip back into my bag.

"Tonight sounds great," I say, looking up. "I'll bring the camera."

After dinner Dad offered to clean up so I'm having a bath. I've lined up every decent beauty item I own on the windowsill: exfoliating scrub with hemp and sea salt, fake tan wipes, new razors, some tea-tree spot stick, coconut lotion, and lastly my new bikini-line hair removal cream. I could really do without the embarrassment at March's house later if we're up close and she notices that I'm less groomed than most.

I start ripping packets and folding open paper instructions with my wet hands, determined not to be left behind the curve again. I'm not sure how much hair to take off so I keep my underwear on as a guide, but then all the tucking and folding goes wrong so I whip my pants off only to find the two sides of my lady garden are unevenly slathered in cream. I'm bent over assessing the sorry-looking triangle that's definitely more scalene than isosceles when it hits me: I might as well bite the bullet and go the whole hog. I set my phone alarm for eight minutes as advised and get to work exfoliating the rest of me.

By the time I've finished scrubbing elbows, knees, and ankles, I'm so worn out I have to sit down on the edge of the bath. Steam has fogged up the mirror, which might be a good thing. There's no way I don't look like a plucked chicken. Finally, the timer sounds and I hop into the shower to hose myself down but I've only put my head under the warm water when there's a loud thump on the door.

"Vetty!" It's Arial.

"What?" I shout grumpily, turning the water off.

"Can I come in?" She's already sitting on the toilet.

"And what if I'd said no?"

She smiles, then picks up a packet of razors from the floor. "Oh, can I use one?" she says, standing again and slinging her left leg onto the bath, pulling up her leggings. "I'm getting man legs. Look!"

242

I stare down at the downy fluff on her bruised shins. I want to tell her she's bonkers and that she shouldn't be worrying about any of that rubbish but I'm hardly in a position to reassure her about anything right now. Besides, my teeth are chattering.

"What do you want, Arial?" I don't try to hide my frustration.

"Oh," she says, deadly serious again. "A beam."

I wasn't expecting an actual answer and certainly not this one. "For gymnastics?"

She nods. "Grace has one! I know Dad hasn't got any money, so I was thinking for Christmas maybe, if you and Wendy chipped in?"

"Arial, it's August?" She rolls her eyes at this like it's beside the point and I'm left working out how to deflate her tiny dream as gently as I can. It isn't easy standing here naked, barely concealed by the shower door. I decide to take the practical approach. "I expect most beams are longer—" I stop. My whole down-there area is starting to tingle. "...than your entire bedroom."

Now the tingling's more like a burning sensation.

"Oh, and can I get a crop top? Like an underwear one, but not like a bra."

I've got to wash this cream off! "Um, can we talk about this later?"

She sighs. "Okay. And by the way, I've already checked beam lengths with Siri, so you know."

"Fine, whatever! Get out!"

"There's no need to be mean!" she shouts, leaving the door wide open.

26

I set off to March's place on foot, with a half-empty back-pack of clothes and Pez's camera heavy around my neck. The camera feels like armor, some kind of simultaneous protector and strength giver, and I lift it to my face occasionally to snap amusing shop signs or faces made by dirty gum on the pavement. Having no pubic hair feels weird. It's kind of raw as I walk but then it's also surprisingly exciting to have done something so drastic.

March lives on the top floor of a small high-rise off Junction Road and I crouch down, taking a photo of it glistening against the bright blue sky.

I feel comfortable as soon as I'm through the door. From the outside it looked like any other flat, but inside it's cozy and colorful.

"Alright," she says, reaching to give me a hug but the camera gets in the way.

"Sorry!" I say, glancing down. "Thought I might start on those photos, if you're up for it?"

"Awesome," she says, pottering off to the tiny kitchen, where she yanks some green leaves from a plant by the window and tosses them into an ornate metal pot. She sloshes water inside and gives it a stir; then she takes two delicate glasses with gold rims down from a shelf and spoons a dollop of honey into each one. "Mum says we should keep these glasses for special occasions," she says, handing me one before clinking her own off it. "But I say, today is special!" Then she reaches into a cupboard and takes out a packet of Tunnock's caramel bars. "You like these, I've noticed," she says, throwing one to me. "Good taste," she says as soon as I've caught it.

I follow her into her bedroom, which is no bigger than Arial's and even messier. There's stuff everywhere: lights hang from the bedframe and there are posters all over the walls. An old mannequin, wearing angel wings, lies horizontally across the top of the wardrobe.

"She had to go somewhere," she says, following my eyes. The dressing table is covered with pencil cups and Post-its as well as eyeshadow palettes and a shiny old baked-bean can full of makeup brushes. There's a large mirror with photos and scraps of paper jammed into every inch of its wooden frame. On the wall behind it are study charts and exam timetables, colored in neon stripes. I lean over to read one about biology. "I'd take them down but they took ages," she says, catching me looking. "Anyway, I'm proud of them." Then, with one giant swoop of her arm, clothes fly onto the floor as she clears the bed. "Sit down," she says, patting the thick bedspread before bouncing back up. Then she thumbs the screen of her phone before slotting it into a small dock on the bookshelf.

Music starts to play and she stands there, eyes closed, hands twisting to each side then rising slowly above her head like a belly dancer's. I don't know the song but the girl's voice is like smoke and honey but also powerful too, and as March starts to dance her T-shirt rises up and up and I glimpse the soft curve of her stomach underneath. She sings along, like she's truly lost in the music. It's all strangely mesmerizing until suddenly she stops, as though snapped from a spell.

"Sorry," she says. "I think I'm in love with Jorja Smith. She sings about stuff that matters. Her voice could heal the world." I don't know who Jorja is or what's going on but I nod like I get it, like part of me might already understand. I open my mouth to ask about the singer, but March is talking again. "She does it her way too. Like, she's sexy on her own terms. She just is who she is and it's such a . . . force," March says, looking at me like she's trying to find something in my face I'm not sure is there. I pick up my tea to take a sip. "But you're a bit like that, aren't you?"

I place the glass down without drinking. "Um, what?"

"Come on. You are," she says, smiling and making my heart pound. My mouth is inexplicably dry and I'm not sure my voice works so I attempt another tiny drink of my tea, but it's too hot and then I laugh because it's all I can do. I can't believe anyone would think to put me in the same sentence as the word "sexy." It seems ridiculous and yet I can't deny the tiny thrill rippling through me.

Thankfully she's up again, looking in the wardrobe, humming along as she flings things over her head and onto the bed. She pulls out an army shirt and turns around, holding it up against her chest, her eyes traveling between the shirt and me and then back.

"Yeah, you're right," she says, slotting the hanger back onto the rail like I've expressed an opinion. Then she reaches deep into a shelf up high. "This would be nice with your hair," she says, throwing something into my lap.

I hold up the vintage-looking lace top as though I'm really looking at it, but I feel spaced still.

"And how about this for me?" she says, waving something gold-colored in the air. Before I can answer, she's undressing. "You've got to see it on." Her T-shirt flies to the floor. Next, she's rolling her jeans down her legs. They're so tight she has to peel them off and soon she's standing there in her underwear. She kicks off her socks and turns around. That's when I see, just inside the lace panel of her panties, unmistakable tufts of dark hair.

It's not like I meant to look—I didn't, but it was impossible not to see and my heart plummets. I pretend to pick something up from the floor, reaching for my backpack and rooting around in it for a while, feeling like a complete idiot for turning myself into a plucked chicken.

"What did Pez say in his text?" she says. "You know, earlier?"

I put the backpack down and sit straighter. "Oh, he was checking times for tomorrow," I say, reaching for the vintage top and smoothing it over my knees.

March yanks what's beginning to look like a dress over her chest and then examines herself in the mirror before turning around. "What's happening tomorrow? Besides us becoming famous."

"He's agreed to look after Arial for a few hours."

She sits down on the bed. "So that you can take this job?"

247

I nod. "That's so decent of him," she says, biting the nail of her thumb. "His heart has always been in the right place. Even at the beginning when we first met, he'd listen like no one else. I wish—" She stops. I can't look at her. If I do, I might open my mouth and that's the last thing anyone needs right now. Not just because I promised I wouldn't, but if I told March the truth, that Pez has a problem with porn, not with her, I don't know what she'd do. She could be disgusted or judgmental and I'd hate that, but if I'm really honest, part of me is more panicked that she'd be supportive, that she'd get it and know *all* the right things to say. Either way all this loveliness between us could be lost. Suddenly she's standing up and rolling herself out of the dress. "It's cool," she says, stepping back into her jeans, doing tiny jumps up and down to fasten the top button. "I get it. You've already said you can't say and I'm not going to push it."

I meet her eye. "Thanks."

She nods at the camera around my neck. "So, is that thing an ornament or are you actually going to use it?" she asks.

I look down and lift the camera to my face. Holding it in front of my eye helps my breath settle. I focus the lens; then I get up and move to the window, pulling back the blind.

"Wait, wait," she says, reaching for the mannequin on top of the wardrobe. She lifts it down and strikes poses as though dancing with it.

"Nice," I say, moving farther back to the light.

"I can smize too, watch!" she says, giving it the whole Tyra Banks. I keep snapping, adjusting the aperture and shutter speed as she moves around.

Her movements are so free and natural I start to wonder whether she was like this when she took those pictures for Pez. Or was she all posed and pouty. Staged sexy, like something he asked for to get turned on. My heart races and I try to stop thinking how it would feel if it was me she was posing for, gripping the camera tighter in my hand.

"How about this?" she says, putting on the angel wings and sitting at her desk. I take a few shots as she stares pensively into the mirror, eyes far away; then she purses her lips and that single dimple pierces her cheek. She's just dicking around but she looks so beautiful my chest starts to hurt. I let the camera drop around my neck.

"Nailed it," I say, sitting down on the bed.

Thankfully she gets up. "I have an idea," she says. "Mum's got an old jean jacket. It's small on me but it would look ace on you. I'll go grab it," she says, disappearing out the door.

I lie back on the bed and stare at the ceiling.

27

It's exactly 6:15 a.m. when I turn onto Camden Road. I've never been up and out this early, but I'm meeting March at the Overground train station in five minutes and I'm not planning on being late. I'm wearing Viv's old denim jacket and a brown suede miniskirt that belonged to Mum. The waistband is rubbing but my T-shirt is soft and familiar.

When I arrive, March is already outside. We take the stairs to the empty platform and it's just us sitting there, sharing a cereal bar, with London all to ourselves. If you were to edit out the dirty chicken boxes and the pigeon nibbling on last night's puke, it could feel like we're already in a movie.

We get to Acton Central, follow the directions on March's phone, and soon we arrive at an abandoned parking lot, full of trucks and large white vans. We ask someone where Matt is and then make our way to his office, which is one of many white trailers parked up in the middle of the huge yard.

"Come in," a raspy voice shouts and when we step inside, a small man wearing a flat cap looks up from his laptop with an unlit cigarette dangling from his mouth. He smiles and hands us some forms to sign; then he points out the window at a large bus two vehicles up. "The girls from wardrobe will check you out," he says. "Grab breakfast afterward and sit on the bus until you're called."

"Wardrobe" is an enormous truck racked out with double-decker rails down both sides. The lady who looks like she's in charge walks over and starts examining me.

"I love this look for the rave scenes tomorrow, but today you'll need to wear these," she says, holding up a green school uniform with a skirt, shirt, and tie. Then she pushes a pair of the ugliest brown shoes I've ever seen along the shelf. "And try these on for size." My heart sinks until I see the cardigan March has been given to wear over a pair of mustard corduroy dungarees. Guess it could be worse.

Once dressed in our super unflattering clothes, we line up for breakfast along with other people who look like they've stepped back in time. March goes for scrambled eggs and I get some oatmeal; then we make tea in polystyrene cups and sit on the top deck of the stationary London bus.

"Look on the next page," March says, flicking through the letter-size call sheet in front of her. "It's the dialogue from the scenes they're filming today." Her lips move as she traces her finger over the words; then she puts her hands on her hips and flicks her head back like some comedy gangster. "*Aye, Gerry,*" she says, reading a line from the script out loud, "*you're the big man around town.*" I expect she thinks she's doing a Belfast accent but it doesn't sound like one. "You read the next line," she says, stabbing the page. I look over my shoulder to see whether the people at the table behind are watching. "Don't mind them," she says. "Go on!"

I clear my throat. "*Wise up, McCreevy, no one gives a . . .*" I can hardly get the words out I'm laughing so much. "*. . . no one gives a monkey's about your sectarian shite. It's Friday night for Christ's sake.*"

March explodes. "Where are you from?"

Somehow, we manage to keep going, reading aloud across the table, laughing like hyenas at the state of ourselves. Whatever else happens today, I've already had the best time.

The set is only a few streets from the unit base but we travel by minibus. The road we're filming on is closed to traffic at both ends and all the modern cars have been replaced with old bangers and the shop signs have been changed too. I've never been to Belfast, but I'd definitely believe we're in some kind of time warp that's not today, or London. We're standing around when the actors arrive on set and run lines with the director on the other side of the street. March points to the guy leaning against the old Ford.

"I recognize him from TV," she says. "D'you?" I shrug. "Look, he's getting into the car. D'you reckon he's Gerry *the big man*?"

She does her atrocious accent again and when most of the camera department turns to look at us I have to bite my cheeks not to laugh. We're introduced to the first AD next and she runs through the scene with us. Turns out it's not enormously different from our dramatization on the top of the bus: basically, two Northern Irish guys have a banter before one drives away. That's literally it, but I spend the morning walking up and down outside a betting shop with a boy our age named Ben, who is carrying a football. March is on the other side of the road, pushing an ancient old stroller in the opposite direction.

After lunch, Matt tells us we're on standby for the afternoon, which means we get to sit around on the top deck of the bus again and drink even more tea.

"I can't believe we're being paid for this," March says as we sit down.

Ben and the girl who was cycling a bike in the same scene are at the table opposite. "Can we join you?" the girl says. She's older than us, maybe eighteen, but not much more.

March taps her hand on the tabletop. "Course," she says.

The girl budges in beside me and Ben sits beside March. "I'm Lizzie," she says. "And it's not a competition . . ." She holds up her hands and looks around. "But my sweat suit definitely wins outfit of the day."

I like Lizzie already.

"I'd totally wear that," March says. "I'll swap it with you for my bockety stroller, which, by the way, doesn't even have a baby inside it."

We laugh at this for ages. I'm laughing because it's funny and she says "bockety" in an Irish accent, just like Viv, but I suspect Lizzie and Ben are laughing because they want to be nice to March. I wonder whether she knows the effect that she has on people? I think she must.

"How long do we have to sit around up here?" Ben says.

Lizzie shrugs. "Could be hours."

"I don't suppose anyone brought a pack of cards," March says.

She's joking but suddenly Lizzie gets up and returns seconds later, holding the end of her sweat suit top like a sack, which she shakes out onto the table. Mini cookie packets spill everywhere. "Who's up for two truths and a lie?" she says, squeezing in again.

"Me!" I say quickly. I'm surprised by my enthusiasm but there's something about the fact that we're all stuck here on this bus in our old-fashioned clothes that makes this seem like a genuinely fun idea. "It's not like we've got anything else to do," I add. March and Ben quickly grumble in agreement.

"Right," Lizzie says, handing out cookies like a card dealer. "Everyone knows how to play? You have to give three statements about yourself. Two of them should be true, and one of them should be a complete lie. And we have to guess the lie, obviously." She takes out her phone and opens the stopwatch. "No going easy on friends, now," she says, looking at me and March.

"What's with the cookies?" I ask.

"Whoever gets it wrong forfeits a pack to the person who's it," she says. "And the first to lose all their cookies has to"—she looks up, like she's thinking—"has to do the next scene with two whole Oreos in their mouth, while the camera is rolling!" She claps her hands. "Maybe three."

"No way I'm getting fired!" March says.

Lizzie winks at her. "Better think of some good truths, then."

"Let's just start," Ben says, stockpiling chocolate digestives, but he wins the draw and then sits on his hands in silence.

"Today, Ben!" Lizzie says.

"Um ..." he starts. "I'm left-handed and I can ... touch my nose with my tongue. And ... I had an operation to pin my ears back when I was six."

Lizzie rolls her eyes. "None of those things really tells us anything. We're supposed to be getting to know one another," she says. "At least one of the options should be a bit juicy—even if it's a lie."

Ben bites his lip and looks cautiously around. "Okay," he says. "I might be obsessed with my math camp counselor."

March turns to him, mouth open. "Whoa!"

"I've written him an email," Ben says. "But I'm not sure if—"

"You're going to send it?" March says, in a way that would suggest this might be the WORST idea ever, and when Ben doesn't answer all the muscles in my body go tight.

Lizzie face-palms. "Guys, can we focus, please." She leans across to Ben. "Okay, you were brilliantly on point there, but the extra detail about your crush *kinda* gave the game away."

Ben's head drops; then he lifts it, smiling. "At least it was juicy."

Lizzie places a hand on his shoulder. "True," she says, "but maybe I should start. Practice round?" Ben nods and she rubs her hands together. "So ... I lost my virginity on a train in Belgium last summer. I have an ... *outie* belly button ... and I played clarinet for years." Everyone exchanges looks like they get it; then she taps the timer on her phone.

"I read somewhere that ninety percent of people have *innies*, so statistically ..." March says, scratching her head, "the belly button has a high chance of being the lie!"

Lizzie smiles and moves on to me. I think March is right,

255

but I'm not going to just agree with her and because I don't really want to probe what Lizzie may or may not have done on Belgian public transport, I say, "The clarinet?" She wiggles her brows then moves on to Ben.

"You didn't really lose your virginity on a train in Belgium last summer," he says, deadpan.

"Correct!" she cries. "Technically, we were still in France!" Ben giggles at this, a lot. "Okay, let's go clockwise," she says, pointing to March. "Which makes it your turn."

"Oh, right," March says, sitting back. "So . . . I can . . . break-dance." She speaks slowly. "I peed in the pool at a swimming party in Year Nine, and . . . I once sent an ex a load of nude selfies wearing only my mum's leopard-print stilettos." She covers her eyes, peeking out between her fingers to set the timer on Lizzie's phone. She hits Start.

I sit up, trying not to picture March in those photos, but then I realize she's just called Pez an ex already and I'm hit by a pang of something like sadness . . . for him. The timer goes before anyone has answered. "C'mon," March says, folding her arms across her chest. "Which one's the lie?"

"No way a girl like you has pissed in a pool," Ben says.

Lizzie's mouth twists. "Mate, everyone has pissed in a pool," she says. "I reckon it's the photos. I don't doubt you sent them. I'm just not buying the stilettos."

March leans across the table to me. "Vetty?" she says, lifting her eyebrows. "Which is it?"

I stare back at her. "I've never seen you break-dance."

"Ha!" she says, raising her hand to Ben who high-fives it. "I've never peed in a pool! At least not since reaching double digits. And, Lizzie, sadly those stilettos were real.

Amateur hour of me. I'd never do it now. I'm still terrified the shots will turn up online one day." She shakes her head, shivering at the thought of it, and I have a sudden urge to defend Pez here. "Ladies, your cookies, please," she says then, holding her hand out. "Jammie Dodgers preferred."

I slide a packet of custard creams across the table without looking at her. "Wait!" Ben says, intercepting them. "Really they should get to see a windmill demo before handing over the goods." He shakes the cookies in front of March's face.

"There's no room for windmills up here," she says, laughing.

Ben looks like he might protest when the radio downstairs crackles. I can't make out what it says but he hops up. "We're back on!" he shouts.

Lizzie finishes lining up her Oreos then tips them over like dominoes. "Let's do this," she says, shoving one in her mouth before leaping from her seat.

I follow down the stairs behind March but as soon as we're off the bus and the others have scarpered off, I turn to her. "He wouldn't do that, you know."

She stops licking the frosting from the middle of her Jammie Dodger. "Huh?"

"Pez. He wouldn't put those pictures of you online."

Her hand drops and her face scrunches up. "What are you talking about, Vetty?"

Up ahead, our minibus parks outside Matt's trailer. "Forget it," I say, walking over. "I'm just saying you don't need to worry. That's all—"

"Wait!" she says, pulling my arm. "Back there, in the game,

I wasn't talking about pictures I sent Pez." She tilts her face a few times like she's reading mine. "The photos I sent him . . . they were—" She stops. "They were of my face!"

My mouth drops open. I should stop but I can't. "And the video?"

She shakes her head, like she can't believe I'm asking. I can't believe it either and my cheeks are starting to chargrill. "Jesus! It was some stupid Boomerang. I was doing a hand-stand against a hay bale. Mum took it. She didn't even get the timing right." She draws her lower lip between her teeth. "Why did you assume any of those were nudes?"

"I didn't," I say, but her eyes narrow. "I misunderstood. Sorry." I tighten my ponytail and take a step back, but she looms forward.

"Has anyone else made similar assumptions?" she asks.

Um . . . yes, clearly Rob did. He sounded so sure when he told me and now I'm entirely beet-red-of-face and possibly more confused than when this conversation started. So, this means Pez asked March for photos of her *face*? It sounds almost too innocent to be true. Unless . . . I dunno, I guess it's possible he was lonely and just wanted to see her. It's not only possible, it's kind of lovely, and I've got the uneasy feeling that I may have underestimated what March means to him. And him to her. God, this is embarrassing. I swallow hard. "No," I say, "it was me who jumped to conclusions."

She studies me for a while. "And so what if I'd sent him a picture of my bits? Seriously, so what?"

"Exactly! I just meant that if you *had*, Pez wouldn't share them online. He's not like that. That's what I'm saying."

She puts her hands in her dungaree pockets and lifts her face to the sky like she's thinking. "Sully pestered me for nudes for like . . . forever. He used to call me frigid because I wouldn't, but he kept on asking and when I finally did— he told all his friends I was a skank." She tilts her face and looks right into my eyes. "Have you ever felt like you can't win?" she says. "Because I have, and I'm so over it."

28

It's the first day filming the rave scene this morning. The warehouse setup looks amazing but it's nothing like as much fun as yesterday. The location is a long bus ride away, and because March was sent back to the costume truck for a different jacket after breakfast, we've been separated, which means we've spent the whole morning on different sides of this enormous building. I'm still embarrassed about the photo showdown and today is Mum's anniversary too, so of all the days to be alone with my thoughts, it's not the greatest.

The entire space has been blacked out apart from the strobe lights that move with the music, so it's impossible to see anything or anyone apart from the people nearby. When the first AD shouts "Rolling!" into the loudspeaker it means the cameras are on, so we have to dance, and we have to keep moving until we hear "Cut!" Mostly I copy the moves that people around me are doing so it's reasonably straight-forward, but it's not exactly a laugh. I keep hoping March will appear by my side, as though her presence alone will make me feel less guilty about all the assumptions I made and magically less lonely too, but she never does and now we've been released in different groups for lunch.

I choose lasagna and sit on the top of the bus alone, staring at my phone. When it rings, I jump on it. "Where are you?" I say, assuming it's her.

"Vetty?" It's Rob.

I let my fork drop onto my plate. "Hey," I say.

"Everything okay?"

Um . . . not really. I'd quite like to blame him for getting me in hot water with March yesterday but the more I've thought about it, the more I see I let my mind run wild. "Yeah, I thought you were someone else, that's all."

"Oh," he says. "Sure there's nothing up? You haven't messaged in a while."

"Nah," I say and I picture his eyes squinting like they're hurt.

"Well, I just wanted to hear your voice," he says and I immediately feel bad, like I should say something to explain my silence. "I've been working, that's all. I'm in West London. On this film."

"Yeah, course," he says. "Met any famous actors yet?"

"I don't recognize any of them."

"Must be unheard of," he says with a laugh that's short but warm; then I hear his breath at the other end.

"Um . . . Rob. Can I ask you something?"

"Sure," he says.

"You know the photos and video of March, the ones that Pez has on his phone?"

"Yeah," he says, like he can't believe I'm still going on about them.

I can't let it drop until he knows the truth. "Well, what made you think they were . . . nudes and stuff?"

"Um . . . he did," he says. "Like, duh."

"Pez said it? Like, he actually said she was naked in them?"

"He didn't have to," Rob says. "It was obvious. Kyle took his phone the day she sent them, and Pez went ballistic. You should have seen it. There was no way in hell he was letting any of us see them."

I sigh. "So, you . . . assumed—"

"C'mon, Vetty. You know what those two are like. The way they—"

"Rob!" I say, cutting him off. "They were just pictures. Photos of her face . . . photos with her clothes . . . on."

"On?" he says.

"Yeah, on! I'm only telling you so you stop mouthing off about it."

"Oh," he says. "Oh, man. You're sure?"

"God, yes! I'm positive."

There's a funny noise down the line like he's sucking air in through his teeth. "Okay. Okay, I hear you," he says. Then everything goes quiet and I watch my lunch getting cold. "I was calling to see if you'd like to come over tonight. Mum's working and Tom's with my dad. So . . ." He stops.

The silence that follows this feels loaded, suggestive almost, and while it's nice to feel wanted, I don't feel like hanging out with Rob tonight. He's not someone I want to spend Mum's anniversary with. "Sorry," I say. "Watching Arial."

"Right," he says, sounding disappointed. "Well, we're all heading to Primrose Hill Saturday night, if you're up for it?"

"Um . . . sure."

"Nice," he says. "We're meeting around eight. So, I'll see you there?"

"Shall I see if Pez is up for it?"

He sighs. "I tried calling him but guess what? He didn't answer," he says. "Because he never answers."

"Maybe I'll talk to him?"

"Sure, but good luck."

"K. See you tomorrow."

"K. Bye."

I dial Pez's number. "Hey!"

"What's up?" he says, like I've woken him.

"Not much. It's pretty boring today, to be honest."

I picture him sitting up. "So, I was right?" I almost hear him smile.

"I didn't say that. What you doing?"

"I'm at yours, watching *Stranger Things*," he says.

"Episode?"

"Just started season two," he says.

"And was *I* right?"

"It's so freaking good," he says. "But that's the difference between us. See, I'm big enough to say *yes*." He laughs. "Man, all that eighties shit is sweet."

"And you haven't seen their Ghostbuster outfits yet."

"Jeez, girl, stop talking," he says; then he stops. "But it's not just the retro stuff, is it? It's them. The way those kids are."

It's us, I want to say. Pez has been Mike Wheeler in my head for a long time but I can't work out whether I'm

Eleven or Will Byers and something catches in my throat. "Did Arial get off all right?"

"Yeah," he says. "Bought her some Nerds on the way, though. A banana is not a proper snack. You should know that."

"You dick." He laughs and it's so nice. Then Matt's voice comes over a walkie-talkie on a neighboring table, ushering supporting cast back to the bus. People around me start getting up. "I better go."

"Cool," he says. "See you later."

We only wrapped ten minutes ago but we're already on the train. March is going to Amira's tonight and she didn't want to hang around. "Come with me," she says as we take our seats.

I'm so pleased she asked but I shake my head. "It's my mum's anniversary."

Her mouth opens. "Oh," she says, inching closer on the seat. "D'you do anything?" she says. "To mark it?"

I shrug. "Nah. Dad's working late and I'm not up for putting on a face tonight, to be honest."

She leans in. "I get that," she says. "But if you ever think of something you'd like to do, maybe next year or whatever, I'd be up for joining you. If you want company, that is." Then she smiles with her mouth closed and I have to turn away in case my eyes leak. The cars of another train fill the window and all I can do is nod as they whizz by.

She knows I can't talk yet and starts on telling me about her day. "Lizzie and Ben were on my bus so I sat with them at lunch, but we didn't play any games without you."

I manage to smile at this. "Rob called me," I say. "He said everyone's meeting up tomorrow night."

"Yeah, Amira messaged. Gonna come?"

I nod. "I've been thinking about asking Pez to come too." I check her eyes and she bites at the nail on her thumb. "But how would you feel if I did?"

She sighs. "Depends, I guess. I'd like to see him. I just don't want to have to deal with any more weirdness."

"He doesn't want any weirdness either. In fact, I think he'd be as eager to clear the air as you."

She's taking this in, when her phone rings. "Hey," she says into the handset, like her mind is still on Pez, not the call. I can't make out Amira's words, but she takes a while saying them. "I'll be at yours by eight. Let's talk about it then." March hangs up then sighs. "Exam results party's next week. It's all she can talk about."

Results! I blow out my cheeks. "I hope to god I manage to scrape by."

Pez and Arial are watching *The Goonies* when I get in and I flop down on the couch beside them. Before I've said anything, Arial shushes me, then reaches across for my hand and tucks it under her arm. Pez glances at me with a half nod and then returns to the TV. "Figured *Stranger Things* was a bit scary," he says, "but I'm continuing the eighties theme in your honor."

I give him my best smirk, then lie there for a moment watching the two of them watching. I'd forgotten how much yelling they did in this film.

I get up and stand by the counter. "Anyone eaten?" I ask,

and they both shake their heads, eyes still glued to the TV screen. "Guess I'll make pesto pasta, then." I grumble it to myself, boiling the kettle and clattering around in the low cupboard for a clean pot. When I stand up Pez is sitting at the countertop opposite me.

"I know what day it is," he whispers, flicking a tube of dry penne across at me. "And I feel bad for two reasons."

"Um . . . thanks for remembering, but why feel bad?"

"Well, you ended up checking in on me on the day that I'd planned to check in on you, that's the first thing. And," he says, "I ended up not mentioning it. I was going to, on the phone earlier, but then . . . you were at work and stuff."

I look at the silk tree outside the window, then toss the dried pasta back at him. "D'you ever feel like everything has changed?"

He smooths his hand down the back of his head, nodding. "Not even *The Goonies* seems that good anymore," he says while reaching over the couch for his phone, which has started to buzz somewhere on the seat. He looks at the screen and kills the call.

"Who was that?" I ask.

He huffs. "Rob."

I turn around and open the fridge. "Maybe he's just trying to be nice?"

"Mmm . . ." he says. "Rob's rarely just . . . nice. Sure, he's got his strong points but more often than not, he's after something." I plunk the jar of pesto down and eyeball him. "Trust me," he says, before spinning his stool around to watch the TV. I stare at the back of his head, thinking about this. "Anyway," Pez says then. "I haven't seen him since I bolted from his party. Honestly don't think I can face him . . . or any of them."

I shake too much pasta into the pot. "But you seem . . . stronger."

"A little," he says, shifting around.

"Well that's good, isn't it?"

He sighs. "It's been good to be here . . . to have a reason to stay out of my room."

"Is your iMac still in there?"

He nods. "I play a lot of *Warhammer*. I won't lie. I've been trying to read but it's making me exhausted and I feel so . . . flat." He looks up. "I don't know if it's a good idea for me to be around people at the moment. Especially March."

My gut twists. "But I think she'd appreciate some reassurance. Right now, she's convinced *she's* the problem."

This clicks. I can tell by his eyes. "But I don't want to use her as a guinea pig to gauge whether or not I'm okay."

"You don't have to. A chat, that's all." While I want March to be comforted, I'd be lying if I said I wanted much more than reassurance to happen between them.

"Maybe," he says. "I'm so . . . shaky—" He stops and looks up. "I think I'm going to need some help, Vetty."

It's such a relief to hear this. "Yeah?"

"I don't want to hide away forever," he says. I freeze, for a few reasons, one of them being I don't want to hide myself away either, and yet here I am, twisted in two, torn between him and March and while he's here, being all honest about his feelings, I'm still lying about mine. "I need to talk to someone," he says.

I force myself to focus back on him. "Maybe Luna?" I say, walking around the counter, closer to him, but he shrugs and looks away. "Or even Harland?" He snorts at this. "C'mon, Pez, they love you and they'll have noticed that you haven't been yourself. I bet they'd be more supportive than you think."

"I was thinking maybe someone . . . professional."

"Oh. Good."

"Anyway, Mum's never around," he says.

"She'd make time," I say, "if you told her you need her."

"Maybe," he says. Then his eyes briefly close and when he opens them he asks, "How's she doing?"

"March?" My voice trembles. "Good, I think. She's going to Amira's tonight to plan exam results parties. You know . . . the kind of normal stuff we should probably be thinking about too. Look, I'm sure what happened at Rob's seems much bigger in your head than it does to any of them. They just want to see you." There's a tiny glint in his eye, like he's thinking about it. I hear singing and I spin around to the front door, where Dad stands armed with pizza boxes. "You're back!"

Arial hops up from the couch. "I'll get plates!"

Dad plants a kiss on my cheek. "Good day?" he says, spreading out his feast like the hunter returned. I mumble something like *fine*. "Anniversaries are a bitch," he says quietly into my ear before sliding a box across the counter toward Pez. I should have known he'd remember; he always does. "Hawaiian with NO mushroom, for Mr. Boyd." Then he looks back, doing the tiniest wink that's just for me, and I smile.

Pez tears off a heavy slice of pizza and I lean over, planting my face between him and the food on its way to his mouth. "Well? Are you gonna come?"

He swoops around, avoiding eye contact. "Guess I'll have binged the rest of *Stranger Things* by this time on Saturday," he says, popping a pineapple chunk in his mouth. "And you got my back, right?"

I reach my hand out, taking his. "Always."

29

I meet March outside the station as usual. We're wearing the same clothes as yesterday like we were told. She looks happy, giddy almost. "We better not get split up today," she says. "Seriously. Let's make sure we get on the minibus together after breakfast." She leans in. "Got it?"

I nod and bite my lip at the same time.

"What's up?" she says.

"He's gonna come out, tomorrow night."

She shifts around in her seat, smiling. "I know," she says.

"He called you?"

"No, but we've been texting, all night."

"Yeah?" She nods. "What did he say?"

"Not that much, but the stuff he did say felt honest." My eyes must widen for her to keep going. "Just that his head's been in a bad place and that he's sorry . . . for not being in touch."

My shoulders sink some. "Well, that's good. Isn't it?"

She sighs and picks her nails in her lap. "We've agreed not to be together," she says, looking up. "At least not until he's in a better place."

"Oh," I say. "And you're okay with that?"

"Maybe I should feel sad, but honestly, I'm relieved. At least things are clear and it already feels like the pressure is off." She turns to look out the window, but I catch the side of her smile. "Maybe it'll be nice to be his friend for a while."

It's the same setup as yesterday but we're positioned closer to the stage, right by the front where the DJ decks are. The first AD describes the action through her megaphone again. "Listen up," she says, standing on a speaker close to us. "We're going to be moving about a lot and going in tight for some sequences. It's really important that you ignore the camera as it moves about the floor. Understood?" She says this really loud and everyone shouts Yes! "Talk among yourselves and act natural. The camera can't hear you so don't worry about your Belfast accents." This gets a laugh. "Okay, everybody, it's 1992, you're in love with yourselves and everyone around you." She shouts this out and although it's only 8:15 a.m. people start blowing the whistles around their necks and cheering like crazy.

Me and March spend the next four hours dancing while the same music as yesterday plays on a loop. This might sound like torture but it's surprisingly uplifting and dreamy, like we're all in a deep hypnotic trance. When we break for lunch, I'm so tired I pick the first thing from each menu, which happens to be the curry followed by something called "school lunch dessert;" then we flop into some seats downstairs on the bus and eat our main courses in easy, exhausted silence.

"Hey," March says once she's finished. "Did I tell you Mum's starting a master's?"

"Nope," I say, taking a mouthful of what is basically apple crisp from my giant bowl and shaking my head.

"Social justice and community action," she says. "Starting in October. It'll take her three years but she's wanted to do it for ages. She's got a degree in science from Dublin and everything, but she couldn't afford it until she got this scholarship from the refugee action charity she's been working with." Then she dips her spoon into my dessert, beaming at me. "She paid the deposit yesterday, or rather *I* paid the deposit."

I put my spoon down. "March, that's the best."

"Isn't it," she says, ditching her fruit salad before quickly taking another bite from my bowl. "Ohmygod!" she says. "That tastes like nothing I've ever eaten at school." Then she goes in for another giant scoop. "Seriously," she says. "It's sick."

Her mouth is still full when she loads another spoon and waves it at me to eat. I take it and smile. I'm not sure whether the apple crisp tastes *that* good, but March is clearly just happy: about her mum, about Pez being in touch, and maybe even this job, and it's so nice to see her like this. We take turns devouring the remains of the bowl and by one o'clock we're off the bus and back on it again.

First AD lady explains that the Steadicam is out this afternoon so we wait around while the director and the man with the camera strapped to his body follow the actor through the crowd several times. We're supposed to stay still for this, but March keeps making faces at me as they establish a path that comes right by where we're standing.

March leans in. "We're going to be on camera," she says, bouncing up and down once they've passed.

I don't care about being on camera. I'm just ready to dance again. The first AD stands on a box and repeats the brief from earlier through her megaphone but it's safe to say every raver in this hot, dark warehouse has it nailed by now.

The music fires up and we start to move. Unlike yesterday, when the camera stopped and started, the music is on continually as the Steadicam works its way around. I watch March dance, moving her hands around like she did in her bedroom, and I think about what she said about me being sexy on my own terms, like that singer, and suddenly I'm dancing, losing myself in the rhythm. Everybody around us seems to be smiling and I'm surprised at how unself-conscious I feel dancing around sober in the middle of the afternoon in my borrowed clothes. I'm sweating from the heat of the lights, the bodies, and the energy of all the movement. I went to spin class with Fran once and it felt a lot like this. My sneakers are sticky on the floor but nothing will stop me dancing now.

March has tied the yellow tracksuit top she was given around her waist and she's wearing a white vest underneath. I notice the shine on her shoulders as she moves under the light. Her eyes close and her face turns up to the ceiling. The tiny muscles around her eyes flex like she's feeling every beat and she mouths the words along with the music. I close my eyes and tilt my head up too, feeling the bass throb up from the floor. That's when her fingers take my hand and she raises our arms in the air. Either we've magically become actors or we really are under some kind of

273

spell. We face the DJ now, moving forward and back, up and down together; then we're opposite each other, swaying as the beat changes. She turns to me, stepping so close that our bodies touch all the way down, chest against chest. My stomach flips as we whirl around together, each of us with one hand held aloft, her black eyes staring into mine.

I look down at her half-open mouth, watching the space between her teeth, my head filling with thoughts of how it would feel to touch her lips. I blush, praying that my face is already too red for anyone to notice under the lights. I go to say something, anything to stop me thinking like this, but her breath brushes against my ear. I'm expecting her voice. I'm waiting for words, when her cheek lands softly on mine. We couldn't be any closer. There's no distance, she's right there, and as I breathe in the faint peppermint of her gum our mouths meet. I hold my lips closed, concentrating on the warm rush rising up from the lowest part of me, and I shut my eyes to feel it more. We move together slowly and I'm burning, melting, entirely in my body, like I've finally worked out how to widen the aperture and slow the shutter speed down, stretching out time and blurring it into something extraordinary. I open my mouth and her tongue lightly scoops the space inside. Then, as one of her hands lands on my waist and the other pushes against my hair, a wave crashes inside my chest, drenching every part of me. This is a kiss. This is what it feels like.

My heart fills, swelling like an airship this time. Nothing about what we're doing makes sense and yet it feels so right. I try to stop the thoughts twirling behind my eyes as I kiss her back, trying to focus only on the pressure as she pushes up against me and we kiss and we kiss and we kiss. I want to feel this so badly and I'm wondering whether real life could ever be like this, when the music stops and March slowly pulls away. She's less than a step from me but I miss the feel of her already. It takes a few seconds for my eyes to focus and when they do I see that hers are clear again.

"That's a wrap, everybody!" The first AD shouts and she keeps talking, saying more stuff, but the volume inside my head has been turned down and everything around us falls away.

We sit side by side on the train.

The car is packed and March is chatting on like nothing has changed. Nothing's changed except there's an octopus swimming around my insides. My lips still tingle where she kissed them, but while she looks calm and composed, I'm almost breathless with a longing I never asked for. March is my friend and I don't want to feel like this. I don't know what to do with the energy in my legs. Maybe I should get up and run?

March closes her mouth mid-sentence and turns to face me. "You're not even listening, are you?" she says. I'm afraid to look up in case she reads the panic in my eyes. Should I worry about the trouble I'm in or simply enjoy the fluttery lightness in my chest? "S'alright," she says then, placing a warm hand on my knee.

What the hell have we done? What have I done to Pez's heart, and to my own? She shuffles in. "You okay?" she says. I smell that peppermint again; it's mixed with vanilla and a pain starts between my legs, crawling up under my ribs. It's all so much more than I want to feel but it isn't a choice.

I shift around on my seat, moving my backpack between my legs. "I think it's best we don't say anything to anyone about—"

She laughs. "The kiss!" she says, like it was a joke, and it stings.

"I mean it," I whisper. "Can we keep it to ourselves?"

"Course," she says, swinging her knees to the side to let someone pass. "And relax. It was fun to pretend for a bit but it's not like it was a big deal."

The train pulls out of Hampstead Heath station and I look away, out of the far window, sliding my palms down my skirt as traffic and high-rises pass in a blur. I feel her look at me a number of times, but we don't say much for the rest of the journey and when we pull into Kentish Town West, I grab my backpack and quickly push up off the seat. "Well, see you."

For some reason, she stands too. "We could get ready together tomorrow night?"

"I told Pez I'd call for him on the way." My words tremble but if she notices she lets it pass.

"Okay," she says, smiling. "I'll come to yours and then you'll be there when I see Pez again, so it'll be . . . easier."

"Cool." I grin back as hard as I can. "Sounds like fun."

The flat looks empty when I walk in but the door to the yard is open and I head on through the living room toward it. I stop by the open door, staring outside and blinking into the sun. Pez is sitting on the wall beside the silk tree, wearing one of his old baseball caps, watching Arial do front and back walkovers on a wooden railroad tie that's been turned on its side. Pez sees me and lifts his hand off his thigh in a wave but I can't look at him yet, knowing what I've just done, and I walk toward Arial.

"Vetty!" she says, pulling herself vertical. "Look, my very own beam!" She claps her hands together. "Pez carried it over from his yard all by himself." She's standing by my feet, waiting for me to say something, but my conscience has swallowed my vocal cords.

Pez jumps off the wall. "A superstar, isn't she?" I open my mouth, but no words come out. Arial cartwheels off but Pez steps closer, moving me back off the grass. "What's up with you?" he whispers.

"I'm fine," I say. "And the beam's awesome." When I look up he's making that face. The one that says *I know you really stole those Haribo, Helvetica*, and I slump down onto the wall in the shade.

After a long minute he walks inside. I stand up and follow him. "I've gotta run," he says, grabbing his backpack. "I'm having a chat with Mum."

"Wait!" I say and he turns back. "You mean, *the* chat?"

He shrugs. "Let's see," he says, but then he tilts his head, looking right at me, sunlight from the yard making his eyes tight. "Eleven in *Stranger Things* called it," he says. "Because *friends don't lie*." Then he walks off to the hall door.

I'm too stunned to say anything, and he's gone before I can wish him luck.

★ ★ ★

My eyes latch on to a fine crack in the plaster above my bed. It's after midnight but I can't sleep. I open my laptop and type "BISEXUAL" into Google. 194,000,000 results in 0.93 seconds. *Okay . . .*

I scan the Wikipedia definition—sexually attracted to both men and women—tick. I then move on to articles underneath that talk about definitions and advice and dos and don'ts and coming-out tips, until I land on an "Am I Bisexual?" quiz and even though I know the answer I click on it and start scrolling through the simple questions, taking care to be as honest as I can.

Result: Sounds like you might be bisexual!

SHARE YOUR RESULT

SHARE

TWEET

You're open to dating and/or having sex with either gender. Continue exploring and discovering what you're comfortable with . . . It doesn't have to look the same for every person you're attracted to. If you're ready, check out how to come out to friends and family.

Oh really? Ya think!

Share your result? I laugh out loud. Yeah, that's the trickier part, isn't it? Then I sit up and lean against the window, peering out into the night. It's completely dark. Nothing stirs apart from Old Giles's gray cat, who is prowling along Pez's front wall. I watch her slink around a streetlight then curl herself up against the black pole of the residents' parking sign, wrapping and unwrapping her tail, writhing in some mysterious pleasure. It's her usual sultry show.

I push away from the window and sit on the edge of the bed, trying to shake the restlessness from my limbs. I stare at my T-shirt and bare legs in the half light, listening for sounds that aren't there: no hum of pipes, no creaks or slow footsteps above my head. The flat is quiet, soft, silent. Then I think about tomorrow night and I try to think about seeing Rob and the prospect of kissing him again. I focus on the smell of coconut shower gel as he leaned against me on the couch. I'm concentrating hard but all I get is Doritos, and then in my mouth I taste peppermint and my head fills with vanilla and I know that although I'm attracted to him, the connection is nothing like it is with March. I didn't need to take a quiz to know this is real. I can't stop thinking about how it felt to kiss her.

I run my hands down my belly and under the elastic rim of my underwear, watching my face as my fingers search the space between my legs. Whatever I'm doing feels good and soon I'm not thinking at all. A rushing sensation starts somewhere deep inside me, close to my stomach, and it's intense and new, so new I dash to my door, and even though everyone is asleep, I lock it. I pull my underwear down and tip onto my knees, moving my fingers in small circles until I'm only my body, allowing my mind into places I've never really let it linger in before.

Soon I'm sweaty and dizzy and I throw my head back as my body writhes and twists, but I don't stop. I'm sure I'm about to pee or die or something because the sensation is there and everywhere, building and building until finally

I'm creased double, frozen, hand slammed against the mirror. Every little part of me cramped up tight, face twitching, mouth silently open as my hand slides slowly down the glass, just like Kate Winslet's in *Titanic* only mine comes to rest on grubby Minions stickers, but who cares because OH. MY. GOD.

I crawl onto the bed and wait for my breath to settle. When it does, my mind and body are so very still and I lie there for a long time, enjoying how strange it is to feel this calm and excited at once.

30

I lie in bed thinking about last night and I'm awake a good
ten minutes before I reach for my phone. As soon as I do, I
sit up because there on the home screen sits a text from Pez
that I missed last night.

Maybe for the best

That's all it says, so I swipe across, finding the earlier
messages he sent too.

Mum went out
Our "chat" never happened
Maybe for the best

I drop the phone onto the bed. *Jesus, Luna!* How can it
be so hard for her to see that Pez is reaching out? I'd try
talking to her, only that could upset Pez and it's not my
place. And she's Luna Boyd after all. I text back something
as supportive as my guilty conscience will allow.

Then I drag myself up, staring at my face in the mirror,
turning it from side to side, searching for something that

wasn't there yesterday. Some sort of sign. I move forward and back to check, but no; still the same heart-shaped face with wonky bushy brows I went to bed with. I haven't changed in the night but I still take Pez's camera from the shelf and hold it to my eye, examining myself in the mirror from behind the lens, hoping it might see something I don't.

I hold myself straight and take in my reflection. It's been a while since I've looked at myself half-naked like this. I mean *really* looked, at all of me. I adjust the light and then focus on how my right shoulder sits higher up than the left, then I catch the new roundness to my hips and then snap some images of the hairs on my thighs catching the sunlight like tiny flecks of spun gold. Then I set the timer and position the camera on a high shelf so it might catch me in profile as I stare at my reflection. Just a photo of me, for me, and I stand and wait but I don't know how long it's auto-set for and then, as I turn to check why nothing has happened—FLASH! It catches me looking right at the lens.

I shuffle into the kitchen, where Dad and Arial are at the counter, already dressed. "Here she is," Dad says, jangling his car keys.

I check the clock on the microwave: 9:18. "It's Saturday, right?"

Arial jumps down. "Emergency food shop," she says. "There's literally NOTHING to eat."

It's not the first time this has happened since we moved back. I look to Dad, who is by the recycling, shuffling through junk mail like he doesn't want to think about whose job this really is either. "Five minutes," I shout out. "I need to jump in the shower."

Of course, everyone in Camden Town is doing their weekly shopping this morning and traffic is backed up in the fruit aisle. Arial flees down the hard shoulder on a quest for bananas while Dad waddles along beside me looking lost. "D'you have the list?" he says, eyes ahead.

I stop pushing. "I'm supposed to write the list too?"

"Just asking," he says, slinging a bag of apples inside our cart. I spot a gap by the potatoes and tell Dad I'll cover the dairy aisle if he finishes off the vegetables. It's too cold to sulk among the yogurts for long so I head off in search of bread, cookies, or the warmth of some comforting carbohydrate. I stomp along, wondering how the highs of my early hours could have crash-landed so quickly. I see Dad holding a bunch of carrots and a sack of potatoes as I pass the detergents, but I wheel on by, slinking into the cereal aisle for more alone time. I'm happily comparing the prices of mueslis when Arial skids up and tips a ton of brightly packaged crap from her arms into the vast cavity of our cart. Then she turns her head in wait while I lean over and rummage through her stuff. I hold up a four-pack of Snickers YoCrunch and some string cheese.

"Please, please, please!" she says, hands clasped.

I let them drop and quickly fish out the variety pack of cereals she's just swept from a nearby shelf. "Put these back," I say, handing them to her.

She climbs on the front and leans over the cart. "Why?"

"Because I've already got Raisin Bran . . . and Cheerios."

"C'mon, Vee!"

"They're full of sugar," I say, pointing to the shelf they came from.

She jumps down. "You say no to everything." She says it under her breath.

I jerk the cart toward me. "Um, no, I don't."

Her eyes squint and her chin juts forward. "Yeah, you do," she says. "Even Mum would've said yes *sometimes*." Then she storms off, passing Dad, who is standing at the end of the aisle like an apparition.

He walks toward me and drops the vegetables and some toilet paper into the cart; then he checks my eyes, looking at me questioningly. I go to say something about how unfair everything is but my lip quivers and I turn away. "Hey," he says, squaring my shoulders back to face him.

"She thinks I'm mean but I'm not." My voice shakes. "And she's in my face the whole time, asking questions."

I feel his arm around me. "You had your own questions at that age, far as I recall."

My eyes fill up. "She expects me to know *everything*! But I don't." My legs turn to jelly and I collapse down into a gap in the Crunchy Nut boxes on the bottom shelf. "And . . . I miss Mum." I whisper it as warm tears stream down my face.

Dad slides the Frosted Flakes boxes along, plunking himself down beside me, and the shelf buckles under his weight. "Me too." He wipes his eye as he says this and if it's possible this makes me feel worse. "But Mum didn't have all the answers either. None of us do."

I snort. "That's comforting."

"Look," he says. "I don't need to tell you how much I'm

284

winging it as a dad. A lot of the time, I haven't got a clue. I told Wendy last week that I'm afraid I'm getting worse."

I shoot him a look. "What did she say?"

He snorts. "Stuff about you girls growing up and your needs changing. It was very sensible and Wendy-like, but the bottom line is, I'm your dad and Arial's your sister. It's not up to you to parent her. Somewhat terrifyingly, that's my job."

I almost smile. "It's not that I mind her asking me that . . . stuff—" I take a huge, rickety breath. "I just wish I was better at it. I wish I could be more like Mum."

He shuffles along and leans his shoulder into mine. "You are," he says. "More than you know." Then he squeezes my knee. "Ever wonder why she loved fonts so much?"

I shrug. "No."

"She aspired to their neatness and their order. She loved them because they were everything she wasn't. Remember her handwriting? Illegible, right?" It's true. It was, and I sweep at my nose with my sleeve, bobbing my head up and down. "Real life," he says, "is crazy and messy and brilliant, like your mother and like you." He looks into my eyes and sighs. "Let's just try to be there for Arial," he says. "Thankfully, I think she wants that more than she wants answers." I try to smile but I'm so choked up my face can't do it. "And for what it's worth," he says, taking my hand, "you're doing a wonderful job."

I'm drying my hair in my barely recognizable bedroom, flipping through photos on the camera, when Dad knocks. "Want me to put out some snacks for when your friends come over?"

I frown. "Snacks?"

"We've got those Ritz crackers, or maybe some . . . chips?"

"Seriously, Dad?" I almost laugh, but his eyes are so soft, like he really is just trying to be nice.

Then he shoves his hands into his jeans pockets and looks around. "Well, it seems like you found the vacuum anyway," he says, backing out the door.

I return to the camera and the wonky self-portrait I took earlier is there. At first I disliked how startled I look, and I almost deleted it, but the blurry deer-in-the-headlights thing is kind of growing on me. The doorbell goes. I leap up to answer it but Arial gets there first.

"It's Pez!" she screams.

I walk out and drag him back into my room, where he circles, staring at the photos I've stuck up on my wall. Finally, he sits, but it's a while before he speaks. "How long before they get here?"

I'm looking for leggings in an overstuffed drawer. "March said they'd come over around eight."

"It's after quarter to!"

I stop tugging. "Ohmygod, relax."

"I'm nervous about seeing her, that's all," he says, standing again.

"Thought you both decided not to be together for a while?"

"Yeah," he says, staring at an old photo of Mum. "But the last time I saw her . . . well, you remember. I left her on Rob's bed half-dressed before bolting out the door. It's not an easy one to come back from."

"No, guess not. Sorry," I say, yanking a top over my head. Pez slots his phone into my speaker dock and starts scrolling. "Don't suppose you've managed to have that chat with Luna?"

He shrugs. "She starts night shoots tonight, so she slept late."

"But you told her you wanted to talk?"

His head drops. "Not in so many words." Then he slumps against the wall. "You sure it's a good idea for me to come out tonight?"

"Yeah," I say. "Everything's okay with you and March, isn't it?"

He nods. "I mean, she wanted to know where she stands, which I get, but she didn't push me." He looks down at his shoes again. "She's a bit special, is the truth."

"She is." As soon as I've said it he looks up at me and in that moment I have the strangest feeling, like he senses how much March means to me too. I turn to the mirror and start lining up makeup brushes.

"It's the others though, you know?"

"You mean Rob, Kyle—"

"All of them," he says. "I'm afraid it'll come up and I'm not prepared for how to handle it."

I pop my mascara wand back into the tube and turn around. "March was the only one you owed an explanation to and that's sorted, so you don't need to worry. I think the rest of them will just be happy to see you."

He sighs, looking at me full force. "What did I do without you?" he says, stooping to lean his forehead on my shoulder. "Actually, don't answer that," he adds, standing straight again. "Less said about it the better."

I return to the mirror, trying to scrape my hair up, but it's all bumpy.

"So," he says after a while. "Have you been speaking with Rob?"

I give up on the high pony and try it down with a severe middle part. "Said we'd see him there."

"You know what I mean," he says. "What's going on there?"

I turn back. "He asked me to come over to his house on Thursday night."

"And?"

"It was Mum's anniversary and—"

"It's not like Rob to have girls over to his place. Maybe he actually likes you."

"What's that supposed to mean?"

"Sorry for being cynical," he says, "but the bloke's not known for developing *feelings*. Would you have gone if it was a different night?"

I sit down to think about this. Maybe I would have but after everything that's happened in the past forty-eight hours, it's obvious that whatever I feel for Rob doesn't compare to the connection I have with March.

"Probably not . . ." I say, trailing off. Then I pick up a lipstick, and as I open and close the lid it seems so clear that I must end whatever it is I've kind of started with Rob. I know in my heart it's right but I'm nervous about how to do this when whatever it is we're doing seems so casual.

I'm trying on the new lipstick when Arial knocks at the door. "Your friends are here!" she shouts.

I turn to Pez. "Okay?" I say, and he nods. "I've got your back. Got mine?"

"Always," he says.

I drag him up off the bed with one hand. "Right," I say, grabbing my bag with the other. "Let's do this."

31

Arial is circling March and Amira, studying them like exhibits in a museum, not even pretending to be discreet. She sees me and Pez and she gives us the equivalent of a thumbs-up with only her eyes. It's quite something. I walk over and hug them both quickly, but Pez hangs back, holding up his hand in a small wave. I spin back to Arial, who is still watching us. "I see you've met my little sister." Arial waves at them again and soon Dad is up from the couch before I can stop him. "And this"—he's already shaking their hands—"is my dad." I think about being embarrassed but I have too many other things on my mind. Besides, March and Amira are being so nice I quickly push his cringy enthusiasm out of my head. "C'mon," I say, tugging on March's jacket. "Let's get out of here."

Outside, Pez unlocks his bike from the gate and wheels it up ahead to the road. March follows him and I watch from a few strides behind as they fall into step. She's on the right, wearing a Supreme hoodie she told me was fake over a minidress and she looks comfy and casual. He's on the left, jeans low and high-tops fresh like always. Still, I can't help but notice their movements and how different they are from the first time I saw them together by the canal. Pez's swagger has long gone and March's steps have changed to a different pace and watching them now I see that the envy I first felt wasn't jealousy over Pez, as I wanted to believe, but a pull toward her. At the junction with Camden Road, he shifts his bike around to the other side so it's no longer between them and he walks on, wheeling it along with his left hand. Their voices are soft and it's impossible not to see the tenderness between them.

"Here," Amira says, pulling a bottle of Smirnoff out of her bag. "Let's have some of this." She stops and cracks the cap. "I bought it for the party next week, but then, why wait?" She checks my face, then lifts the bottle to her mouth. "*Ughh . . .*" she says, grimacing as the vodka goes down. Then she nods up at March. "See, she's not taking any chances."

I turn to her. "Huh?"

Amira laughs. "If that dress doesn't get him back, let's check his pulse."

I try to laugh too but it tumbles out awkwardly. "I'm not sure it's like that," I say, but she looks at me like I've lost it.

We walk behind them the rest of the way, taking small swigs from her bottle in turn. I'm neither drunk nor sober but my mind begins to speed, everything inside and around me going that bit faster. Once we reach the bridge at Chalk Farm Amira breaks into a run, but as soon as we hit Regent's Park Road my breath catches and I have to slow down. Last time I was on this street was with Mum and the memory pushes up against my chest.

I force my feet to move and Pez turns back and wheels up beside me, trailing along slowly, like he knows. We walk

290

on in silence; the shops with their striped awnings and window displays are as charming as I remember. Night is falling and the lights inside the tall white houses are starting to come on. Pubs and cafés line the road all the way to the park and the tables outside are filled with well-dressed people enjoying the last of the evening sun. Even the dogs around here look pleased with themselves.

Outside the newsstand Amira hands me her bag. "I can't drink any more of that straight. It's poison," she says, before disappearing into the bright light behind her. March bounces on the step outside, telling Pez all about the film set. She's in full flight and he wheels back and forth, drinking in her every word.

My mind wanders back to that day when I was here with Mum. It was cold, December maybe, and we sat in the window of that café by the butcher. Mum hadn't yet told me that she was sick, but that was probably why I was allowed to have hot chocolate *and* apple pie after my lunch. We'd recently watched that movie, *Amélie*, together, the one about the lonely but kindhearted waitress in Paris, and I'd cut myself bangs like hers and had taken to speaking with a not-so-slight French accent. As I breathily ordered my tuna *sahn-weech*, Mum looked on smiling. Rather than being embarrassed by my odd behavior, it was like she enjoyed it. She never minded stuff like that. She let me be me.

Amira reappears with a liter bottle of Fanta under her arm and soon everyone's bounding on toward the park, but my feet are still slow, like they're stuck to the pavement. We pass the Greek restaurant and I catch the eye of a young girl as her mum pours her lemonade. I stare through the window at her—*grab her hand and never let it go*—and try to laser-beam the words through the glass as I pass by. The others have already reached the gates and I have to run to catch up, wriggling through the liquor-store crowd and dodging their swollen bags, heavy with cans. Inside the park, clusters of horizontal bodies cover the hill.

Ahead, farther up, Pez and March chat away, her head briefly leaning on his shoulder. My heart surges—pleased for him and yet still wishing it could be my head on her shoulder or her head on mine. Is there a word for feeling this anxious but happy at the same time?

When I reach the summit, Amira is dialing Nick, so I turn around to take in the view: all of London stretched into one incredible skyline, and my spine tingles at the sight. It's impossible not to marvel at the shapes and spikes rising up out of the waning light and I pick out the Shard, the BT Tower, St. Paul's, and the London Eye. I feel calmer up here, steadier.

"I *am* waving!" Amira says. "Stand up so I can see you."

I look down the far side and Nick appears amid a large crowd of bodies halfway down the hill, holding his phone to his ear. He moves out to the edge and we amble toward him. He leans in and gives us both a hug and this feels good. We sit down on the grass, huddled together as some lazy-sounding hip-hop thuds the ground underneath us. Lucas raises his can and even Kyle smiles. Then I spot Rob, farther off, pushing himself up and quickly moving toward us.

"A bit late," he says, smiling. "But look, boys, she's here." He looks pleased to see me but as he gets closer I smell beer mixed with some kind of aftershave and I'm suddenly disappointed to see he's wasted already. I don't want to be with him. I feel this so strongly and I don't know how I should act around him now.

"Hey," I say, nodding at his can. "Started early?"

He plunks himself down. "Why not?"

March screams somewhere close by. She's riding Pez's bike as he follows on foot behind. She's hurtling toward us but she sticks her feet out just in time.

"I can't believe we got this dressed up to sit on the grass," she says, climbing off the bike and pulling down the end of her dress.

Kyle takes her in. "Your efforts weren't wasted."

March dummy-kicks his back before working her way around the group, hugging everyone as she goes. Eventually she settles down beside Pez, who is kneeling a little farther up and slapping hands with Nick. I notice he hasn't come over to give Rob his usual handshake, but they share a small nod, which might be enough. Lucas shuffles in and everyone follows suit and soon we're all sitting in a messy circle with Amira in the middle.

"Dig in!" she says, lining up bottles and snacks from her bag and placing them in the center. Then she starts chatting to Nick, while Lucas does impressions for Pez and Kyle, and March, who sits opposite them, tosses her head back laughing. Pez catches me looking and I know by the tiny squeeze of his eyes that he feels at ease, almost happy, and my shoulders sink with something like relief. At least I did the right thing convincing him to come out.

Then Rob sidles up to me, landing a tiny kiss on my ear, and I quickly turn around.

"What's up?" he says, tousled hair high off his face and his pale brow shining with sweat.

I shake my head. "Nothing, just—" How do I play this? I can't tell him it's over with us before it's begun, and not HERE, but it doesn't feel right to go along like I'm into it either.

Thankfully I hear March just in time. "How about that game, Vetty," she says, clapping her hands. "The one we played on the bus last week."

I swing back into the center of the group. "Two truths and a lie?"

She bounces on her knees. "That's it!" she says, turning to the others. "So, we all take turns to say three things about ourselves, one of which is a lie."

Lucas looks confused. "Then what?"

"The others have to guess which one isn't true. But only one guess."

Kyle looks up. "Is this a drinking game?"

"Why not?" she says, taking Pez's Mars Milk and Lucas's beer and straightening them against Amira's bottle of vodka in the middle. "Whoever gets it right first has a turn next and the rest of you must drink! Who's in? Raise your hands," she says. As her wrists twist, her glittery nails sparkle in the half dark. Lucas pumps his arm into the air and Kyle follows suit. Amira claps her hands and Rob, Nick, and Pez smile like they're up for it. "All right," March says excitedly, and everyone huddles in close. "Shall I kick things off, so you get the idea?"

"Just start already," says Rob.

"Behave," she says, firing him a look; then she takes a breath and stares up, thinking. "So, I've . . . never read a

Harry Potter book, I did violin up to Grade Five, and I'm allergic to fish."

Amira spins around. "Everyone's read Harry Potter."

March shoves her. "So, that's your answer?"

"Yeah!" Amira says, laughing. "That's my answer."

"I'm calling violin," says Nick, and March drums her hands on her thighs, eyeballing the rest of us in turn.

"Harry Potter!" Lucas shouts out.

She looks to Pez, eyes soft. "Well?" she says.

He stares at her like he's really thinking. I know that look so well. "I've seen your old violin," he says. Her eyebrows rise and I suddenly remember her spicy seafood dish at the Korean place in Chinatown.

"The fish is the lie!" I shout it out.

She clicks her fingers and squints at me in a way that makes my cheeks burn. "Bingo!" she says. "I knew Vetty would get it." Then she winks. "The rest of you must drink!" she says, lifting her legs, and her feet do a dance on the grass.

"C'mon, let's keep it moving," Amira shouts.

March looks around the circle. "Vetty, you won, so it should be your turn."

I sit on my fists. "Um . . . okay," I say. "So, I can . . . do a cartwheel one-handed, I've never broken a bone, and I own an autographed LA Dodgers baseball shirt with my name on the back."

Everyone screws up their faces. Everyone except Pez, that is. "Easy," he says.

"Not for everyone," I say, sticking my tongue out at him, and he pouts back and the childish ridiculousness of this moment makes my insides feel all warm. Rob tries to push in closer like he somehow notices whatever is passing between me and Pez, but there genuinely isn't much room and he's left sitting slightly on the edge.

"My cousin carries an EpiPen because of her nut allergy," Lucas says.

"Keep up, man," says Nick. "We've moved on."

"Oh, right," Lucas says, taking another sip, then sitting up.

"Cartwheel," Rob shouts. "But I'm only saying this so you have to prove me wrong." Then he makes a suggestive face that's kind of hilarious.

"Yeah, cartwheel!" says Nick.

Amira bounces up too. "Cartwheel!"

"K, cartwheel!" says March.

"So, you're all saying cartwheel?"

"Except me!" shouts Pez.

"Well, maybe you should be disqualified on grounds of inside information." When I look up Kyle is shaking his head. "Broken bones," he says, and everyone turns to him. "That's the lie." From his tone, it's like he's talking about something else.

Rob muscles in, turning his back on Kyle. "Well?" Rob says, waving his hand over my face. "Which is it?"

"Actually, Kyle's right," I say, "and Pez would have been too. I broke my arm when I was ten." Everyone reaches in for drinks. Nick swigs from the vodka first and Lucas guzzles a beer, finishing one bottle before opening another. Kyle slinks back onto the grass and cracks a fresh can.

"Well, I need to see this one-handed cartwheel to believe it," Rob says, eyeing me like it's a dare. For some reason I

296

feel like a challenge and next thing I'm standing, raising both arms high up to the night.

"Do it, do it!" March shouts.

I tilt myself upside down, but the grass is squishier than I expected and the hill even steeper and my other hand lands to take the fall and I collapse into an embarrassing heap. Everyone laughs, even me. "Wait, wait!" I say, righting myself. Going downhill wasn't such a good idea and I raise my arms again in the opposite direction and this attempt works. When I land on my feet, everyone cheers. I sit down, next to March this time. "You were saying, Rob?"

My botched gymnastics display must have ruined whatever was going on with my hair because March leans across and fixes it. "Sort yourself out, love," she says, tucking a loose strand behind my ear. I notice Kyle move in, watching us.

"My go next!" Rob shouts out.

Lucas spins around. "Wait your turn."

"C'mon," says Rob. "I've got a good one."

Kyle dusts off his hands. "My go," he says. "And mine's way better." He reaches for the vodka and takes a long drink, like it's water. "Okay," he says, faltering as he sits back down. "So, I'm color-blind, yeah?" Then he clears his throat. "I've got six toes on my right foot, and I've . . . just taken Rob to the cleaners. Smashed that bet, I did."

Rob crushes his empty can before shoving Kyle hard. "What *is* your problem?"

Kyle sits up. "The bet was to turn her," he says, looking over as March adjusts the strap of my top, which hasn't quite returned to where it started before my cartwheeling exhibit. Her fingers feel suddenly cold on my skin.

Lucas elbows Kyle. "Shut up, man."

Rob flicks a lighter at Kyle's head. "You prick!"

Nick looks up. "What bet?"

"Rob's lesbian challenge," Kyle says, looking at me, and for the first time ever I can see into his eyes, but I don't want to look. "So, Pez told Rob he had no chance with you because you're a lesbian and that, but big Rob here was convinced he could turn you. I was having a laugh. Rob was the one who made it an actual bet."

I stare at Rob, gripping my thighs like I'm in a car that's about to crash. "Is this true?"

Rob looks up from the grass. "Um ... come here," he says quietly, reaching for my arm. I pull back and he rises to his knees, holding up his hands. "Listen, I can explain, yeah?"

I sense Pez stand opposite, but Nick puts his arm out, stopping him. I can't believe this is happening. I swallow. "Go on."

"At the start it was a bet," Rob says. "But then—"

"Are you fucking kidding me?" Pez shouts; then he's up, lurching at Rob. Flecks of saliva fly from Pez's mouth as he pushes Rob back into the grass. "Where's your respect? You sick, twisted prick—"

Rob scuttles backward. "Oh, *I'm* sick and twisted?" he says.

Pez's face hardens; then he closes his eyes for a moment, and when they open, he's squinting. "What's that supposed to mean?"

"It means I'm not taking that from *you*," Rob says, grinding the words with his teeth as he tries to sit up. "The guy who watches so much fucked-up porn his mum calls me up, crying because she's afraid her son's a pervert." I freeze. Nobody moves, except Rob, who has managed to pull himself up to his knees again. His demented-looking eyes move around the circle before stopping on March. "It's time you knew what he's really like and what he expects of you," he says, before turning to me with both his hands up. "And Vetty," he says. "How d'you feel about him spending so much time alone with your little sister now? Doesn't feel right, does it? Because Pez isn't right." I glare back at him, rage ricocheting around my rib cage. This crop top's too tight suddenly and I'm like the Hulk about to burst from his shirt. The more I stare at Rob the more I swell with anger. I don't know what words to use first, but I refuse to look away until my gaze has scorched him through. Everything blurs. There's so much to say my tongue thickens and I can't speak.

Out of the corner of my eye, I see Pez lift his bike from the grass.

"Wait," Lucas shouts, jumping up. "Wait!" he cries, but Pez is already wheeling his bike down the hill.

I stand up and scan the path below, but Pez has disappeared in the dark. I scoop my backpack off the ground and swing it at Rob, who ducks, but I swing again, connecting with his shoulder this time, hitting him hard. "How dare you!" I shout it out, backing away before I turn to run up the hill, scrambling all the way to the top, where my eyes frantically search the shadows below. I finally make out Pez, weaving through a group of girls who walk along the path holding hands, and now he's mounting his bike.

I sprint down the hill and I don't stop until I've almost

reached the park gates, hoping I'll intercept him there. Here I am, chasing him again, but it really is all my fault this time. I convinced him to come out. I told him it would be okay, but everything has blown up in the worst way possible. Afraid he'll turn back if he sees me, I stand under a tree, ears cocked, waiting for the delicate thrum of his spokes in the dark. My brain thumps between my ears, my heart too. I look around to see his BMX speeding toward me and my feet step out onto the path, my arms spread wide, knowing he'll have to stop. I'm so sure, I close my eyes, imagining myself back on those pegs, my arms around his shoulders, me, tall like the BT Tower as he steers us through the streets. I'm even feeling the heat as I lean into his back and that's when the soft tick of his wheels gets close for real and my eyes ping open. He's zooming toward me, red hoodie zipped to his chin, but he doesn't stop and just like Elliott in *E.T.* he soars up and up. My eyes clamp shut and wheels skid and screech and . . . thud!

Silence.

A terrible

black

hole

of absolute quiet.

An alarm is sounding, loud and close. Too close. I look up and before my feet have a chance to move my heart lurches toward a large blue car, stopped in the middle of the road. My hands slap against the cold glass of its window, behind which long hair lies tossed over an inflated airbag. Inside, a woman's head lifts in slow motion, but I don't wait to see her face. My hands swat along the side of the car, to the hood, then to the road, where one of Pez's long, red arms is thrown out wide. My legs crumple and I drop to my knees, reaching for him, but my hand falls short on the warm black tarmac.

Half of him lies hidden under the car and the other half looks up at the night. One eye's closed, an eyebrow arched in surprise, but his throat is loose and relaxed, peaceful almost, as a tiny trail of blood trickles from the side of his mouth. For a moment, it's like I'm not crouched here on the road; I'm up in the sky staring down at the car like it's a swimming pool I see from an airplane window and I see myself, leaning in, as if this will reveal the other half of his body, the side that's hidden. It's not all of him. I place my hand on his cheek.

"I didn't see him," a woman's voice cries. "I didn't see him," she repeats. "He came from nowhere. I've called an ambulance."

His boyish wrist peeks out from the end of his sleeve and I rest two fingers where his hand meets his arm. *Please, Pez, we can't be separated again. Please!* I don't know or care if I'm talking out loud as I press down deeper on his skin, closing my eyes. When I feel the gentle throb underneath I raise his heavy hand in mine and lift it to my wet cheek.

PART FIVE

It's always darkest before the dawn

32

The ambulance doors slam and when we start to move my eyes clamp shut. The light inside is so bright it hurts and it's easier to concentrate on what the paramedic is saying when I can't see all the terrifying things around me.

"Pre-alert the ICU," he shouts into the front. "Sixteen-year-old male, high-energy injuries to his left-hand side. Altered consciousness. Abnormal work of breathing." My eyes open at this and I stare at Pez lying strapped to a stretcher, completely still, his face pale and lips tinged blue. The paramedic leans over him, hands quick, as more words fire fast from his mouth. "Low oxygen saturation. Reduced breath sounds. Hemodynamically unstable." He glances at the small watch attached to his breast pocket. "ETA 23:56," he says, covering Pez's mouth and nose with an oxygen mask, which is hooked up to a stand with a small airbag above it. The bag expands and contracts in sync with Pez's breathing but his chest heaves faster and faster, as though he can't get enough of what's inside.

"He can't breathe properly. Can he? Can he breathe?" The questions sputter from my mouth.

The paramedic turns his face to mine without speaking and I see by the tiny movement of his lips that he's counting.

"Breathing rate thirty-eight," he says, to whom I'm not sure; then he presses his lips together before opening them again. "I'm Mo," he says, looking at me. "We're doing all we can."

Pez groans like a wounded animal and I spin around. Mo does too and I follow the wires surrounding Pez's face and body, trying to make sense of where they all lead.

"This one is monitoring his heart," Mo says. I nod, concentrating on the beeps I hear, but each sound seems to follow the last too quick, and I can't tell which thumps are my own and which beat through the machine that Pez is connected to. Our hearts are tangled and I curse myself for treating them both so recklessly.

Mo drags Pez's eyelids up one by one, shining a tiny flashlight inside and flooding them with light. "Has he taken any drugs?" he asks, shooting me a quick look. I shake my head. "Alcohol?"

"No," I say, wishing away the taste of the vodka lingering in my own mouth.

"Any allergies?"

"No."

"Is he on any medication?"

Mo's questions come quick but I'm almost as fast. "No. Don't think so."

"Next of kin?" My mouth opens but I stop. His head tilts. "Please," he says. "Your friend is sixteen. We'll need an adult to communicate on his behalf."

I swallow down the lump in my throat. "His mum, but she's working." I stumble on the words.

"Is his dad at home?" I shake my head. "Then I need Mum's number."

I slide Pez's phone from the pocket of his hoodie. I find Luna under "Mum" and I hold out the phone.

"His mum is Luna Boyd." I feel like a dick for pointing this out, like Luna's fame is remotely relevant now, but I want to warn Mo that she might not answer because of it. His eyes widen the teensiest bit but his fingers continue ripping open the packet of a very long needle.

"I'm putting in a drip," he says, taking out the shiny syringe, and I watch as a drop of Pez's blood leaks onto the spotless white gauze. Mo scans the various machines then lifts his head, leaning into the front of the ambulance again. "No response but no deterioration with fluids," he says. "Blood pressure still low."

Oh god, please, please let him be okay.

Please, god.

Please.

We leave a dark parking lot and burst into a hallway of holy hospital light. Mo and the other paramedic wheel Pez along a corridor and I scuttle after them as doors swing wide behind us and people press themselves to walls as we pass. The journey seems endless but then we come to a sudden stop in the center of a strange room, empty of other beds but teeming with people wearing plastic aprons over what look like blue pajamas. The doctors who treated Mum wore these same blue scrubs and the sight of them wallops me in the gut.

Doctors dive on Pez like he's the accidental star in some TV drama and soon he's hidden by bent blue bodies and I'm left listening as beeps and blips merge with the buzzing inside my pocket and the loud tick of the clock that hangs on the wall. The big hand is minutes from midnight and it strikes me that Pez might not see tomorrow and I stand, stuck to the ground, frozen by this thought, for what could be an eternity or merely seconds because time has instantly lost all meaning.

A warm hand grips my arm. "I'll take you somewhere quiet where you can wait," says a soft voice. An older nurse with kind eyes places the same warm hand on my back and steers me along the corridor outside.

I run my fingertips along the plastic couch as I look around the four small walls the kind nurse called the "relatives' room." There's an identical couch opposite and a wooden table in between. A mug of tea sits half-drunk alongside a mound of tissues, dampened by a stranger's tears. Every sound inside and outside the room makes me jump, so I stand up and pace the floor. Of course, Luna didn't pick up when Mo called but he left her a message and I've followed it up with several of my own. The signal seems patchy down here so Dad said he'd keep trying her. I log on to the hospital Wi-Fi and my messages open to the ones Pez sent last night.

Mum went out
Our "chat" never happened
Maybe for the best

I scroll up and see the shrugging emoji guy I missed this morning.

I keep going, scanning every one of the messages Pez has ever sent me. I go right back to the September after Mum died, a few days after I started my new school. I read, then reread every word he wrote since I moved away, remembering how much I treasured each and every one of his lame jokes and stupid memes. In my head, I answered every one of them, but it's clear from the evidence in my hand that I only answered half. Maybe less. How did I not notice how much harder he worked? How did I not see how much reaching he did when all I did was move further away? How did I not see what was written underneath his words?

My phone screen lights up and my heart leaps but it's from March.

> **Vetty, can't get you. We saw the ambulance. Nick has pez's bike. Tell me you're both OK. xxxxxxxxxxxx**

My thumbs start to move . . .

> **At the hospital waiting for luna. He's . . .** I stop and consider what words to use. **with the doctors**

I hit Send; then I'm thinking about adding a kiss but the door has opened and the kind nurse is standing there framed in the bright light. "How is he?" I ask, springing up.

She steps inside. "He's in critical condition," she says, "but we've got the trauma team consultant here. Any word from his mum yet?"

My eyes drop downward to my unsent kiss. "The reception is bad."

She points to an ancient-looking phone that hangs on the wall. "Give her another try. You can dial straight out."

I walk over and lift the receiver.

33

I hear Luna's voice before I see her. I drag back the heavy door to the relatives' room and she's standing in the corridor wearing a smart navy suit, opposite a woman I haven't seen before in blue scrubs. Luna somehow senses me there and reaches her left hand toward me without taking her eyes off the woman in front. I stare at her outstretched fingers, but something stops me from taking them and her arm falls back by her side.

"We're worried about his breathing," the woman, who I've worked out is the trauma consultant, says. "He has a hemopneumothorax: a collapsed lung with blood in it, basically. He's lost a lot of blood and we need to do a CT scan to see where he's bleeding from, whether we can stop it, and why he's unconscious."

With the same rejected hand Luna grips the consultant's arm. "But he's going to be okay?" she asks as both of us step closer.

The consultant edges back, tapping Luna's wrist. "We put a large drain into his left lung and this has stabilized his breathing for the moment but he also has free fluid in his abdomen." A deep sigh follows and I don't like how long she's taking to choose her words. "A bleed can be life-threatening," she says, "unless we identify the source and stop it." She moves toward the relatives' room and pushes open the door. "Have a seat," she says with a tight smile. "I'll update you straight after the scan." Then the door shuts and her footsteps move briskly off.

I'm awake in my worst nightmare.

Luna sits briefly on the plastic couch and then stands again. I'm waiting for a barrage of her questions but she paces the room with her hand against her mouth. Finally, she sits and stays seated but she still doesn't speak and the only sound is her polished nails drumming the seat beside her.

I turn my face to the wall, heart aching for all the stuff I didn't say to Pez while I still could.

Luna clears her throat and I look over, noticing for the first time the lanyard around her neck, and I squint to read *Detective Rebecca Riley* printed across the front; it's the name of the character she plays in *Darkzone*. Pez is having his brain scanned, his stomach is full of blood, but then perhaps this could as easily be a scene from a TV program that Luna is acting in, for work.

Then, like she's suddenly remembered her lines, her mouth opens. "How did he seem?" she says. "You know, before it happened?"

I examine her eyes, trying to work out whether she wants the truth or whether it even matters what she wants. Heat burns up my insides.

"Scared," I say eventually, and she sits up, repeating the word like it's foreign. "He didn't want to come out tonight

311

but I told him everything would be fine. I should have seen it."

She leans farther forward, tiny lines crinkling the sides of her eyes. "Seen what?"

"How fragile he was—" I stop and cover my face with my hands because I don't know how to say what needs to be said without destroying her.

"Please," she says, voice trembling. "I need your help to piece all this together."

I let my hands drop. "It's him we need to piece together," I say, looking at her. "Haven't you noticed how sad he is sometimes?"

Her brow furrows. "Yes," she whispers. "I have."

"Well, it's like . . ."

"Go on," she says, tugging at my words like she sees there's more.

I stare at the *Darkzone* ID, which has settled in the crease of her lap. "It's like he got stuck playing the one role," I say. "Forgetting about the rest of him . . . the Pez who is dreamy and funny and . . . gentle. Like he's forgotten he can still play those parts, and maybe I . . . maybe we forgot too."

She goes to speak but then presses her lips together like she thinks better of it and we both stare at the floor, listening to the fridge endlessly humming its one long electrical note. "I've been concerned about him for a while," she says. "Everything that's been going on with Harland and me . . ." She gnaws on a knuckle on her left hand. "It's been so diffi-cult to get him to talk." She removes a bottle of water from her bag and takes a sip. The bottle is a funny square shape with a pink flower on it, the same as the silk tree in our yard, and I'm suddenly thirsty too. "He's so distant," she says. "And he's online the whole time, lost in his phone or his computer, and I don't know how to reach him or whether he wants me to at all."

I try to drink down her words but they're hard to swallow and soon it's as though I might choke. "But—" I say, shoving the table between us with my knees so I can stand, but the table won't budge. In fact, it appears to be bolted to the floor and I'm left looming over her in a half crouch but for some reason the stupid table's refusal to move makes me more determined. "It's not the internet making Pez distant. He goes online because he's lonely. He goes there to feel better, or not to feel at all."

She sits back into the seat. "But that's not . . ." she says, looking up. "I mean, it's hardly the solution."

Like *now* she's some parenting expert. "No! It doesn't even work, not anymore, but he's had no one to talk to. No one."

Luna's head barely moves but her eyes are latched on to mine as she breathes hard through her nose. Then her eyes fall shut like it's all sinking in, and when she opens them again, they're wet. She takes a tissue from her bag and dabs at them, looking at me for a long time as tears splotch onto the wooden tabletop below us. "I just wish I knew what to do." She whispers it in such a way that I'm certain she's not acting.

"He wanted to talk to you." This comes out a bit too loud and I sit down, lowering my voice. "He's been trying. If you guys do split up, he'll still need you, both of you. Possibly even more."

She places her knuckle to her lips for a long time. "I didn't know where to start. I don't," she says. "I don't know what to say to him sometimes."

"You could just . . . be there?" The words tumble into the space between us and I picture Dad crouched down in the grocery store between the Frosted Flakes and the Crunchy Nut. I look up. "I think that's what he needs more than anything."

Then the door pushes open behind Luna's head, startling us both into standing. "Please sit," the consultant says, perching on the couch beside Luna. "His scan shows four fractured ribs on his left side. These punctured his lung and have torn his spleen." She's watching only Luna. "There's a significant amount of blood inside his abdomen and the only way we can manage that is with emergency surgery to remove his spleen and more blood transfusions. The surgical intensive care teams are managing him now. He'll go to the operating theater tonight."

"His breathing," I say. "Can he breathe?"

She turns to me. "We've got a tube in his left lung and another in his throat," she says. "He is connected to a ventilator, which is helping him along."

Luna starts to sob and the consultant reaches over and places a hand on her knee. "The good news is that there doesn't appear to be a brain injury," she says. "But we're still concerned about the bleeding. It's the priority."

Tears spill from Luna's eyes. "Can I see him?"

The consultant nods. "Yes, briefly," she says. "He won't be able to respond because of the tube and the painkillers but you can talk to him, of course."

Luna stands and I follow the two women out the door, stumbling behind wordlessly along the corridor until we reach the ICU. Luna squirts antibacterial gel into her hands and the consultant tilts her head at me. "Immediate family only, I'm afraid."

Her words are soft but my stomach drops. "But when—"

"Once he's out of intensive care," she says.

Luna reaches her hand out and this time I let her take mine. "Get some sleep. I'll call you as soon as there's news," she says, smoothing down my hair. "And thank you," she says, taking a breath and pulling me close.

I peer inside the glass panel after them and there he is, in the center of the room, lying on a big red mattress, head wedged between two orange blocks with a collar around his neck.

Sleep? Like I could even close my eyes.

34

Within minutes, I'm walking along Euston Road alone, squinting half-dazed at the few people I see and peering up at empty office buildings and motionless cranes that reach high into the sky. It's almost dawn, no longer night and not yet day, and it feels like precious, stolen time. My eyes are a tiny camera with its own aperture and shutter speed, changing the light and playing with depth of field as foreground and background alternately blur and blend before me. Gradually the light wins and geometrical blocks of pink-tinged sky emerge over the British Library as I pass by. With quick blinks the stark lines of St. Pancras sharpen in the new sun. I'm halfway home before I remember to call Dad.

He exhales into the handset after one ring. "Vetty, y'okay? How is he?" he says quickly.

"Still in ICU." My voice catches. "I'm on my way."

"With Luna?" he says.

"No, I'm walking."

The bed creaks. "At this hour? No!" he says. "Not after—" He stops. "Look, wait by reception," he says. "I'll be there in ten minutes."

"I'm almost on York Way." My voice is calm.

"Jesus, Vetty, it's five o'clock in the morning." I picture him sitting up and rubbing his eyes.

"Dad, you can't leave Arial. Besides, it's bright now and I need to walk."

"Okay," he says after a while, softening like he might understand something of the hugeness that happened tonight. "But don't hang up. Okay?"

"Okay."

"Just slide the phone back into your pocket. I'll be here if you need me."

I take a right onto our street from Agar Grove and Dad is standing outside the flat in his old fleece bathrobe. He wraps me in his arms and carries me inside like I'm in a dream. We sit at the kitchen counter, where I drink the hot tea he's made and nibble on cold toast as birds begin to chirp noisily outside the window. We talk about stuff me and Dad never talk about, like all the months when Mum was sick and how much we both hate hospitals. It's almost seven when my head has slowed enough to think of sleep.

"How about we hold off telling Arial, just until we get the call to say that he's out of ICU?" he says.

I kiss his forehead. "Sure," I say, leaving him alone with his coffee. The sound of soft singing stops me as I pass Arial's room. She's obviously got headphones on and she's gloriously off-key. Whatever she's listening to must be turned up loud because she doesn't turn around when I open the door. She's lying on her stomach and I walk over and lie down on my back beside her. She flicks one of her large white headphones away from her ear. "Before you say anything, Dad finished the Cheerios, not me," she says, repositioning her earpiece and singing along more quietly but still blissfully unaware of how everything has changed in the night. She lifts her head and takes in last night's clothes that I'm still wearing. "You wore that exact top yesterday," she says. "That's kinda gross."

My heart tugs. I don't want the ordinariness of her morning to end and I've got a wild, illogical urge to read her a story, to lock us in this moment. I reach for the dog-eared copy of *Anne of Green Gables* on her bedside table but I'm afraid she'll say no, so I pick up *Wow, I'm Amazing!* from underneath and flick through it idly while I work out what to do. It opens to a chapter called "Body Talk" and I shuffle up on the pillow, almost sitting, and scan the page of positive vibes and scribbly diagrams listing the waxing, shaving, plucking, epilating, and hair-removal-cream options, along with pros and cons for each. I clear my throat. Arial stops singing to watch me.

"Because something is written in a book doesn't automatically mean that it's right," I say. She pulls her headphones fully off so they sit around her neck and she peers into my lap. "I mean, these are suggestions, not rules," I say, waving my hand down the page.

She cocks one eyebrow. "Okay . . . ?" she says, dragging the word out long.

"So, when *I'm Amazing!* or whatever talks about ways to shave your legs, it doesn't mean you *have* to do it." I close the book. "Because there will be lots of books . . . and TV shows and films and Instagram and friends and they'll all say different stuff. But none of them can tell you how to be you. Whatever way you want to girl is up to you."

Her head shrinks back. "You're being a bit weird, Vee."

I take a deep breath. "Well, it's important I tell you this stuff."

She rubs her eyes and looks at her bedside clock. "Now?" she asks. I nod. "Um . . . why?"

"Because I didn't tell you before and . . ." I lower my voice. ". . . And I think Mum would have."

She rolls onto her left, resting her head on the heel of her hand, but she watches me and says nothing so I lie back, staring at a patch of damp on the ceiling, thinking about my conversation with Luna in the hospital. Finally, I roll my head to hers. "Arial, you know I'm here for you?" Her head dips down. I was hoping for something more convincing and I prop myself up onto my elbows. "And if you ever want to talk about stuff, just tell me. Yeah?"

"Cool," she says, scrolling through songs on the screen.

"And I'm sorry for being shitty before."

She lifts her chin cautiously. "You weren't *that* shitty."

"Yeah, I was, but . . . thanks for saying I wasn't."

"S'okay," she says, picking up her iPad. "And not being rude, but . . . is that it?" She's about to put her headphones back on when I hold up a hand.

"There is one more thing."

She pretends to scroll through her music library again but she's listening. "Uh-huh."

"It's just . . . well, I've been working some stuff out lately, for myself, and it's—" Her eyebrows rise. "Your book talked about gay people, which is cool and everything, but some

319

girls and some boys are attracted to boys *and* to girls."

She looks up. "Both?"

"Yeah, like they don't differentiate—well they might, a bit. How exactly that works varies, I'm sure, but I guess some people can simply be attracted to people." The words flow from my mouth and I take a minute to let them soak in.

"So . . .?" she says, not unkind or impatient, more like she might be vaguely interested as to where I'm going with this.

"So, some people fall for who they fall for."

"And what's that got to do with me?"

"Just saying whoever you choose to love is okay."

She looks up. "Would Mum have said that?"

I let my head drop back and reach out to place my hand on her lovely face. "Yeah," I say. "I think so."

Later . . .

His is the only bed in the small room and he lies unmoving, chest exposed with a big tube, which is still connected to some kind of plastic box with water bubbling in it, sticking out from his side. I lean over him, trying to take it all in. There's a long, white bandage with spots of dried blood down his stomach and a different colored tube on the other side, hooked up to another bag of something I don't understand. A huge mask covers his mouth and inside his lips have lost their volume. I can still see his eyes but they're closed and sunken. It's another version of Pez entirely.

"He's sleeping but you can sit with him." I spin my face to the door, where the kind nurse stands, stretching plastic gloves over her hands. "I've come to change the bandage on his chest," she says, "but you chat away."

"Can he hear me?"

"Of course," she says. "He's on strong painkillers, that's all." I can tell by how quickly her smile comes that it's one she has to use a lot. She lines up shiny tools on the silver cart beside the bed and expertly unfurls a bright-white bandage against Pez's tight brown skin. When she's finished she fills a jug with water and leaves it by Pez's bed. "Drink some," she says. "When you come back tomorrow he'll be on the ward and you might even get a cup of tea there." Then the door closes behind her.

I find Pez's hand in the sheets and lean over to see his face better. "Nice gown," I say. "Off-the-shoulder. You've got your own room too, which just means you were in a real state when you got here last night. It's not that you're special or anything. Okay, that was a joke." I sit down. "Mum was in a place like this. Not this hospital, but a similar intensive care unit, and I don't like being here much, so you're going to have to do something about getting better . . . really quick." I squeeze his hand. "That nice nurse said you can hear me, so I hope you're listening."

I think I see his nose twitch inside his mask and I stand up again and it definitely creases, just tiny crinkles, but I'm sure of it and I rest my head on his lap. "No more shame, Pez. You hear me? So much stuff has become clearer while you slept and I'm not going to live hiding half my heart anymore. It's all of me and all of you. No more secrets, for either of us. No more."

I find his hand again and that's when his warm, rough fingers squeeze mine.

35

On my way out from the bathroom I lean into the living room to read the kitchen clock, and that's when I see Wendy's unmistakable curls springing up over the back of the sofa. She's sitting there, staring at the TV that's not on.

"Wend?"

She stands and turns back. "Hey!" she says. "Arial said you were in the shower so I just . . ." She trails off.

I tuck my towel in and make my way toward her. Usually we'd hug but I'm sort of dripping wet so we lower down onto seat cushions opposite each other. Her face is tanned, and she smells like sunscreen or a new perfume I don't recognize. I'd be lying if I said things weren't a bit awkward. "When did you get back?"

"Last night," she says. "Late."

I look around. "Did you stay here?"

She shakes her head. "An Airbnb on the square. It's really a shed in someone's yard . . ." She does a forced eye-roll. "But a really nice shed," she adds.

"Where's Fran?"

"Doing a course in town. Social media marketing, for the business."

"Arial could give her a tutorial for free," I say, trying to smile. "Actually, where is she? Where's Dad? He did take the day off, right?"

"They're at the trampoline park," Wendy says, placing her hands on her knees. "Listen, I just wanted to say . . . well, a few things really, but first." She puts her hand on my arm. "I'm so sorry about Pez."

"Thanks."

"I know you're going to the hospital but maybe we could grab some breakfast first?"

"Sure," I say. Visiting hours start at eleven. "I just need to drop by the café to ask Viv if I can come in late today, after seeing Pez."

Wendy shrugs. "Great. Let's eat there, then."

"Um . . ."

"Makes sense, no?"

"I guess . . ." I check the clock again: 8:54. If we leave quickly then we could be finished by the time March gets in at ten.

We talk about Pez for most of the way there but the silence that follows feels awkward. "So, Venice?" I say. "Did you do the whole gelato on a gondola thing?"

"Of course," she says.

"And Fran made it to that exhibition at the Guggenheim?" I'm talking too fast. Wendy starts an involved take on modernist kinetic art, which I'm sure is fascinating but we've reached the café and I'm too busy squinting in the window, making sure March hasn't decided to arrive early, to take any of it in. Wendy's head tilts in a concerned manner so I stand straight and look her right in the eye.

"Hope you took lots of photos," I say. "In fact, any sign of your wedding pictures yet?"

She makes a face that's hard to read. "Um . . . yeah. We got the files yesterday."

"Wow! That's so great. Are they amazing?" I'm blabbering.

"Actually," she says, "we were disappointed."

My eyes ping back to hers. "Disappointed?"

She shakes her head. "A bit. Only because there were no photos of just the two of us together. At least none that we really liked."

"Not one?"

She clicks her tongue. "There was lots of fun . . . reportage, but—" Wendy breaks off and turns to watch me watching Viv, who is setting a pot of tea down on the other side of the glass. "Everything okay, Vetty?" she asks at the exact moment that Viv looks up.

I step toward the door. "So, this is it," I say, pushing inside.

Wendy follows me and lifts a menu from the counter. "How about over there?" she says, pointing to a spot right by the window.

My heart sinks but I follow behind, praying she can eat quick. I've only just sat down when Viv grabs me in a strange half hug, where she's standing but I'm still sitting.

"Vetty!" she says, letting go. "I didn't expect to see you today. How's Pez doing?"

"He came out of the ICU last night and—" I stop and start nodding up at her. I want to say more but I'm afraid I'll cry. Talking to Viv like this in front of Wendy makes everything feel so . . . real.

She gives my shoulder a small squeeze and then her hand extends to Wendy. "I'm Viv. Technically, I'm the boss," she says, before giving a little snort.

Wendy laughs. "Wendy," she says. "Vetty's aunt."

Viv smiles warmly. "Well, what can I get you, girls?"

"Oh," I say, "I wanted to ask first whether it would be okay to start at one o'clock today. I could stay until six."

Her hand lands on my shoulder again. "Vetty, love," she says, "you're not working today."

"I'm not?"

Her hand pats my sweater. "March told me you were at the hospital half the night on Saturday and I'm sure you'll be back in there today. We've got it covered here."

I swallow, then sneak a quick look at Wendy to see whether the name March has registered with her. If it has, she's not showing it. "Thanks, Viv."

"Pop in tomorrow and let us know how you both are. Won't you?"

I nod. "Course."

"So," Viv says, handing each of us a menu. "What'll it be?"

Wendy flips the laminated card around several times, scanning each side, and it's a torturous minute before she speaks. "Poached eggs and avocado on rye with a . . . side of bacon," she says finally. "Oh, and a mint tea, please."

I steal a glimpse at my phone: 9:24. "Just a hot chocolate for me. Thanks."

Viv slots our menus back and walks off with a smile. Wendy gives me a look. "What?" I say. "I'm not hungry." Wendy scoots her chair in closer, eyes wide and waiting.

"Okay, March works here too. She starts at ten. I'm kind of hoping we don't have to see her."

Wendy sighs. "I'm sorry, you should have said—we can go somewhere else?"

I shrug. "We've ordered now. And it's not that I don't want you to meet her. Just not yet."

Then she looks at me knowingly. "I've been thinking about you since the wedding," she says.

I scratch a piece of dried egg yolk off the tabletop, which is kind of gross, but I keep at it until it's gone. "Not sure that's what you're supposed to do on a honeymoon in Venice, but whatever." My voice flatlines but she looks wistfully out the window like she doesn't notice.

"We sat on the veranda at the Gritti Palace on our first night, reliving the fun, drinking stupidly expensive Bellinis with the Basilica di Santa Maria della Salute in the background."

"Sounds more like it."

She turns to me. "It was all pinch-me beautiful, until I told Fran about the chat you *tried* to have with me." Her hand reaches across the table. "I hope you don't mind that I shared that with her?"

I consider being pissed off, but it's hardly a shocker that Wendy tells Fran everything. Besides, that chat has been like an elephant sitting between us and I'm as eager as she is to clear the air. I'd just prefer it wasn't right here, in the café, now. I shake my head.

"Good," she says. "Because I couldn't stop thinking about it. I couldn't shake the feeling that I'd got my approach all wrong and when I was telling her about what you were trying to say, about being interested in both girls and boys, all I could picture was me NOT hearing you."

"It's okay," I say softly.

Her forehead creases. "You were right to be upset, Vetty."

"I thought you'd . . . understand."

"I'm sorry," she says. "I assumed that you were coming to terms with being a lesbian, I guess because that's my experience. But that was wrong of me. You were trying to tell me something else and I didn't mean to stifle you. I'd never—"

"I didn't explain it properly. I couldn't . . . then."

Wendy's about to say something, when Viv arrives with our order on a tray. She places Wendy's tea down in front of her, then gently lands my hot chocolate before setting the plate of breakfast in front of Wend. Then she's gone.

"When I told your grandmother," Wendy says, lifting the lid off her teapot and giving it a stir, "I was older than you. I'd already finished college, and to be honest, I was sure she knew I wasn't going to be bringing home a husband anytime soon."

I lift my mug to my mouth and take a quick sip. "Did she know?"

"If she did, she pretended not to. She cried a lot."

"Because she was . . . upset?"

"Just . . . worried, I think." Wendy lifts the pepper and grinds it over her eggs. "It was twenty-five years ago," she says, lifting her cutlery. "She'd been led to believe that gay people were . . . promiscuous, that they struggled with commitment. She was afraid my life would be harder." She places her knife and fork back down and lifts her head to the ceiling. "But there I was, twenty-five years later, being just like her, unable to hear what you were telling

328

me." She reaches out and gently touches my hair. "I'm ready to listen now. If you still want me to?"

I watch her split an egg and I swallow hard. "That day, when you asked me whether there was anyone special, it was hard to answer this because there wasn't one person; there were two."

Her fork stops in front of her mouth. "And one of those was . . . March?"

I nod. "The other turned out to be a mouth-breather, but that's another story."

She chews for a while. "I'm sorry; if I'd known I really wouldn't have made you come here . . . which would have been a shame because these eggs—" She raises her arm and presses her forefinger against the thumb on her right hand. *Perfect!* I can't help but smile. "So, what makes March so special?" she whispers, leaning in.

I take a bite of her bacon while I consider. Even thinking about March makes the tips of my ears feel hot but I huddle in too. "Her energy," I say. "The way she lives with her whole heart and the way . . . I can be me around her. She could be in magazines she's that pretty, but it's all the stuff you can't see that draws me in." I sit back; my head is spinning.

Wendy's eyes glisten. She's watching me carefully. "And does March know how you feel?"

I shake my head. "She's my friend."

Wendy breathes out for a long time before nudging her plate forward. "Real friendship is not for the fainthearted."

I snort. "Dad says stuff like that. But neither of you ever played Truth or Dare at Freya's house." Wendy cowers down, face cringing like she can tell something bad is coming next. "It was ages ago," I say. "Year Eight. Me and Jess were sleeping over and Freya dared us to pick someone in our class who we'd kiss. Jess said Tom Whitehead and I knew this was a huge secret and so I figured we were going for it, and I . . ." I squeeze my eyes shut. ". . . I said I'd kiss the face off Matilda Lessing." For a moment Wendy is silent. She says literally nothing, and I open my eyes.

"You really said 'kiss the face off'?"

"Actual words."

She scrunches up her eyes like she gets it. "Oh, Vetty," she says.

"I pretended I was joking, of course, and they sort of laughed but something changed. When we were going to sleep, I didn't feel like I was welcome in the huge double bed anymore. I don't want to lose another friend."

Wendy knits her fingers in mine. "But you didn't lose Jess and Freya."

"No, but I didn't tell them the truth either."

She looks out at a couple chatting as they pass. "It's not easy," she says. "It takes a lot of bravery just to be ourselves." She squeezes our hands together, then lets go to drink a mouthful of her tea. "Ooh, that was a good line. Think about it while I nip to the bathroom. How are we doing for time?"

I quickly check my phone—9:51—and hold it out for her to read.

She stands, then looks around for the bathroom. "Two minutes," she says. I pick up my bag and race to the till to pay.

Viv waves her hand before I've asked for the bill. "It's on me."

"Please, Viv," I say. "That's so kind but I want to, really."

She clicks her tongue then rings up our order. "At least let me get the drinks," she says. I take a ten out of my purse. "Keep the change," I say, handing over the note.

She drops the coins in our tip jar. "Well, we appreciate that," she says, smiling at me. "See you tomorrow, love."

I run to the entrance, smiling, but the door opens and March strolls inside, already wearing her apron and sporting the biggest pineapple yet on the top of her head.

I brake before our bodies crash and she looks up. "Vetty!" she says, not "alright?" which I notice. Next thing I look down at her hand, holding mine. "What are you doing here? Mum said she was giving you the day off." She tugs on one of my fingers and I think of Kyle on Saturday night and what he'd say if he were watching us now. Can everyone tell how I feel about her? Is it *that* obvious? Would she hold my hand like this or look into my eyes the way she does if she knew the truth about how I feel? "Wanna step outside?" she asks, already undoing her apron loops and heading for the door. I follow. Once we're on the street she turns around. "So, how's he doing today?"

I shrug. "I'm on my way in now."

"Of course," she says. "Any news on when they'll let him go home?"

"At least five days, they said, all going well, but at least he's . . ." I trail off. I can't stomach the end of that sentence so I look down, pretending to check the time on my phone. "I've got to run. I want to be there as soon as he—"

Her face falls. "Y'okay?" she asks. I nod. "Well, call me later, yeah?" I nod again and she grabs me in a quick hug.

"Give him that from me," she says before making for the café door as Wendy walks out of it.

"You did not just buy me breakfast," Wendy says, putting her jacket back on and fumbling in her purse at the same time. March turns back briefly and Wendy looks up as the door closes behind her. I start to walk. "So . . .?" Wendy says, quickly following behind. "That was—"

I speed up. "Uh-huh."

36

I spot him at the far end of the room, propped up behind the half-drawn curtain. At least he's in an ordinary ward now and it's a lot less sci-fi-blockbuster and more familiar-Sunday-night-TV-drama. When he looks up at me the relief is almost too much.

"Hey," he whispers as I get closer. I take the camera off and lean in to hug him. "Watch the left side," he says, flinching and then carefully repositioning a pillow. I go to sit on the chair next to his bed but Luna's jacket is already draped over the back. "She's on a call," he says. "She'll be ages."

I take a seat and shunt closer to the bed. There's so much to say I don't know where to begin. "How you doing?" I do my absolute best to sound casual. "I mean, apart from the internal bleeding and the agony of your broken ribs."

"You won't believe how much it hurts to cough."

"Did you tell the doctor?"

He nods. "She's been in to check my drains. Says I need another X-ray, but she thinks I'll live." His voice sounds so weak but he smiles and I smile too. Then he winces and I can see that the tiniest movement is painful.

"Dad and Arial say hi. She's already made celebratory

pancake batter for when you get back." The sides of his mouth tug upward. "It's in the fridge."

"Tell her thanks," he says, but he's looking at the camera at the bottom of the bed. His camera. I reach for it and hold it to my face.

"Just one?" I say, peering through the lens. "Then I'll put it away. D'you mind?"

"Not sure I'm looking my best," he says. "But go on." He's thin and pale, but his eyes are bright, and he looks almost himself again, which is saying something given that he's covered in wires and wearing a hospital gown. I move the f-stop and adjust the shutter speed, snapping away until he raises his hand. "Enough!" he says, turning his face, but I shoot one last pic because that's the one.

I nod to Luna's bag. "How is she?"

He sniffs. "Happy I'm alive."

"Me too," I say, reaching for his hand. "Everyone is. I've had so many messages. Even March—" He startles at her name, then lies back and stares at the ceiling. I shouldn't have mentioned her so quickly. I've hit him with reality too soon.

"Does she hate me now?" he says.

I shake my head and he twists his neck to look down at me. "No," I say. "She doesn't. Not at all." Tears pool in my eyes. It's guilt. It's everything.

"Hey," he says, his hand squeezing mine. "Y'okay?"

I suck in a deep breath. "I promised myself . . . that if you came through this—"

"Steady," he says, raising our clasped hands like he's already reached peak emotion from me today.

"I'm serious, Pez. I promised myself that if you were okay, I'd never keep secrets between us again and it's just . . ."

"Vetty?" he says, trying to find my eye and smiling like it's me who needs support and I can't stomach how wrong this is.

"I kissed her." I blurt it out, then squeeze my eyes shut. When I open them, his eyes are wide and staring right at me.

"Kissed her?" he says. "March?"

I nod.

When my head dips he slides his hand from mine, confirming everything I've feared. "I had to say it, Pez. I couldn't not tell you."

He tries to sit up, but he can't, and he jabs at some remote control and the bed shudders, making him suddenly more upright. Then he turns his head and stares into the space on the opposite side of his bed. I watch his chest rise and fall in agonizing silence until the blue curtain is suddenly swept back and the lovely nurse from the other night is standing there, holding a tray.

"There you are," she says, placing it on the table next to Pez's bed before swinging it around so it sits across the bed, directly in front of him. "Try and get some of this lunch into you," she says, removing the plastic lid. "And would you look?" she says, eyeing Pez while nodding at me. "Hasn't she brought the color back to your cheeks already." With that she leaves, but it's some time before I can form words.

"Pez, say something, please."

Thick steam rises from his food. He waves it away, then rolls his head to me.

"When?"

I swallow. "On our last day on the film. I'd already persuaded you to come out, and because I knew the kiss meant nothing to her, I tried to pretend it meant nothing to me, but I should have told you."

His head drops back onto the pillow. "Then why didn't you?"

"Because . . . it was her." My voice shakes and I jam my hands between my knees to stop them from trembling too. Everything, apart from the shrill of machines and the beep of a nearby monitor, has gone quiet again. "And—"

"And you still kissed her?" he says, eyes tight.

"It all happened so quick," I say. "I didn't plan it." He frowns. "She's the first girl I've kissed and I feel awful, for you and for us, that it happened with her. Pez, I'm so sorry."

He reaches for his fork, then prods at the chicken breast on his plate before attempting to break some of it off. The chicken is too tough so he switches hands but he can't manage to hold the knife with his other. Still he severs away with his fork, grimacing from the effort; then he finally gives up.

"So, you like her now?"

I stand and gently free the cutlery from his hands. He watches as I cut the chicken into neat morsels; then I stab a piece and mix it with a mouthful of rice and hold it in front of his lips. Without taking his eyes off me, he swallows. Quickly his mouth opens for more. I shovel in bite after bite and he gulps it all down.

I pull away. "You need to chew!"

He makes a face. "You wouldn't chew this either, and like

it's indigestion I'm worried about," he says; then he opens his mouth more cautiously. I start to feed him again, slowly, and he eats silently until the plate is almost empty. Then he swigs some water and lies back, spent of what little energy he had. "Guess she'll never look at me again anyway."

"That's not true."

"Maybe not," he says. "But either way, I need to get my head together before I can try being with anyone else again." He looks at me. "So, how long have you known . . . that you like girls?"

"I dunno," I say, refilling his glass with water and sitting back down. "Maybe forever? Or at least since George. You remember? I sort of felt like you knew. It wasn't like I kept it a secret . . . not then anyway."

He shrugs. "Guess you've never been like other girls." As soon as he says this my body stiffens against the plastic chair. "What?" he asks, like he can tell.

I lean back, looking up. "You have no idea how much I've stressed about those words, 'not like other girls,'" I say. His eyebrows rise. "Seriously, I tortured myself trying to work out exactly what you meant when you said I was 'different.'"

He tries to sit up again. "Did I say that, that you were different?"

Did he? Maybe this was my word and not his. "Dunno."

"All I meant is that you're not like other girls to me." He looks over. "I'm different with you and I feel different about myself when I'm with you. It wasn't about how you are . . . as a girl. Sorry, it's hard to describe." I roll my eyes, like this detail he is taking such care to explain isn't *that* important, but the truth is I appreciate it more than I can

337

put into words. "I never said to Rob or Kyle that you were a lesbian. I would never."

I nod. "I know."

He looks relieved. "And thanks for telling me," he says. "Coming out must be a big deal and I get that. I'm happy you trust me."

I'd never have gotten here had he not poured his heart out. "You trusted me first."

He smiles. "Well, I'm here, whenever." He nods at the wires sprouting from his body. "Well, I don't plan on being in this bed forever, but you get what I mean." This is quickly followed by another painful grimace as he tucks the pillow in again. "So," he says after a while. "Have you told Wendy you're gay?"

I bite my lip. I've been thinking a lot about labels lately and which is right for me and whether they're even important. I've spent years worrying that my heart was greedier and more reckless than everyone else's, but I know now that this isn't true and it helps. I just love how I love. "I'm not gay."

His forehead creases. "But—"

I shake my head. "The way I've felt about boys is real too."

"Oh," he says, before raking his bottom lip with his teeth. "I wish you could have talked to me. Only so you weren't worrying about this on your own."

"I was going to, when I got back, but then . . . March turned up in July. And then there was that kiss with Rob." He recoils, not from pain this time. "Mouth-breather, I know." He smiles at the *Stranger Things* reference, so I do too. "And everything I didn't want to feel just confirmed how real all those feelings are. Truth is, I'm pretty sure I'm bisexual."

It's the first time I've said the word aloud like this and it hangs in the air between us. I wait for it to hit the ground, but it floats off like a feather and I feel my lips curve into a smile.

He watches me carefully. "So, that's it? Simple as that?" he says, smiling like he's making it clear that he's messing around.

I shrug. "Or as complicated."

He strokes his chin in a way that in any other situation would be funny. "D'you mind if I ask?" he says shyly. "Is there one . . . you know, guys or girls, that you like better?"

I watch an elderly man being lifted into a wheelchair on the other side of the room. "I honestly don't know if it's about better," I say. "I've been attracted to so few people in that way that it's hard to be sure, and they've each been different. With Rob it was mostly physical I think."

"That's reassuring," he says, deadpan.

"But when I hung out with March, I wanted to spend more and more time with her, because it was like we were vibrating on the same frequency. At least that's how it feels now, if that makes sense?"

He looks like he's thinking. "If it does to you, that's enough." He nods at the yogurt in the corner of his tray. "Open that for me?"

I stand up and peel off the foil lid, spooning a bite of pink mousse into his mouth. For a moment he looks skeptical, like he's not sure about the taste, but then he raises his chin, opening his mouth for more, then swallows and lies back. "It makes sense," he says then. "When my head was all dark I asked March to send me a photo of her face because it was the nicest thing I could think of. When I needed something good to focus on I'd just stare at her." He shakes his head like he's embarrassed but this might be the sweetest thing I've ever heard. I'm thinking about how much March would like to hear it one day, when I notice Pez staring over my head.

Harland's face is framed in the rectangular panel of glass. The door slowly opens and Harland pushes inside, followed closely by Luna. I stand, quickly checking Pez's eyes for a reaction.

Even with Harland's long strides it takes time for him to cover the length of the room and as he approaches I squeeze Pez's hand three times in mine. Harland doesn't take his eyes off Pez. He watches Pez like he's the only thing in the room and I wonder how it could have taken everything that's happened for him to see his son like this.

When Harland reaches us he stands on the opposite side of the bed from me.

"Hi, Dad," Pez says quietly. I've never heard him call Harland Dad. The shock of it touches Harland too and he drops to his knees, looking up at Pez. Then like it's almost too much, he slumps forward, tipping like a domino onto the pillow, the one that Pez so carefully positioned earlier.

"I came as quick as I could," he says.

Pez blinks a few times and I stand there silently taking them in, but when Luna's hand lands on Harland's back it's time for me to go.

I stride down the corridor toward the elevators, feeling for the first time in a long time like I know where I'm headed.

The door opens as I arrive, which for a moment seems to confirm this new sense of direction—until Rob steps out carrying a laptop under one arm and holding a large bottle of Gatorade with the other.

I move toward him, barely hesitating, forcing him back into the elevator, hoping it will swallow him up again, but as I turn and make for the corridor, the huge, silver doors slide shut, sealing us both inside.

Rob slams his hand against the number five and we surge up. "Just, is he conscious?" he says.

I'm trapped, all the way to the top floor. "No thanks to you." I snort.

"Please!" He raises the arm with the Gatorade. "I want to apologize."

"You're way past that," I snap. "Anyway, Luna and Harland are in with him now, so when we finally get out of here, you still can't go in there."

He slumps against the wall with a sigh. "Look, I've been a royal asshole."

I turn my face away. "Oh, you think?"

"Okay," he says. "So, what Kyle said was true; the whole trying-to-get-with-you thing started as a bet. I wanted one over on Pez. I wanted to prove him wrong, for once. But after I talked to you—"

"This isn't about me, Rob! You humiliated Pez, in front of everyone. How could you say those things?" His chin drops. "His mum—his mother!—confides in you about something *that* important and you—" I throw my hands up. "You're supposed to be his friend."

The doors open on the third floor and a hospital porter

wheels a woman and her drip inside the elevator, pushing Rob and me farther back into the space.

Rob's eyes close. "I know," he whispers. "But . . . he hasn't been that much of a friend either lately."

I lean in. "Maybe not, but unlike everyone else, Rob, you had some idea as to why. But hey, that didn't stop you throwing him under the bus. Did it?"

Rob stares at his shoes. "No," he says quietly.

The doors open on the fifth floor and the porter wheels the lady out. I reach over and hit the button marked G. "So, you never wanted to kiss me?"

He swallows. "I was . . . nervous."

I blow out my cheeks. "Please!"

"I swear!" he says. "I thought it would be weird. I've never done anything like that, but—"

"Anything like . . . kissing?"

He squirms. "You know what I mean."

"Um . . . no, I don't. Please elaborate."

"Well, I'd never kissed anyone, like . . . gay before."

Ugh, I can't even . . . We ride to the ground floor in silence, me with my fists clenched, working out whether or not I should bother setting Rob straight on what my sexuality is and isn't. When the doors open I stomp out toward the main exit.

He follows behind. "Please, hear me out," he says. We're back in the fresh air before I face him. "Look," he says, "it stopped being about the bet." I fold my arms across my chest. "I swear," he says, clearing his throat. "I liked it when we'd talk, and that time we kissed, it felt like there was something there. I guess I realized that I liked you. You know, genuinely." It's all sounding a bit too remarkable to be a compliment. "See, there's something about you that's . . ." He stops.

I roll my eyes and spin on my heel. "I've got to go," I say, hurtling along the side street toward Tottenham Court Road. There is no way on earth I'm letting Rob see a smile on my face, in case he decides it might have something to do with him.

"Seriously," he says, catching up. "I get why Pez thinks so much of you."

I cross the road to the bus stop, where I look up, pretending to read the times, letting my breath settle before speaking again. "Well, that's real nice of you and all, Rob, but it turns out, I wasn't fully myself with you, so I'm not sure how much of me you've seen."

"Oh," he says just as a number 24 bus pulls up.

I hop on, then quickly turn back. "You're going to have to work hard to earn Pez's trust again. He's hurt, and no one could blame him, so give him space." I tap my Oyster card, staring down at Rob as he nods up from the curb. "And, so you know, I'm not finished being angry with you," I say. "Not even close."

Then, in another exquisitely timed move from Transport for London, the doors shut in time with my mouth, whizzing me and my delicious last word toward home.

37

I wake to a ping and reach for my phone. Amira has added me to a group called "Exam Results Night." It's just me, her, March, Nick, and three numbers I don't recognize. At least Rob won't be there. The screen flashes with a message from Amira.

> Hope it's not too soon to send this but we can start here on Thursday night. Who's in?

I've hardly thought about school or exam results all summer, and since the accident they seem less important now. I think about replying but there's something I need to do first. Soon as I've dialed, it goes straight to voice mail.

"Alright, it's me. Leave a message."

"Hey, March, just wondering whether you fancy trying that Shake Stop place after work today. Well, um . . . if you do . . . I'll be there at five. Okay, bye."

I hang up, then scroll back through my photo library to find the selfie she took of us eating our Korean surprises on a bench in Chinatown. I look like I've been electrocuted and March has splotches of sauce on her chin, face all screwed up. Looking at us makes me think about what Wendy said about not having one wedding shot of her and Fran that they both really liked. I swipe frantically right back to early June and the night they danced along to Lauryn Hill in their kitchen as I watched from the court-yard outside on the other side of the glass doors.

I stare at the image and I'm not sure whether it's techni-cally any good, but there's something about how private it looks. They stand apart but their hands are held together, silhouettes bold against the bright kitchen light and all of it framed by the darkness outside the window. You can barely see their faces but you know it's them and you can almost see everything they're feeling in that moment.

I stroll up Kentish Town Road to Snappy Snaps with the sun warm on my face and it feels good to be alone on the busy street. Oiled by the movement of my limbs and the gentle wind that brushes my arms and legs, my thoughts seem looser, and I manage for at least four minutes not to think about whether or not March will turn up at five.

I walk inside and show the woman behind the desk the photo of Wendy and Fran and then I select the image size and she shows me how she can adjust the lighting effect on her monitor in a way that the self-service machines can't. I select a plain black frame and then she tells me to take a seat.

I'm flipping through my phone and saving my new school's email and phone number when the Snappy Snaps woman returns to the counter at the back, sliding the framed print over it. I walk up and examine it more closely; then I stand back, almost to the door, to take it in.

"Everything all right?" she asks, like there might be a problem.

I can't move. I can't drag my eyes away. The contrast is so much sharper than it was on my phone. "It's perfect," I say, searching for my debit card. Then I carefully lift it down and walk out onto the street, holding it proudly under my arm. I'm in such a spin, getting off the bus and galloping toward the main shopping street, I almost don't see March waving at me from the window of Shake Stop. I step closer to the glass to check that it's her; then I turn the corner and stroll inside. As soon as I'm through the door, she waves from her seat.

"Alright," she says, like only she can. "Thought I'd nab us a booth." I slide along and sit down, carefully tucking the framed photo in behind my back.

A waitress appears, hovering a stylus over her device. "I'm Cathy, I'm your server today, may I take your order?" She says all this without looking up.

March hands me a menu, which I quickly scan. So Shake Stop is basically an expensive Shakeaway but with more comfortable chairs.

"Um . . ." My eyes race through the chocolate bars, then the sweets, and then the fruit options. "Could I please have a . . . Toblerone, After Eight, and Skittles super-blend." The waitress looks up at me; then she and March share a look.

"Just a mango lassi for me," March says. The waitress stabs her device several times then vanishes. March leans in. "So . . . how's he doing?"

I sniff. "Complaining about the food."

She smiles. "That's a relief. I mean, that's got to be a good sign, right?"

"Yeah," I say. "For sure."

She picks up her phone. "Amira has asked us to her house on Thursday night. Did you see?"

I nod. "I'll see how I feel. If that's okay?"

"Course," she says. "And so you know, it'll only be us and a couple of friends from school. No Rob."

"I saw."

"So, you could come anytime. Thing is, Amira's dad doesn't let us drink so we might move on quite early. Don't know what time you wanna come, so make sure you call."

"I'd like to see how I feel."

"Sure, babe," she says. "Nervous about your exam results?"

She has no idea how nervous I am just sitting here, trying to work out what I'm about to say. The corner of Fran and Wendy's framed photo is jutting into my back, reminding me it's there. I think about showing March, but if I veer off topic I might chicken out. "Um . . . a bit."

"Yeah, me too. I worked hard though; at least I can say that." When I look up she's pinching skin from the cuticle on her thumb. For once, there's no bright-colored polish on her nails. They look bitten down. "Hey, can I ask?" she says. "Is it true, what Rob said, about Pez and the porn?"

I sit back. There must be some military term for what Rob did: scoring maximum damage in one hit. "Is everyone talking about that?" Her face doesn't move. "He's afraid everyone thinks he's some kind of pervert now."

She slowly lets air out of her nose but shakes her head. "That's not what I think. It's just . . . hearing it like that . . . It sounded serious and I'm wondering if he's okay."

"It's true that it's a problem," I say. "But it's not how Rob

347

was making it sound. He was wrong to make out that Pez is twisted in any way, because he's not. He was hurting, and that's—"

I stop because I'm picturing him, lying on the road, bike and body twisted, and my teeth begin to chatter like I'm cold.

Her hand lands on my shoulder. "Vetty?" she says. "You're crying?"

I look up. "I don't want to lie to you anymore. I don't want to hide."

Her beautiful face changes. "Okay?"

"It wasn't just a bit of fun for me. The kiss," I say, wiping my eye with my sleeve. "It wasn't fun because I really like you."

Her eyes flash wide and she looks at me for a long time, studying my face like she might see how hard it was for me to say this, and everything inside me stirs up and up until I'm liquid inside. She moves her hand along the table in front and spreads her fingers wide on the tabletop. It looks like she's about to say something, when the waitress arrives with our drinks.

March pulls her hand back and drags her mango lassi closer to her. "I had no idea you felt that way," she whispers once the waitress has left. "Well," she says, circling the straw with the tip of her finger. "Maybe I did, a bit. But I thought that was more . . . mutual appreciation, you know?" It's hard to watch her mouth and my eyes fall downward toward my strange, mud-colored shake. "I shouldn't have kissed you," she says. "I'm sorry."

I sit back in my chair. "Don't be. I know you don't feel the same. I needed to say it because I needed to be truthful."

I take a sip of my drink. "I hope you don't feel weird about it, that's all."

Everything falls quiet and she sucks in a long breath. "Being your friend," she says, ". . . is everything. And not just because of the obvious stuff, like you love Tunnock's caramel bars and *Friday Night Lights* almost as much as I do." Her hand reaches out to mine. "If you're okay that we're just friends then it changes nothing," she says softly. I look into her eyes and for some reason I believe her. "There's no world in which we can't figure this out."

I feel my insides settle. "Thanks," I say, taking another sip.

She dabs her mouth, dubiously eyeing my shake. "That nice?" she asks.

I shake my head, trying to swallow, but it's hard. "It's . . . gross."

She reaches across and takes a big sip, then looks at me like she wants to vom. "Oh god," she says, leaning in for one more sip. "That's legit rank."

I laugh, and she does too, and soon we're both in hysterics, like my revolting drink is so much funnier than it is, but god, it feels good.

38
One week later...

Pez leans against the white willow tree. "Do you hear that?" he says.

A radio plays somewhere close by. "The music?"

"No," he says, closing his eyes. "Birds singing. They're so . . . loud." I lie down on the warm grass, eyes closed like his, listening to the chirping above our heads. After a while, Pez sits up and takes a blue freezer bag out of his backpack. "Hey, it's for you?" he says, handing it to me. I sit up and take out the rectangular, cream card, examining it. It's the program from Wendy and Fran's wedding. "Other side," he says.

I turn it over and stare at myself on the train, looking out the window. It's a beautifully detailed portrait of my face in scratchy black ink and I run my fingers down paper me, tracing the grooves where his pen has pressed into the card. I look up at him, sitting cross-legged under our tree in the shade, and my heart swells.

"Do you like it?" he asks. I nod and I keep nodding because I can't think of words.

"Well, happy birthday," he says, standing the drawing up beside him, against the trunk of the tree. I look at my face again and see that it's the second picture of me in existence that I really like. I reach over and hug him tight. He's a bit stiff but I don't care. "Ouch!" he cries. "I'm still injured, remember."

I let go and grab the large package from behind my back. "I want to show you something too," I say, dragging it between us and opening out the brown paper on the grass. "It's a wedding gift for Fran and Wendy. A late one. They're heading back to Somerset today so I thought I'd drop it off."

He holds it up and stares at it a moment. "Where did you take it?"

"Outside their kitchen. On my phone."

He peers around it. "It's like you stole it."

I smile, because I kind of did. "I'll never forget how lovely it was to watch them dancing. I'm kind of hoping they might feel this way again when they see it."

"Sweet," he says, lifting the frame closer to his face; then he places it gently back on the grass and looks up at me. "Helvetica Lake?"

I blow a stray hair off my face, cringing. "It's pretentious to sign it, right? But I thought, with the mount and—"

"No," he says. "It's nice to see your full name. That's all."

"You don't think it's lame?" I ask.

He shakes his head. "It's great. It's you."

"I've changed my honors subjects too." His eyebrows arch. "I've swapped out sociology for photography."

A huge grin takes over his face; then he nudges my arm. "I'm proud of you, girl," he says in a stupid funny voice that makes me feel absurdly happy.

"You seem better," I say. "How was it with Doctor What's-his-name?"

"David," he says in the same silly voice. "And technically he's a therapist, not a doctor, and he takes no shit, but he's okay."

"Hey, I'm proud of you too."

"Thank you," he says, more slowly and seriously than I was expecting. "It was tough to start off, but once I said a load of stuff out loud, things got kind of easier. I've told him I need to be normal again before school starts."

He snorts then like he knows how stupid this sounds. I wrap my arms around my knees and watch some kids messing around on the swings. "At the start of this summer I wanted that too, you know . . . normal? But now I just want something real."

His head dips. "I hear you," he says. "I hope one day all that stuff will feel . . . normal again."

I take in his face. "What stuff?"

He sighs and looks away. "There's so much pressure and I don't know how I'll be. Like I don't know if I'll be able to just kiss someone again and for it to ever feel . . . natural." He trails off and I feel him follow my eyes as I watch the kids who are on the slide. What Pez said gets me thinking about the night of the wedding when he mentioned how physical everything is. He starts to shift around on the grass like he can read my mind or else he regrets what he's just said because when I open my mouth he moves his face, like he's afraid what I'm about to say will hurt.

"There are other ways"—I reach for his hand—"to

352

touch someone. Like, there are different paths to our heads and our hearts, like you said that night in Somerset—"

"I was a mess then," he says, tugging a loose thread on his jeans. "It wasn't that deep."

I nudge him with my shoulder. "You said it, Pez. I heard you, and I'd like to—"

"What?" He looks at me.

"I'd like you to feel what it's like."

"What what's like?" he says.

"The feeling . . . the closeness?"

"So, you've scored some magic drugs?"

I ignore this and inch in. "Perhaps . . . I could kiss you? Er, feel free to say no, but . . . I'd like you to remember what it's like to kiss someone who cares about you. It won't be like it was with her, and I'm not trying to make it like that. Just to . . . remember what that closeness feels like. I haven't kissed that many people so it's not like I'm saying I'm any good—"

He goes to stand but stops. "You're serious?" he says.

I shrug.

"You've finally gone nuts." He says it so sincerely, I think he's genuinely worried for me, which is funny because I've rarely felt saner. I pick up the bottle of Mars Milk from the side of his backpack and take a drink.

"It doesn't have to be weird," I say, wiping my mouth. "We've done it before."

"Four years ago," he says.

"Well, yeah."

"And you made me pretend to be our tennis teacher."

"This time it's got nothing to do with George, I promise."

He laughs, then leans in, frowning. "What kind of kissing are you talking about?"

I stare at his forehead, creased into that perfect Wi-Fi sign. It's comforting to see this in a way I can't explain. I wonder if he even knows it's there. "I dunno, just a kiss."

"Um . . . all right, then," he says.

I get a flash of how bizarre this should feel but doesn't.

"I'm going to count to three and then I'm going to do it. You all right with that?" I ask. He dips his head. "So," I say, taking both his hands, and I feel them shaking in mine. "I'm going to count backward, from three down to one, and when I—"

Then his face moves closer and his skin is against my skin. Traces of the rough stubble above his top lip brush against mine and the tip of his nose is cold against my cheek. My mouth feels small on his and I keep it closed. His lips are fixed and I leave them there and it's a few seconds before I kiss him back. I'm wondering if he'll pull away, but he leans in and kisses me again and his lips feel wet now, mine do too, and our mouths open into each other's. I'm not thinking of anyone else. I'm focused only on Pez and I no longer hear the nearby children or the birds or the music drifting from an open window. It's as though a stethoscope sits over my ears and all I can hear is the pounding of our two hearts.

He pulls away and I straighten but he shifts closer on the grass toward me. I lean into him and when our lips touch this time my eyes open because it's not that kind of kiss. There's a tiny drag as he pulls away and I watch as his mouth closes and he bites his lower lip.

"So," he says, wiping his mouth with his arm, "guess that was okay." He puts his arm around my shoulder and pulls me close as the two kids from the swings pelt past us on their way to the bench. I could sit like this forever. This is everything. This is enough.

"Yeah," I say. "Was all right."

He smiles and grabs his bag. "C'mon, we should eat. Your call, birthday girl."

"What about that expensive pizza place with the tables outside?"

His hand reaches for mine. "Pushing it!" he says, dragging me up.

"Wendy's Airbnb is only up the road," I say, lifting the photo from where it's standing against the trunk of the tree.

Pez checks his phone. "Something we have to do first," he says, taking the photo and slotting it under his arm. "I'll carry it."

It feels good to walk together and we fall quickly into step. It's the best kind of quiet; nobody needs to speak and still everything feels easy.

We cross Camden Road and turn into Rochester Place and my legs start to tingle as we pass the gates to the terrace gardens where we sat after he crashed Harland's car. We keep going all the way to Kentish Town Road and turn right, past the church and the pub and the drugstore, wandering on up past the Tesco Express toward Nando's. Here he comes to a stop.

"I've got an idea," he says, untying the shirt from around his waist. "Put this on." I hold up the shirt. "Here," he says, "let me." He takes it by the sleeves and lifts it to my face, covering my eyes before tying the sleeves in a knot behind my head. I feel his hands on my shoulders as he starts to spin me gently around and around. "Now," he says, taking my hand. "Keep walking."

"Um . . . what are we doing?" I say. But the truth is, I know.

"It's a game," he says, "You have to guess."

"We've turned back." I say this but really we've come 360 degrees and we're almost opposite the post office, coming up to Snappy Snaps, and we'll keep going all the way up the road, and soon we'll walk into Clementine's. And Dad and Arial will be there, along with March and Viv, and Wendy and Fran and Nick and Amira and Lucas and even Jess, who I'm back in touch with properly now and who's been asking weirdly specific details about train times.

Maybe Stevie Wonder will sing "Happy Birthday" as I walk in the door and Dad will present the rainbow cake I overheard him tell Arial about. He's been so keen to show his support since he found out and he's nothing if not on the nose, that man. Only Wendy will have explained the whole bi-colors thing to him by now too and he'll no doubt be completely thrown by it all. Then Pez will stand over the seventeen flickering flames saying, *Go on, Vetty, blow!* and I know that as I close my eyes and make a wish I'll always remember this day because today I am ready. Today is my launch point. Today I am real.

Acknowledgments

Hannah Sandford, I've got to start with you. Stephen King put it best when he said, "To write is human, to edit is divine." Your notes are eerily sharp and insightful, but most thrilling and disturbing of all is that you are always right. Always! Your talent is otherworldly. This was a tough book to weight correctly, but you stood by patiently as I hacked away, ever trusting that those tender teenagers were in there somewhere. A huge, heartfelt thank-you. I am extraordinarily grateful.

Rebecca McNally, publishing director of children's books at Bloomsbury, thank you for giving this book such a wonderful home. Hali Baumstein and the outstanding editorial team at Bloomsbury USA, thank you for your A-game professionalism.

Extra special thanks to Marianne Gunn O'Connor, my magical superpowered agent. You are an enduring force of joy and support. Thank you for always believing in me. Thanks too to Paddy O'Doherty and Vicki Satlow for the ongoing encouragement.

This book is dedicated to Vivienne Griffin, my first best friend. For the girl you were and the uniquely brilliant woman you are. You've been gladdening life since we were six years old. This book is all about the special connections we're lucky to find in life, the kind of friends with whom we can truly be ourselves, and the vulnerability that underpins these cherished bonds. This story is for all the luminous women who embolden me daily, especially my dearest Jessica Parker. I don't know what I'd do without our superlative chats and those late-night cartwheels. It's for the incomparable Irish women who've long galvanized me and kept me sane, and for all my knock-down, fabulous Somerset friends, with notable high fives for the kick-ass runners with whom I share mud-soaked therapy sessions in the rain. I love you all.

For the gorgeous community of authors, bloggers, readers, and booksellers who championed *No Filter*. Particular thanks must go to Mariella Frostrup, Rowan Coleman, Jackie Lynam, Sue Leonard, and Manor Books, Malahide. I am more grateful than you could possibly know. To Daisy Woods, thank you, for generously allowing me to pick your dazzling teenage brain. To Ian and Renate Larkin for kindly indulging my Clifton-life fantasy last August.

To Niamh, my big sister, thank you for your invaluable expertise on all things medical. Everyone should be lucky enough to have a doctor in the family. Hi to baby Dara too, for showing up in our world and simply being delicious. To my magnificent mother, Maura, my inimitable well of wisdom, your love follows me everywhere. Thank you for always being there.

Alfie and Mabel, my beloved children. I have no idea what we did to deserve you two, but hey, thanks for being you. You're just THE BEST. If you ever read this, just skip the cringy bits. And for the record, I don't love the dog more. ★**waves**★ Hi, Mildred!

And always, always my husband, Alan, my first reader, my forever love, the one who makes everything feel possible. Thank you!

Finally, for everyone who relates to this book. You're the reason it was written.